CONSTANTINOPLE
END OF EMPIRE

First published in Great Britain by Black Apollo Press, 2009
Copyright © Haig Tahta 2009
A CIP catalogue record of this book is available at the British Library.
ISBN: 9781 900355 66 7

CONSTANTINOPLE
End of Empire

HAIG TAHTA

BLACK
APOLLO
PRESS

This book is dedicated to Lara and to all the victims of officially sanctioned ethnic cleansing of the twentieth century.

CONTENTS

INTRODUCTION

This third novel in the trilogy covers the experiences of several families in the city of Constantinople from the outbreak of the Great War in 1914 to the treaty of Lausanne in 1923. It begins immediately from the end of the second volume – entitled *Constantinople 1920*. This short synopsis will hopefully give the reader, who may not have read the previous two volumes, some background to aid in his/her enjoyment and understanding.

The first novel – *April 1915* – is set in the Ottoman Empire at a critical moment following its fatal decision to join the Great War in 1914, on the German side. Olga, an Armenian girl, and Selim, a Turkish young man, were deeply and quite impossibly in love – a love certain to be doomed. Harry, a British Naval officer is present at the drama of the Gallipoli landings. The day before that fateful invasion, the fathers of the two Armenian families involved in the story are arrested and deported, eventually surviving by the skin of their teeth.

The second volume begins three years after the end of the first novel. The Ottomans have lost the War. The capital city, the underlying theme of the trilogy, is occupied by the British army. The historical background to this second volume is the Greco-Turkish War, moving from the ill-fated landing of the Greek army in Smyrna to the decisive battle of the Sakarya, and the fall and burning of Smyrna.

The novel starts with the arrival in Constantinople of a

Russian family – the countess Natalya Androvna and her two sons Nicolai 22, and Alexei 14. They have fled from Sevastopol in the great 'White' Russian exodus as the Red Army poured into the Crimea. In the city, this Russian family eventually meet and interact with the Avakians – the Armenian family of four daughters and a son – the principal protagonists of the first volume.

Olga, the second daughter has matured as a result of her work for three years as a nurse in the great Turkish military hospital at Scutari. She is clearly still in love with Selim but in view of the hostility of both families, they are only able to meet rarely and the relationship remains unresolved and unfulfilled. Sima, the eldest daughter, is currently 'walking out' with George,a very suitable young Armenian merchant of her own class and background. Nerissa, now twenty, is at University. Taking advantage of the more permissive atmosphere after the War, she is continuing what she considers to be a platonic relationship with Vahan, while he is becoming increasingly emotionally drawn to her.

Sima – the practical eldest sister, always a cynic where 'love' is concerned, finds herself falling in love with Nicolai, the penniless, now stateless Russian aristocrat just arrived from the Crimea. Eventually she drops her suitable young man and in contrast to poor Olga, her father – Karekin Avakian – and mother accept the situation. Karekin takes on the charming Alexei as an office helper to take the place of his son Haik, who is going with Paramaz, an orphan who survived the 1915 massacres, to Smyrna to open a branch office of the merchant house.

Having been present at the evacuation of Sevastopol and involved with the escape of Nicolai and the Androvs, Harry now also becomes involved with the Avakians. He has become a special naval liaison officer to the British Commanding Officer of the Constantinople garrison – General Harington.

Paramaz is introduced – the same age as Haik (17 at the start – 19 by the end). He is an Armenian orphan from the catastrophe of 1915. He was taken in and given a job and a home by Karekin after the war, and his dramatic story is a reminder of the massacres of 1915, dealt with in the first novel. A complex character, his traumatic experiences have left him confused and morally flawed.

The whole story climaxes with the great defeat of the Greek army in Central Anatolia, their frantic retreat, and the entry of the victorious Turkish army into Smyrna. Many of the characters are gathered in this city. Selim, an officer again but now serving with the Turkish Nationalists, has been there clandestinely for some months; and before the end he is reunited with Olga who, unknown to him, has been working as a nurse at the Ottoman Imperial Hospital and at the Armenian Hospital in Smyrna. Finally their love is consummated and they have three wonderful months living together during the last few weeks of the dying Greek administration.

The drama unfolds. Mikael, fleeing with the Greek army passes through and is living with a Greek family during these four days. Paramaz, in all the turmoil of the looting, pillaging and killing of the days after the arrival of the Turkish army, shoots (accidentally? or on purpose?) the young Haik, who dies in the street. The great fire of Smyrna, one of the great consuming fires of history, breaks out and rages for days, as the city burns. Harry – now a captain of one of the destroyers in the British fleet anchored in the great Bay – picks up survivors in the waters against the orders of his Admiral. Selim, wounded and in great pain dies in the fire as it sweeps through the Armenian quarter. Olga, distraught and in despair, is only saved by a Turkish journalist who takes her, unconscious, to his home in the untouched Turkish quarter, where he rapes her during the night.

In this Gotterdammerung finale, Mikael gets away on an Italian ship with his Greek lover. Paramaz also escapes on a British ship clutching a baby he has saved. Constantinople waits anxiously for news.

CHAPTER 1

Spiro

"Oh my God – Spiro! Spiro, my son! Get up! Wake up, get up quickly!"

Spiro woke up with a start and looked up at his distraught mother. As soon as she saw that he was awake, she stopped shaking him and hurried out of the room. For a moment he simply sat up and rubbed sleep from his eyes thinking that he must have overslept. But then he smelt the unmistakeable odour of smoke and fire and became aware of cries and shouts in the house from different members of his large extended family.

Jumping out of bed, he grabbed his short pants and a previously worn long-sleeved shirt. Hopping about on one foot and then the other, he pulled up his trousers and struggled into the shirt. He glanced out of the tiny window of his room, but this faced into the courtyard of their large house and nothing appeared to be out of the ordinary. However the smell of smoke and burning was beginning to pervade everything.

Just as he slipped on his sandals – the whole process of dressing had only taken a few moments - his elder brother, Costas, came running in.

"Well done Spiro – listen, grab what you want to take with you and come down fast. We have to leave right away. The fire will be upon us within the hour. Come on, come on!"

Spiro was still not entirely awake and could not take in what was going on. 'What fire?' he thought. However, at not quite 12-years-old, he was used to doing what he was told by his elders without much question. He looked round the little room, which had been his alone for as long as he could remember and wondered what his brother had meant when he had said, 'Grab what you want to take with you.' He didn't have anything, did he?

But Spiro stopped wondering about it all as he could clearly hear the disturbing sounds of the family shouting and yelling in the hall downstairs. He shook his head and took a quick look round. It was either luck or a latent maturity which made him snatch up his thick sheepskin coat, a recent gift from one of his uncles; then with one last look at the room he ran out and down the narrow stairs.

Downstairs in the spacious hall of the large house which had been the Pantelis home for generations, Spiro saw the whole of his extended family milling about arguing, waving their arms, shouting, gathering up all sorts of unlikely items, then putting them straight down again. Babies, unchanged and yelling at the turmoil they sensed all around them, were held by young girls or their mothers. Some of the women were crying and standing about helplessly, but others were bustling in and out, piling up things of all sorts by the front door – blankets, pots and pans, a clock, a small carpet, a picture. This heavy iron door, which had been so solidly locked and bolted against the Turkish soldiers who had been roaming the streets for the last few difficult days, was now wide open and Spiro could see out into the street. His eyes opened wide with anxiety and for the first time that morning, he felt fear. In the distance he saw great billowing clouds of thick black smoke moving towards the houses on the other side of the street. Every so often sheets of bright red flame burned brightly in their midst.

No one took much notice of Spiro as he stood at the side near the door clutching his coat and trying to make sense of the chaos. Somehow the sight of all the adults in his life acting in panic, even irrationally, was more frightening for Spiro than all the smoke and flames in the distance. He had to pee – it was beginning to trickle. He ran back into the courtyard and relieved himself, easing some of the tension.

Smyrna was burning!

Only a few days before, after the defeat and total collapse of the Greek army in the Anatolian interior, Spiro had watched in the streets as ragged and exhausted Greek soldiers had arrived and fled westwards. He had looked on as individual soldiers, judging instinctively which was the Greek quarter in the polyglot town, had knocked at his mother's door begging for some food. Bread, cheese, olives and fruit of all kinds were handed out unstintingly to any soldier who requested help. For Spiro, this was all an exciting change from the routine of his daily life in the town where he was born.

Spiro was old enough to know that his mother's family had lived in Smyrna for generations. He lived in the middle of the Greek quarter – his friends and all his neighbours were Greek. He went to a Greek school, attended the Greek Orthodox Church on Sundays, when made to by his mother, and spoke Greek. But he also spoke Turkish. All the men in the family, including his own father, wore the fez, symbolic of the fact that they were all Ottoman citizens, part of the population of a polyglot and multi-cultural empire which had ruled the whole of this part of the world for centuries.

Spiro had never directly experienced ethnic or religious discrimination, though he knew that the official religion of the state was Islam, and that he and his family were, to that extent, second-class citizens. However, while his spoken Turkish was not the refined Ottoman Turkish of the great capital city of Constantinople to the north, it was fluent and quite adequate to deal with all the other little boys, regardless of race, who ran barefoot around the streets and the busy quays of this great port.

Christos Pantelis, Spiro's father, was a fairly affluent and successful merchant dealing with the export of the prolific dried fruits of the area. He was the paterfamilias of a large house in the Greek quarter on the other side of the Rue des Franques, not far from the quayside. The household included not only his immediate family - his wife Agape and his two sons, Costas, just seventeen, and Spiro, almost twelve - but also several relatives and their children, unattached aunts, as well as old nannies and aged servants.

Two years earlier, when he was only nine, Spiro had been present on the quayside, with almost the whole of the rest of this large family, for the arrival of Auntie Elena, the wife of a deceased uncle he had never known, together with her two small children. They were refugees of the Russian civil war and were from one of the fast disappearing Greek communities around the Black sea coast – in this case Odessa. As often happened in large extended families like his, he had been required to look out for these two little cousins. Andreas, though four years younger, was cheerfully tolerated and allowed to join in with all his friends who ran around the quays. He ignored the little girl Anya, though he never refused to carry her when necessary.

On the day, about a week ago, that he had watched the retreating Greek soldiers pouring through the town, a Sergeant from the 42nd Evzones had called at the house in the afternoon and had been welcomed with great excitement by Auntie Elena. His name was Mikael. During the eventful four or five days before this morning, when he had awoken to face the fire, Spiro had come to understand that Mikael, who seemed to sleep in the same room as Auntie Elena and his little cousins, was an Armenian. Spiro, of course, knew perfectly well about Armenians – the boys ran about the streets barefoot just like he and his Greek friends, though there were less of them; they lived in a different part of the town immediately alongside the Greek quarter, and they went to a different church. Spiro did not think too deeply about all the different races that lived in his town, the Jews, Turks, and Europeans – but if challenged, he would have said that the Armenians were a sort of 'Greek' who spoke a different language and went to a different kind of church. Armenian priests and Greek papas looked very similar as they walked about the town and had the same musty incense smell about them. Centuries of sterile arguments raging between those clerics about the nature of Christ meant nothing to Spiro.

Although he had been born an Ottoman citizen, for the last

three years he had been living under a Greek administration. Since 1919, at the invitation primarily of the British Prime Minister, a Greek army, escorted into the harbour by British destroyers, had occupied the town. War had raged between the Greek and Turkish nationalist forces in the interior ever since, while the hapless Ottoman government in Constantinople had watched with ever-increasing impotence. But here in Smyrna, the population had ignored the war and life had gone joyfully on. For Spiro, during all these formative years of his life, the police in the streets were Greek, the holy days were orthodox and the military ships in the bay were friendly allies.

Spiro was an observant lad, sensitive to the somewhat contra-dictory signals coming from the adults. He was aware that a crisis was brewing in the family even before the Greek soldiers came swarming through the city, followed immediately by desperate refugees from the interior. He found it difficult to comprehend the creeping fear and panic he sensed among the adults as the Turkish army poured into town. Sheltered from the sight of all the looting and smashing of shop windows in the Rue des Franques, the rape and break-ins in the Armenian quarter, and the haphazard killings everywhere, he only knew that he was being kept strictly indoors and not allowed out at all. He resented the fact that Sergeant Mikael took his two little cousins out with him twice, when he himself was not allowed to put a step beyond the bolted front door. How could he begin to understand why an innocent, good-looking eleven-year-old boy, uncircum-cised and an obvious *giavour*, would be at such risk in streets filled with inflamed and undisciplined Turkish soldiers.

And all the time the adults argued among themselves, inces-santly and with shrill emphasis. They seemed to be divided into two completely contrary groups. One group came out forcefully with statements, all of which Spiro understood and with which he could nod his head and agree, such as –

"We are Ottoman citizens aren't we? We've lived here for generations. Since 1908 we have even provided soldiers for the Ottoman army. Why should...."

"This town has always been a great entrepot throughout the

days of the empire, why shouldn't it continue? Surely the Turks will want us to carry on and bring in wealth as before."

"We've always lived together for four hundred years, haven't we? A bit of unpleasantness occasionally but...."

"What about all those allied ships in the harbour with all their heavy guns...?

"Kemal Pasha has said that no one is to be harmed...."

Meanwhile there were others in the family who said totally different things with which Spiro also found himself nodding in agreement –

"But, listen, they'll seek revenge for the unfortunate incidents which took place when our army landed...."

"What about all those villages burned as the army fled...."

"These soldiers in the streets are not like the old Ottoman regulars, many of them are guerrilla thugs and...."

"For God's sake all of you! Haven't you seen the dead bodies in the Armenian quarter?"

But now, Smyrna was burning.

All argument had ceased and the family were preparing, chaotically, to leave. Spiro had already seen Mikael, holding a weeping Anya in his arms, and Aunt Elena, holding tight to Andreas, pass decisively out of the front door and into the street. Elena was carrying a shabby leather suitcase, which Spiro recognised as the one she had clutched two years before when she first arrived. The noise of the approaching fire could now be heard drowning out most of the shrieks and yelling going on around him. Spiro felt that he had been standing by the front door for hours, though it could only have been a few minutes. Costas and his father, carrying an assortment of things that they had haphazardly picked up from the items deposited at the side by the women, hurried to the front door and shouted out to everyone that they all had to leave – "Now! – Now!"

Spiro went out into the street and saw for the first time that hundreds of others were also running out of their houses and making for the quays and the sea. The terrifying sight of the smoke and the flames, moving inexorably towards them from the south and east, overshadowed the screaming and the chaos.

Agape, clutching a bundle of things Spiro could not make out, came running out of the house as Costas and his father kept shouting to everyone still inside to leave. His mother was in tears and clearly distressed, but she was no longer in a state of panic. In one hand she had a bundle of blankets with things inside. In the other hand, she was also holding a short skirt, a headscarf and a faded yellow blouse. She thrust these into Spiro's hands, then, grabbing his other hand, they began running up the street, followed closely by Cristos and Costas and the rest of the family. Mikael and Elena had already disappeared.

Spiro was now very frightened. He urgently needed to pee again, even though it was only a few minutes since he had last done so. His mother hurried him along the streets. The fire behind them was advancing implacably – with hundreds running ahead of it like a flock of sheep, or a horde of lemmings, all moving towards the seafront. There was no real thought or planning in the Pantelis family, any more than there was in any other part of the panic-stricken population. It was pure chance that drove the family towards the Point in the north.

In Smyrna, the waters of the great bay come right up to the quayside, lapping only six inches below the road that runs for about two miles all the way from the sheltered harbour right up to the Point. The only things separating the road from the sea were bollards placed every few metres where boats would have been tied up in more normal times.

The fire was by now moving due west directly towards the harbour. The buildings along the seafront, taller than the town behind, were not yet alight and were screening the sight of the approaching flames from the thousands already milling on the quayside between the buildings and the sea.

As they reached the seafront, Spiro and his mother sank to the ground by the roadside catching their breath. But Spiro, curiosity overcoming fear, stood up again and sidled over to his brother. He looked back at the quayside to the south with its crowds of people and, at that moment, a great penetrating scream rang out. He involuntarily wet his pants as he grabbed hold of Costas' hand. The scream, heard for miles out at sea, continued and Spiro saw with horror that all the buildings on the seafront had almost simultaneously burst into flames. He could no longer hold what little urine was left, but he was scarcely aware of the trickle down his legs as he looked on with horror at the terrible scene being enacted before his eyes. All around him the watching crowd moaned and shrieked, surging back and forth in terror.

The entire city was ablaze. It burned for hour after hour, and for the rest of that day, the whole of the next night, and then the following day, but all that Spiro could take in were the shrieks of the women and children and the wails of the crowds further down the corniche, who had nowhere left to go save to fall or be pushed into the sea. The heat down near the harbour was so great that some of the pathetic suitcases and bundles, grasped tightly by these thousands of now homeless people, spontaneously combusted.

But at last those families clustered near the Point in the north could see that the fire was not going to reach them and the tension eased somewhat. Bodies were floating in the sea – swimmers were still desperately trying to get to boats lying idle in the bay, though most were refused access, slipping away from the trailing ropes and adding to the bodies in the water.

Spiro huddled up against his mother with his brother Costas holding him tight on the other side. Two whole days passed like this during which Spiro lay half asleep for much of the time, his mind numbed and overwhelmed by the sights and sounds around him. They had no food of any kind and only a little water carefully brought by Costas. Spiro could scarcely take in what was happening. Turkish soldiers, no longer with any discipline at all, wandered through the crowds, particularly at night, robbing and picking out girls to take to one side to rape, idly slaughtering, without thought, any male who had the temerity to try and intervene.

The weekend finally arrived. The smell of the fire and of the burned flesh of thousands still hung over the remains of the city, mixed with the faint odour of military petrol, proving indisputably that the fire had been deliberately started in the first place. The entire Greek and Armenian quarters of the city, together with most of the European quarter, were a mass of rubble and cinders from which wisps of smoke still rose. A quarter of a million people stood, sat, or lay slumped on the ground on a narrow strip of roadway between the sea on one side and the smouldering ruins of the city on the other.

The crowds milling about on the quays, hungry, exhausted and still in a state of hysteria, were now faced with a new crisis. That weekend, a proclamation issued by the Turkish authorities was posted all over the quayside. From a small solitary aeroplane, leaflets setting out the declaration rained down over the many thousands still apathetically huddled on the seafront.

"All Greek and Armenian males of, or approaching, military age, are to be treated as prisoners of war and driven into the interior. All remaining Greeks or Armenians, old men, women and children, must be gone within two weeks. If not departed by then, they too will be driven into the interior."

Driven into the interior! Deported! Everyone knew perfectly well what that actually meant in practice – endless lines of exhausted people, putting one foot in front of the other, dragging themselves on till most of them had died. So they had to be gone within two weeks.

But gone where? How?

CHAPTER 2

Olga

Olga never learned the name of the man who had first rescued her and then raped her. His fortuitous presence in the street outside the front door had saved her from one of two equally terrible fates. As she had run from the house trying to get help for her stricken lover Selim, she would certainly have been shot by one of the three soldiers to whom she had appealed. One soldier was already going for his rifle as she passed out before him, and would have fired if this Turkish civilian had not picked her up bodily, thrown her over his shoulder like a sack of potatoes, and run off with her, winking at the men as he went. In this way, he had also saved her from the fast approaching flames, which in the end destroyed the whole of Smyrna with the exception of the old Turkish quarter. The flames had raged through the city destroying everything in their path. They had burnt her Turkish lover, Selim, to death, and had consumed the broken body of her brother Haik, lying dead in the street a short distance away.

After the Turkish Smyrniote effendi had at last left her lying broken and ravished on the straw in his stable, Olga had wept and wept. She sobbed not for herself, not for the pain and humiliation of what had happened, but for the final and irrevocable loss of the man she had loved for six years, and with whom she had at last discovered fulfilment and a deep happiness in these last few months.

But tears and sobbing can only last so long before eventually giving way to a numb acquiescence. There was, of course, no question of any sleep for the rest of that terrible night, but as the dawn light found its way through the wide cracks of the stable door into the ramshackle wooden shack in which she lay, Olga's tears finally dried up. The Avakian spirit began to stir in her and she sat up and looked around.

As she had been completely unconscious when hurried away from the flames engulfing the Armenian quarter, she was not entirely clear as to where she might now be. However, it was apparent that she was in some kind of outbuilding in the Turkish quarter of the city, one that had housed animals of one sort or another. This meant, surely, that her rescuer – or abuser – was likely to be a fairly substantial householder, not only to own a house, but a stable. Now that she was beginning to think more clearly, she also recalled that he had in fact been fairly well dressed.

However, the reawakening of her spirit, replacing the despair of the night before, did not mean that she had recovered her strength. She had not slept all night nor eaten anything for hours, and she realised that she was getting thirsty. She fell back on the straw and eventually fell into a troubled sleep which lasted most of the rest of the day.

As the afternoon of this second day began to come to an end, Olga finally found the strength to stand up. Her dress, soiled and crumpled, was still intact, but her underwear was torn and thrown aside. Olga made no attempt to recover these, but smoothed her dress down as best she could before trying the door. It was locked, but the whole structure was so flimsy and worm-eaten, where the door was attached to the framework, that it would not need much effort to break it down. But it would probably make a lot of noise and in addition, at this stage, she did not feel she had the energy to try.

A rusty dripping tap in the corner, provided her with some water as she lapped at it – though this only seemed to increase her thirst. Sometime in the late afternoon she heard movement outside for the first time and could hear some conversation, but it was subdued and soon the sounds moved off into the distance. Striving to hear through the cracks in the door, Olga became aware that there was a change in the background noise she had heard over the last 24 hours. The continuous crashing, hissing and rumbling of the huge fire could no longer be heard.

Olga decided that even though she might well have to suffer another night of shame and humiliation, it would be fatal to try and break out during the day when people were more likely to be around. She would make her escape attempt in the early hours of the following morning.

As night fell, Olga lay waiting with nerves stretched to breaking point, listening for every little sound that might herald the arrival of the man. She was almost dozing off again when there was a rattling at the door and a creak as it was slowly pushed open. It was dark outside and Olga could see nothing. She waited in an agony of suspense, her body quivering in anticipation of what was coming.

Nothing happened – nothing moved.

There were some more mysterious sounds that she could not place and then, with the same creak, the door seemed to have shut again. Olga almost screamed out loud. Was the man in the barn or had he gone? She waited for almost twenty minutes before she plucked up the courage to crawl to the door, carefully feeling her way aided by the many cracks in the wooden walls.

Standing just inside the door was a pottery pitcher of cold water and an old earthenware plate on which was a loaf of bread and some wizened olives. Olga never knew who it was who had both rescued her and then raped her. She never knew what had persuaded him to leave her alone that second night, to give her some sustenance, and finally,she realised, to leave the door unlocked.

The relief released another flood of emotions and Olga wept again. Then she ate the food, drank down all the water and waited for the dawn.

As the sun came up, Olga quietly pushed the door ajar and looked out. It was very early in the morning, but was already quite light. She saw a courtyard with a fairly substantial wooden house with a second storey on the one side, and some trees and a bedraggled hedge on the other. On the far side of the court-yard opposite, she could see a narrow cobbled street with a line of ramshackle houses.

Olga took a deep breath. There was nobody about as far as she could see. There was an unusual smell in the air. She sniffed and immediately recognised the distinctive smell of burnt wood and cinders, but above that easily recognisable odour, there was another sickly smell she could not place – somewhat like the smell of charred bad pork.

Olga had difficulty taking that first step out of the old shed. It was as if she was wary of stepping out into the open air; as if she could not bear to face the accusing gaze of others; as if she did not want to leave the spurious sanctuary of the shed. Of course no subject had ever been taboo in the Avakian household once they were in full spate, and rape as a problem had been discussed in the abstract. The general consensus had been that women subjected to such an experience felt soiled and suffered the guilt of the victim. But Olga found that she had no such feelings. She was ashamed that she was naked under her crumpled dress, but her emotions were so bound up with the death of Selim, that the rape during that first night lost its meaning. At the same time, to complicate her feelings further, she was aware that the man who had so casually violated her had also saved her life.

Olga took her first step out into the open. But once that first timid step had been taken, she began walking quickly through the courtyard and was almost running when she came out into the little street. She did not know exactly where she was. She knew the Turkish quarter of Smyrna straggled up the hillside to the ruined Byzantine castle at the top, so all she had to do to get to the town centre was to walk downhill.

As she walked down the twisting, narrow, cobbled street, though her mind was in a turmoil, she was no longer reflecting unduly on her own horrific experiences, and she began looking about her as she passed others who were also up early. She was by now so bedraggled, so shabby with such dirty, soot-laden features, that no one gave her a second glance. Eventually the crazily twisting little street turned sharply right, for the first time leading straight downhill, and it was at this point, as she turned the corner and looked straight down on the town, that Olga stopped and stared in horrified amazement.

The whole of the rest of the town stretching right up to the Point in the distant north lay out before her, including the great bay filled with ships of all kinds. The whole city was a mass of rubble with smoke still rising in wisps from piles of charred timber and stones. The strange smell Olga had noticed before struck her again and, in a sudden flash of recognition, she knew what it was. It was the smell of burnt human flesh.

Feeling faint, Olga went over to the side of the street and leaned against the wall of a house. She could not make out any landmarks or any details other than the flattened city and the ships in the bay beyond. She could not see the thousands upon thousands huddled along the quays stretching all the way from the inner harbour right up to the Point. It seemed to her as if there were no more people left in the town. But Turkish men were walking up and down, going about their early morning business and muttering 'salaams' as they passed. This in itself was unusual. Unveiled as she was, shamelessly standing in the public street in the heart of the Turkish quarter – on any other day she would have attracted disapproving looks instead of the muttered morning greetings.

Olga stood on that street for some time. Apart from the muttered greetings and the blessings of Allah passed to each other, the increasing numbers of townspeople in the streets were subdued, silent and apprehensive. There was no sense of triumph or sadistic pleasure for the fate of their fellow-citizens. The academics, the poets and the intellectual politicians might be glorying in the triumph of the national principle: Turkey for the Turks alone; one pure and unadulterated people; one culture. But the ordinary people were dazed and anxious. They already missed the Greek grocer down the road, the Jewish baker, everything they had known and been comfortable with for years. Certainly they had envied the wealthier *giavours*, they may even have disliked them. But faced with the direct consequences of this enforced ethnic cleansing, to their own surprise, they were quiet and saddened. These people had a strong residual respect for the old tolerant multi-cultural Ottoman ideal. However, nationalist propaganda and the shrill teaching of the academics would soon be settimg them straight.

Looking down and searching for some comforting landmark, Olga saw at last where she had to go. Down at the bottom of the hill on the edge of the Turkish quarter, still completely intact and standing proudly upright, was the Imperial Ottoman Hospital – her old employer. Desperate now that she had a clear destination, worried for the first time that she might be arrested or worse before she could reach the hospital, she hurried down the hill.

The hospital was the first place she had seen which was busy and had a sense of normalcy, despite the emergency atmosphere. It was now the only functioning hospital in the city and it was crowded and in a state of noisy confusion. The nervous and harassed staff were scurrying about. Crowds of people accompanying relatives with major or minor burns, were milling about trying to get their attention. Everyone there was either a Turk or a Jew – there was not a single Greek or Armenian. Olga, however, saw only people hurting and in need. She was soon recognised; it had after all only been less than a week since she was last on duty. A uniform of sorts was found for her. No one questioned her appearance – it was almost the norm at this point.

Olga threw herself into the work, refusing to take more than a few hours sleep every so often. She questioned nothing and did not bother to find out what may have been happening elsewhere in the town. She bandaged, she sewed up wounds, she made up beds, she held people's hands as doctors operated with the minimum of drugs available. She cleaned up urine and excrement, she comforted complete strangers and occasionally she even found herself sharing a joke and smiling.

But however hard she worked, however hard she concentrated on all the patients whom she tended and comforted, she could not hide from herself the knowledge that she was pregnant. She was a nurse, she knew with certainty that the baby growing inside her was Selim's. It was not, nor could it possibly have been, the issue of the unknown Turk who had casually raped her during that terrible night only a day or two previously. It was not self-delusion – she could work out the days easily enough. She knew that she was carrying Selim's baby.

CHAPTER 3

Paramaz and George

Paramaz held on tight to the baby entrusted to him by its dying mother on the quayside, as one of the ship's boats from HMS *Iron Duke* pulled up at the point where he had carefully positioned himself. He leant over and handed down the baby into the arms of the stunned sailor without giving him a chance to say anything, and then clambered aboard himself, pulling the dazed George after him. The young midshipman in charge of this boat called out from the front,

"Are you British subjects?"

Paramaz, who spoke no English, but only Turkish and Armenian with a smattering of Greek, said nothing, simply taking the now squalling baby back from the sailor. But George at last came out of his stupor and called out,

"Certainly, sir ... Cyprus ... but no documents, all gone in the fire."

The young officer nodded and began asking the same question to all the others crowding up to the boat, desperate to get on board.

As the great fire of September 1922 raged unchecked for days, the Italian and French warships anchored in the bay had sent out boat after boat to pick up survivors in the waters, and as many of the panic-stricken people milling about on the quaysides trapped between the fire and the sea that they could safely taken on board. The French consulate had even set up a small desk on the quayside at which officials were handing out visas and passes for their boats to anyone who could speak a few words of French, and who claimed to have French connections.

Throughout all this time, the British Admiral – Sir Osmond de Beauvoir Brock – aboard his flagship HMS *Iron Duke*, was adamant in his orders that no one was to be offered any shelter or space on any of the ships under his command, which was the largest contingent of the allied fleet in the harbour. He insisted that it would break the promise of neutrality he had made a few days earlier to the new Turkish governor, as the Turkish army poured into the town. The men of the British fleet had become restive and almost mutinous as they watched helplessly while the city burned and old men, the sick, women and children, jumped or were pushed into the sea as the fire spread inexorably, forcing the fleeing Greek and Armenian sections of the Ottoman population onto the long, but mercifully wide, quayside of Smyrna.

At the moment of greatest horror, during the night, a ramshackle rowing boat crowded with desperate refugees had pulled up alongside the *Iron Duke*. The sailors had, under orders, thrown down buckets of water to prevent any one attempting to clamber up the ropes. This particular boat had then overturned like so many others in the bay, immediately drowning almost all the occupants, while some swam away to a more prolonged death. One young girl arrived near the destroyer commanded by Captain Harry Bridgeman. She was clearly exhausted and about to expire. A grizzled old sailor from this ship had removed his coat and boots and jumped overboard to hold her up. The rest of the men were restless and the Captain – Harry – immediately ordered all boats away with orders not only to pick up the sailor and the girl, but also to pick up any survivors in the near vicinity in danger of drowning in the water.

The admiral was furious when this was seen from the deck of the *Iron Duke* and promised a court-martial. However, by the following morning, with the waters filled with dead bodies and still more desperate and exhausted swimmers, he had relented and, persuaded by his executive officer, he changed his orders. His captains were now given the right to send out boats not only to pick up swimmers but also people on the quays. But clearly there had to be some discrimination. There were over 200,000 people along the corniche – the ships could only take a limited number, so there had to be a show of taking only people with some connection, however tenuous, to Great Britain; hence the midshipman's question to George and Paramaz.

Paramaz was an Armenian orphan who had survived the terrible deportations and mass killings of his people in Eastern Anatolia in 1915, when only 12 years-old. Two years previously, he had been plucked out of the back streets of Aleppo and taken in, given work and a home, by the Avakian family, a wealthy merchant family of Constantinople. His traumatic experiences had included witnessing the death of one of his little sisters and the casual abduction of the other. He had then been forced to watch the rape and murder of his mother. Now 19 years of age, he had been in Smyrna working for the family firm of Avakian Levonian et Cie, managed locally by George Levonian, with the help of Haik, the son of Karekin Avakian, the benefactor who had taken him in from the streets of Aleppo.

Haik had been killed by shots fired by Paramaz just before the start of the great fire, during the state of lawlessness in the Armenian quarter which accompanied the arrival of the Turkish nationalist army. Paramaz had fired three shots up the street, supposedly aimed at three Turkish soldiers who had emerged from a house with valuables they had looted after raping the women inside. As they stumbled out, loaded up with goods and buttoning up their trousers, they had come face to face with a distraught Haik, who had hesitated for a fateful moment before reacting. Each of the shots fired by Paramaz had slammed into Haik's chest as he turned away from the soldiers, who were already pulling out their own rifles. Had Paramaz aimed at the soldiers or at Haik? Had his envy and dislike of Haik, whose actions were now putting both their lives in jeopardy, affected his aim? What had been in his mind as he had pulled the trigger three times? Whatever the truth, Paramaz had acted swiftly as Haik died, running up and removing from the dead body the money-belt containing gold coins, which he knew Haik had saved as they fled, giving a few to the soldiers and offering some to a Turkish civilian who had witnessed what had been going on, but who declined the offer.

Now on board the *Iron Duke*, squeezed into a crowded mess-room, he sat on the floor cuddling and rocking the baby. The clothes in which the baby was wrapped were filthy, wet with urine and weak watery excrement. Stinking and shrieking it might be, yet Paramaz held the baby tight, rocking and crooning as he had seen his mother do with his long-dead baby sisters all those years ago. There were now a few women on board this otherwise all-male battleship, but Paramaz refused to pass on the baby to anyone else. He seemed to need the infant as much as it needed him.

Eventually, a sailor appeared with a cup of warm milk. George, lying exhausted alongside and still dazed, thanked him and handed the cup up to Paramaz. For some time Paramaz was unable to get the baby to drink. The baby needed to suck not swallow. Paramaz finally hit on the idea of dipping his little finger in the milk and letting the baby suck on it. It was a tedious and lengthy process, but Paramaz, normally impatient, managed to get the baby fed.

The same sailor who had brought the milk came back some time later to see how 'mother and child' were faring. With George translating, Paramaz asked for some water to clean the infant, who was clearly uncomfortable, quite apart from the smell. The water had arrived, and the sailor, whose name Paramaz never learned, stood watching, with curiosity and concern, as Paramaz unwound the sodden, despoiled rags in which the baby was clothed. When the baby was finally naked, the three of them discovered, for the first time, that it was a boy.

The sailor had also brought a clean kitchen cloth and Paramaz set about washing the baby boy with the cold water, paying no heed either to the baby's lusty yells or the fact that he was himself getting wet. It was clear that the wet clothes, would have to be thrown away. George had no need to translate. Off went the sailor, grinning with an odd pleasure at all that was happening. He returned quickly with a pile of somewhat moth-eaten, but clean, woollen vests and a large drawing pin – begged borrowed or stolen from some store.

Both George and the sailor now began enthusiastically tearing them into large strips while Paramaz rocked and crooned at the now clean and nude baby boy in his arms. Once the vest tearing was complete, Paramaz gathered some round the little boy's legs, tying them round the waist. All three adults burst into wide grins as the baby gurgled for the first time, and then seemed to smile.

Paramaz lost all sense of time as the *Iron Duke* steamed north. His consciousness was directed solely on the baby boy in his arms.

George lay still, slowly emerging from the daze into which he had fallen from the moment the great fire had started. He took no notice of the people around him, but went over and over in his mind the events that had led to this point; his failure, somehow, to arrange for the escape of his staff, even though he had been aware of the approaching crisis. It was he who, over a year ago, had persuaded his father's partner – Karekin Avakian – to dispatch the two 19 year-olds, Paramaz and Karekin's own son, Haik, to Smyrna. And now Haik was dead – and it was he who was going to have to explain, even though he didn't know how it had happened.

Then there was Olga! He was not, of course, in way responsible for her presence in Smyrna and he had no idea what might have happened to her. Nevertheless, he was the one who would have to tell her parents something. How were they going to cope? They would be facing the certain loss of their only son and the uncertainty of what might have happened to their second daughter. George had difficulty in articulating his feelings, and was acutely sensitive to the thought of pain to others. How was he going to communicate the death of Haik to his family?

His thoughts turned to Sima, the eldest of the four daughters of the Avakian family to whom he had almost been engaged, and with whom he had fallen in love at the very moment she had rejected him. Then, again, the image of Haik – a young man he had been deeply fond of – would drift into his mind, bringing silent tears. These thoughts went round and round in his head, giving him no rest. The loss of the offices, and the complete destruction of the warehouse and all its goods, belonging to the family firm set up by his own father and Karekin, never crossed his mind for an instant. Both families were merchant-adventurers. This sort of financial catastrophe was part of the stock-in-trade of any active merchant house. But the loss of an only son – a cheerful, friendly boy with all his life before him – that was different.

Then at last the fleet passed through the Dardanelles and arrived in the waters facing the incomparably dramatic shoreline of the city of Constantinople. This city, the capital of a great Christian empire for over a thousand years, then the capital of an equally great Muslim empire for almost a further five hundred, the seat of the longest-lasting caliphate in Muslim history, was currently under the administration of a third empire – the British – at the height of its imperial reach.

Admiral Brock could not wait to tidy up his flagship and be rid of all the refugees he had reluctantly taken on board. Ironically, this was one of the small advantages for the assorted mixture of civilians huddled in various corners of the ship. The admiral – commander of all the British warships throughout the eastern Mediterranean – was in a position to demand immediate attention from the local authorities and their British advisors – and so it was that the *Iron Duke* was one of the first boats to start off-loading all its homeless humanity.

George and Paramaz stepped off the launch at the Eminonu quayside, rather than at the busy quays under the Galata bridge. Those quays, humming with all the furious hooting and tooting of the ferries jockeying for position, brought throngs of passengers from the villages up and down the straits on both continents or direct from the towns on the Asian side.

Together with all the others from the launch, they were whisked away immediately by a small group of polite Ottoman policemen, and led into a temporary building. This was manned by several Ottoman bureaucrats – effendim in civilian suits wearing the ubiquitous fez – who sat behind a line of desks. Behind them, watching the proceedings, and occasionally intervening, were two British army officers. Paramaz and George, neither of whom had been in Bolis now for over a year, noticed a subtle change had arisen in the relationship between the conquerors of the city and the Ottoman civil servants. The Turks were that bit more assertive, a little bit more independent, while the British officers seemed less sure of their authority.

The baby had begun squalling again and, perhaps as a result, George and Paramaz found that they were among the first to be interviewed. Unafraid for themselves as George had had the foresight to grab his papers before fleeing from the office, they knew they might have difficulty with the baby.

"I see – Paramaz Avakian and George Levonian. Are you from Stamboul?"

"Yes sir", George was doing all the talking. "Here look, you can see that I was born in Bebek."

"Excuse me, effendi" – old Ottoman officials, unlike the new breed of nationalists, were always unfailingly polite – "I do of course see the papers, but we are faced with people presenting forged or stolen documents. You may only land and remain here if you are Ottoman citizens born in this city."

"My parents are here and could vouch for me if necessary."

"Very well. Your papers are clearly in order. What about you sir?"

Paramaz, rocking the baby to and fro, unable to quell its continued wailing and uncomfortably aware of the wetness of the rags round its upper legs, stared back at the official. George said quickly in his upper-class Ottoman Turkish speech which had already impressed the official –

"He is the adopted son of Karekin Avakian, one of the important merchants of the city."

"And why can't he answer for himself?"

"Sir, I am having difficulty with my baby – I'm sorry – but yes that is indeed so. I live in Makrikoy."

The official immediately recognised Paramaz's peasant Anatolian Turkish accent. Only a few months ago his lip might have curled in good-natured contempt, but times were changing. As Mustapha Kemal's nationalist armies of Anatolian peasants were closing in on the old city, the words 'Anadolu Turk' were for the first time in five hundred years no longer pejorative. The once-mighty city of Constantinople, which had effortlessly dominated Asia Minor for centuries, was fearfully awaiting the arrival of this avenging Anatolian army. The official nodded at the baby who continued to cry out in that high-pitched scream guaranteed by evolution to upset every human within earshot –

"And the baby?"

George again quickly intervened.

"Oh, effendi bey, his wife died during the evacuation of Smyrna and he has been distraught ever since as you can see, and he has had to look after the baby all this time on his own without the help of its mother's milk."

Paramaz marvelled at the speed and clarity of George's answers. He looked at the official who was clearly looking for some excuse to refuse entry at least to this Armenian peasant.

The British officer who had overheard George's last remark as he passed, had stopped behind him. Paramaz, meanwhile, suddenly thought of his 'wife', the wife George had conjured up for him and who had died in the terrible death of Ottoman Smyrna. Without knowing quite why or for what, Paramaz began weeping silently. He wept not only for the baby's mother, but also for the wife he never had.

The British officer murmured something to the official who shrugged.

"You may leave effendim."

Wearily, they walked out into the sunshine. Paramaz, who had been unable to weep at the rape and slaughter of his mother, in front of his very eyes, or at his sister's deaths, and whose tears had dried up forever all those years ago, wept silently, tears running down his cheeks. He held the baby tightly to his chest, until the baby's cries subsided. Paramaz released his grip and rocked the baby back and forth, back and forth.

All around them the life of the city pulsated. They saw the Galata bridge with its crowds toing and froing, with more trams and 'otomobils' than they remembered from a year ago and less animals – but still one of the great crossing bridges of the world. As Paramaz's tears at last dried up, George considered what he had to do first. He wanted above all to go home to see his mother and sister, or at least to go to the Levonian offices in Pera and be enfolded in his father's arms. But the matter of Haik's death and Olga's uncertain fate had to be dealt with first. But how?

"Paramaz – are you all right? Good. What will you do now?"

"I'll go home – the only home I know – to the Avakians and try to tell them all that has happened."

"And the baby?"

"He is mine" replied Paramaz fiercely. "I will look after him. I will see to him – I will see to him."

"But for God's sake – how, how?"

Paramaz was silent, looking down at the now sleeping bundle. Then without a further word, he stretched out his free hand, touched George gently on the shoulder, held it there for a long moment, settled the baby firmly on his hip and turned with the clear intention of walking back up to Sirkedji station.

If George wondered fleetingly how Paramaz was going to pay for the trip back to Makrikoy, he said nothing, but simply watched as Paramaz turned to go up to the station. Emotionally drained, George stood for some moments longer, ignoring all the busy crowds around him, but then making up his mind, he hurried after Paramaz.

At Makrikoy, alighting at the Cobancesme station, Paramaz and George took a carriage up the hill to the Avakian home instead of walking. It was midday, the baby was at last asleep, exhausted by lack of food and discomfort. Of the family, only Armineh was at home when Paramaz found the bell and rang. Talin opened the door, took one look at Paramaz and screamed out loud. Armineh and Marie bustled out into the Hall in a rush.

Paramaz walked in – dirty – dishevelled – hungry, and with a fierce look of despair in his eyes. He was followed by George, who was unable to look anyone in the eye, but simply stared down at the floor. Armineh took one look at each of them and realised the worst at once. She did not need to be told. Haik was not with them, so….. Her heart pounded, and she could scarcely stand up. Marie, equally distressed, came forward and held her.

"And Haik, Paramaz, – my son Haik? – my son?"

"I am sorry, Armineh-hanum. I am so sorry. Oh God, your son is dead – shot – and then surely consumed by the flames."

Armineh stood still. She did not faint, though her heart was beating so fast she was almost overcome. She couldn't take it all in – there was a mist before her eyes. She swayed and almost collapsed, but was held tight by Marie – her son, her only son.

And at last Paramaz, who was, after all, still only 19, gave way to the sheer horror of all that had happened to him, of all the terrible things he himself had done. In his mind, he had almost satisfied himself that the shooting of Haik had been an accident, but he was now reminded that that could not apply to the shots he had aimed at the shadowy figure of Selim.

He burst into tears – no longer silent, but deep throbbing sobs. This triggered something in Armineh, who began howling, almost like an animal in pain. This went on for some moments -

an eternity for both of them - as Marie looked on helplessly, herself distraught at the thought of the fifteen years she had helped to look after this boy, who she would never see ever again; but then at last all the noise woke up the baby, who began screaming.

Armineh stopped at once and her eyes cleared and focused on the bundle in Paramaz's arms

"For God's sake, Paramaz, what is that?"

Paramaz stopped sobbing, pulled himself together and looking down at the screaming bundle in his arms said,

"A baby, Digin Armineh, a baby. I have to look after it – it's a little boy."

Paramaz stood looking at the women, and then for the first time bent forward and kissed the child. He slowly rocked the little boy to calm him down, all the while explaining how he had come to look after him. Paramaz was no fool. He knew that in the long run he would be unable to care for the child in his arms without help. As his voice finally died away, he waited. He thought about Haik and Selim and his part in their deaths. He remembered his mother and his two little sisters and the way they had died. He waited in the long pause that followed the end of his story, continuing to cradle the baby in his arms.

The silence dragged on.

Then, Armineh shook her head and tried to dry her tears with the back of her sleeve. She walked forward as if in a dream, freeing herself from Marie's support, and taking the little boy from Paramaz's arms, she looked at him with tears still running down her face. She had not cradled a child for over ten years. Holding herself stiffly upright, she passed the baby over to Marie and said,

"Come along Marie, this little man needs a good bath, some nice clean clothes and a warm drink."

Armineh turned to go up the great stairs of the Avakian house, but it was all too much, even for her indomitable spirit. As she set foot on the first step, she sagged, her eyes shot up into her head and she fell back in a faint into the arms of George, who had been a silent witness throughout, and anticipating what was about to happen, rushed forward to catch her.

CHAPTER 4

Harry

Harry had never thought of himself as being particularly sensitive or introverted. His father, Colonel William Bridgeman, always so careful to hide from his only son any feelings of sentiment, or love, had encouraged him to remain cool and unemotional in all circumstances, and to avoid any demonstrative display. The unfortunate man, himself the product of a 19th century upbringing, had only ever kissed his son in the middle of the night; looking down on the sleeping boy, fearful that he would awake and catch him in a moment of weakness.

The minor public school Harry had attended – a 19th century Arnoldian copy of Eton – had reinforced this attitude by encouraging self-sufficiency in its young boys. This was achieved by inculcating a strong, muscular Christianity, backed up by liberal thrashings. This had the desired effect of persuading the boys to despise tears and any sign of weakness.

Harry had the innate strength of character to stand up to this regime without turning into a bully himself. As he grew physically bigger and stronger, he was prepared to oppose the atmosphere of bullying and contempt for the weak and vulnerable, which was such a feature of his schooldays. Boys brought up during the privileged days of Edwardian England were regularly beaten, in order to ensure they became God-fearing Christians, prepared to go out into the world and fight for King and Country without question. Harry received his full share of punishment, but it had not changed his basic nature. He conformed not because he had to, or because it was more comfortable to do so, but because he had worked out for himself that it was a fairly reasonable philosophy if kept within bounds.

Having become a naval officer, despite opposition from his

father – an Army man who had followed generations of Bridgemans as Army officers – Harry had seen active service through the war and the immediate years following the different armistices of 1918. From the start of the Gallipoli campaign of April 1915, he had been stationed with the fleet in the Eastern Mediterranean. He had witnessed the pointless and banal death of Rupert Brooke on a remote Greek island in the Aegean. He had been with the fleet delivering the army onto the beaches of the Dardanelles. He had been present at the harrowing scenes of the evacuation of the White Russians from Sevastopol. He had witnessed the effects of modern warfare in a variety of situations, but had never seen anything like the burning of Smyrna. As the captain of the destroyer HMS *Lion*, lying with the rest of the fleet in the great bay, he had disobeyed orders and picked up as many survivors from the sea, as his ship could safely carry. He and his men watched helplessly while the city burned for two more days. The quaysides filled up with thousands and thousands of despairing human beings, mostly women and children, trapped between the great fire and the waters of the harbour, while some of the ships of the large allied fleet stationed in the bay, continued to stand idly by.

The smell of burning wood and other building materials, mixed with the unmistakeable odour of burned human flesh, was seared into his memory. For the further two or three days that the British fleet remained in the Bay of Smyrna, Harry, together with all the other sailors, had to listen each night as moans and prayers arose from the crowds in their thousands milling about on the seafront with nowhere to go – caught between the burnt and red-hot cinders of the city behind them and the sea at their front.

Once night fell, the undisciplined Turkish troops began their orgy of rape, slaughter and robbery, moving at will through the helpless crowds. This in turn caused the crowds to start screaming and the screams and shrieks went on for hour after hour. On the British flagship – the *Iron Duke* – the navy bands would play operatic arias and Strauss waltzes all night on the orders of Admiral Sir Osmond de Beauvoir Brock. Trying to be as charitable as possible, Harry believed it might have been ordered by the Admiral in the vain hope of keeping up morale – but its actual effect was simply to drown out the sounds of horror coming from the shore.

Eventually the Admiral had relented and changed his orders, allowing ships from his fleet to take on those in danger of drowning together with a few refugees from the shore. As the fires at last began to die down, the Allied ships began to leave the bay. The British fleet steamed away heading for Constantinople. As the bay emptied, Harry, already in a state of considerable emotional turmoil, looked back and saw the line of Ottoman citizens along the seashore, numbering at least 200,000, raise their hands forward in a pointless gesture of supplication. A final moan rose from the crowd as the ships slowly turned away and headed out towards the open sea.

A cry of pain from one person is a tragic enough sound. The same sound from over 200,000 desperate souls makes a noise that carries a long way, a sound any sensitive human being would remember all their lives – and so it was with Harry. This cool British naval officer, brought up in the best traditions of duty and service, a model of calm and discipline, an inspiration to the men under his command, began to have fearful nightmares. Years of service and training came to his aid, and his command was handled impeccably, but his mind would not rest. The Fleet finally arrived in the waters off the wonderful shoreline of the city of Constantinople.

Once the British Admiral of the fleet had reversed his orders on the third day of the fire, swimmers had been picked up by many of the British captains, who had also sent boats to pick up some of the destitute from the shore. Accordingly the fleet now held a large number of refugees from the dying city of Smyrna – a mere drop in the ocean of course, but nevertheless some lives saved. One by one the ships' launches carried their few survivors to the shore, off-loading them at the Eminonu quayside where the Ottoman authorities had set up a reception area, supervised by the British occupation administration. Harry sent the 200 or so people he had rescued to the shore. He then ordered a major clean-up of the ship.

Harry had clashed once before with his commanding officer – Admiral Brock – when he had dared to question the racist and xenophobic attitudes of the American High Commissioner at a dinner the Admiral had been hosting on the *Iron Duke*, thus causing the Admiral some embarassment. He knew that he would be court-martialled for the decision he had made in Smyrna the night of the outbreak of the great fire. But he was quite calm and clear in his own mind that he had acted correctly, not only as a human being, but also fully within the traditions of an officer of the Royal Navy.

Classically educated, Harry knew there had been many great destructive fires in history deliberately started by humans – the total destruction of Carthage by the Romans came to mind. But in Carthage there had been no great line of battleships moored beside the city looking on as the city burned; a situation for which their own governments had been largely responsible. Furthermore, Harry thought, the vengeful Romans had at least first removed all the surviving civilians from the city.

Harry thought that weeks might well pass before he would hear about any court-martial. But he was wrong.

On the very first day of the arrival of the fleet in Constantinople, Admiral Brock had gone to pay a visit to the American High Commissioner at Constantinople – Admiral Mark Bristol. Bristol was an outspoken American whose anti-semitic jibes, and constant disparaging remarks about the devious Greeks and Armenians, pained the aristocratic British Admiral. Still, his own views were on the whole fairly similar, the only difference being that Bristol openly proclaimed his beliefs to the world; Brock was more diplomatic.

"My dear Bristol I have to confirm that the whole thing was a terrible affair. There were still thousands of refugees on the seafront with the whole of the city burned behind them."

"Admiral Brock, I am quite convinced that the depiction of events by those returning from Smyrna is totally unbalanced, both as to who was responsible and the numbers actually killed."

"Well sir, I won't argue with you, but I have to repeat that several of my officers quite clearly saw Turkish soldiers, even officers, pouring petrol on properties not yet burned – and even on the quaysides amongst the civilian refugees."

"Rubbish, man, rubbish! It is clear to me that the burning of the city was an accident. My own opinion is that after the Turkish army entered the city – in total discipline I would remind you – some Armenians and Greeks decided to burn their own houses so they couldn't be occupied by anyone else. All this nonsense about petrol is a total fabrication, take it from me. Anyway, it was only when the wind arose that the whole city went up in smoke."

In fairness to Admiral Brock, he did not agree with the opinionated Bristol, whose prejudices about the subject races of the Ottoman Empire were well-known to all, but he was not prepared to argue. He had gone to seek Bristol's cooperation for a possible joint approach to the Turkish nationalists regarding the refugees still lining the seafront at Smyrna, and needed to play along with the man's prejudices. He failed, but in the course of discussing the matter further, Harry's name came up and Brock inadvertently let out the facts of Harry's decision to pick up survivors from the bay when he had been given clear orders not to do so. Bristol was emphatic –

"My dear Admiral, you cannot allow the matter to rest for even a day. I remember him – an argumentative troublemaker, I seem to recall, without any idea of the real issues at stake here. I suspect he's the type ready to spread lies about the events in Smyrna and to inflame the press on the matter. I would muzzle him immediately, before any other of your officers get ideas above their station."

Admiral Brock came away from the meeting without any support from the American for any joint approach to the Kemalists over the situation in Smyrna. He had an instinctive distaste for Bristol's bourgeois vulgarity and bigotry, but where Harry was concerned, he thought that Bristol was probably right. It was necessary for Harry to be removed here and now from command, even before any court-martial could be convened.

Within another day, Brock had radioed the Admiralty in London setting out briefly the circumstances and recommending, indeed insisting on, an early court-martial, either here in Constantinople or in London. The answer from London was immediate. As so many of the witnesses were likely to be stationed in Constantinople, the court-martial would be held there at a venue to be decided and a senior officer would be appointed to preside. Meanwhile Captain Bridgeman was to be on suspended leave with full pay, without any loss of rank or privileges.

Some days later, Harry's replacement, nominated by the Admiral, was piped aboard. Having folded up all his uniforms and placed all his personal belongings in several suitcases, Harry shook hands with all the ship's officers and left on the ship's launch. This landed Harry at the Galata Bridge alongside all the ferries busily shunting in and out, picking up and setting down their passengers from the little towns up and down the straits. Having lived so long in and around the city, he knew what he was about. He hired two porters and walked up the iron stairs onto the bridge.

The Galata Bridge!

This bridge across the entrance to the Golden Horn, connecting old Stamboul to Pera and Galata was the hub of the Ottoman world. It was filled with all the races of the empire crossing from one side to the other; Turkish hanums predominantly veiled but some women with open countenances, from whose faces the more old-fashioned male citizens averted their gaze; Armenian and Greek merchants now suddenly wearing the fez again after three years of trilbys and panama hats; elderly Ottoman Turks unfailingly polite and wearing the fez; young Turkish men swaggering triumphantly, all sporting Enver-style moustaches but, ironically, no longer wearing the fez; peasants from eastern Thrace riding donkeys; British officers, still in command, but no longer with local ladies in tow; Kurdish porters, Jewish rabbis, Albanian riff-raff, former Russian soldiers,

donkeys, camels, trams clattering across and more and more
motorcars. Harry had seen it all before. He loved it, but he had
important things to do and couldn't linger. Deciding against the
Pera Palace Hotel, he ordered the horse cab to go to the Park
Otel on Taksim.

Harry was clear in his mind that he must do something about
the nightmares he was having. The keenest impression that
remained with him from his days by the Bay of Smyrna, binoculars trained on the seafront, was a deep, abiding feeling of
shame. This was not the horror of men fighting in the ghastly
conditions of trench warfare; it was not the sight of men blinded
by gas forming a line to stumble back sightless from the front; it
was not bodies lying bleeding and dying in the war. He was able
to cope with all that – he was after all a seasoned officer experienced in the terrible realities of war. But Smyrna was different.
He couldn't analyse it. There had been four fleets in the harbour
– British, French, Italian and American. All had been filled with
healthy and active young men, of whom he was one. Meanwhile
on the seafront, there had been old men, women of all ages,
children and babies, all in deep distress and no young men to
help them at all.

Harry did not hate anyone – he did not blame anyone – he
just felt deep shame for being on the side of those who, to all
intents and purposes, did nothing – nothing at all – to redress
the balance. He knew that he had to do something – if necessary,
go back to what was left of Smyrna if he could – to get rid of this
sense of shame.

Harry acted quickly and decisively. Going on any British ship
would be out of the question. However over the years, Harry had
made contacts with many shipmates and captains. Within a few
hours of arriving at the hotel, he had already checked on, and
given up on, a series of possible freighters, none of whose
captains were thinking of going back to Smyrna, despite the
rumours of large quantities of baled tobacco standing unburnt,
waiting to be picked up for profitable delivery.

Eventually, by the afternoon, he heard that an American

destroyer – the USS *Lawrence* – was planning to leave the city for Smyrna the very next day to check on possible further American citizens requiring evacuation. Harry, still in uniform, hired a private motorboat and had himself taken alongside. He knew the captain from previous encounters at the bar of the Pera Palace. It did not take him long to persuade the man to let him travel on the *Lawrence* as an observer – promising to come aboard in civilian clothes. He said that he knew Smyrna well and would be willing to help, if necessary, to pick up any US citizens.

Harry arranged to come on board the next afternoon just before the ship was to sail. The die was cast – Harry felt excited though how he might be able to help was still unclear. He had the whole of the next morning free so he decided to go and visit his friends the Avakian family in the suburb of Makrikoy.

CHAPTER 5

The Avakians in Crisis

Armineh had fainted from the sheer emotional strain of the news. However, once recovered, she knew she would have to cope. Within minutes after first making sure that Marie and Talin were able to look after the baby, she went upstairs to her own bedroom on her own two feet. George simply looked round helplessly and then departed quickly, leaving Paramaz standing alone in the middle of the hall staring into space.

Once in her own room, Armineh lay back on the bed and gave way to her grief. "My son – my only son – oh my darling boy, my son, my son." This was repeated in a low murmur over and over again. The thought that she would never see his cheerful smiling face, that she would never again have to get him to tuck in his shirt or do up his tie or stop talking incessantly, devastated her, and her tears flowed and flowed.

But, after almost two hours had passed, the tears dried up and she began to think of all those for whom she was responsible. Sima would surely be all right – she had her all-consuming love for Nicolai to fall back on. But – oh God – Nerissa! How would Nerissa manage? She had to be strong for her. Seta, on the other hand, was young, she would bounce back, but Nerissa could collapse completely if not treated with care. Armineh got up, washed and began to think. In the end she knew she would manage her children – but she was not so sure that she could manage her husband. He would not say a word – he would stand there stiff and unbending and only she would know how much he suffered. How could she comfort him? What could she say to him?

Armineh contemplated all the possibilities. Then she remembered the baby that Paramaz had brought back from Smyrna. How would Karekin react? And Paramaz himself – how was it possible that Haik had been shot while Paramaz appeared to have got away without a scratch? Could she bear never knowing for sure what had *really* happened? And where was Olga? Her mind raced back and forth as she lay back on the bed again and at last sank into a merciful hour's sleep.

When she awoke, she knew she had to act, She got up, brushed her hair, dressed carefully avoiding any suggestion of black and came downstairs. Paramaz, Marie and Talin had clearly been listening out for her and each stood by the dining table outside the kitchen door.

"Now, Marie, what's happened to the baby?"

"Madame, I've put him in the old nursery – he's fast asleep."

"What's his name, Paramaz?"

"I don't know, Digin Armineh, I just don't know. The mother handed him to me just before she died on that damned quayside."

"Don't swear, Paramaz," said Armineh automatically. "Where is George?"

"He's gone home."

"Talin – pull yourself together girl. Go and fill some bottles with warm milk, Marie will show you how. We must wait until my husband returns to decide what should be done about the baby"

"I won't let him go – I won't let him go," Paramaz cried out.

"Paramaz, calm down, calm down and don't raise your voice

like that."

"I'm sorry Digin Armineh – I'm sorry," murmured Paramaz.

"It's not a question of who will be looking after him," continued Armineh. "It's the problem of officialdom – bureaucracy. In this day and age, even in all this chaos, you can't just add a baby to a family without doing something about it with the necessary authorities. Karekin will know what to do."

Armineh was able to get some small comfort from slipping into her role as family manager. She knew that activity would help push the reality of her son's death to the back of her mind, but these thoughts were only just below the surface. And then – oh God what about Olga?

"Paramaz – what about Olga – what happened to her, do you know?"

"I really don't know; but I can tell you that in those last terrible days she was with Selim and …"

"What was Selim doing there?"

"I don't know – Oh God, I really don't know. I…" And Paramaz covered his face with his hands.

Armineh had never liked Paramaz much. She had always been suspicious of him and was instinctively aware that he had once caused some distress to Seta. But now she could see that he was in a state of genuine anguish, and she decided not to press him further.

"Now listen carefully Paramaz. I want you to go now and find Vahan. He will be in the bazaar at the Asadourian shop. Explain the circumstances to him and tell him that I would be very grateful if he could make a point of coming here before Miss Nerissa gets back from her classes. Then go round to Karekin's office. Listen carefully. Don't see him, and if by chance you do, say nothing – just leave a message that his wife needs him and asks him to come home as soon as possible. Now – go. Don't worry about the baby, we'll look after him."

Armineh had it all worked out in her mind. Vahan, Nerissa's good friend and a favourite in the Avakian family, would be here to give support to Nerissa when she got back from University. Sima would be back soon and once over the shock, she would help with Karekin once he arrived. Armineh waited. She knew that Karekin would know at once what had happened the moment he entered the house.

It is not necessary to chronicle in voyeuristic and harrowing detail all aspects of the Avakian grief, person by person, over the next two days. There was Sima, who, like all eldest sisters in large extended families, had had to hold Haik's hand from when he was a few years old, had helped him to take his first fumbling steps, had relieved her mother from time to time carrying him and had taken him to school during those terrible days in 1915. He had been closest to Nerissa with whom he had played when they were both little. She wept and wept as she recalled that only he had listened patiently when she needed someone to pour out all her teenage angst. Then there was Seta, mercifully too young to suffer long from grief. Finally there was Karekin. Mixed in with the terrible anguish over the death of his only son, was the inchoate guilt of the survivor – 'Asvadz, asvadzim why did I survive in 1915 only to send my only son to his death seven years later'.

Above all, the whole process of grieving was made more difficult, not only because there was no body, but also because there had been no clear and coherent account of how Haik had died. For two days Karekin stayed at home, and they all sat round the table for hours talking about Haik, remembering him and in Avakian fashion even breaking into argument as to when and how some event in his life had taken place. Armineh and Karekin dozed in each other's arms and slowly the family came to terms with the death.

Then on the fourth day, Karekin gathered the family round the dining table after breakfast. He invited Paramaz and Marie to sit down as well. When everyone was seated, Karekin turned to Paramaz and said –

"Before we talk about the baby, I want to hear from you now the exact details of my son's death. I want it all in detail please from the moment you and he left the Kapamadjian house."

"Karekin effendi, I must explain that the situation in the

Armenian quarter during that day and the following night was terrible. It was not only shops that were being broken into and looted. Bands of soldiers were breaking down the doors of private houses – particularly the larger houses – rushing in, killing any males they found and raping and then often killing the girls and women. Then they would leave, taking with them anything of value they could lay their hands on."

"We heard that the Turkish army had been well-disciplined."

"Maybe on the first couple of days when the cavalry initially entered the town – but once the infantry poured in, with all the guerrillas and hangers-on, it was a different story."

"The American High Commissioner – what's his name? – ah yes Admiral Bristol – has let it be known that all the murder and looting started the moment the Greek governor and police left and before the Turkish army arrived – an arrival that he said relieved the situation."

"That's simply not true, Karekin effendi. It's a clear and deliberate lie and there is absolutely no evidence for it. I saw with my own eyes that for the two days after the Greek administration left and before the Turkish army arrived the streets were completely quiet and orderly. Businesses were open and there was no animosity whatsoever between the ethnic communities. The port was operating normally and tobacco was being loaded right up to the moment of the entry of the Turkish army. I saw no rioting or killing or looting of any kind."

"Ah well, never mind – please go on."

"Haik and I decided that we had better get to the harbour and meet up with George, who as you know lived in a flat above the offices. But first Haik insisted that we go to pick up Olga – or at least make sure that she was all right."

"Yes, yes – he would," muttered the family.

"Where then was Olga living?" said Karekin. "Wasn't she at one of the two hospitals at which she was working?"

At this point Paramaz hesitated for the first time. It did not need a shrewd appreciation of his character for it to be clear to all that he was measuring his next words carefully.

"Karekin effendi, I was not aware at the time but it seems that

Haik knew that Olga had taken a small suite of rooms in a private house near the Armenian hospital."

"Very well – get on with it."

"Er – it's a little difficult to explain, sir, ...but when we got to the house Olga was not able to come with us directly...."

"Why, Paramaz, why for god's sake? What the blazes are you trying to say"

"Because Selim was with her and he was badly wounded and couldn't move or be moved."

"Selim – Selim – what are you talking about, lad. Selim..." Karekin spluttered and could hardly speak.

Armineh, who together with both Sima and Nerissa, had already worked out for themselves from hints picked up from Paramaz that Olga had been living with Selim in those last days of Ottoman Smyrna, looked directly at her husband and said –

"My soul, my dearest – Selim Kemal – Olga's friend – you must remember."

"But what the hell was he doing in Smyrna, or did he arrive with the Turkish army. Oh God where is she now – Paramaz for God's sake, tell me."

But now Paramaz had again become distressed. Tears came to his eyes as he blurted out,

"I don't know – I just don't know!"

Karekin immediately calmed down and looked at Paramaz, who cast his eyes down muttering apologies.

"Well go on."

"Haik and I went out in order to find a cart to help in moving Selim to one of the hospitals. There were many lying about in the streets brought in by refugees from the outlying villages who were now on the quayside. Haik immediately saw one further up the road, and before I could say anything he ran forward to get it. But it turned out to have been taken by some Turkish soldiers who were looting the house outside which it was standing. They came out just as Haik went running up to take hold of the cart. The soldiers dropped their loot, pulled out their rifles as Haik turned to run back. But it was too late – too late. Three shots rang out and I saw Haik fall dead. I had been walking forward too, but I turned to run. They chased after me, but I got away through some back streets and eventually found my way to George."

There was a long, drawn out silence as everyone tried to imagine the scene.

"And what about Olga?"

"I don't know," said Paramaz. He put his head into his hands and began crying. No one had ever seen Paramaz cry like that before, except Armineh who had already been surprised by his tears on the first day.

Karekin stared at Paramaz. He wanted to strike somebody – anybody – and Paramaz was the closest to hand. He felt Armineh's hand touching his arm lightly. He swallowed his anger, took a deep breath and nodded at Armineh to confirm that he was in control of himself. However he felt sure as he stared at Paramaz that there was something lying unsaid between them.

"Well – let's now talk about the baby. What do you know of him Paramaz? I understand that you don't even know his name or whether he has been baptized yet. I presume that it was an Armenian mother to whom you were talking. Speak up boy, speak up, I can't hear you."

Paramaz was now in a state bordering on the terror he suffered on that terrible seafront. Lie upon lie was ensnaring him as he muttered –

"Yes, effendi bey, I think so...I think so..."

All his original contempt, indeed almost hatred, for this elite liberal family who had come to his rescue, lay in ruins as his mind swirled round and round the events of those last few days in Smyrna. It was an accident, wasn't it? An accident that had resulted in his being the hand that had shot the only son of this family, each one of whom had only ever showed him kindness. Now he sat looking away from this man whom, in his ignorance, he had dismissed as a liberal weakling.

Karekin could hardly contain himself. Everyone was uncomfortably aware that there was more to the story than Paramaz was disclosing. But both Armineh and the two elder girls thought that it was an unusual delicacy on his part. They considered that maybe Paramaz wanted to avoid making Olga's liaison with Selim too clear to Karekin. Armineh intervened at this point, and reducing the tension, said –

"Karekin, my soul, what are we to do about the baby?"

"My darling, I have already thought it out. He is to remain with us of course. I don't even care if he turns out to have been a Turk. I am proposing to register the boy as an Armenian orphan, whom I am adopting as our son."

There was another long silence as everyone looked into their hearts at how this decision might affect them. Paramaz, unable even now to control his tears stood up, walked to the end of the table in the silence that had followed and knelt on both knees by Karekin's side. He got hold of Karekin's hand and tried to lift it to his lips in a gesture of humility and respect. But Karekin pulled it away before the gesture could be completed.

"Karekin effendi, I want you to give the wages you pay me towards the cost of looking after this baby."

Karekin was about to refuse, even to laugh at the absurdity of the suggestion, when he caught sight of Armineh. He knew that look and he immediately held back the cutting remark he was about to make. Armineh, meanwhile, got up from her chair and said quietly –

"That is generous of you Paramaz, we will think further and...." But at this precise moment there was a ring at the front door.

"Must be someone who knows where our bell is," said Nerissa automatically.

Talin ran out of the kitchen and went to open the door. In walked Harry in civilian clothes. He passed his hat to Talin with a smile and then walked forward as everyone stared.

Harry could see at once that there was an atmosphere of crisis and that the family were in some sort of conclave. For a start, it was unusual for Karekin to be at home at this hour. He said at once –

"Oh dear, I am very sorry everyone. I've come at the wrong time I can see. Please excuse me."

THE AVAKIANS IN CRISIS 51

The language immediately turned to English in that effortless, automatic way which was such a feature of the Bolsetsi.

"No, no, my boy. Come in, come in" said Karekin, who was fairly relieved that the distressing family business could now be set aside for the moment at least. Giving Harry no time to refuse, he said – "I think it would be a good time for some coffee don't you think? Shekerli?"

Harry mumbled his thanks and then went round to shake hands with Armineh. Seta, whose eyes were red and who had clearly been crying, jumped up and ran into Harry's arms. Harry lifted her and she hugged him, but then started crying again and ran out of the room as Harry put her down. After all this time, Harry was no longer the slightest bit embarrassed at the emotional excesses of the Avakians. He smiled and nodded at Sima and Nerissa on the other side of the table.

By mutual consent, all sat down again round the table as Paramaz and Talin left, and Marie went into the kitchen to make the coffee.

It didn't take long for Harry to be told the dreadful news about Haik in Smyrna. Harry had always been a good listener and he did not interrupt as the story related by Paramaz unfolded. Then, to everyone's amazement, he told them of his own experiences – the voyage to Smyrna of HMS *Lion* to join the fleet already there – the events that had occurred in the bay – and his witnessing of the terrible fire, which had engulfed the city. Finally he came out with his second surprise of the morning.

"You know, I am going back there this very afternoon or tomorrow at the latest. I am haunted by the sight of all those people lining the seafront, waiting. I will do what I can."

Harry had said nothing about the pending court-martial or his own predicament, though in the circumstances, none of the Avakians thought to question him. Everyone round the table was quick to realise what this revelation might mean. They waited for Karekin to speak.

"Harry, my boy, I wonder if you could do something for us if you get the chance. As we just explained, Olga, too, was in that ill-fated city a week ago. She was working three days a week at the Imperial Ottoman Hospital, and three days a week at the Armenian hospital. We have had no news of her at all. Paramaz saw her on the last day before the fire broke out but can give us no further information as to what may have happened to her. Please if you have the time, could you kindly make some enquiries as best you can at both hospitals and see if you can find anything out."

"But my dear friends, of course, of course, I will consider it my primary task."

Harry soon had to take his leave once the gharry had been called up for him. The girls came up and kissed him warmly. Harry shook Karekin's hand, and then for the first time in their relationship gave Armineh a chaste kiss on the cheek.

Harry boarded the USS *Lawrence* that same afternoon. The ship left for the Dardanelles and the Aegean Sea some time after.

CHAPTER 6

Waiting for Ships

Nothing in Spiro's short life could have prepared him for the ordeal that he now faced and which lasted for over ten days, huddled on the quayside at the Point in Smyrna. He spent a lot of the time with his head buried in his mother's lap, not wanting to see too much of what was going on around him. He slept a lot during the day from a mixture of hunger and exhaustion.

For two whole days the fire burned uncontrollably. The entire city was ablaze. On both those nights, Spiro found it difficult to sleep as the whole harbour was lit up, bathing the whole bay in a sinister daytime glow. Thousands of now homeless citizens of Ottoman Smyrna surged up and down the quays, never able to get far due to the pressure of numbers. Spiro heard the shrieks and screams of the women and children unable to get away from the heat – a heat which had already caused some of the allied ships to turn and move further away from the shoreline.

By the weekend, the fires were beginning to burn themselves

out, largely due to the fact there was nothing left to burn. But the brutality and random killing by the Turkish soldiery during the nights continued unabated, as they wandered amongst the refugees. Any males older than 14 or younger than 50 were grabbed and marched off, or executed on the spot. Spiro couldn't help but watch as a group armed with clubs, including not only uniformed soldiers but also an officer, fell on a man and clubbed him to death not more than 50 feet away from him. Spiro could hear the bones snap. Eventually the body was nonchalantly kicked into the sea, after it was searched for any valuables. "Ermeni" ('Armenian') said one of the men to no one in particular, as if that in itself was sufficient explanation – and the group moved on.

It was shortly after this incident that Agape, almost hysterical with fear, produced the short skirt and blouse she had grabbed before leaving the house.

"Spiro, come here and stand behind me against the wall. Take off your shirt and pants and put these on."

"Mama – no – why?" and Spiro backed away from his mother whose wild eyes and dishevelled hair scared him.

"Listen, it's your only hope. Can't you see that they are killing all the men. Do it, just do it!"

Fortunately at this point Costas, who was sitting, trying to keep as low a profile as possible, saw what was going on and called out –

"Mother, don't be so ridiculous. It's dangerous enough for him being a young boy – but if he becomes a girl, he'll be taken aside for certain."

Spiro did not understand what his mother and brother were going on about – but he pulled away from his mother's grasp. She burst into tears afresh, unable to make up her mind what was for the best. Standing in the middle of all that horror and confusion, she finally let go of the pathetic bundle of girls clothing which fell to the ground and soon disintegrated under the feet of the passing crowds.

Shortly after that, both his brother and his father were finally singled out by a party of somewhat better disciplined soldiers, led by a competent officer, and were grabbed. Agape jumped up and clung on to her husband, crying out unintelligibly. She was roughly pulled away as Spiro's father, head down, a look of shame crossing his face at his inability to resist, was led away. This had given a moment for Costas to lean down and embrace Spiro and to whisper – "Goodbye, little man – look after our mother". Then he too was pulled away and they both joined a group of males – all Greeks – and were marched away. Costas managed to look back just before they turned the corner. Spiro, whose eyes were glued to him the whole time saw a little smile, a wave of the hand and then nothing.

The days passed. Now the crowds of 200,000 souls, containing a few old men over 50, but otherwise mostly women and children, waited, huddled in desperation, squatting, lying on the hard road, leaning against the remaining walls which by now had lost their terrible heat. No food, precious little water and above all no ships. Mustapha Kemal's ultimatum was shortly due to expire. Once it did, all that would be left was deportation to the interior – days and weeks of weary trekking to nowhere with little food and no hope; the Armenian deportations of 1915 all over again – a planned programme of deliberate long-drawn-out extermination.

Meanwhile the whole of Greece was in deep mourning. The main buildings in the cities were draped in black. Everywhere black sheets were hanging out of windows, black ribbons were tied round carriages and round people's arms. Flags were flying at half mast. The lively restaurants on the seafronts or in the towns played no music of any sort, and the atmosphere on the streets and in the cafes was feverish and explosive. The King did not emerge in public and the government was nervous and shaky.

There was not a soul in the whole kingdom unaffected by the plight of the more than a quarter million surviving Greeks waiting for rescue from the ruins of Smyrna and the sea. But where were the ships? Where was the political will to do something about it? The Greek state had the largest merchant marine capacity in the entire Mediterranean. The Turkish nationalists did not possess any fleet at all, not a single ship. Nevertheless, no ships appeared in the bay of Smyrna.

As if to underline the lack of any initiative from Athenian officialdom, at some time on the Monday, after Costas and his father had been marched off, never to be heard of again, a shabby little freighter manoeuvred its way into the harbour. She was flying the flag of the defunct Tsarist empire, and had calmly sailed down from Constantinople, past all the increasingly irrelevant naval might of the British and French fleets and so into Smyrna. No one knew the nationality of the captain who yelled at everyone in a stentorian voice that could be heard up and down the quay in a mixture of bad English and even worse Greek. Yet, ignoring all the bales of tobacco waiting to be profitably taken aboard, he took off as many of the desperate refugees as the ship could safely hold, and sailed away to Piraeus.

In all the chaos, selfishness and bureaucratic obscurantism displayed by the Greek administration of the time, one announcement at last stood out to save the honour, if nothing more, of the catastrophic Royalist government in its dying days. Greece made it clear that desperate though her situation was, bankrupt, overcrowded and defeated, now one of the poorest nations in Europe, she would nevertheless be prepared to accept within her borders any refugee from the Anatolian debacle, any former Ottoman citizen be they Greek, Armenian, Jew or any other nationality. In contrast to this noble declaration, many homeless Smyrniotes of different ethnic backgrounds who escaped and eventually managed to make it to the richest country in the world, were turned back from Ellis Island.

Still no ships!

Meanwhile the victorious Turkish soldiers had clear license to rob and rape, almost as if it was part of official policy to reward them after the end of a hard campaign. Appeasement was pointless, for when eventually those troops wandering the quaysides were withdrawn, fresh soldiers arrived repeating the previous excesses with renewed vigour. No girls between the ages of 13 and 30 were safe, and by the end, when the count was finally taken, for every hundred old men, women and children that managed to survive, only two were women in that age group.

Robbery too continued enthusiastically. The pathetic bundles of clothes and carpets and the flimsy suitcases had been opened and searched over and over again. There was nothing left. At the same time, the age limit of the girls being grabbed was rising at one end and falling at the other.

A certain amount of food was trickling down. Several American private citizens – working for organisations like the Red Cross or the YMCA, or other relief groups, were carrying out acts of kindness and charity, often with some personal danger to themselves. These private citizens, together with the personal initiative of American sailors, often acting against orders, managed to save the honour of the United States, an honour which Admiral Bristol was doing so much to besmirch. Contrary to all the reports that he was actually receiving from his own officers, on the 22nd September, Bristol sent the following cable for use by the State Department in Washington to pass on to the American media –

"The killings in Smyrna are only by individuals or small bands of rowdies. During fire some unavoidable deaths by drowning as people attempted to swim to boats in the harbour – but few. People massed on quay to escape fire are guarded by Turkish troops. Total deaths not exceeding two thousand."

At the sharp end of the weasel words of all such carefully worded cables, Spiro had no idea what the world's great leaders were doing to end a tragedy that affected him personally and which was growing daily to epic proportions. He was nearly 12 years-old and was perfectly well aware of the menace implicit in the proximity of all these undisciplined soldiers. The so-called 'Turkish troops guarding the people' were, in fact, wading through the desperate crowds picking out young girls and looking for valuables amongst the few remaining personal effects clutched by old women. He could hardly recognise his own mother, who seemed to have aged ten years in under a week, and whose staring eyes barely concealed approaching insanity. There were no longer tears for her husband and her eldest son – these had dried up as the matter of survival for herself and Spiro took precedence.

Still no ships and over a quarter of a million people standing or lying along a two-mile stretch of seafront – waiting – waiting – as Mustapha Kemal's ultimatum was due to expire in less than a week.

Early on the Sunday morning of the 24th September, less than nine days after the fire had burnt itself out, Spiro rose from another night of restless, troubled sleep. Even so early in the morning, people were already shuffling about. The seafront had become a reeking sewer, but the water system was miraculously still operating, and there were stand pipes from which water could usually be persuaded to trickle.

Agape also awoke, parched and in need of water. Spiro borrowed a tin can from an old woman lying alongside them, and rising up out of the mass of still sleeping bodies lying around him, he went to fetch some water from a standpipe right by the sea on the other side of the quay. He could see some allied military ships in the great bay fairly far out, all at anchor, all just waiting. There was one ship arriving – an American destroyer surely, as Spiro could pick out the Stars and Stripes.

Picking his way carefully between sleeping and, in some cases, lifeless bodies, he approached the water pipe, tin can ready. And then, out of the blue, a figure that he had not noticed before, who had been crouching as he ferreted through an old tin suitcase, stood up. It was a Turkish soldier, but Spiro had no idea whether he was an officer, guerrilla, regular infantryman or chete irregular. But he immediately saw the man's gleaming eyes looking directly at him, and turned to run. Too late – the soldier jumped forward, grabbed him, with an oath on his lips, and in so doing, tore off Spiro's threadbare shirt, which came away in his hands. Spiro didn't scream – he was terrified but somehow his vocal chords didn't work. He wriggled in the man's grasp and tried to pull away. However, though he himself did not scream, a scream did ring out. Agape, distraught, hair dishevelled, dirty and until then lying exhausted on the ground, had jumped up, flung herself across the road right onto the pair, pulling at Spiro to drag him free.

Who knows what the soldier had intended in tearing off Spiro's shirt – but in any event, the intervention of Agape changed everything. With another violent oath, the soldier let go of Spiro and pulled out a pistol. As Spiro staggered away and turned to look back, the soldier shot Agape full in the face from only a foot away. Frozen to the spot, Spiro saw his mother's face blown wide open, blood and gore splattering over her and the people all around. Only seconds passed before more screams rang out from these people, now fully awake. The soldier, without another glance at the blood-spattered body of the woman slumped before him, turned back towards Spiro. Nearly senseless with fear, and now almost naked, Spiro turned in the only direction left to him and jumped off the quay straight into the sea. More shots rang out. Spiro tried swimming underwater as long as he could. He could hear the sound of more bullets pinging into the water around him as he swam – but he was going to have to surface soon.

CHAPTER 7

Admiral Jennings

Throughout those terrible days when no government authority of any kind appeared to be ready to undertake any sort of relief effort, a handful of American citizens were doing their best to fight the nightmare, which was threatening to overwhelm the whole of the Greek and Armenian communities still caught on the quayside of Smyrna. Against the clear and specific orders emanating from the U.S High Commissioner in Constantinople

– Admiral Bristol – these private citizens handed out American flags to parties of Armenian orphans, young boys and girls. Holding them bravely aloft, they were often ignored by the wandering predatory soldiers. Time and again, at some personal danger and considerable inconvenience, they handed out food and offered personal protection to elderly Greek widows who sat waiting.

One of these civilians, Asa Jennings, originally an ordained Methodist minister from New York, wrote in his diary on one of those interminable nights –

"I have seen old men, women and even children whipped, robbed, shot, stabbed and drowned. It seemed to me as though the awful, agonising, hopeless shrieks for help would haunt me forever."

For Admiral Bristol, this comment was just another exaggerated claim from a hysterical man on the spot. But in fact, Asa Jennings was a quiet, dispassionate man, not given in any way to exaggeration or hysterics.

Jennings was a frail and unassuming man, only just over five feet tall. Unlike other short men, he did not make up for his diminutive stature by loud or aggressive behaviour. He seemed doomed to stand on the sidelines in the shadow of others more boastful and arrogant than himself. He had given up his position as a Methodist minister, but he had not lost his faith. He was not a missionary, but he was driven by the same moral imperative to act, that was so noticeable in late 19th century missionaries. This moral certainty was allied to a calm clarity as to how human beings should act towards each other.

After leaving New York, Jennings joined the YMCA and had been working for them for some time. He had taken up the job of Secretary of the Boys Section in Smyrna some months previously. As it happened, both of his superiors had gone on leave and he had been left in sole charge at this dramatic and vital moment. As the great fire had finally burnt itself out, Jennings was a witness to everything that was happening. Although safe during the fire in one of the northern suburbs, he had seen how the Turkish occupation had turned so viciously on the population after their original entry into the town. Jennings was by nature friendly with everyone and had become acquainted with a wealthy Greek property owner who had had the foresight to take his family on a belated summer holiday as soon as he heard of the battle at which the Greek army had been so totally defeated and broken. Before leaving, he had offered Jennings one of his large houses at the Point for use as a centre to feed the refugees from the interior, already beginning to pour into the town.

As soon as the fire had burned out, leaving most of the buildings at the Point intact, Jennings had immediately taken over the building and had stocked it with all the provisions he could get hold of. By dint of sheer persistence, he also acquired another Greek-owned building next door and stocked it, too, with basic foodstuffs; all this within a day or two. Spiro was not to know it, but most of the food that trickled down to him during those days came from these two houses. Once he had stocked the two buildings, Jennings hoisted the American flag on each house as an added precaution against the marauding soldiery. Within hours, this resulted in the American vice-consul rushing down to confront him,

"You can't raise the American flag here – we have orders to remain strictly neutral."

"Yes, of course I see that – I am so sorry. However this is my house and if I wish to fly the American flag over it, I will do so."

"You are jeopardising our relations with the Turks – you must take it down, I absolutely insist."

"I do apologise once again for having to go against your wishes – but I don't intend to do so."

"This is not a question of wishes, you stupid man – this is an order from your government – haul it down!"

Jennings turned away, leaving the assistant consul, spluttering and almost apoplectic with rage. Defeated by Jennings' intransigence, he returned to the temporary quarters where the consulate had been relocated, now that the original had burnt down. That night he sent a telegram to Bristol referring to Jennings' activities as 'totally irresponsible'. Bristol telegraphed back stating that the US government required Jennings to cease his activities.

Jennings quietly ignored them both – the food continued to trickle out, and Jennings began to take more and more personal responsibility for dealing with the events unfolding around him. Soon the two houses, proudly flying the Stars and Stripes, became a centre for the pregnant women and children who had lost their parents.

American sailors, still patroling ashore after the other allies had left, also intervened, where possible. If they saw Turkish soldiers leading away a young girl, they would claim the girl was a girlfriend. The Turks, embued with that extraordinary politeness, learnt as part of the old Ottoman culture, would often let the girls go. After all, there were plenty of others. The sailors would then bring them back to Jennings' two houses – which eventually held more than a thousand souls.

This practice was of course deeply frowned upon by the US officials still in Smyrna – but in every case the naval officer in charge of the patrol would look away, pursuing some other matter until the confrontation had ended.

When standing up against authority – an authority you have accepted all your life – it is the first step that counts. Jennings had always deferred to authority. But the certain knowledge that he was right and morally justified in his actions, and that his government in the person of Admiral Bristol was wrong, gave him an ever-increasing determination as the crisis unfolded. He found that he was now giving orders to all and sundry, without a moment's hesitation. On the fourth night after the fire had subsided, he accepted an invitation to dinner from the captain of an American naval vessel in the bay, and duly went onboard. As he arrived and was being directed to the captain's cabin, some shots were heard coming from the shore. Everyone went to the side and looked out. In the ship's lights, lit for the arrival of the ship's launch carrying Jennings from the shore, a figure could be seen swimming towards the ship. The lights were making the swimmer a target for Turkish soldiers on the quayside, and the sailors immediately turned them off. The swimmer could however still be seen by everyone, obviously exhausted and still some way from the ship. No one moved. Jennings called out –

"For God's sake, why don't you lower a boat?"

"Sir, of course we would normally, but without specific orders we don't dare, in view of government policy."

"Then go and get some orders – get on with it man."

"But sir, it's no use – no officer could give the order – it would have to be entered into the ship's log, and then he would be in trouble on the neutrality issue."

"Then damn it – I'll give the order. Now – now – push off the boat and quickly!" Jennings' anger and agitation was obvious from his choice of words – words he would never normally use. Much to his surprise, the men jumped to it. The boat was lowered and rowed out to the swimmer, now clearly in difficulties, and returned with a young girl, of about fifteen. She was somewhat unceremoniously dumped on the deck at Jennings' feet. At that point an officer on duty walked by, saw at once what was going on, turned and smartly strode away in the opposite direction.

The girl was gently wrapped in blankets by the young American sailors and she soon opened her eyes. Seeing a whole host of strange men gazing down at her, she brought her hand up to her mouth to stifle a scream. As soon as she realised that she was among people who would not harm her, she visibly relaxed and began crying softly. The men averted their eyes and looked at Jennings, who said before being led to the captain's cabin –

"Please look after her till I return and I'll take her back with me on your launch. Don't worry she will be all right."

But these were all single episodes, mere drops in the ocean of misery. Unless the world's governments, or at least one government, took a decisive step, a tragedy of immense proportions was about to occur. Jennings prayed. Everyone was praying. Ships! Where were the world's ships? The whole mass of humanity lining the seafront, now beginning to die from exhaustion and lack of food, waited – and Kemal's ultimatum was due to run out within a week.

Then on the Wednesday morning – the day Harry was

visiting the Avakians in Makrikoy – Asa Jennings woke up with a desperate urge to save at least the thousand or so women and children now under his care in the two commandeered houses. He had become friendly with the captain of another US destroyer in the harbour, and managed to persuade him to lend him the use of a manned ship's launch to look for accommodation on those ships still remaining.

As he went round the great bay, he eventually came alongside an Italian cargo liner – 'the *Constantinopoli*' – a good name, he thought. Jennings stood and shouted up –

"Do you have any refugees on board."

"No, sir, we are empty."

"Oh my God, are you saying that this great ship is standing empty. Can you take in some refugees?"

"Wait sir, let me go and fetch the captain."

Jennings waited and began thinking of what he could say to the captain when he finally appeared.

"Good morning, sir, I am the captain. I am under orders to pick up what cargo I can and move on to Constantinople, where a consignment is waiting for me. However I have no orders to take on any refugees."

"Captain, I am prepared to pay you the equivalent of any cargo to take about a thousand refugees to Mtilini, which is on your way," said Jennings. He hesitated a moment, then added – "And I'll pay an extra bonus for your personal trouble."

"I would, sir, willingly – but I can't without some sort of specific orders, or at least some official confirmation that I won't get into trouble."

"Well, would you accept such confirmation from the Italian Consul here in Smyrna."

"Yes, if he can also get permission from the Turkish authorities for me to move alongside."

Jennings worked all the rest of the day and through the night, getting the necessary orders and permits, arranging the docking of the ship, packing up all his thousand charges, moving them on board, paying the captain from the dwindling money of the Association and then finally coming on board himself. On the following morning, the *Constantinopoli* pulled away from the quay with all Jennings' refugees from the two houses on board, together with quite a few others who had managed to infiltrate themselves into the groups going up the gangplanks. Turkish soldiers stood by, even at this last moment grabbing any valuables and dragging out any young male who looked close to military age, but otherwise not impeding the evacuation.

Jennings himself collapsed in exhaustion onto the bunk in the cabin the Italian captain had allotted to him. There, this little man, this unassuming Napoleon of the waves, gave way to tears – tears of what? – joy or grief or simply plain exhaustion. He fell fast asleep.

When the *Constantinopoli* reached the Greek island of Mtilini, it was already late in the afternoon. All the refugees hurried down the gangplank. On shore they were welcomed by the Red Cross, which had already been telegraphed by Jennings from the ship confirming their arrival. As the liner prepared to move on to the city for which it had been named, Jennings also left the ship. Refreshed by six or seven hours sleep, he now saw another chance. Lying in the harbour were twenty large transport vessels, all moored alongside each other. These were the ships, which the Greek government had chartered to evacuate the remains of the Greek army, as it fled to the coast a few weeks ago.

Jennings approached the Greek general in overall command of this transport fleet, who had sauntered onto the quay and was watching as the refugees filed away. They went into the general's office – the general having witnessed the deference and gratitude of the refugees towards Jennings. Jennings, no longer overawed by officers of whatever rank said –

"Couldn't all these ships be sent to Smyrna to take off all the refugees stranded along the seafront? Look general, if those people are still there when Kemal's ultimatum runs out they will simply be marched off into the interior, and you know what that means."

"My dear sir, I have no idea where your authority lies, but I saw your disembarking refugees, and their relief and gratitude, and I would be prepared to send say seven – one-third of the fleet – if I had a written guarantee that they would be safe, and that the Turks would not try to grab them for their own use before the refugees boarded."

"General, the US is prepared to escort the ships in and out of the harbour"

"But see here – er – Mr. Jennings, that says nothing about protection in case the Turks try to seize the ships once docked."

"Look General, I will personally accompany the ships in and out of the harbour."

"Er… Mr. Jennings – I don't want to appear difficult, but I don't really know who you are or what authority you have. I simply can't take the responsibility."

Jennings fumed. To him it all looked so simple. Here, were 20 empty transport vessels – there, were over 200,000 miserable people waiting for ships. Without them, they were likely to die. Jennings had no authority, no influence, no governmental power – but he did have deep compassion and enormous determination.

There followed a series of wireless messages sent in Greek naval code, back and forth between Athens and Mtilini, which when looked at coldly as they appeared in the official register, read as follows –

"In the name of humanity send the 20 ships now lying idle here in Mtilini to evacuate starving Greek refugees standing on the quayside in Smyrna." Signed Asa Jennings.

"Who the hell is Asa Jennings?"

"US citizen – Chairman of the American Relief Committee."

Jennings always claimed that this was not really a lie, as he formed the Committee as he spoke, and as the only US citizen on the island he was of course its chairman.

"Please note – Prime Minister has called a cabinet meeting and will reply further shortly." was the reply. Then about an hour later –

"What protection is offered?" Signed Prime Minister of Greece."

"Two American destroyers are in the bay and will escort ships in and out of the harbour." Signed Asa Jennings.

"Will American destroyers protect ships if the Turks attempt to seize them."

"No time to discuss details – stated guarantees should be more than sufficient."

Jennings knew that he was on shaky ground. He had already discussed the situation with the captain of the USS *Edsall*, one of the American destroyers in Smyrna, who had confirmed that he saw no conflict of orders in escorting ships of any nation in and out of the harbour for humanitarian purposes. But to intervene in a conflict that might break out on the dockside – that was different. As the exchanges continued it soon became clear that the Greek cabinet, only a few days short of itself falling, was not prepared to take the risk.

It was then that this small, self-effacing citizen, defied all the complacent bureaucratic governments of the world and took a major personal risk. The next two messages read as follows –

"If no favourable reply received by 6.00 pm this evening I will wire openly so that all wireless stations throughout the Mediterranean will pick up the message that Turkish authorities had given permission, that American navy had guaranteed protection, yet Greek government would still not permit Greek ships lying idle in Mtilini to save Greek and Armenian lives awaiting almost certain death in Smyrna."

The reply coming well before the 6.00pm deadline read – *"All ships in the Aegean placed under your command for the sole purpose of removing refugees from Smyrna."*

Jennings had – to all intents and purposes – just been made Admiral of the entire Greek fleet.

By midnight, Jennings had chosen one of the captains of the 20 transport ships as the lead ship. Ten of the others were ready to sail immediately. Jennings arranged for this lead ship to haul down its Greek flag and raise an American flag. And so it was that Jennings lead his mercy fleet of a further ten ships out of Mtilini heading for Smyrna.

About halfway to Smyrna, some hours out of Mtilini, the fleet was met by the USS *Lawrence* – the destroyer from Constantinople on which Harry had managed to get a place. Harry had been unable to sleep and was on deck as the *Lawrence* came alongside the transport ship, sporting an American flag from its topmast. Both ships stood to. Harry heard the following exchange over the megaphones –

"Asa Jennings – can you hear me. I've heard of your mission. Would you prefer to ride the rest of the way with us? We will be there much quicker."

"Thank you sir. A very kind offer. But I have given my word to the Prime Minister of Greece that I would be with the first ship to enter the harbour. I will see you there. Go with God."

The ships parted and the *Lawrence* sped away on its course for Smyrna.

The Greek transport fleet entered Smyrna late the next morning, an hour or two after the *Lawrence* had arrived. Dark clouds still lay over the town and the smell of the fire was still strong. As the convoy closed in, all that could be seen of the city were the gaunt remains of buildings going back up from the seafront, their black and charred debris silhouetted against the hills behind. Then in the front, at the water's edge between those remains and the sea, lay a long line of suffering human beings, waiting, praying for the arrival of ships. As the fleet approached Jennings saw that every face was turned towards them. Sick people had struggled to stand upright. Women held up small children, and every one of them – every single one – held out their hands towards the lead ship with Jennings on the bridge, as if willing with their hands to guide the ships in.

Then a long moan, the last of the terrible sounds that had

arisen for over ten days from this same crowd, reached Jennings, who stood staring straight ahead on the deck. At the site, Jennings could take no more. He struggled down to his cabin and wept uncontrollably.

Jennings took off 15,000 refugees from Smyrna that day. After offloading them in Mtilini, he returned two days later with 17 ships and took off another 43,000. And finally, shamed by the initiative of this quiet, private citizen, a huge cargo fleet chartered by the British government arrived and took off the remaining 120,000.

CHAPTER 8

Harry and Olga

After the meeting in mid-sea between the USS *Lawrence* and the first Jennings fleet, Harry had still been unable to fall asleep. As Harry walked up and down the deck of the American vessel, he pondered his situation. He saw at once how at last, with all his experience of ships, there was a clear way in which he could help. When the Jennings' fleet reached Smyrna, it would have to dock and there would be quite a problem of loading and unloading. He had no idea what the attitude of the Turks might be, but whatever happened, there would have to be some organising as the ships docked one by one. Harry knew that he would never forget the nightmare of those two days of fire, nor the screams and distress from the people he witnessed massed on the quays of Smyrna. But now, as he anticipated the practical help he knew he would be able to provide, the cloud of personal hurt and shame began to lift.

The *Lawrence* sailed into the great Bay of Smyrna and began moving towards the Point. It could clearly be seen from the bay that the fire had not reached as far north as this and the buildings, including two houses ostentatiously flying the Stars and

Stripes, were still largely intact. Harry gripped the rail and gazed at the same piteous sight of massed crowds lining the seafront that Jennings was to see later that morning.

As the ship came to a halt about two hundred yards from the shoreline, Harry and a sailor beside him heard a faint cry below them – it was more like a squeak than a shout – but it was just enough to make them both look down. There in the sea, swimming aimlessly, going round and round in circles, and clearly at the end of his strength, was a young, almost naked, boy.

Harry shouted out to drop a line. However the sailors did not need any urging. Despite the orders they had received, they had already begun dropping a line to the struggling figure. They shouted down at him to get him to focus. The boy looked up at the shouting men and got hold of the rope. He held on tight as willing hands hauled him up and dumped him on the deck. The boy was naked, but for ragged pants, and he was shivering not only with the cold, but also in a state of shock.

It was Spiro.

Sometime later Harry heard Spiro's story. After diving into the sea he had begun swimming towards the new ship he had seen that morning coming into the harbour. Spiro admitted that he was well aware that other survivors of the fire had tried getting aboard ships at anchor in the bay, but had been refused access. With little alternative, he thought it would be worth trying to go towards a newly arriving vessel. He simply swam towards the new arrival. He had, however, miscalculated the speed at which the *Lawrence* was approaching, not taking into account that it would be slowing down. His remaining strength, already sapped by the days of deprivation on the quay, began to give out. But for the moment, all Harry saw was a shivering naked child looking around with huge anxious eyes at the young seamen gathered round him.

A sailor hurried up with a thick coarse blanket, which he handed to Harry. Harry knelt and wrapped it round the child who had still not said a word. He then looked back up at the sailors. Making sure that there were no officers in view, they signalled to Harry and, without speaking, pointed to one of the lifeboats slung along the side. Harry lifted the child, who seemed to be much lighter than his age suggested, and carried him to the lifeboat. There one of the sailors unloosened a corner of the tarpaulin covering the boat. Harry gently lay the child inside. Bending down and speaking in his poor Turkish mixed with a few words of classical Greek, he indicated that he would be safe there for the moment and that food and water would be brought.

It was unlikely that Spiro understood much of Harry's Turkish, and definitely not a word of Harry's public school ancient Greek – but the sympathetic body language came through. Up to this point, he had not really considered the death of his mother. After his own close brush with death, exhausted from the emotional turmoil of the last few hours and days, within a few moments he fell fast asleep.

Harry carefully closed the tarpaulin on the inner side of the lifeboat, then stretching over, he lifted and pulled back the corner of the tarpaulin on the sea side, where it could not be seen from the deck. The men watched silently. Harry turned and facing them said firmly –

"I take full responsibility for having placed the boy here. Any help that anyone gave me was under my personal order."

Who knows what these young Americans thought of this Englishman's presumption that he had the right to give orders to anybody on this ship, but they said nothing.

Within two hours, the Jennings fleet turned up and Harry, too, heard that great moan from the crowds as the lead ship made it to the quayside. Harry had already gone ashore and was one of the first up the gangplank. Although wearing civilian clothes, ten years as an officer in the Royal Navy gave Harry a natural authority, which he exercised to the full. He asked for Asa Jennings as if he was a personal friend.

"Where is my friend Asa, Captain? I understand that he is aboard this ship."

"Yes, sir. He has been with us throughout, but he went down to his cabin shortly after we entered the bay."

"Why? He's not ill is he?"

"No sir, I believe it may have been the sight of all those

desperate people on the quays that undid him."

"Well, well. Can I take him down a mug of tea from your galley?"

Tea! Tea! – all you English ever think about is tea. Look, come and get some whisky from my store."

Some minutes later, Harry made it down to Jennings' cabin with a mug of hot tea and a tumbler of whisky. Jennings was already up. He had wiped away his tears and he had carefully dressed as formally as possible in order to face the inevitable bureaucratic difficulties, which he believed were unavoidable. Harry had been right – a hot strong tea was just what Jennings needed to face up to the many hours of negotiation that were now needed.

Harry introduced himself and after ten minutes, he and Jennings had divided up between them their responsibilities. Within another 20 minutes, Harry was already on the shore directing lines of refugees and helping them past the barriers that the Turks had already raised. The danger was for any man who looked more than 14 or younger than 40. Any suspected within this age group were dragged out and led away to the sound of the screams and entreaties of their female relations.

Neither Harry nor Jennings raised a finger or lodged a single protest against all this, even when boys of 14 were singled out. The Turks had always made it clear to Jennings that they would accept the embarkation of all the old men, the sick, and the women and children – indeed they were now positively anxious that they should go – but not of any males of, or even approaching, military age. These were to be treated as prisoners of war – a war which for the moment was still going on. Neither Harry nor Jennings saw any reason to jeopardise the rest of the mission for what, from the Turkish point of view, was a reasonable objection.

But the grabbing of girls and young women, for a different purpose, was another matter. Turkish officers were present, and Harry appealed to one or another of them when the girl chosen looked particularly young. He was almost always met with unfailing politeness in the old Ottoman manner, rather than the arrogance of the new nationalists. But in the end, throughout the day, he only 'saved' a handful. In any event, there were less and less of this age group of women amongst the refugees shuffling aboard.

Harry worked all day, hour after hour, without rest. He carried babies – he directed people to water – he helped old men who could scarcely walk – he comforted children who had lost their parents, speaking in a mixture of incomprehensible classical Greek and poor, but at least understood, Turkish. On one unforgettable occasion, he even helped to ease the passage of a baby into the world. A woman in the last stages of pregnancy went into labour right in front of him. She had shuffled out of the queue, a mute appeal in her eyes, that Harry had immediately understood. Talking now entirely in Turkish, as he had come to realise that no one understood his schoolboy Greek, he comforted the woman and assured her that he would get her back on board a ship whatever happened.

Two more elderly women joined him to help, as the baby was born into these extraordinary surroundings. "A boy – a boy." Harry grinned and laughed out loud – "No way of military age – no way". Once all was settled and the baby washed and in its mother's arms, Harry personally escorted the women back into the shuffling line, through the guards and onto the gangplank of the next ship. Weak though she still was from the birth, she struggled up, desperate to get on board.

"What is your name sir?" said the woman shyly, clutching tightly onto her squalling baby, as she turned for a moment before stepping onto the deck.

"Harry – madame."

"My boy's name will be Hari," she said as she stepped onto the deck and out of sight.

It was already late in the afternoon when the boats could take no more. Jennings was as exhausted as Harry, but both men were on fire with adrenalin – excitement – testosterone – whatever, both with the same sheer delight in what they had worked for and achieved over the last ten hours. They shook hands as Jennings clambered up the gangplank of the last ship, confirming that he would be back within a day or two at the most. At the top, as the gangplank was drawn up, Jennings turned and raised his hand in a modest friendly salute. Harry could not help himself – he stood firmly at attention and saluted in the military manner as the ship pulled away.

That night, Harry took a short stroll as far as he could go into the burnt areas of the city. His mind turned to the promise he had given the Avakians. As he picked his way through the ravaged Greek and then Armenian quarters, he soon saw there was simply no way that anyone could have survived in the Armenian quarter. The cathedral was a completely blackened shell and no building resembling what may have been the Armenian Hospital stood anywhere nearby. That night, Harry slept in one of the two Jennings safe houses, still supposedly under the protection of the Stars and Stripes, despite every effort of the US vice-consul here in the town, and Bristol back in Constantinople, to have the flag pulled down.

Exhausted but content, Harry had his first undisturbed night's sleep in ten days. In the morning, as everyone waited in the hope that Jennings would get through again soon, Harry decided to try the Imperial Ottoman Hospital in the south. He knew he couldn't face the long walk, through all the miserable humanity on the corniche, to the Konak in the south and the untouched Turkish quarter. But movement inland from the Point, and then round to the south, was now open to all, so long as they were not Greek or Armenian. Harry got the Captain of the *Lawrence*, by now a close friend, to persuade the American consul to lend him the consulate car and a driver to take him through the eastern suburbs and back down to the Konak.

When they arrived at Watchtower Square, Harry arranged for the car to pick him up at three o'clock in the afternoon from the same spot – a time well before Jennings could possibly have returned with any more ships. As the consulate driver departed, Harry turned and stared at the Konak with its great red and white Turkish nationalist flag hanging from the balcony. He recalled how only two weeks ago he had attended upon General Noureddin with Admiral Brock in this same building, when they were asking for permission for British naval patrols to land – and that was surely only a few hours before the city was torched.

Standing in the middle of the square, Harry suddenly felt conspicuously aware that there were eyes all round watching his every move. Probably not true, but in the nervous, feverish atmosphere of the town, with the looming tragedy on the seafront still not played out, it was perfectly understandable. Harry hurried to the side of the government building and into the cobbled, straggling streets leading up to the Turkish quarter. Picturesque but squalid, with many old Ottoman houses, their wooden latticed balcony windows and their graceful lines still intact, it presented a dramatic contrast to the burnt charnel house that was the modern city, with its European, Greek and Armenian quarters completely razed to the ground.

Harry walked through this part of the city, which he had never visited, savouring the quiet, the normality of a town seemingly untouched by the terrible events that had taken place less than a mile away. But Harry was no longer the cool, emotionally reserved British officer of even a month ago. He noted something that he would probably never have remarked upon before. Almost all the Turkish inhabitants who passed him on one side or another had the same sadness in their eyes. Harry was aware there had been no love lost between these same people and the Greeks and Armenians of the modern city below. Yet there was no triumphalism in the eyes of these citizens, as they glanced down on the ruined churches and buildings of their previous neighbours.

Something of the spirit of the city had been irrevocably lost forever. Though that lost spirit might have been partly *giavour,* these people, not yet brainwashed by the fanatical adherents of the one-people nation-state concept, seemed somehow bereft, in an indescribable way.

Harry finally walked back down to the Imperial Ottoman Hospital – still fully intact and flourishing. He made his way to the reception desk, manned by a veiled Turkish lady. Politely, in his still rather poor Turkish, Harry asked after a Nurse Avakian. The receptionist, Harry could not tell her age, looked somewhat cursorily at a list and then shook her head.

"I'm sorry effendi there is no such person on our staff."

"Please madam, could you look into this further as I know that she was working here for three days a week, every week, for the last year."

"Ah, yes – here she is – but effendi she left on the 9th September to attend her next three day duties at the Armenian Hospital, and well...er...well... you see ...."

"I'm sorry madame – I do understand. I won't trouble you further."

Harry turned away, thinking of what he would have to report to the Avakians once he returned. Then, reflecting that this receptionist was probably quite new and had not been working here prior to the arrival of the Turkish army in the city, he turned back and tried just once more –

"Madam, it might be that she is here under the name 'Olga hanum'.

Again the veiled lady shook her head – but just at that moment a nurse was passing. She overheard Harry repeat the words 'Olga hanum'. Speaking impeccable Ottoman Turkish – probably from Stamboul – she said to Harry –

"Oh! Are you looking for Olga? She is on duty, but if you wait here, I'll get her to come down when she has finished."

Harry was already in a state of euphoria. His 12 solid hours work yesterday, helping 15,000 refugees board the transport ships, had already given him a happiness he had not known for weeks. Now, he experienced an overflowing sense of joy – not so much at locating Olga, as with the enormous relief and pleasure he would bring her suffering family, who had befriended him so unstintingly. Sitting in the hospital waiting room, he was basking in this warm, almost self-congratulatory mood, when Olga ran in, breathless with joy at seeing a friend from the past for the first time since the end of the fire.

Harry stood at once, but Olga didn't stop, running straight at him and holding him tight. There, in the middle of the busy waiting-room, in the midst of people hurrying in and out, Harry dropped the hat he had been holding and twisting around in his hands and brought up his own arms. Without thinking, he enfolded this extraordinary girl, squeezing her to him, as hot tears ran down Olga's cheeks, dropping onto his neat white shirt collar.

It didn't last for more than a moment. Olga was shaking with quiet sobs. They were not akin to the many tears she had shed since the death of Selim. These were tears of relief in the embrace of a family friend from her previous life in Bolis. All the emotional turmoil, lying repressed and dormant since she had returned to work at the hospital, came flooding out. It was the first instance of happiness she had experienced since that terrible moment when she was forced to abandon her lover to the terrible flames of the Great Fire of Smyrna.

Harry's immediate reaction was bound up with his own feeling of satisfaction from the achievements of the day before. It wasn't long before his engrained sense of propriety kicked in and he pulled away. He stood back and held Olga at arm's length smiling as her tears of sadness and of hope, continued to flow.

Drying her eyes, she began to laugh. She squeezed Harry's hand and telling him to wait, hurried off to get permission to leave for an hour or two. They walked out together and she took him to a café, still intact and miraculously serving coffee, in a side street a little way up the hillside. They had a lot to tell each other and it all came tumbling out, but it was not just the facts of what had happened. Harry poured out all his feelings about the great fire, about the plight of the countless refugees still milling about on the quaysides and about his own efforts. He did not refer to the court-martial. For her part, Olga talked about Selim, about the arrival of Haik and Paramaz and about the horrors of the approaching fire and her rescue by a passing Smyrniote Turk. She did not refer to the rape.

They could hardly get their words out fast enough as they interrupted themselves and each other. Aware of the passing time and the imminent return of the embassy car to the Watchtower Square, Harry tried to persuade Olga to pick up her things and go back with him to the Point that same evening. But she said she could not just walk out and abandon them like that but would have to make proper arrangements for resigning. She thought that they would probably be quite happy, even relieved, to let her go – she was perhaps the only Armenian left in Smyrna and definitely the only one in the hospital – but it had to be done properly. As they prepared to leave the café, it was agreed that she would accept his invitation to go back with him to Bolis on the *Lawrence* when it left in a day or two.

Harry paid the bill and they left the café to walk back to the hospital. Olga's eyes were shining as she began to imagine a return to normal life. She didn't think directly of the baby she was carrying. But the knowledge that she would soon be seeing her mother made it all seem possible. As they approached the hospital gates, when everything had been settled, and all the necessary arrangements had been made for their next meeting, she finally said –

"Oh Harry, what about Haik and the others, do you know what happened to them?"

In all the elation, Harry had temporarily forgotten about Haik. He was going to have to tell her the truth and to repeat to her what he had been told when he had gone to the Avakians. He hated spoiling the euphoria, but he knew it was necessary.

"Olga, walk down to the Konak with me please – while we wait, I'll tell you everything I know."

As they waited for the car, mercifully late, Olga heard the news. But she had already expended all her tears, so as Harry talked, she simply bowed her head and stared at the road. When he was finished, she looked up at him and said –

"I knew it deep down, I knew it all the time. Whatever happened, Haik would always have come back to me if it had been physically possible for him. I knew. I knew that he would never have voluntarily abandoned me – only death prevented it."

Saying that, Olga stretched up, gave Harry a little kiss on the cheek, smiled, and walked away back to the hospital as the consulate car finally arrived.

CHAPTER 9

Satenig – Rehia

One of the consequences arising from the strict separation of the sexes that existed in wealthy Moslem households was the physical division of the house into public areas and those that were 'haram' – forbidden to all males except the husband. This was a cultural attitude that applied throughout the interior of the Empire, even amongst wealthier Greeks and Armenians. In this respect, they aped the dominant Ottoman customs. A further side effect was that the males of the household, apart of course from the husband, had no idea what was going on amongst the women.

This of course did not apply to the elite of Constantinople of whatever race or religion. Nevertheless, even in Constantinople the household of Garabed Asadourian presented another problem for Vahan in his courtship of Nerissa Avakian. Vahan was the eldest son of Garabed Asadourian, and since the terrible events that befell the womenfolk of the family during the 1915 deportations, the little Asadourian establishment in the small townhouse just off Taksim was an entirely male household. This made it difficult for Vahan as there would be no female present if Nerissa was ever inviteed to visit.

Vahan's mother and all his Aunts and elder sisters had disap-peared in the second wave of deportations and massacres that had struck Caesaria – Kayseri – which had been the family home for generations.

On the 24th April 1915, Garabed had been arrested, like so many other leading Armenians, and had only just managed to survive the ensuing bloodshed. Vahan had been a student at Istanbul university at the time and had automatically become an officer in the Ottoman army, once war was declared in November 1914. After the arrest and deportation of his father, he managed to send proof of his status as an officer back home to his mother. Accordingly, she and the other women left in the house, together with the 16 year-old Raffi, Vahan's younger brother, had been exempted from the first deportation order, which had resulted in the deaths of over three-quarters of the old men, women and children of the Armenian population of the town.

But matters in the town had gone from bad to worse and, within the year, further deportation orders were issued. This required that all the remaining Armenians left in the town, the families of officers, and the Protestants and Catholics previously spared, were hounded out of town. Without even the practical help of Raffi, who had run away from the clutches of the police many months before, all the women left in the house had been forced to leave and to join the last wave of Armenians forced on to one of the many death marches setting out in the winter months of 1916.

This particular final group, containing no males save some ancient grandfathers, did not even make it as far as Malatya, which was the assembly point for most of these death marches. Most people ordered out of the homes they had lived in for centuries, simply disappeared one way or another as they passed by indifferent villagers, stumbling, like so many others, through the empty spaces of Eastern Anatolia; dying of hunger, thirst, mindless killings and exhaustion as they passed.

As deportation order after order went out from Talaat's ministry, this was the story of community after community stretching out from Caesaria eastwards to the Russian frontier. This was a planned extermination in the search for a one-people, one-culture, one-religion, nation-state, required by the nationalists to replace the ramshackle, but basically tolerant Empire, that appeared to have failed so miserably.

Neither Vahan, living in Constantinople throughout this terrible period, nor his brother Raffi, living incognito and hand-to-mouth in the interior, nor Garabed who had survived and managed to reach Aleppo, had any idea what might have happened to their womenfolk. And now in the fourth year of the peace, following the Armistice of Mudros, they still did not know for certain and no longer had any expectation that they ever would.

The situation in the Asadourian house in Caesaria for the two weeks immediately prior to the arrest and deportation of Garabed in April 1915, had been tense and full of foreboding. Even though the Armenian community had no idea what was about to befall them, the knowledge – the worst-kept secret of the whole war – that the Allies were about to invade somewhere in the Straits left everyone in an anxious and fearful state. Garabed, in any case, had to stay at home as he recovered from the beating, suffered at the hands of the police. It was during those troubled days that he and Mariam had sought solace in each other's arms more deeply than ever before, and when confidences were privately exchanged between them.

In that month, Mariam was already three months pregnant, but she had not yet told Garabed, who hadn't noticed. Mariam was small and had never shown much change in her appearance, when carrying her other children, until about the sixth month. Mariam's last child – a sister six years younger than Raffi - had been born ten years earlier. Mariam was over 40 years-old, and had assumed she was unlikely to have any more children. An odd feeling of shame accompanied the realisation that she was pregnant, so she had hidden the news for as long as possible. In those last two weeks of their life together, she whispered the news to Garabed. To her surprise and pleasure, Garabed was delighted, though more than a little worried whether she would be able to cope, particularly in the light of the worsening political situation.

Only three days after he heard the news, on the day before the landings in Gallipoli, Garabed was arrested. He was sent away the next day and he never saw his wife again.

Mariam was six months pregnant when Raffi was forced to flee. It was hardly surprising the 16 year-old Raffi never realised that his mother was pregnant. The effects of the arrest and disappearance of his father, compounded by the first wave of deportations, left him as the head of a house full of women. There was his mother, some unmarried sisters, elderly women of the extended household and some abandoned neighbours who had been taken in. Some of the older women had to be lifted in and out of their beds and looked after. This left him exhausted, with no time or inclination to look beyond the next moment.

Unknown, therefore, to any of the three men in the family – although Garabed had been told of the pregnancy – Mariam gave birth to a little girl, a little prematurely, in the autumn of 1915 at the family house in Caesaria. The infant was about seven or eight months old, healthy and already weaned, when the last round-up took place. With no time to prepare – no carts – no donkeys – with shabby suitcases and some rolled-up bedding, the remaining women and young children began the dreary, deadly trek out of the town and towards the east, heading for Malatya, and ultimately for the Arab vilayet of Syria.

But this final pathetic group, guarded by a motley assort-ment, without any pretence of proper organisation or discipline, was not destined to get further than a few days march from the town. On the outskirts of a small village halfway between Kayseri and Burgan, the few so-called gendarmes, mostly criminals let out of prison for the purpose, having already looted all the shabby suitcases, torn away the gold rings and hidden any coins they could find, herded the women into a circle and murdered them. Mariam held her little girl to whom she had already given the name – Satenig – tight to her breast as the shooting began. Although she was standing in the middle of the shivering group, she was one of the first to die, sinking under the bodies of those falling on top of her.

But Satenig never got a bullet.

The guards who carried out this particular slaughter were violent, uneducated men, petty criminals, chosen from amongst those languishing in the prisons of the town. They had never intended to go more than a few days walk from their home town. They were also, however, slipshod and careless in carrying out their murderous task. They never bothered to go round finishing off the twitching bodies of their victims. And so it was that even though the baby was howling feebly, buried under the dead bodies, they sauntered off with their loot and with their blood-lust assuaged. These killers had not only been brain-washed by the race hatred spread by Talaat's ministry, but there was also for them an element of class hatred and envy as well.

However, not only the baby survived. Digin Arabian, one of the women, also escaped. She had fainted in sheer terror as she saw the rifles raised and the bullets fired. She fell and, like little Satenig, found herself buried beneath dead bodies.

After half an hour spent quaking with terror, only just able to breathe, and soaked in blood, this woman – Nouritza Arabian – crawled out from under the bodies and looked around in a daze. The flies were already gathering around a scene of terrible desolation. It was then she heard the crying of the baby. Fearful as she was, desperate to get away from the awful carnage, she could not ignore the cries and forced herself to find the child amongst the inert bodies. She had to prise her out of the arms of Mariam, still holding her tightly in the rigor of death.

Amongst this last pathetic group of old women and children that had left Caesaria only three days previously, Satenig had been the only baby and Nouritza knew who she was and who the parents were. She had even talked with Mariam several times during the few days of the march.

Holding Satenig tight and trying to soothe her increasingly plaintive weeping, she staggered away as fast as she could from this place of death. She was exhausted and without any means of looking after herself, never mind a helpless infant. As she stumbled on, the moment came when she was at the end of her strength. What could she do? The path she was blindly following was clearly used. Riddled with guilt but quite unable to go another step carrying the child, she lay Satenig down on the path by the side of a bush. She could see a large village, almost a small town in the distance down the hillside – surely someone would come by and rescue the child. Would it be better or worse for them to be found together? She couldn't think straight. Still covered in the browning stains of blood, traumatised by what she had just witnessed, she stood up and staggered down the hillside.

This was still an area of settled habitations, unlike the wild and empty regions further east where most of the deported Armenians perished. Eventually, a shepherd grazing the village sheep came by. Satenig, abandoned and already missing the warmth of the human contact, was crying again and moving feebly. The shepherd – a Turk rather than a Kurd – looked down at the child, now crawling and being gently nuzzled by one of his sheep. This man was not a criminal from one of the slums of the cities, he was not a nationalist academic nor an Ittihad fanatic for a one-people state. He was a simple man who honoured Allah. He realised immediately that this must be a 'giavour' child abandoned on one of the death marches. But first and foremost, it was an innocent child.

He picked her up, managed to give her some sheep's milk and carried her down to the overgrown village of Chehan, which Nouritza had seen down in the valley. Before delivering the sheep to their various owners, he laid her down on the steps of one of the small town's two mosques. Satenig was now more than just bedraggled. Her clothes were wet and stinking. Although capable of crawling about, exhaustion, dirt and lack of food had affected her and she lay there mewling feebly, making efforts to sit up, but falling back immediately. She had a plain wooden cross with a blue stone hanging from her neck, and this, together with her clothes, identified her as an Armenian.

Chehan was a large village, almost a small town, unusual in having two mosques, and many people did pass by, glancing away from the child lying on the steps. In due course, someone reported the matter to the local gendarmerie. Omar, a married man of about 40 years of age, a sergeant in the police force, put on his belt and sauntered down to see what was going on. As it happened, Omar and his wife Gulmaz had not been able to have any children. He looked down at Satenig who was still howling, not only because she was dirty, tired and hungry, but because she was missing the comfort of human contact. Satenig looked up at the looming face of Omar peering down at her, raised her arms towards him. Omar was touched. He too saw only a child not a giavour. He bent down and picked her up, stinking and dirty as she was. As soon as Satenig found herself in this man's arms, she immediately stopped yelling.

Omar carried the child back to his home, where a spirited conversation took place between himself and his wife.

"My revered husband, what exactly do you want me to do with this child?"

"Gulmaz, we have no children. This is obviously an abandoned baby – couldn't we look after it?"

"I am nearly 40, husband, I am far too old to look after a baby. My mother is no longer alive and I wouldn't know what to do. No, no it's impossible."

"Very well, very well – but at least for tonight. I can't take it back to headquarters at this hour. Come Gulmaz we can't leave it out during the night."

"Of course not, Omar. But listen it is a giavour child – look at that cross – I'm not going spend my declining years looking after a giavour. But very well, just for tonight. Go and speak to Vicdan hanum next door and ask her to come in so that she can help me. She has had lots of children. I wouldn't know where to start. It might help if she could bring some of her children's old clothes, if she still has some."

And so it was that that night, Satenig, the daughter of Garabed and Mariam Asadourian of Caeseria was fed, cleaned and clothed and fell asleep in the house of Omar the police sergeant of Chehan and his wife Gulmaz.

The next morning Omar left to report what had happened at the police station and to get instructions about what should be done with the infant. Gulmaz fed the child with some porridge but took care, as she explained to Omar, not to hold her or give her any sign of affection. Satenig could sit up and even manage a spoon. After drinking some water she sat and stared at Gulmaz with huge brown eyes. Gulmaz took her out into the street. It was still winter, but it happened to be a warm sunny morning presaging the coming spring. Gulmaz sat herself down on the top step as usual taking in the sun, putting the child down in the dusty earth-packed street. Her neighbour Vicdan, who had done most of the work the night before, came out and sat across on her own front steps as the little girl crawled about playing with the stones on the street between the two women.

It was no more than half an hour later, as the two women chatted and watched the little girl that two policemen arrived.

They had been sent by the officer on duty to pick up the little girl and bring her back to the police station where they were still discussing what was to be done with the infant.

The two women said nothing as the two men came up. But Satenig, who had been sitting playing with the stones, gave one look at the two uniformed men and, with surprising speed, crawled over to Gulmaz and crept under her long black skirt. Then holding on tightly, she peeped out at the two men. Gulmaz, at first taken aback, looked down at the child hiding under her skirt. She then grabbed up the little girl and cuddling her for the first time, glared at the two uniformed policemen, both of whom she knew very well.

"Well. What do you two want?"

"Gulmaz Hanum, your respected husband has asked us to come and collect the child, abandoned last night on the steps of the mosque. We are to bring her back to headquarters."

"Nonsense. I will be looking after the little girl. Since Allah has seen fit to send her to me, I will bring her up in the true faith."

"But Hanum" said one of the two, thoroughly confused, "you told your husband that you didn't want to look after a giavour child and that … ."

"Rubbish. Go and tell my husband and your officer that the child is ours and that her name is… er… is…Rehia."

The two men departed in bemusement. As they turned away, Gulmaz lifted Satenig to her lips and gave her a kiss. Vicdan too waddled across and gave the child a hug.

And so it was that Satenig became Rehia and was brought up as the little daughter of Omar, the town's police sergeant, and Gulmaz his formidable wife. She was loved and mothered and had the best of food and clothes. She called her mother Gulmaz 'Ana' of course, and, when she started speaking, spoke only Turkish. Her father, Omar, was fiercely protective of her and delighted in the child. Omar, was not particularly pious, but the rituals of the house were Muslim. As the years passed and Rehia grew, she knew only that she had a loving father and mother who doted on her. She knew and accepted as natural that they waited for the call to evening prayer from the nearby minaret before they could sit down to their evening meal.

This would have been the end of the story of little Satenig/Rehia except for one further matter. Nouritza Arabian, against all the odds, had also survived. Staggering into this same village she had managed to find shelter and some food for a day or two. Although known to be a giavour refugee from the big city, she had then been able to find a lowly domestic post with an up-and-coming Turkish family who needed a servant. They wished to have a mature woman who could read and write and teach their children, rather than a village girl, and Nouritza was ideal and also very cheap.

Not much was secret and private in this small town and Nouritza soon came to hear about the arrival of the giavour baby, found under a bush near the village and adopted by the village police sergeant. She watched from afar the growth of the child – now known as Rehia. This had all happened in 1916 and Nouritza remained silent as six years passed and the world outside changed.

CHAPTER 10

Constantinople on the Edge

The world's desire – Micklegard – the largest city in the European world for centuries – the Imperial capital of three empires, the eastern Roman, the Byzantine and the Ottoman was in complete turmoil and enveloped in an atmosphere of fear. The total collapse of the Greek forces in Anatolia was worrying enough for a substantial number in the city; the fall of the second city of the empire which followed was worse; but the total destruction of that city, Smyrna, in one of the great fires of history, together with the reported looting, rape and robbery gave rise to wholesale panic.

The Imperial city had arrogantly lorded it over the peasants and humble farmers of Anatolia for over a thousand years. All their wealth, their excess produce, and the sweat of their labour had gone to feed the rulers of the city – from Roman senators to Byzantine Emperors and Ottoman Sultans. Now the city faced an avenging army, which had already shown its complete disdain for the great urban centres of culture and civilisation by the sacking and burning of Smyrna.

As the facts of what had actually happened at Smyrna became widely known, the enormous fire-power of the allied fleets gathered in the Marmara sea and at anchor in the straits, with their huge twelve-inch guns, suddenly seemed irrelevant. For 20 years, the Great Powers of Europe, highly influenced by the theories of Mahan on the importance of sea power, had spent a large proportion of their military budgets on expensive battle-ships. Now, the victorious Turks, marching north from the great debacle in Smyrna, were about to show up the limitations of sea power.

Not one of those huge monsters of the sea would be able to prevent even one of those Anatolian soldiers from burning another small village. And as this avenging army marched north-wards, it seemed increasingly unlikely that any of these big ships would be able to prevent it from crossing the narrow straits and pouring into the city. Yet the Turkish nationalist forces did not possess a single military vessel.

Throughout history, the straits not only formed the sea passage between the Euxine world and the Mediterranean, but also represented the bridge between Asia and Europe. Constantinople, dominating those straits and symbolising centuries of civilisation, waited, like a tired and raddled old painted lady, for the mayhem to come. Rape she could contemplate, but not the destruction of all the goods she owned, her buildings, her infrastructure, her ancient beauty, her traditions and culture. The city trembled.

It would all be decided in a matter of days. Every day counted, every moment was important. Every decision, every telegram was going to make a difference. Anything could have happened. Nothing was inevitable. Everyone in Constantinople was on edge. Even the Turkish half of the population felt anxious in the midst of the triumph of their forces. Young men drove round the town with pictures of Kemal in their cars, shouting out slogans exactly like the Greek youths had done two years before. Turkish nationalist flags were everywhere, streaming in the wind from all the windows. But their elders sat in the cafés smoking their narghiles, thinking nostalgically of the dying glories of the Ottomans. Like many Stamboulis, they worried in their hearts about what might happen if all those unspeakable unwashed peasants of the interior were let loose on their beloved paradise on earth.

Karekin in Makrikoy could grieve no longer. He remained dissatisfied with Paramaz's recital of what had happened in Smyrna, but he could not put his finger on the cause of his doubts. Many people had died at Smyrna. Perhaps it was the absence of a body on which to focus his grief. Realising the importance of ritual in these matters, even though he himself thought it was all mumbo-jumbo, he arranged for the family to have a private mass heard, and the very next day he went back to the office.

The whole basis for the operation of the business partnership of Avakian and Levonian had disappeared with the defeat of the Greek army and the destruction of Smyrna. The earlier ending of the 'arrangement' between his eldest daughter Sima and George, the only son of Hovannes Levonian, added to the likely estrangement of the two families. But for the moment, there were too many other problems looming for any decision on this aspect of his business to be made or even discussed. Karekin simply threw himself into work in order to distract himself from his personal worries.

Despite the fact that he had been one of the first of the prominent Armenians to be arrested and deported in April 1915, Karekin had never been an active Armenian nationalist. He considered the Armenian Revolutionary Federation (ARF) irresponsible and mindless, simply mouthing the same fashionable nationalistic slogans that they were hearing from all the other European fanatics demanding a 'one people, one culture, one nation' state. They repeated these platitudes without any thought as to whether their demands were suitable or achievable in the present circumstances. He believed that as a political party, they had totally disregarded the peculiarly vulnerable position of the Armenian peasantry of the interior, where Armenians were everywhere in the minority with only a few exceptions.

Karekin was, and always had been, a supporter of the old Ottoman ideal of a multi-cultural, multi-ethnic Empire based on geography and economic convenience, rather than on any one exclusive ethnicity. Having talked several times to Selim, he knew it was likely he would have been in complete agreement with Nazim, Selim's father, if he had ever had the chance to meet him.

However, even Karekin could now see that the current Ottoman rump government, totally dependent as it was on the British military presence, was inevitably slipping away into the dustbin of history. Almost all the possibilities for the city, seriously considered only a few months before, were no longer feasible. The solution of a reformed, liberal Ottoman revival, perhaps with Mustapha Kemal as the power behind the throne, was fading fast. Turning Constantinople – a city situated both in Europe and Asia – into an international city, perhaps the seat of the new League of Nations, had long since been dismissed by the Eurocentric western powers. But what other possibilities were left? Kemal had already decreed that Ankara would be the capital of the new exclusive nation-state that he was creating. Over half a million Greeks had already fled from the old Ionian coastline. What about the half million Christians of the city – was it all going to end in a tragedy similar to Smyrna?

Karekin was in a quandary. It was not just a matter of politics. His own daily life, and that of all the people for whose welfare he was responsible, was going to be directly affected by whatever happened in the next few weeks. If the Greeks had to leave, what about the Russians, like Sima's beloved Nicolai and his young brother Alexei who was still working in Karekin's office? What about the 100,000 Armenians of the city – were they to be dealt with like the 20,000 Armenians of Smyrna? Surely impossible, there was no such thing as an Armenian quarter in Bolis, but what... then?

If there was to be a Smyrna solution, shouldn't he take his family away. But where could they go? There was too little time. Whatever was going to happen was going to happen within days, if not hours. And so, like everyone else, Karekin did nothing. He continued going to work, and remained cool and rational, as far as his family was concerned. He refused to call on a God in whom he didn't believe, but he was happy to join his talkative family in discussing all the possible alternatives round the dining table. He took great care to calm the fears expressed by Nerissa and Seta, who brought back lurid tales, of what they heard about Smyrna, from university and school. Nevertheless, he did not try to hide anything, giving his opinions with total honesty and ignoring attempts by Armineh to shield the girls from the realities facing them all.

The problem for Tim Harington, the British commander of the allied forces occupying Constantinople, was quite different. He had to balance two different agendas in his mind. On the one hand, he was the representative of the British government, the military servant of the London politicians, and accordingly was required to carry out as best he could the imperial requirements of British policy. On the other hand, he felt a personal responsibility for this unique city, which he had come to love over the years of his mission here. When the Greek Royalist government had made a tentative move to take over the city only a few months previously, in an attempt to escape from the dilemma of their own creation in Smyrna and Anatolia, Harington had not waited for any instructions from London. He acted immediately and decisively to prevent it happening. He had appreciated at once how catastrophic an attempted Greek military conquest of the city would be. It was not a question of who would win in the end, it was the certainty of the terrible damage that would result. Any kind of modern military campaign would spell doom to this architectural and cultural jewel, built over centuries.

At the same time he was responsible for the ordinary soldiers under his command. Following the complete and unexpected defeat of the Greek army, the road to Constantinople now lay wide open for the nationalist army. To all intents and purposes, there were only two obstacles standing in the way. First, was the continued presence of the large British fleet under Admiral Brock. But what precisely could this huge fleet do except bombard everybody, soldier and civilian alike? It could not take or hold any ground. The second obstacle was Harington, himself, in command of about 5,000 men.

Positioned astride the route coming up from Smyrna, sitting in the town of Chanak on the Asiatic side of the Dardanelles, was a small British garrison. The French and Italians had already made their peace with the Turkish nationalists and had withdrawn their small contingents. From the 14th September onwards, almost 40,000 highly motivated Turkish troops began to move north from Smyrna. At any time, these forces were in a position to attack both the small British garrison at Chanak and, ultimately, Constantinople itself.

Harington did possess one of the important qualities necessary in any military leader – unflappability. He immediately started to strengthen the garrison, backed up by the guns of the fleet behind, to withstand any attack, short of an all-out offensive by the whole Turkish army,. He called on reinforcements to be sent from Egypt and Malta. But he could see how perilous the situation had become. If hostilities did break out between his forces and Kemal's, he would probably end up evacuating the city under fire, but holding on to Chanak and the Gallipoli peninsula by his fingernails. Officially his task was to make the tactical 'on-the-spot' decisions, but the vagaries of the telegraph system, and the speed at which events were unfolding, often meant that he had to make strategic decisions as well. The exact opposite was happening in London. The existence of the telegraph tempted the decision-makers there to interfere with the immediate tactical decisions that had to be made on the spot, rather than concentrating on the major strategic ones that were urgently required.

In London, the collapse of the Greeks and the dramatic destruction of Smyrna had led to an immediate political crisis which got steadily worse, as the triumphant Turkish army drew closer day by day to Chanak and Constantinople. The principal players in London were Lloyd George the Prime Minister, Lord Curzon the aristocratic foreign minister, and Churchill the architect of the original Gallipoli campaign.

Lloyd George based almost all his views on affairs in the Eastern Mediterranean on a mixture of a Gladstonian dislike of the Turks, and ideas taken from the bible, particularly the Old Testament. While he had been unhappy with the Greek Royalist government that had ousted his friend Venizelos, he had no time at all for the Turks. Curzon and the officials at the Foreign Office, though less anti-Turk, were currently angry at the abandonment of the alliance by the French and Italians, and their support for the Turkish position, which appeared to verge on treachery. Churchill, who was in no way anti-Turk, resented the challenge to British prestige, and believed that to restore its credibility, the government had to act boldly in the Straits and be seen to do so. Even the Conservative partners in the coalition, who were more conciliatory, agreed that firmness of purpose had to be demonstrated. Churchill, and the others who thought like him, believed that to back down in front of what was still thought of as an Asiatic, Moslem army would be fatal for the prestige and power of the British Empire.

Finally, there was the all-important matter of what was wanted by the Turkish government in Ankara – for such it now was. Despite every effort made by the British to put some backbone into the rump Ottoman government in Constantinople, it was increasingly clear that Mohammed VI, and his court of aging ministers, now counted for almost nothing. The real issue was Mustapha Kemal's demands. Kemal was somewhat ambivalent on the issue of Stamboul. He had already decreed that Ankara was to be the capital of the new Turkey. So where did that leave the old imperial capital?

Contrary to the puritan image he tried to promote in public, he had always enjoyed the life in Constantinople, frequenting its bars and other places of entertainment and becoming an accomplished dancer of all the latest western dances. The atmosphere created by his victories might be intense and puritanical, but he himself was no bigoted prude.

There was no longer a question of who was going to have Constantinople. The four years since the British occupied the city had seen all sorts of possibilities come and go. But once the fatal decision had been taken to let the Greeks land in Smyrna, the resulting Turkish backlash, and the nationalist revival in Anatolia, meant that the city was going to become Turkish again, sooner or later.

The real problem now was the issue of the minorities. What was to become of the half-million Greeks, Armenians, Jews and others in the city?

Kemal was quite clear on most of the issues still outstanding between nationalist Turkey on the one hand, and the allied powers on the other. When a peace was eventually negotiated to bring the state of war between the Ottoman Empire and the Allies to an end, there were certain matters on which he would stand completely firm. The hated 'capitulations' had to go – Eastern Thrace and Adrianople on the European side had to return to Turkey – all foreign troops had to leave Constantinople – above all, Kemal was not prepared to allow any of the Ionian Greeks who had fled from Smyrna and its hinterland to return. Kemal may not have been personally responsible for the decision to burn down the Christian quarters of Smyrna, but like the pragmatist that he was, he was happy to profit from the new situation resulting from it.

But on the matter of the Christians and Jews of Constantinople, the attitude of Ankara, and Kemal, was still in the balance.

Only the British Empire, with Harington as its representative, stood between Kemal and all he wanted. If it came to a military confrontation, the chances of the matter being settled by some form of 'Smyrna' solution, was high. On the other hand, if the British simply gave in and retired, it would surely herald the beginning of the end of their Empire.

Meanwhile the Avakians, like all the rest of the citizens of Constantinople, waited.

CHAPTER 11

Vahan's Decision

When the end of the Great War came in the closing months of 1918, it took quite a time before the changed circumstances and the new atmosphere created by the conflict penetrated the remoter villages and small towns of the interior. Inertia in human affairs is strong, and Nouritza Arabian was no different in this respect to those living around her. Her lowly work with the Kazim family had given her a measure of contentment. Of course she would never forget the past, her previous life in Caesaria and the horrors of the final deportation orders, which had forced her out of the only home she had ever known. How could she ever forget the terror of the three-day trek, culminating in the final denouement, when everyone around her was slaughtered, and only she and the baby daughter of Mariam Asadourian had survived.

But she was grateful for the shelter she had been given, and slowly as the Kazim children grew, life settled into an acceptable routine. She taught them the Arabic script of the Turkish language and looked after them whenever their parents were away. As the family became more affluent and acquired more servants, her status in the family improved and she became a sort of honorary grannie.

All this time, she kept an eye on little Rehia – the adopted daughter of the town's police sergeant Omar, and his wife Gulmaz hanum. Apart from making an effort to become acquainted with them, she was careful not to say anything about Rehia's past.

Three separate but connected occurrences, which happened

as the years passed after the end of the war, changed all this. The first event, which was the catalyst for her eventual decision, occurred in the winter of 1920, when the friendly and popular police sergeant caught a bad chill, when called out to intervene in a brawl between a husband and his wife in the middle of the night. He lingered on for a few days and then died, surrounded by his grieving neighbours and his wife, and attended also by his only child – Rehia.

Within the next year Gulmaz hanum, left alone as a wealthy widow, married again – this time to a younger man, Orhan, a soldier in the old Ottoman army who had retired after the war. Orhan had married a young village girl by whom he had already had two children. Old Ottoman law still prevailed in these parts, and Muslim men were allowed to have more than one wife. So there was nothing to prevent this young man from taking Gulmaz under his wing, or at least marrying her for her money and property. Gulmaz was no fool; she was perfectly aware what lay behind the offer of marriage. In the end, the life of a second wife was preferable to that of a widow. It was a trade-off: male protection in return for sharing her property.

Gulmaz remained a warm and good mother. To Rehia, Gulmaz was always her 'ana' – her beloved mother. But inevitably things changed. The new father of the family had children of his own and wasn't interested in this precocious little girl of five or six years of age. The first wife – a simple village girl, much younger than Gulmaz, posed no problem at all. Indeed, if anything, she looked up to the well respected Gulmaz, but she had her own two children, and there were inevitable tensions between them and Rehia, a strong-willed child, spoiled by Omar's doting affection.

Orhan knew of course, as did everyone else, that Rehia was an Armenian infant found abandoned by the side of a footpath outside the town. Yet such was the basic goodwill of the ordinary townsfolk, no hint of this had ever been given either to outsiders or to the other children in the little town. So it was that Rehia had no idea of where she had come from or who she really was, believing herself to be the beloved only daughter of Omar – the policeman.

Orhan was not a hard or unreasonable man, but he felt the need to establish his position vis-à-vis his new second wife. It was necessary to make it clear to the village community that he was the man, the head of his household. Unfortunately, the point of contention between him and Gulmaz was nearly always little Rehia, and the whole town was aware of it.

As was Nouritza Arabian.

The final event which triggered her decision was when she heard about a law, passed by the increasingly impotent Ottoman government in Constantinople, to the effect that any Armenian orphans taken in by Turkish families during the terrible events of 1915, had to be returned to any close relatives of the child who made themselves known and who made a proper claim. It was one thing to pass such a law, quite another to enforce it in the lawless conditions of the Anatolian interior. Either way, it wouldn't have crossed Nouritza's mind to do anything about it if Omar had still been alive. At last, these events combined in Nouritza's mind and she decided to act.

As a 'gesaratsi' from the previous Armenian community of Caesaria, she knew of the well-known and well-to-do Asadourian family. She was aware that their eldest son had been in Bolis at the time of the deportations. She had no idea if any of them had survived, but she had been with Mariam throughout the last three days of the dreadful trek, helping her to carry the baby Satenig, and talking with her until the end.

Although she had achieved a measure of ease with the Kazim family, she missed her people, her community, her old religion and the customs of her youth. Accordingly, she had warned the family that as soon as the political situation improved and permitted easier and safer travel, she intended to go to Stamboul and seek out any of her own relatives who might be survivors. With the steady extension of the Ankara government's control, easier travel was already available. So it was that she came to write a letter addressed to the Asadourian family. She sent it care of the address of the Armenian Relief Organisation in Constantinople, known to all the Armenians still left alive in

Eastern Anatolia, for assisting in the recovery of Armenian children taken in by sympathetic Turkish families during the terrible deportations. The letter read –

"Sireli Asadourianner,

My name is Nouritza Arabian and I live in the village of Chehan, which is on the road between Kayseri and Burgan. I was with your wife/mother Mariam when we were forced to leave Kayseri six years ago. I am sure that you know that she and all the rest of her family were killed only three days after we all left.

Out of our whole group only I survived, as did your baby daughter/sister – Satenig. She had survived the shootings by the guards and I was able to pick her out of Mariam's arms after the soldiers had gone. We eventually came to this town. Here the baby was taken in and adopted by a good man – Omar and his wife Gulmaz. I myself took work with another family and I have watched as the little girl, who was given the name Rehia, grew up. She is now about six years old. No one has ever told her that she is an Armenian – but all the rest of the village knows and Gulmaz hanum still has the wooden cross which was round the neck of the baby.

Omar, the father, who doted on the child, has died and Gulmaz hanum has remarried a man who has children of his own.

I don't know if any of your family has survived. Mariam told me that her eldest son – Vahan I think – was living in Bolis. I am myself proposing to come to Bolis once the countryside is more settled. My address here is at the top of this letter and if I get any reply I will try to persuade everyone that Rehia could come with me if you should so desire. Although Gulmaz hanum undoubtedly still loves the child, she may be prepared to let her go in view of her remarriage and of the new law as to Armenian orphans.

However I would warn you that Rehia has no knowledge at all of her antecedents. She loves her ana and believes that she is her child. I doubt if I myself could persuade her to accompany me. Although she does know me as an Armenian, in order to protect the general village consensus that she should be left in ignorance of who she is, I have never approached her on this matter.

I await hearing in the hope that one of the family is alive."

This letter was eventually delivered to the little house in Taksim where the Asadourians lived, arriving on Saturday the 16th September. This was the day that Vahan had been called away to the Avakian's home in the morning to be with Nerissa, when she was given the news of the Haik's death. Vahan had been fond of Haik and was as upset as the rest of them when he heard the news, but he had understood that Nerissa's distress took precedence and held back his own tears. Armineh's instincts were right – Nerissa had turned to Vahan who had been sitting next to her when the news had been broken, and had buried her face in his shoulder. Poor Vahan. Nerissa, always sensitive to her own and her family's feelings, never considered for a moment that Vahan might have feelings for her as well. She pulled away fairly soon. Vahan's presence had been a great help, as Armineh knew it would be, but aching to hold Nerissa in his arms to comfort her, he found he could only offer words of sympathy.

When Vahan arrived home that evening he was met by the bombshell which had burst on the Asadourian home. The family gathered in the little sitting room. The four men sat: Garabed, stern and with his stick held between his legs, sat on one side of the fire which had been lit despite the fairly benign weather; Vahan and his younger brother Raffi sat on the other side;18 year-old Ara, who had been saved by Garabed in terrible circumstances during the massacres of 1915, and who now lived with the family as the 'adopted' brother of the others, sat near the door. Garabed slowly read out Nouritza Arabian's letter again.

"Baba – could this possibly be true" said Vahan once he had taken it all in.

"Impossible, brother, impossible! I was there, remember, for at least two months after baba had been deported and I saw no sign of mother being pregnant. It's nonsense – some sort of attempt to get money out of us. I..." said Raffi.

"Well I'm not so sure brother, the letter reads so...."

"Enough boys, enough" said Garabed looking down at the floor. Mariam whispered to me only a week before my arrest that she was already about four months pregnant."

"But baba, it's simply not...."

"Enough Raffi – you were only 16 at the time and you are not known, even now, for being very observant of other people and their feelings. Mariam was certainly pregnant in April 1915. This lady could not have known that Mariam had already told me. Her story rings true. It seems that I have a daughter and you, my sons, have a sister who has miraculously survived."

Everyone sat, silently absorbing the implications of the letter and Garabed's additional information, which he had kept to himself all these years. Then at last Garabed slowly got up and said –

"I am tired. Tomorrow is Sunday and as you know, I will be away all Sunday and the next day. This is a matter we must all think about, and decide what to do. I am sorry, Vahan, to hear about the distress in the Avakian family. I never met the young lad who died in Smyrna, but by your accounts he was likely to have turned into a good man. I understand that you have already invited that clever young lady, Miss Nerissa, to come here after University classes on Tuesday. I have no objection to her being here when we decide on this matter. I have always found her very understanding. It might be a good thing for us to have some female insight into our problem."

"Very well, father. I won't stop her from coming."

"So, everyone, we'll talk about all this on Tuesday. Meanwhile Raffi, it will be your task to find out if it is physically possible yet for anyone to travel either to or from this town...er...

whatever it's called... oh yes, Chehan. You, Vahan, will look into the legal position and also, as an alternative, whether there is any way we can send money to this woman. Once we have all the facts we'll discuss it further when I get back on Tuesday."

And with that the family meeting broke up.

Nerissa was still grieving on the Tuesday she had agreed to go to tea to the Asadourians. But she had duly returned to her classes at university the day before, and she was no longer subject to sudden and involuntary tears. There was still no news of Olga, which added to the worry, as she tried to contend with her grief for Haik. But she was looking forward to her outing to the Asadourians, recognising that it would take her out of her own troubles into another family environment. She had never quite got over her awe of Garabed effendi – but he was always so charming to her in an old-fashioned way that she would always end up totally disarmed by him. She still harboured a strong feeling of physical attraction to the extroverted, somewhat crude, but totally alive Raffi. However she was slowly coming to accept that this 'chemistry' was not reciprocated and was not really the 'love' she was always looking for.

When she arrived, only Vahan was at home. Ara opened the door to her and welcomed her in in his old-fashioned flowery manner. Vahan came bounding down from his room and gave her a chaste kiss on the cheek. In the sitting room, Nerissa sat on the edge of a chair. After a few short words of explanation, Vahan handed her Nouritza's letter, written, of course, in Turkish. Nerissa read it through quickly, then looked up at Vahan with eyes wide open in surprise.

"It's quite true my sweet, it seems that baba knew that mother was pregnant when he was arrested in April."

"But..."

"Listen, I believe I can hear Raffi and father coming in now. Please read it again slowly and carefully as we are going to discuss it together."

Ara already had tea prepared. Conversation, which had been in Armenian till then, switched immediately to Turkish once Garabed, who couldn't speak Armenian, came in. Tea was brought in and for some time the talk ranged over the uncertainties of the current political situation, each of them contemplating the imminent arrival of the nationalist armies, each of them careful not to refer to what had happened in Smyrna. Garabed had noticed the letter in Nerissa's hands when he came in, and eventually, as Ara cleared up, he raised the issue facing the family.

"Now, what are we going to do about this little girl – Satenig."

Raffi immediately burst out without any hesitation–

"Father, there is no difficulty, no doubt at all. It is perfectly possible now that the nationalists are in full control of the whole of Anatolia to get through to Kayseri. From there, whoever goes can easily hire horses and get through within hours to this little town. One of us must go at once and rescue this little girl."

"Baba" said Vahan, "I am not so sure. Her name – the only name she has ever known – is Rehia. Since she was six months-old, she has only known this woman, Gulmaz, as her mother. She has been brought up as a Turkish girl in a little Anatolian town in the middle of nowhere. Imagine the distress it will cause if she is dragged away from the only mother she has ever known."

"How can you say or even think such a thing," Raffi interrupted excitedly. "She is an Armenian whose mother was murdered by Turks. Are we now to leave her in the hands of other Turks, as if rewarding them for slaughtering the rest of her family?"

"Raffi, you can't group people together like that as if they were all the same. The Turks who murdered your mother aren't the same people who saved and brought up your sister," said Nerissa, speaking for the first time.

At this point, partly to forestall Raffi who was getting excited and was about to answer Nerissa's point, Garabed intervened.

"Well Miss Nerissa you may be right, but what then do you suggest we do."

"Garabed effendi, I have no doubt that Vahan is right. Rushing off and taking the little girl away from the only mother she knows is going to be very distressing for her. According to this letter, she has no idea that she is a foundling and that Omar and Gulmaz are not her real mother and father. However, young children are very resilient. She will weep, she may rage, but in the end if she meets with new love and tenderness she will recover."

"She is Armenian, she is entitled to know her own people and her own culture," shouted Raffi.

"Oh for heaven's sake brother, forget this 'she is Armenian' stuff. As of this moment, she is Turkish – all her culture is Turkish and even her name is Turkish. Instead Raffi, say to me – 'She is my sister, she is my sister, the only sister that I can now ever have'."

Raffi looked at Vahan for a long moment and then nodded and finally said –

"One thing is clear. There is no way this little girl is going to leave with this Nouritza woman. One of us will have to go and bring them both back. I know the area well and I would be prepared to do it."

There was a long silence as everyone thought some more. Garabed, still leaning on his stick, looked at his two sons and said –

"Have either of you considered how we, a totally male household, are going to look after a little girl of six in this house?"

"Oh father, come on, we'll manage" said Vahan. "Love is all that matters in the long run, and that is a commodity that can be given by men just as much as by women. All we need is to employ a good woman to be here when we can't be. But look – it is impossible for Raffi to go. You know, brother, that while you are more resourceful and practical than me, you have little tact and a hasty temper. You'll end up alienating everybody and forcing..."

"Don't give me all that diplomacy nonsense. I've got far more strength in my little finger than..."

"That's enough " called out Garabed, as Nerissa began cringing, as she usually did, when passions took over from reasoned argument.

"We are talking about my daughter...my own daughter. Oh God, the last gift of my wife." Garabed's voice shook for a moment and tears stood in his eyes. Then he continued firmly –

"I agree with all of you. Raffi, you are correct that we must move heaven and earth to try to get her back. You, Miss Nerissa, are also correct in pointing out that it needs to be done as gently and carefully as possible, and she is not to be torn roughly from her mother. And finally I agree with you Vahan that you are the only one who can do it. Can you manage?"

"Yes of course. But I insist that I will make my own decision when I see the situation in Chehan. I will force no one."

Then at last for the first time Ara, who had been leaning

against the wall listening, at last spoke up –

"Father, Vahan will need some help. Let me go with him."

And so it was that two days later, Vahan and Ara set sail for the port of Mersin, not much more than 150 miles from Kayseri. At the same time, a letter was penned marked 'urgent' to Nouritza Asadourian at the address given at the top of her letter, informing her of their impending arrival possibly within the week, or, at most, ten days.

Nerissa was escorted back to Sirkedji station by Vahan at the end of the afternoon. For the first time in her life, she considered how other families, too, had love and anger mixed up in their relationships; how other families, too, could be sensitive to each other. Above all, she found herself thinking for the first time of Vahan not just as a family friend, her brother's saviour, a good dancing partner, but as someone with beliefs and passions which, she found, she shared.

CHAPTER 12

Olga Arrives Home

Jennings' second trip, this time with seventeen of the Greek transport ships from Mtilini, returned to Smyrna on the 25th. It departed in the evening of the same day with 43,000 souls on board. Harry worked all day, helping to shepherd the now shattered, and drearily apathetic refugees through the Turkish checkpoints and onto the ships. Olga offered to help, but short of putting on an American or British uniform of some sort, she was so obviously Armenian, it would have been positively unhelpful and even dangerous. Accordingly, Olga spent the day working as usual at the Ottoman Hospital, whilst preparing to leave the next day when the *Lawrence* was due to sail. Harry had lent her some money so she could buy some clothes, but she had been unable to find anything. Only the Turkish residential quarter had remained untouched by the great fire. The main bazaar and the Jewish quarter had burnt down alongside the rest. There were no shops left in the town.

Having cleared the position with the Captain of the *Lawrence*, Harry came with the Consulate car to pick her up the next morning. The USS *Lawrence* sailed out of the great bay at noon and at last, apart from the still unburied, blackened corpse of Haik, there were no Avakians left in the ruins of the once thriving city of Smyrna.

The matter of the naked boy hidden in one of the ship's lifeboats had not, as yet, been resolved. The sailors had carefully fed him and provided water, under the impression that the Captain had no idea what was going on. In fact, there was not a single officer on board who was not aware of the existence of the boy, and the circumstances in which he had come to be on board. Within two hours of leaving the Bay of Smyrna, the Captain asked Harry and Olga to attend a meeting in the officer's mess together with his own senior men.

"Captain Bridgeman, I have called this meeting because we have to decide a few issues before we reach Constantinople."

"Certainly sir, I understand perfectly."

"First there is the matter of this young lady – er – Miss Avakian. Will there be any difficulty in her disembarking when we arrive?"

"Captain," interrupted Olga, "I am an Ottoman citizen, born in, and a lifelong resident of, Constantinople. My father will no doubt be available, if necessary, to vouch for me."

"I can confirm this, sir, as I know the family well," said Harry.

"Very well, thank you. However, we have a more serious matter to think about. What about this young Greek boy whose arrival on board this ship, against all current standing orders, was largely your responsibility Captain Bridgeman."

"Yes sir – I'm sorry. I seem to be disobeying orders on a daily basis these days, having followed them scrupulously all my life until now."

"Look, Harry – I don't care about all that. I have not called this meeting to criticise you, or to try and get rid of any responsibility. The question I need to consider is how we are to deal with this when we reach Constantinople. The situation there is very critical – neither the British nor any of the Ottoman officials are going to allow any Smyrniote Greek to land in the town. The whole question of the Ionian refugees is currently a political hot potato."

At this point the discussion became general as various possibilities were mooted and considered. One thing was crystal clear – it was going to be quite impossible for the Captain to escort the boy ashore in his official capacity, as this would run the risk of involving not only him, but the whole crew of the *Lawrence*, in an official enquiry.

One of the American officers said –

"Look, the boy's name is Spiro. For heaven's sake stop calling him 'the boy' all the time. We know Spiro can swim, after all he swam out to us didn't he? Let him slip off the boat during the night when we anchor and swim ashore."

"My God Vergil, he's only 11 – what will he do when he arrives penniless and almost naked on the shore."

"Well, I wasn't suggesting that. We could give him some clothing and some money in a waterproof pouch. He's 12, he'll get by. Anyway, anything is better than losing him to bureaucratic officials anxious to play everything by the book."

"Listen", said another officer, "he's a bright lad, what about letting him stay aboard as a cabin boy. He'll learn English fast enough, and we can let him off if he wants to leave whenever we next touch at a Greek port."

This seemed to be a generally acceptable solution, but then the Captain interjected in the midst of a chorus of "ayes" –

"I'm sorry but that's impossible. I have to inform you that I've been promoted and have to report for a new assignment when we reach Constantinople. A new Captain will be taking over, and there is no way that he is going to accept that position. There is no 'cabin boy' post on this ship, and none of us could contemplate trying to hide the situation when a new Captain takes over. I'm afraid that he is either going to have to swim or to take his chances with Turkish officialdom. After all, the Brits are still there – surely the worst that could happen is that he will be deported – which simply means sending him to Greece."

There was a short silence, broken by Olga, whose female voice took everyone by surprise.

"Sir, I have spoken to Spiro. He is indeed a bright lad. But he is terrified of being handed back to Turkish policemen. He sees little difference between the Turkish uniforms that he encountered during those terrible last few days in Smyrna, and the Turkish uniforms that he will have to face there in the city. My suggestion is that I take responsibility for him. I will say that I brought Spiro on board with me when I arranged my return to my home city. Spiro is an Armenian relative who has been working as my servant and helper for about a year, and he helped to bring my luggage on board. I'll bluff it through. He already knows a few words of street Armenian. I'll manage, gentlemen, I'll manage. And if it fails, as was already said, the worst that can happen is for him to be deported after all – but at least none of you will be to blame."

"But, Miss, there must be some risk to you this way."

"No – no way. There is absolutely no risk, I can assure you. Just leave it to me."

And in saying this, with her steady and certain conviction, Olga was not merely covering over any possible danger. She really did believe, with all the arrogance and self-confidence of her class and background, that no one would disbelieve or question her. She was yet to appreciate the changed circumstances in which elitist Ottoman Christians were going to have to live in the future.

Harry looked across at Olga, seeing for the first time, not just a strikingly beautiful and elegant woman whose company he had always enjoyed, but a woman who possessed a spirited and forceful character, with a morality similar to his own. He felt the same glow as he had at that first meeting at the hospital – a glow which he had put down to the pleasure he knew he would have in telling the family the good news when he got back, but which now.....

In the silence that greeted Olga's last statement. Harry said –

"She will manage, gentlemen – she will do it."

The Captain stood up.

"That is a very fair offer, Miss Avakian, for which I thank you. Let the boy out of that infernal lifeboat, and arrange for him to be berthed with Miss Avakian in her cabin. And Arthur – for god's sake – get the ship's tailor to make up some basic clothes for him. We can't have Miss Avakian being attended by a naked boy, even if he is only 11 or 12."

And with that, the meeting broke up.

As the USS *Lawrence* slowly moved up the Dardanelles Harry could see the frenetic activity of the many British naval vessels patrolling the area. As they passed Chanak on the right, and the Gallipoli peninsula on the left, Harry pulled out his binoculars and tried to work out what was going on. But having been away from the centre of affairs now for over a week, he had no idea of the looming crisis that was arising as Kemal's victorious army came closer and closer to this point, where the Straits were less than a mile across and where Xerxes had thrown across his bridge of boats over two thousand years ago.

The *Lawrence* arrived in the waters off Constantinople on the 27th September. Almost all official business had virtually stopped. Kemal's army had arrived on the Asian shore, and advance parties were even now taunting British troops across the lines at Chanak. Of course, neither Olga nor Harry were aware of any of this tension, and found that despite all their worries Olga had only minimal difficulty in negotiating her entry, once she had established that she was a bona fide Ottoman citizen from Constantinople. Olga was proved right. There were still no officious nationalist officers at Eminonu; they were still the Ottoman bureaucrats of the old school. Inefficient they might be, but they were polite and well mannered. Olga explained what was the truth, namely that she had lost her 'nufus' and other papers in the fire; however, she could produce her papers from the Imperial Ottoman hospital, showing that she had been working there until only a few days previously.

The officer nodded and gave scarcely a second glance at the servant boy accompanying her. Like everyone else in the city, his mind was concentrated on the approach of Kemal's army. Harry, meanwhile, had been waved through immediately. He said he would wait for her at Sirkedji station.

From the moment that Nerissa had returned from university on the day that Paramaz and George had returned from Smyrna, she had been in a state of anxious confusion. The devastating grief for the death of her brother had been followed, once she had returned to her classes, by the alarming reports going round the university, of the horrific scenes in Smyrna before, during and after the fire. Vahan, her friend and dancing partner, had been on hand at the worst moment, when she was told of the death of Haik, and his presence had comforted her. What Nerissa really craved was physical comfort. Deep down, she wanted to curl up in her father's arms.

But Karekin could not quite contemplate taking his clever twenty-year-old daughter into his arms as of old. Determined to be honest, and imagining that this daughter, always so combative and engaged in the discussions that took place around the family table, simply needed to sort things out in her own mind, he kept his comments about his own fears, to a minimum. Armineh, who had long since given up cuddling her elder daughters, had her time cut out seeing to the 13 year-old Seta, taking her onto her arms and calming her fears fuelled by school gossip. But neither Nerissa nor her parents imagined that she could have done with the same.

Meanwhile Vahan wanted nothing more than to hold her in his arms, and not just on the dance floor. Why then did Nerissa hold back? She had now seen her sensible elder sister, Sima, fall head over heels into a romantic attachment with an impoverished Russian refugee. This, despite the fact that Sima had always argued the importance of choosing your life partner for all sorts of reasons, but never just for love. This had been a permanent argument among the three girls, with Olga and Nerissa claiming that what was important in any relationship was that spark of 'love' – they called it chemistry – between couples before any marriage could be contemplated. Sima, on the other hand had always claimed that what was important were common background, common culture, mutual understanding about the bringing up of children; then love might or might not come later.

Yet, in the end, Sima had rejected the eminently suitable George, the perfect match, with whom she had been 'going out' for years, in favour of the 'chemistry' she had always affected to despise.

Now Nerissa could see that Sima was deeply happy and content in her relationship with Nicolai, and this reinforced her own certainty that what was important was love – a spark she didn't feel with the shy, introverted, former music student with whom she had been going dancing since the end of the war. She had been visiting the all-male Asadourian household ever since that first day when she had been introduced to the old father – Garabed. She felt then, she was more romantically attracted to the brash and extrovert younger brother, Raffi, than to Vahan himself. Yet she had absolutely nothing in common with Raffi and she knew it.

Meanwhile, this bright intellectual girl, who carefully analysed day by day, both her own feelings and those of her family, remained unconscious of the fact that Vahan, with whom she continued to have long and intimate conversations, had fallen in love with her. For his part Vahan, who still remembered the very first time he had smiled at her all those years ago at that afternoon tea at Tokatlians, where Olga and Selim first held hands, could no longer contemplate his future without her. Feeling her coolness towards him, he didn't know how to react. His brother Raffi could have told him, in cruder terms, but that was not in his nature.

Only Nerissa was at home when Olga and Harry arrived at the house. Olga, excited and bursting with anticipation, rang the bell. She fell upon Talin with kisses when she opened the door, and then burst into the great hall of the Avakian house. The Avakian home was one of the largest in Makrikoy, situated just north of the Vali Effendi racecourse. Most of the life of the family was focused round this hall immediately inside the main door. This was a very large room with a fairly grand staircase opposite the entrance. On the left was the large dining table with the entrance to the kitchen and utility rooms beyond. On the right was a comfortable sitting area by a large open fireplace; there was a door leading to a formal sitting room through which one passed onto a wide veranda, overlooking the large garden with the orchards beyond.

"Mama, everyone, Mama I'm home, I'm home." Olga shouted out.

Nerissa, up in her room working on an essay on Trollope, jumped up, scattering her papers as she did so, and ran out onto the landing. Looking down over the banister she saw a radiant Olga looking up and alongside her Harry with a young boy behind. Nerissa flew downstairs, her hair all over the place, almost tripping and falling in her eagerness, and collapsed with tears of joy into Olga's arms. The two sisters, so different and so often in disagreement, were sobbing out loud with joy. Harry smiled and Spiro gave a little giggle – he of course had seen this sort of thing many times before.

"Where's mother?" Olga said at last.

"Oh Olga, they're all out, they'll be back soon. My soul, what happened, how did you get back, what's the … oh sorry!" she said as she noticed Harry again, and reverting immediately to English in that automatic Bolsetsi manner said – "Look, we must all sit and have some tea."

Nerissa released Olga and turned to extend her hand to Harry. To her surprise he ignored it, and instead, coming forward, he held her and kissed her firmly on both cheeks. Then, stepping back he indicated Spiro, still standing behind him. Spiro hadn't understood a word, neither the Armenian nor the English. Speaking in his poor Turkish, he waved at the lad with a flourish and said –

"May I introduce my friend – Spiro Pantelis effendi."

Spiro did not know where to look; in all his almost 12 years he had never before been referred to as 'effendi'. He coloured bright red and shifted his feet, but then saw Talin, who was giggling, and immediately recovered, grinning at his own discomfiture. Olga, also now talking Turkish, said to Talin –

"Please Talin, sober up and go and fetch some tea and cakes or something – and look after Spiro and give him something to eat – and no teasing, there's a good girl."

Talin still in a fit of giggles indicated to Spiro to follow her and stalked out to the kitchen. Nerissa saw for the first time that the boy was dressed in an extraordinary outfit, which appeared to have been made out of a grown man's sailor suit.

One by one, the rest of the family came in as the afternoon wore on. Seta bounced in with a great burst of joy when she realised who was sitting at the table. Then Armineh and Sima came in together. Armineh just stood and tears flowed soundlessly down her cheeks as Olga jumped up. They held each other tight and cried together for a long time. Finally Karekin arrived, earlier than usual as if he had had a premonition, with Paramaz in tow. He too stood stock still when he entered. Then he held his daughter tightly to him for a time – for an eternity.

Tea gave way to supper and the family remained at the table. The great fire of Smyrna and all the political events leading up to it were ignored as the house rang with the noise of an Avakian family reunion. The discussion was all about the many personal matters which had transpired. Paramaz had not joined them, but the baby boy was brought down by Marie and, gurgling happily, was handed round between the women. Nerissa, notoriously disinterested in babies, passed the little boy straight on to Olga. Seta, sitting on the other side of Olga, expected the child to be passed straight on to her, but was surprised to find that Olga held on to him. She was making all the proper cooing noises that adults indulge in, and cuddled the baby tightly. Armineh also noticed this with surprise, but made no comment.

Inevitably, the conversation kept turning to Selim's presence in Smyrna, and then, as quickly, shying away. Olga wasn't ready to go into all that part of her life. Ironically, she had had no trouble talking about it to Harry on several occasions as they had travelled together. She couldn't quite understand why she was unable to be just as forthright with her own family. She kept prevaricating and changing the subject – but these were Avakians she was dealing with and they persisted.

She was going to have to admit the existence of the relationship. She assumed that Paramaz would have told them that she was – or may have been – living with Selim before the catastrophe. But the Great War had not changed conventions that much, at least not in the Ottoman world. She felt she couldn't blurt out the true facts in front of the whole family just like that – there was, after all, Seta to consider - and on top of that, the family would be embarrassed by Harry's presence. They were not to know that he was already aware that a relationship had existed. She appealed to her mother, saying she would tell all about things 'tomorrow', when she was not quite so overwhelmed by the joy of her return.

Armineh, who had long since interpreted Paramaz's prevarications, and knew that Olga must have been living with Selim during those last few months before the arrival of the Turkish army, immediately intervened. She recognised the element of distress in Olga's evasions and moved the discussion away from this subject. This then was the moment for Harry to get up and declare that he was happy to walk down to the station and did not need the carriage to be called. Reverting to formality while the parents were present, he shook hands with all of them, said goodbye and left.

Olga went up to her room with Nerissa. As they continued to chat together, she could think only of the baby growing inside her. Within a few weeks she knew it would become obvious, to her mother at least, if not to everyone else. She had to decide very soon what she was going to tell Armineh – and more to the point what she could say to Karekin.

As Olga considered her position, it seemed to her

that if she admitted to the baby being Selim's child, conceived naturally and with her loving consent, this would be shameful for Karekin. If, however, she admitted the rape and explained the coming child that way, he would be upset, but not shamed.

What should she do?

CHAPTER 13

Chanak

As the Avakians tried to come to terms with their situation, the Turkish army moved out of Smyrna and headed towards the Imperial City. After almost two thousand years of effortless domination over the native peasantry of Anatolia – whether Greek, Seljuk, Turk or Kurd –– the city was about to be brought sharply and painfully to its knees. This was how it appeared after the horrific events in Smyrna.

The arrogant Western powers, who were treating the defeated Ottoman Empire with greater severity than any of the other combatants, waited to see what Mustafa Kemal would now do. It was as if an old, weak and sickly champion boxer, having at last been knocked out, had risen, kicked the referee, pushed his opponents out of the ring and was now standing with his boxing gloves raised to the cheers of the crowd.

From the point of view of the Western leaders in London Paris and Rome, nothing but a few disunited allied battalions stood in the way of a new invasion of Europe by avenging Turks. In a worst case scenario, they were forced to contemplate a possible resumption of the war, only four years after the triumphant occupation of Constantinople itself.

Mustafa Kemal made it clear that Smyrna was in no way the end of his ambition – he intended to take back Constantinople and planned to be in the city within days. The question was: would this be a magnified repeat of the occupation of Smyrna only a fortnight before? Furthermore, he had made it quite clear that he would not stop at the city, but intended to chase after the Greeks into Europe. His minimum demand was the whole of Eastern Thrace including the town of Adrianople, still occupied by the remnants of the Greek army.

Whether he liked it or not, standing in his way was the British garrison in Constantinople, commanded by the cool figure of General Harington. In addition, Harington also commanded a tiny force – one single battalion – at Chanak, a small port on the

Asian side at the narrowest part of the Dardanelles.

In Constantinople, Harrington had immediately swung into action as soon as he had received news of the collapse of the Greek army and the fall and occupation of Smyrna. The first and most pressing matter he had to deal with was the impending fate of his single battalion stuck out at Chanak. This was an outpost of the 'neutral zone' which the allies had drawn like a ring round Constantinople and the straits. This neutral zone had been accepted by the Sultan's government, which had agreed to respect it, on condition that the allies agreed to defend it. Indeed, only about two or three months previously, the Greeks themselves had threatened to breach this zone with a threat to enter Constantinople from the European side. On that occasion, Harington, backed up by the French and Italian commanders, had thrown troops into the Chatalja lines, making it clear that they would oppose any Greek move. The issue now was whether Harington would do the same against the victorious Kemalists, who of course had never accepted the idea of such a zone.

He would and he did.

On the 15th, as the fires in Smyrna began to die down, he asked the resident French and Italian generals – Generals Charpy and Mombelli – if they would send token detachments of their troops to Chanak, so as to show three flags, instead of one. They agreed to do so, without consulting Paris or Rome at that stage. These token detachments arrived at Chanak and were welcomed with great pomp and circumstance, cheerfully played in by the British garrison band. For the moment, then, there were three flags flying at this little port commanding the straits. In order to control the Dardanelles and allow shipping in and out of the Marmara Sea, and on to Constantinople, holding on at Chanak seemed to be vital.

But by now, as September began to come to a close, the Lloyd George government in London was in a state of nervous tension about the whole position. It seemed to Churchill, Lloyd George and Curzon, the men who counted in this matter, that the French and Italian governments were wavering in their determination to stand up to the Turkish nationalists, and that they might have to face up to the defence of the straits alone. If this did indeed become the position, they felt that defending the European shore was more important than keeping a tenuous hold on Chanak on the Asiatic side. As it became increasingly clear that the French and Italians were going to withdraw, the cabinet advised Harington to withdraw his troops from Chanak.

Harington did not do so; instead he warned Mustafa Kemal's representatives, now openly operating in the city, that the three allies were in agreement and united in their opposition to any attempt to violate the neutral zone. There was already an element of bluff in this, as it seemed that Rome and Paris were about to pull out and leave the British to face the Turkish army alone.

Meanwhile in London, as the situation continued to develop, and it was noted that Harington was not proposing to withdraw from Chanak, the cabinet decided to send a whole division to reinforce him. Harington received this news with enthusiasm and began putting pressure on Charpy to urge his government to reinforce the French contingent as well. But at this juncture, as the Turkish army moved ever closer, the French government finally came off the fence, reversed their policy and ordered Charpy to withdraw all his troops from the area, including the small token detachment at Chanak, as well as all his men in Constantinople. The Italians, who had been negotiating directly with Kemal for some time, eagerly and immediately followed suit. There was now only one flag at Chanak – the flag of the British Empire.

During this period, Harington, while overseeing operations from his office in the Harbiye buildings in Pera, had a house in Tarabya, one of the last of the little towns straggling up the Bosporus at which the ferries from the Galata Bridge stopped. Here, Harington coolly decided to give a formal party as the French and Italians moved out of Chanak, and while the desperate refugees were still waiting on the quaysides of Smyrna, awaiting the arrival of ships. All the allied High Commissioners, the Admirals and the Generals, including of course Charpy and Mombelli, were invited. Both Generals wrote back notes to

Harington begging to be excused as they were so unhappy at being ordered to withdraw and leave Harington on his own. Harington, however, insisted. As all the allied chiefs arrived, amongst them Admiral Bristol, as well as members of the Ottoman court, the pipers of the Irish Guards, standing in full ceremonial uniform in the large entrance hall of the house, played martial airs. There they were – all the great and the good of the Western empires, in whose hands now lay the future of not only the Avakian family and their Bolsetsi friends and relations, but also all of the populations of the old Ottoman Empire.

But this was to be the last occasion that Western Imperial diplomats and officials were going to convene in the city that they had dominated as ambassadors and advisers for nearly a hundred years. The uninvited Turks, the peasant soldiers of Anatolia and their leaders, were closing in. As the guests left, Harington turned to his chief of staff and said –

"By God George, that was a remarkable evening wasn't it?"

"Yes sir, certainly," was the reply, "most successful. Lady Harington is to be congratulated on the smooth arrangements."

"I think we have got them all on board now haven't we?" continued Harington. "They're not going to let that ambitious brigand simply walk into this wonderful old city – they'll rally round you'll see."

"Well you know, sir, they certainly enjoyed themselves, but they are all about to ditch us one way or another. They are all playing devious games of intrigue behind our backs – except of course that idiot Bristol who is at least doing it quite openly."

"Not all of them George, not all of them. General Charpy was in tears when he shook my hand as he left."

"Genuine, sir, or crocodile?"

On the 23rd September – the day that Jennings started taking off his first batch of survivors from the Smyrna quaysides – Turkish cavalry crossed into the neutral zone and approached Chanak. The position there had steadily improved for the British as Harington sent in reinforcements arriving as a result of the earlier decision in London. From a military point of view, the little port could not now be taken without a major effort on the part of the Turkish army. But there were still enormous problems. Hordes of Greek refugees, people who had lived peacefully in the area as Ottoman citizens for generations, had been pouring into the Chanak zone daily. There was a shortage of clean drinking water and it was urgent that they should be evacuated as quickly as possible. Barges had been hired to move them across to the European side and this was being seen to on a daily basis, though many refugees still remained.

The local commander at Chanak was still short of the full complement necessary for a sure defence. However, the battleships and cruisers of the Eastern Mediterranean fleet, with the one exception of the *Iron Duke* still in Constantinople, were anchored in the straits outside Chanak, and all their marines were landed. Harington wisely left the operational control to the local commanders, who decided that of vital importance was convincing the Turks that the British would fight if necessary. He had accordingly placed troops as far forward in the neutral zone as he could – 40 miles or so inland. There stood Captain Petherick, a young officer in command of the Third Kings Own Hussars at the tiny formerly Greek village of Ezine, covering the direct road between Chanak and Smyrna, up which the Turkish army was now marching.

Up rode the Turkish cavalry, fortunately much the best disciplined element in the Turkish nationalist army. The country was rough and hilly, not ideal for cavalry. Harington had given strict orders that no British soldier was to fire a single shot until they themselves had been fired on. The situation was tense – a false order, a trigger-happy trooper, anything could have happened resulting in hostilities, which, once started, would have been almost impossible to stop. However, it became obvious that the Turkish force had received similar orders, and there followed several hours of what might be described as farce, if the possible consequences of a false move had not been so potentially devastating.

Instead of the normal military strategy of camouflaging themselves and concealing their movements from each other, both sides followed the exact opposite tactic of ostentatiously moving around and showing off their strength and determination on the top of the hills around. They were all manoeuvring on almost the same battlefields as the siege of Troy. Here they were, millennia later, still beating their golden shields, waving their swords and shouting defiance at the enemy, as if they were Greek and Trojan heroes.

It was all shadow-boxing and bluff. But it was dangerous brinkmanship, both on the part of London and of Mustafa Kemal, as a minor incident or accident could, at any moment, set off an explosion. It was doubly dangerous because the ensuing crisis had little to do with Constantinople itself, or with the freedom of navigation of the straits, but a lot to do with the way in which the protagonists saw the situation as one of honour and national pride.

This crisis, which followed the burning of Smyrna and the expulsion of the Ottoman Greeks from Anatolia, arose at first because of British fears that the Turks would try to cross into Europe, seize Constantinople and chase the Greeks out of Thrace and further if necessary. But by this date in September, it was already obvious that, one way or another, the British were going to allow Constantinople to revert to the Turks, and possibly Eastern Thrace and Adrianople as well. That being so, what was all this posturing over this little port on the Dardanelles all about?

The reasoning from the British government's point of view was complicated but very pressing. Lloyd George took the traditional Gladsonian liberal view that the return of the Turks into Europe would necessarily mean the return of oppression, corruption and massacres. In view of the Smyrna solution, he was not entirely unjustified in that opinion. Having prevented the Greeks – nominal allies after all – from descending on Constantinople only a few months earlier, Great Britain was surely bound in honour to react in the same way when the Turks, with whom they were technically at war, made a similar attempt.

But finally, and this was the vital psychological aspect, the British political establishment became obsessed with the idea that now that only the British flag remained proudly defiant at Chanak, any supine withdrawal in the face of this Asiatic peasant army would involve an irreparable loss of Imperial prestige, particularly in Moslem India. There was a 'Rorke's Drift' mentality, which, while it had on the whole disappeared from the British public's appetite for glory in the blood, mud and disillusion of the fields of Flanders, still flickered in the Churchillian wing of the political establishment. Furthermore, those romantic Imperialists were probably right in the long run and what was to happen here, and in the great Imperial city in the next few weeks, did spell the beginning of the end of Empire. Before Chanak the British Empire stood at its greatest extent. Within less than thirty years later it was fast disappearing, while the Ottoman Empire had gone altogether.

The Turkish army threatening Chanak, and approaching Constantinople in the north, now numbered over 50,000, without counting the reserves moving up all the time from the interior. The split between the British and French widened and their relationship now reached its nadir since the entente first negotiated 20 years before. The British foreign minister Curzon had met the French premier Poincaré in Paris on the 22nd September, the day before the arrival of the Turkish cavalry in the neutral zone at Chanak.

There at the Quai d'Orsay, in an encounter reported by many observers, Curzon talked of the French having 'abandoned' the British at Chanak. Poincaré, livid with rage, demanded that Curzon withdraw his comments, though they were strictly correct, as the small French contingent had indeed been withdrawn. In any event, Poincaré then lost all control and had shouted and raved at the top of his voice, behaving "like a demented schoolmaster screaming at a guilty schoolboy". He shouted out torrents of abuse in the most insulting manner. Poor Curzon – a grandee aristocrat to his fingertips – the once mighty Viceroy of India – the foreign secretary of Great Britain – was actually trembling. The moment came when he could stand it no longer, and muttering unintelligibly, he rose and stumbled out of the room, collapsing outside into the arms of the British Ambassador.

"My God, Charles," he called out "I just can't bear that horrid little man. I can't bear him." He then burst into tears and wept unashamedly.

Yet, surprisingly, despite all the personal drama, the meeting was fairly successful, once the parties reconvened and apologies were exchanged. A vital seven more days were gained when it was agreed that under the direction of General Harington a conference should be held at Mudania – another sleepy little port, but this time on the Sea of Marmara – with an invitation to Kemal's representatives, to try and fix the necessary arrangements as the Turks advanced towards Constantinople. This was yet to be accepted by the Turkish nationalists, and meanwhile the Turks remained within the neutral zone. Throughout this period, British reinforcements were pouring into Chanak and were now in a well-entrenched position with artillery and naval support and with total air supremacy in the form of a small airforce squadron.

This was the position when the cabinet decided to instruct Harington to deliver a clear ultimatum threatening immediate war unless Mustafa Kemal withdrew. Harington was instructed to notify the Turkish commander in Chanak that unless his troops were withdrawn – 'all the forces at my disposal will fire upon your troops.' Here at last was the crunch. On one side, an old Empire seemingly at the height of its power and prestige, now fearful of what was still thought of as 'an army of orientals'. Meanwhile, on the other side, stood a nationalist force heady with victory after the total defeat of their ancestral enemy and the fall of Smyrna, and equally concerned about the possible loss of momentum if they now voluntarily withdrew.

Harington received his instructions on the 29th September. At the same time, the Admiralty sent instructions to Admiral Brock to destroy all private shipping moored in Constantinople in order to prevent nationalist forces from using them to cross the Bosporus into Europe. All was in the balance and once again, Constantinople waited in dread for the denouement.

CHAPTER 14

The Village of Chehan

It was not quite accurate to describe Chehan as a village. It had two mosques and a permanently manned and staffed police station, and it was larger than any of the one-street villages that abounded in the area. On the other hand, it was not a town. It had several cafés and a restaurant or two. Some of the citizens still owned and kept sheep and perhaps a cow in their backyards. Two separate local shepherds still called at these houses in the mornings, employed to collect the sheep to be taken out to the hills for pasture. Also, unlike a town, there was no public bakery or bread shop – everybody made their own bread.

Well – a village then? However, there was a little school, and that was right next door to the only café, a tiny hole of a building, where the men would sit for hours on stools and chairs on the street just outside the decrepit door, which opened into a gloomy dark room, and which they avoided whenever the weather allowed. There they would sit smoking not very clean narghilés, and sipping at one tiny coffee cup all morning. In the school in the next building, those boys released and paid for by their parents would come and sit cross-legged in rows in front of a crusty old Hodja with a large old-fashioned turban, nodding their heads and repeating endless lines from the Koran. All in Arabic of course, a language none of them really understood.

Orhan's own little boy was not yet old enough, so Rehia did not have to take him to school, and instead played with him all day long running barefoot in and out of the streets. In the house, there were now servants together with what could only be described as 'hangers-on', relatives of Orhan. This meant that Gulmaz only needed to supervise and organise the work and little Rehia was not burdened with any household chores, other than the traditional one for elder daughters to look after the next child down.

Orhan was somewhat lazy – he spent a lot of time at the little café by the school, playing endless games of tavloo with his friends – but he was not mean in any way. He did his best in relation to Rehia and was never cruel. In the culture from which he sprung, girls counted for nothing in any case, and he always considered that Rehia, who had been over-indulged by Omar, was far too noisy and active. She was apt to argue back to adults. If all children should be seen and not heard, it was arguable for men like Orhan in Muslim rural communities, whether little girls should even be seen.

Vahan had left Caesaria, Kayseri, in 1913 to go to University in Stamboul and had never returned in the ten years since. The town lay on the direct road from the coast to the village of Chehan. The morning he and Ara arrived in Kayseri, three days after disembarking at Mersin, Vahan made a tour of the old Armenian quarter and went to look at the old family home, while Ara went off to find a donkey-master. Unlike Raffi, Vahan had not witnessed or personally experienced any of the traumatic events of the great massacres and deportations of 1915 that had struck his people. He walked through the old quarter where he had gone to school, attended church, and run and played in the streets with all the other boys, Turk and Armenian alike, and was devastated by what he saw.

Knowing what had happened in that year from April 1915 to 1916, did not prepare him for the reality. From a thriving community of over 10,000 people, not a single Armenian was left. He had expected to see more physical destruction. Instead, the streets were now eerily empty. One or two of the more modest houses had been re-occupied by squatters, mostly Turks uprooted from other parts of the empire. They had obviously preferred taking over the smaller dwellings, while the grand houses of the wealthier merchants surrounding large courtyards, remained empty and abandoned. The squatters looked sad and the locals clearly avoided going through the streets that had once housed their noisy and bustling neighbours. The professors and the teachers might rant and rave about removing the canker in their midst, the politicians and the gauleiters of the provinces might set about the cleansing that the academic nation-state enthusiasts demanded – but the ordinary, simple townspeople felt that something valuable, even if abrasive, had been cut out of their lives.

Vahan walked slowly past the abandoned homes. Tiles were beginning to fall off the roofs; windows were broken, shutters smashed, doors broken open revealing the empty rooms beyond. Vahan could remember grand receptions in some of these houses, when as a boy he would come and stand with his friends in the street and watch the guests arriving; and as a shy young man, on the eve of leaving for university, he had himself come as one of those guests with his parents.

Vahan felt the brooding silence of the streets. He could see that the present townsfolk – all those who seven or eight years ago had been persuaded to shout *'giavour asiliyor' 'giavour! giavour!'* so mindlessly, now avoided going into the old empty Armenian quarter; perhaps to efface the memories of the throngs of people who had formed the backdrop to their lives a few years before. It was still hot for September. Vahan sat down on a stone bench alongside one of the empty houses and tried to recall his childhood. Surely it hadn't been that bad. He had never felt 'hated.' Admittedly, he went to an all-Armenian school, but he played in the streets with lots of Turkish kids – his mother attended the local 'hamam' with all the other mothers, Turk and Armenian – while his father was a respected 'mukhtar' of the district, and would sit at the cafés with Turkish business acquaintances sharing a hookah. Where then did the hatred come from? How did it arise?

The more he tried to remember the atmosphere of those old Ottoman days of his childhood, the more puzzled he became. There really could be only one answer – the hatred must have been orchestrated. Class envy exists in all societies, he thought, but this had been turned by thoughtless academics into ethnic hatred.

Vahan gave a sigh, rose and walked back through the narrow, silent, cobbled streets to the main bazaar and back into the bustling life of a Turkish provincial town. Ara had found a donkey-master, one Achmet, prepared to accompany them to

Chehan with four donkeys and with spare fodder for the two horses which Vahan and Ara had purchased in Marsin, to take them to Kayseri.

It had taken the old women and children, deported in the early months of 1916, three days to stagger to the point just short of Chehan where they were murdered. It took Vahan's little caravan less than a day, plodding into the village in the early evening. Achmet knew of a family willing, indeed anxious, to give shelter to visitors, especially those with gold from one of the big cities.

It was a delicate situation. Vahan felt that it might be embarrassing, even dangerous for Nouritza Arabian if they approached her first. So, in the morning, he and Ara went to the police station where Omar had been the sergeant. Nationalist fervour had not yet penetrated this little town and they were met with the unfailing politeness of the old Ottoman police. Vahan asked to be directed to the house of Orhan and Gulmaz khatun, and he was given clear directions. However as he turned to leave Ara said –

"Constable effendi, it would be very helpful if you could tell us if Orhan bey is likely to be at home."

"No sir, almost certainly he will not be."

"And where, effendi, would we be able to find him."

"I believe he will be at the café. He is often there in the middle of the day."

"And later," called out one of the other policemen with a chuckle.

"...er ... well yes. You will find the café next to the school just past the mosque – there – down the road."

As they came out into the sunshine Vahan raised his eyebrows at Ara and said simply,

"Why?"

"Well, my brother, I know these people better than you. While it seems clear that this Gulmaz might well be the one who will have the last word – for many reasons we must approach the husband first, because that is how this culture would require us to act. Secondly you must remember that the little girl will likely

THE VILLAGE OF CHEHAN   125

reject us, whatever we do or say and the mother will seek to protect her. We have to go at the matter obliquely – first the husband, then the wife, and only right at the end the little girl."

At the café it was the young Ara who made all the running. Here his country accent became an asset, whereas Vahan's Stambouli Ottoman Turkish was regarded with suspicion. But it was Vahan who ordered the bottle of raki, which went round the few customers and broke the ice. The other men sitting round were ready to follow the lead of Orhan in his response to these strangers. Orhan introduced himself immediately. Neither Vahan nor Ara mentioned the new law regarding Armenian orphans at any stage. The talk, at first lengthy with elaborate greetings and introductions, ever so slowly progressed to the business in hand. As the objective of the strangers emerged, Ara quickly established that Vahan was the little girl's blood brother.

This was a relationship everybody understood and sympathised with, and slowly, as Orhan himself contemplated the matter, everyone began to come round to the logic of the situation and the proposed solution. Without making any reference to money, Vahan let it be known that compensation would be offered for the years the family had cared for the little girl. The men nodded and drank up the second bottle of raki. No one, no one at all, mentioned or referred in any way to the deaths, or the circumstances in which this effendi's little sister had come to be in this out-of-the-way village. Thus the morning passed pleasantly enough.

"You must be totally crazy, husband, out of your mind. Do you think for one moment that I am going to give up my darling Rehia for a few pieces of silver. What are you saying, you must..."

"Calm down, wife, calm down. There is no question of selling the little girl. Come – come. It is her brother who has arrived. Her very own blood brother. You know this is happening all over the countryside – the orphan children who escaped the death marches are being returned to relatives far less closely related than this."

"Pig! This isn't an orphan child we are talking about – it is my baby, my Rehia, whom I have brought up with love and care all her life. I can't let her go to strangers, and I ..."

At this point Gulmaz broke down and began weeping. Orhan took her in his arms, saying she was still young enough to have children of her own with him. Gulmaz knew that Orhan did not care for Rehia. She also knew in her heart that just as she had been unable to have children with Omar, she was unlikely to have them ten years later with Orhan. She wept bitterly and would not be comforted, for she knew that though she was going to put up a fight, unless she could change Orhan's mind, in the end, she would have to give in.

It was eventually decided that Vahan and Ara would be invited to come for coffee the next morning. That afternoon, Vahan at last paid a visit to the Kazim family, where he finally met Nouritza. She had already warned the Kazims of her decision to leave as soon as she could – and here was her chance. She arranged with Vahan that she would accompany him back to Bolis, whether Rehia accompanied them or not.

Everyone in the village was now fully aware of the arrival of these Stambouli strangers – Armenians – relatives of the little Rehia. Everyone in the village sympathised with Orhan. Sooner or later Rehia was going to find out about her real roots, and however it occurred it would be traumatic for her – indeed it was likely that Rehia had already been teased by other children and had an inkling that she was in some way different. But they were also all aware of the strength of will of Gulmaz. Once little Rehia burst into tears and called out 'Ana! Ana!', there would be an explosion and who knew what would happen.

The scene that next morning at the home of Orhan and Gulmaz was distressing – though in the end the person who was most distressed was probably Vahan. It is not easy to grasp fully the mind of Rehia herself who was now nearly seven years old. She raged and wept and clung to her 'Ana'. She shouted that she would not go with these dreadful men. But she was curious as well. She was not acting when she hid her head in Gulmaz's voluminous skirts, but nevertheless peeped out, clearly intrigued by Ara who was a master at making funny faces at her behind Vahan's back. She had been aware that there was some mystery in her birth, and had returned Orhan's indifference towards her with childish dislike.

Vahan made no attempt to explain Ara's presence, save to say that he was his younger bother. Gulmaz, facing the combined opposition of almost everyone crowded into the room, raised objection after objection. How could a young girl of seven travel alone with three men for days down to the coast? This was countered by breaking the news that Nouritza Arabian would be accompanying them all the way to Stamboul. Who could the little Rehia talk to, she did not know a word of Armenian?   But Madam, as you can see, we are all talking Turkish, came Vahan's reply. Who will give her presents, who will clothe and feed her? Then as if in desperation and speaking in real and genuine distress – "Who will love her like I do?"

At this last desperate cry, Vahan, almost in tears himself, rose and came to Gulmaz, and bowing down before her, took her hand, raised it to his lips and kissed it in a gesture of deep respect and emotion.

"Gulmaz hanum, she is my beloved sister, my mother and father's daughter. I will love her like you do all the rest of my life. There, in Stamboul, she will have not only all her family but her own natural father as well. Here everyone knows that she is a giavour child and she now knows it herself. All that she has to sustain her is you. That is worth a lot of course – your love, madam, shines out from your eyes. But here she really has no one else. In Stamboul she will be surrounded by family – father – close friends – her brothers – her community – for all of whom she will be like a miracle sent down by Allah. She is seven. She will always remember you as her 'ana'. Ishallah she will visit you here when she becomes a young lady. I myself will bring her. I know it is hard, but I am sure that you will give her this chance."

There was a long, a very long, silence as Vahan returned to his seat. Vicdan, who had given Rehia her first bath in this village all those years ago, moved across to hold her neighbour tightly. She whispered in her ear. Orhan looked on with wonder. He had

never seen his wife listen to someone for so long without interrupting. The silence dragged on. Rehia, looking on at everything
with her huge brown eyes, had long since gone to sit with
Orhan's young wife. Then at last, as the silence became
deafening, Gulmaz spoke, looking down at the floor -

"Asadour effendi, would you please arrange to send Nouritza
hanum to me later this morning. I know she is fond of Rehia,
and Rehia knows her fairly well. I have things to arrange and
things to say to them both." There was a short pause. "In private
and without all you clumsy men around." Gulmaz glared all
round her in a show of defiant bravado – though her heart was
breaking. She went out of the room and into the women's
quarters, without even looking at Orhan.

Orhan and Vahan quickly came to an arrangement about the
compensation for all Rehia's clothes and bedding and everything
else that had been done for her. It was clear enough to Vahan
that Gulmaz was unlikely to get any of it, or indeed would have
wanted a single penny.

Vahan never got to know what Gulmaz said to Nouritza and
to little Rehia – but the very next day the little caravan moved off.
Achmet had arranged for a double straw pannier to be placed
across the back of one of the stronger donkeys. Rehia's bedding,
and her carefully cleaned and folded clothes, went into one of
the panniers, and Rehia herself balanced the load sitting in the
other pannier peeping out over the edge. Nouritza sat on one of
the other donkeys, Ara and Vahan on their horses, and the
donkey master on the lead donkey with its continually tinkling
bell.

The final parting between Rehia and the only mother she had
ever known had been poignant. Rehia cried and clung to her
mother, but Vahan could see that the true tragedy was with
Gulmaz, who no longer wept, but just gave Rehia one last
embrace, and turned away. Indeed within an hour or so of
leaving the village, Rehia started peering out curiously over the
edge of the pannier. The little caravan moved all day, for five full
days, in order to reach the coast at Mersin. At the end of each day
a camp would be set up. A fire would be prepared and lit by Ara,

who also did the cooking. A tent would be put up for Nouritza and Rehia, while the three men slept out in the open. Nouritza would lay out Rehia's bedding. It was all very exciting, and Rehia had little time to be sad.

Vahan hadn't brought his violin, but his singing voice was an attractive high baritone, and every night after they had all eaten, he would sing lullabies and sad Armenian songs to Rehia who had had no experience of any music at all in the village. On the first night, emotionally and physically exhausted, Rehia had called for her 'ana' and had cried herself to sleep. But as each night passed – helping the ever-cheerful Ara prepare the food – listening with wide-open eyes to Vahan's singing – cuddling up to Nouritza, she began to recover her natural high spirits. During the day, Rehia spent most of her time looking out over the edge of her pannier, except when she was lulled to sleep. Ara would occasionally ride up alongside and tell her a story.

The little party arrived at the port of Mersin without any further problems. Despite the success of the nationalist forces in the west, this was still a fairly lawless region and they were lucky not to have fallen prey to any of the many bandits in the area. They managed to find a berth on a Bulgarian freighter heading for Constantinople within hours of arriving, selling the horses and paying off Achmet.

Two days later, the great mosques of Constantinople – that incomparable shoreline vista – came into view, as the ship steamed up out of the Marmara to its anchorage.

CHAPTER 15

Burhan Celal

Burhan Celal had lived all his life in the city of Smyrna, the principal port of the Ottoman Empire after Constantinople itself. His father, an effendi in the service of the local Ottoman administration, owned a substantial two-storey house in a road running up from the Konak and the harbour to the ruined Byzantine castle perched at the top.

The Turkish quarter was a crazy patchwork of twisting narrow streets and steps straggling up the hillside. Many of the houses, almost all wooden, had great views over the rest of the city below and the wide sweep of the bay beyond. Burhan's father had been a civil servant who had worked at the Konak, the government centre in Watchtower Square.

The home in which Burhan had been brought up was large and square, surrounding an internal open patio in the middle of which was an old covered well. To one side was a side courtyard opening out onto the street in front. This was separated from the neighbour's equally large house on that side by trees and a high flowering line of bushes. At the back of the courtyard was a line of three decrepit wooden outbuildings and on the other side a fine stable for the family's horses and donkeys. Burhan's father had originally kept hens and a sheep in the further outbuilding of the three, but Burhan had got rid of these and that shed was empty and crumbling, as indeed were the other two.

The whole area had narrow twisting streets with small open spaces containing undersized trees and in a number of cases, fountains, decorated with blue and white tiles, donated in the past by some pious gentleman of means. Every so often there were modest mosques with shallow rounded domes and a small low minaret. There were fewer carriages in these streets than down in the wider streets of the Armenian, Greek and Jewish quarters. All the necessary goods, the furniture and other heavy items, were still largely carried by porters, stooped forward with thongs round their foreheads stretching back to hold the goods on their backs, which they steadied with one hand, as they trotted forward calling out "make way, make way!" They would try not to stop or slow down, allowing the momentum from the weight on their backs to carry them forward.

As the only son of a well-to-do father who was an official of the Empire, Burhan went to school at a modern establishment at the bottom of the hill near the bazaar. His father had been a believer in the Tansimat reforms and had supported the attempt to bring the Ottomans firmly into the coming twentieth century.

Without ever overstepping the mark or harbouring any actual treasonous thoughts, Burhan deprecated the reign and character of the odious Abdul Hamid ll, who had almost single-handedly brought the whole reform movement to a grinding halt. Like so many Ottoman citizens, whatever their race or more importantly their religion, Burhan and his father had had to face the difficult questions hovering over the Empire at the end of the nineteenth century. Above all, what was the identity or under-lying principle of this Empire of which they were all part? Was it for instance a Muslim state, whose rationale was Islam, containing as it did the Moslem holy cities, and the Caliph as its ruler?

Neither Burhan nor his father were committed Muslims. The father had attended as a matter of social form, the small local mosque, and he made sure his family conformed to all the rituals and holy observances of the year. However he had many *giavour* acquaintances. There were many Greek and a few Armenian colleagues working in the Konak, and Smyrna itself had never had a clear Moslem majority.

But if the Ottoman Empire was not a state whose identity was purely Moslem – then what? Clearly it was not a Turkish national state. Even after the loss of many of its European possessions by the start of the twentieth century, the Turks still constituted barely thirty per cent of the total. Very well, could it perhaps be defined as a geographic entity uniting many lands and regions, all far better off if organised as a single state? The peoples of the empire, from the Arabs in the south, through many races and religions, to the Macedonians in the west, were so intertwined that a single empire managing them all made obvious social and economic sense. If this was indeed to be the basis for the state, then loyalty to a five hundred year old dynasty with a great historic past made as much sense as anything else.

But that was not very inspiring. Men will die for their religion. They will also die for their nation, for the defense of the tribe. Apply reason, and most sensible people would not die at all.

While it was unlikely that the Greeks were ever a clear

majority in Smyrna, nevertheless, if all the other races and religions and European ex-patriates were included, the Turks were always in a minority. This was why the rest of the empire always referred to Smyrna as 'the giavour city'. Neither Burhan or his father really cared, they were fond of their city and thought of it as theirs, just like everyone else.

The family had a small *ayki* – not really a farm so much as a country cottage with orchards and animals – in a village not far from the city. The neighbours in this village were all Turks, but across the little river at the end of the fields was a 'Greek' village where the religion was Christian Orthodox. It was only religion that separated them – both sets of villagers spoke only Turkish and both sets considered themselves loyal Ottoman subjects.

Burhan was destined to become a civil servant himself and when he was twenty, only a year into the twentieth century, he was sent to Constantinople to stay with relatives and study law – not Koranic law but rather modern jurisprudence. He had long since given up any deep faith. Like his father, but even more loosely, he adhered to the outward forms of Islam, but rarely went to the local mosque for Friday prayers, nor did he take much notice of the strictures of Ramadan.

Before leaving, he and his father had discussed the possibility of buying a property in the European section of the town to which some of the wealthier and more educated Turks were moving, perhaps along the Rue des Franques. In the end for various reasons the idea had died, and it was shortly after that decision was made that the young Burhan had left on one of the many steamers plying between Smyrna and the capital.

Burhan's studies and his life in Constantinople came to an abrupt end after only three years, on the news of the death of his father. Accordingly, he was already back in Smyrna and married to a girl carefully chosen by his mother when the revolution of 1908 broke out. From the start, Burhan was a keen supporter of the Committee of Union and Progress. He shaved regularly, not allowing his beard to grow and he sported an Enver style moustache. Like most Turks of his age and background, he considered the decision of the Ittihad leaders to join the war as an ally of Imperial Germany a terrible mistake, but he never wavered in his support for the government. At the age of 35 on the outbreak of war, he was, of course, eligible for military service, but as an official in the administration of the Smyrna province he was exempt, and so during the war he continued to serve under the excellent original Ottoman Governor - Rahmi Bey – who had fortunately not been replaced by the Ittihad.

Burhan had never had much to do with the non-Turkish people of the city. All of them, Greeks, Armenians, Jews and Kurds all spoke Turkish and all considered themselves to be Ottoman citizens. Unlike the many Greek Orthodox villages in the interior, where the inhabitants did not speak or know the Greek language at all, those of Smyrna spoke good Greek. However, despite all the nationalist fervour and propaganda directed at them from Athens, hardly a single Greek from Smyrna had ever had the slightest desire to leave the city or the empire to go to the small Greek kingdom on the other side of the Aegean. The wealthy were making lots of money as part of a large empire with a lively polyglot people, far larger and more sophisticated than that of the little kingdom. If the poor thought at all of emigrating, it would have been across the Atlantic, not just across the Aegean.

The Armenians, an enclave of about 40,000, were also doing well in Smyrna. Their Archbishop had been on good terms with the old Ottoman Governor, and, in any event, they had nowhere else to go. The Jews, not as wealthy or as sophisticated as their co-religionists in Salonika, were the most ardent supporters of the dynasty which had given them protection and support for so long. Unlike the Armenians, who had been ignited and heavily influenced by Western missionaries and their own unthinking revolutionaries and nationalists, the Jews saw at once that the 1908 revolution could lead back to the start of a dangerous Turkish nationalism, likely to be far worse than any Ottoman excesses against non-Moslems. They remained therefore the staunchest and closest supporters of the Ottoman regime.

Like everyone in Smyrna, Burhan went to Greek grocers, he bought his bread as he made his way home from a Jewish baker, he expected the policeman on the corner to be a Turk, he expected the clerk who served him behind the counter at the Bank to be an Armenian, he employed a Kurd to carry home goods he had purchased. His weekend lasted from Friday prayers, through the Jewish Sabbath to the end of the Christian Sunday. The only difference from life in the capital was that, unlike Constantinople, there were few Turkish women unveiled – but Burhan, knew that even that was probably just a matter of time.

Then, as Burhan was approaching 40 years-old, came the total defeat of the Ottomans and the end of the war. That was bad enough, but then within a year came the single most important event affecting the future of Burhan and everyone else throughout the old Ottoman world, effects which would reverberate throughout the whole of the 20th century. The Greeks of Athens were invited to invade and take over control of Burhan's home town – Smyrna. Led by British destroyers the Greeks landed in 1919 and a Greek governor was installed in the Konak. Burhan lost his job.

In the end there was never any question of the Greeks setting up another Empire – a new Byzantine empire perhaps - with room for many different people and religions. All they were after in Athens was a Greater Greece. Having lost his job, Burhan felt that overnight he had become a second-class citizen, even worse off than his Greek neighbour had been under the non-nationalist Ottomans. Mehmed VI, the impotent Sultan still under British control in Constantinople, wept without stopping for over an hour when he heard the news. He was right to do so, as the Greek occupation spelt the end of his dynasty one way or another, whichever of the two competing nationalities won the now inevitable war.

Burhan had had no real difficulty in surviving through the three years of the Greek administration. He had some capital and there was always the little farm outside the city. The Greek governor, Sterghiades, was a very fair if rather stern man. He was always very careful to be even-handed to all the ethnic communities living in the city under his control, indeed so much so that he became unpopular with his Greek compatriots. Burhan, who had always loved writing, drifted into writing articles for the only Turkish language newspaper in the city, and he became one of their most active reporters. He was an open supporter of the nationalists in Ankara, but he was never persecuted in any way by what was, by and large, an honest and fairly efficient administration. Month by month he lost all respect for the Ottomans, save for a residue of nostalgic regret, as they became increasingly irrelevant to political developments.

By the time of the arrival of the victorious Turkish army in the city, Burhan had been married for over twelve years and had three daughters all aged below eight. He doted on them as any parent would, but he ached for a son. This was still a Moslem society where the head of any family had to be a male, however much females might manage affairs in the background. Burhan's mother had died and the upbringing of the girls was left entirely in the hands of his wife – Nefise. Burhan and Nefise had absolutely nothing in common with each other. For better or for worse, without her husband to modify her views, Burhan's mother had chosen for her son an old-fashioned, strictly brought up girl from the village in which the family had its small farm. Burhan had not thought of objecting in any way, preferring to conform, as he tended to do, to the mores of the time. Nefise had had the prettiness of youth when they married, but had absolutely no education at all, and after the birth of their third daughter she was beginning to turn plump.

Nefise was still veiled if she ever went out of the house. On those very rare occasions that they walked out together, she always walked a step or two behind Burhan. She could not read or write, the old Arabic characters being quite beyond her, and so she was unable to appreciate in any way Burhan's articles, which were read and commented upon by everyone claiming any culture or education in Smyrna.

Without a desk outside the house or any office to go to, Burhan fell into the habit of wandering around the city on most days, taking notes of everything he saw and of all the people he met. Unlike the poorer Turks of the district in which he lived, he did not have that latent envy of the *giavours* of the city who were generally wealthier and better off than the Muslims. He himself certainly had no religious prejudices whatsoever, as he made clear in his increasingly more secular articles – but day by day he drifted into a more and more heady Turkish nationalism. In a sense, this was a contradiction. With all his easy-going tolerance of the other races of his city, it did not cross his mind that the exclusive one-race nation-state, which he passionately espoused, would inevitably sooner or later aim for uniformity and get rid of all this rich diversity.

When on September 9th the Turkish army entered Smyrna, Burhan was delirious with excitement. All the newspapers had closed down, but he was out in the streets making notes on everything he was seeing. He had not been present on that day when an ecstatic Turkish mob, cheering Nur-ed-din the new governor outside the Konak, had dragged the Greek Archbishop Chrysostom from the steps, gouged out his eyes and then literally tore him to pieces. It is just possible that had he been there and witnessed the effect of the mob rule, his own fervent feelings might have been dampened and he might have been saved from the excesses three days later and his subsequent guilt for what occurred.

It was on the evening of Tuesday the 12th September that Burhan was out again in the streets. His excitement was intense – his whole body thrilled to the dramatic events being played out in his city. He had experienced nothing like it any time before in his life. Burhan was not usually insensitive, he was not in any way sadistic, he did not hate anyone enough to wish them ill, he had no thoughtless religious fanaticism; so why was it, as he wandered through the Armenian quarter, that he did not recoil from all the haphazard killing, looting and rape? What was it about journalism that made his eyes alight with animation as his pencil jotted down snippets of impressions as he wandered through the increasingly bloody streets, rather than looking away in revulsion?

He was in this state of euphoric curiosity and overwhelming

tension when he passed the house of Madame Derounian, where Olga and Selim had been living. He was present and saw Haik and Paramaz emerge. He actually nodded at them as they came out. However there appeared to be no one else on the street, so he stopped and watched as Haik had run forward to grab the empty cart standing upright further up the street. Of course he had no idea that this was in order to take the wounded Selim to the hospital. He saw the three Turkish soldiers come out of the house carrying looted property, and he saw them grab at their rifles as they spotted Haik. He witnessed the unknown Paramaz pull out his revolver and aim three shots up the street and then watched as the unknown young man died and the equally unknown Paramaz run up and start rifling the body, even offering Burhan himself some coins.

Burhan remained in a state of intense physical excitement. Jotting down this event, he moved on and continued to survey the complete breakdown of any law and order in the Armenian quarter and the idle killing and rape going on all around him. It was a terrible night, and Burhan was trying to take it all in when he became aware of the great fire starting in the streets behind him. He hurriedly began retracing his steps to get back to the Turkish quarter and found himself back on the street where he had earlier witnessed the killing of the unknown young man. The three soldiers were still there with their cart now piled high with carpets and clothes and other items clearly part of their loot. The huge fire was now not many metres away, shielded at the moment by the houses on the other side of the street. Burhan, who could now see the way out at the other end of the street to the south, hesitated for a moment, and it was at that moment that Olga had run out of the house, the same house from which the two young men had previously emerged.

Burhan's senses were aflame – there was real danger present – only a few moments separated them from being trapped by the flames. Death was staring at them all as the young soldier, having struck the girl so hard she had fallen down unconscious at his feet, pulled out his rifle in order to finish off this Armenian girl, who was gabbling incoherently about a Turkish officer. At this point with only seconds left, Burhan at last acted. Aware that even he was in danger from the inflamed soldiers, he shouted out the only words he could think of which established him as an ally and not another Armenian. Calling out "she will serve me tonight brothers," he lifted up the unconscious young girl and ran off with her over his shoulder, just in front of the approaching flames. He did not take any notice of what happened to the three soldiers as they trundled away with their full cart.

Afterwards, Burhan never sought to excuse himself for his actions when, gasping for breath, he finally got home and threw the still half-conscious girl onto the straw in his decrepit old shed at the side of the house. The passions in the streets, the drama, the haphazard killings, the real danger of death all overwhelmed his basic decency. Crouching beside her, he pulled up the already torn and crumpled dress. He dragged off the underwear and then had his will quickly and without any opposition. When it was over, he stumbled out, locking the barn door behind him, and into his own bedroom.

The following day, with the fire raging all day in the city below, and the huge billowing smoke and flames rising into the sky, with Nefise and his daughters staring out of the window all day, wide-eyed with wonder and anxiety, Burhan sat at his desk. He found that he was unable to write a single word of the famous article about the events of the previous day, that he'd thought would make his worldwide reputation. His notes were all intact, the words were all there, but he could not set down a word. From being a reporter of events, he had become part of the event itself. What had he done? He was a respectable middle-aged man; he had a wife and three daughters, though in a sense all that was irrelevant. His action was despicable whatever his circumstances and regardless of his age. He brooded all day. There was no question of fear – no one would ever reproach him even if he shouted it out from the rooftops – but he remained knotted up with guilt.

When night fell, he waited until it was dark and then went to the kitchen and got a pitcher of water and a plate of bread and olives. He walked to the shed and opened the door, but he lacked the courage to go inside. He knelt and put the pitcher and the plate just inside the door, shut it but left it unlocked, and hurried away.

Burhan did not sleep the whole night. He was at the window at dawn when he saw the dishevelled figure of Olga slip out of the shed and into the street and away. He breathed a sigh of relief – it was over.

But not quite!

Burhan's eldest daughter, an active and lively eight year-old, was playing with her friends a few days later at the edge of the area near the burnt-out former Armenian quarter, when she stumbled and fell into some cinders, still smouldering a day or two after the fire had died down. Screaming with pain she was brought back to the house by a neighbour. Burhan was sitting at his desk, still unable to put pen to paper or to get Tuesday night's events out of his mind. He took her into his arms but saw, at once, that she needed more than a kiss to make it better. He was not going to leave it to anyone else to take her down to the hospital. With the whole Greek, Armenian and European quarters burnt to the ground, the Imperial Ottoman Hospital at the bottom of the hill was the only place where doctors were still working and where wounds or burns could be treated. So with his daughter in his arms, he hurried down the hill.

Burhan, well-off and fairly well-connected, did not have to wait long before his daughter was taken in and her hand and arms treated. Burhan sat and waited for several hours and there, in all that coming and going, in all the confusion and noise of the hospital, he saw Olga, working away grimly and with dedication. He recognised her at once, even in the crisp white uniform. He had no fear, but his guilt, which had never left him, redoubled and became unbearable. At the same time he felt a compassion for what this girl might be feeling.

He made a discreet enquiry and discovered her name. He

then asked the receptionist whether, if he wrote to a nurse at the hospital to thank her for her help, it would be delivered to her personally. He was told firmly that it would be if she was still with them.

Burhan took his daughter home in the evening once she had been treated and seemed to have recovered. He then spent two whole weeks pondering on the letter he intended to send – anonymously of course – to this woman. This was to be in lieu of the famous article that would never now be written. He intended to set out all that had happened on that terrible day and would frankly confess his shame at how the day had ended. It took him ten days of careful thought to cover everything he had seen and every shabby act that had taken place. The shooting of the young man on the street; the removal of the money belt from the dead body; the things he saw later on the Rue des Franques; the atmosphere in the town; his return to that first street once the fire started; and finally the shame of what had occurred when he returned home.

The letter was a masterpiece of his journalistic art – it was undoubtedly one of the best articles he had ever written. It would, however, be seen by only one person. It was only after the letter had been written, addressed to N. (which he imagined was short for nurse) Avakian, and posted to the Imperial Ottoman Hospital that he was able at last to come again to his wife's bedroom.

CHAPTER 16

The Androvs Consider

The defeat of the Greeks and the burning of Smyrna not only had many consequences that would influence the history of the region over the coming century, but also several minor ones affecting many people at the time. One of these was the gloom and panic that overtook 'giavour' Constantinople. The atmosphere of puritan reaction against the gaiety and joy of the last few years quickly led to the closure of many of the Russian and Westernised night-clubs and dance halls. The disappearance of almost all the French and Italian military, the lack of any allied naval personnel, now confined to their ships, the move to take belated summer holidays by large sections of the wealthier Greek community, all meant that there were less and less people coming to the entertainment centres of Pera.

This, in turn was affecting the large Russian émigré population. General Wrangel, with the remnants of his White Russian army had already departed to various adventures in the Balkans and elsewhere. Since arriving from Sevastopol he had been touting his army for use in all the world's trouble spots, and his offers had been taken up, and the army had packed up and left. However, a fairly large Russian civilian element had remained and had drifted into employment as musicians, waiters and waitresses, cooks and washers-up serving the entertainment world of Pera. Here in Pera, for the last three years, the bars, restaurants, dance halls and teashops had been thriving. During most of the five years of the British occupation, Constantinople was probably the liveliest of all the capital cities of Europe.

For all these years it had been party time for the ancient Imperial city. But now its nemesis, in the form of an avenging army of Anatolian peasants, was looming. If that army acted as it did in Smyrna there would be a bloodbath. No one wanted to go dancing anymore as the city waited anxiously. The Russian restaurants, the Russian orchestras, the Russian night-clubs and the Russian brothels all began to close. Even the revered Pera Palace Hotel – the centre for all the Allied officers who had passed through the city on tours of duty – had to start retrenching as the elite local merchant society began staying away and visitors dried up. And so it was that in the middle of all the uncertainty and anxiety affecting the Avakians, Count Nicolai Androv, Sima's Russian fiancée, lost his job as a violinist in the Hotel's saloon orchestra. Overnight, the only income coming in to the Androv household was the small amount that 16 year-old Alexei, Nicolai's younger brother, was bringing in from his work in Karekin's office. His mother, the Countess Natalya Androvna still had a few of her jewels, the carefully saved gold coins and the valuable Rublev icon – but the future looked bleak.

Nicolai knew that Sima, the eldest daughter of one of the major Armenian merchants in the city, had taken an unconventional step in allying herself with him. He was aware that from the point of view of the large Armenian trading community he was only a penniless, now nationless, Russian aristocrat with no prospects of any kind. Karekin's offer the year before of a junior post – an apprenticeship – for Alexei, who was only 15, had been a gesture of support for Sima's choice, which both he and his wife Armineh had come to accept. But as the political situation began to change, so did the position of the Androvs. Nicolai had not spent these last two years just playing the violin and basking in the warmth of a budding romantic attachment. He had also managed to get Nansen passports for all the family. But the moment of reckoning over the future of his mother and young brother, both his responsibility, was now approaching as fast as the oncoming Turkish army.

Karekin was a man who had always surprised his friends and his business acquaintances by his unusual views – unusual for his time and culture. In particular they all looked askance at the way he had chosen to bring up his daughters, all of whom had gone through as full an education process as any boy of the city. But when it had come to the final test of his liberal cross-cultural opinions, he had been unable to accept the possibility that his beautiful daughter might marry a young Turk, even though in many ways he was quite suitable, being an Ottoman citizen of the city as well-connected as he himself. While he had not directly opposed the relationship – that was not his style – he had ignored it and left it to his wife, Armineh, to create the necessary difficulties. Olga was left in no doubt of her father's inner opposition.

In reaction to the realisation of his own failure to live up fully to his own ideals, he had fallen over backwards in accepting Sima's decision to attach herself to the even more unsuitable Nicolai. Karekin pondered the matter as a real philosophic problem. His different attitude to the two suitors of his daughters had certainly not arisen as a result of his opinion on the respective characters of Sima and Olga. He knew that he might have started off by trusting Sima's maturity and intellectual capacity more than Olga's, but he had been aware that Olga had developed, and that difference no longer applied. Well then, perhaps deep down there was a difference in the love he felt for each of these daughters? Ridiculous – he knew that that was certainly not the answer. Did it reflect in any way, then, on the character of the two men involved? That too could not be the reasoning, as he had immediately liked and was at ease with both of them equally. What about religion? But that was surely absurd. Karekin attended church as a matter of cultural form, but he did not believe in any of the dogmas, superstitions, rituals or taboos either of his own religion or that of Islam – both of which he thought too irrational for words. Why, then, had he accepted the penniless Nicolai and rejected Selim?

Karekin never fully worked it out for himself; but he had an inkling. The multi-national Ottoman ideal was collapsing, and all round him the proponents of exclusive one-nation states were each shrieking out their own petty frontier demands by claiming that their particular people could not possibly live with their neighbours within the same state. He sensed that it was all artificial – deliberate hatred for each other created by clever academics, historians and political philosophers, and then taken up by unscrupulous politicians.

Karekin shuddered, because as he thought it all out, as he tried to decide why there had been this great difference in his attitude to his two possible sons-in-law, it became clear to him that he too must have been affected by the deliberate emanation of ethnic hatred spewed out by the Department of the Interior led by the venal Talaat, and which had resulted in the great catastrophe of 1915. If he, a well-educated and sophisticated citizen could be so affected, what possible hope was there for the simple villagers of the interior, who thought that they had lived perfectly amicably, if not always entirely harmoniously, for years with their Greek or Armenian neighbours, but who had been led to believe that really deep down they hated them.

Karekin found himself wishing... but too late - Selim was dead!

On the day that Nicolai received his notice and his last weeks wages, whilst on his way home from the Pera Palace to the Patakis house in Stamboul, he had called in at a small Russian-owned bar and restaurant tucked away on a side street leading down to the Galata bridge. Here at the bar in the almost empty room, he had sat for an hour contemplating his future and chatting to the staff, all of whom were Russians he had known since the flight from the Crimea. Countesses of the Imperial Court washed up dishes in the kitchen, and the cook had previously worked for years in the Imperial Palace at Yalta. The waitresses were no less distinguished. Not so longer ago, one might have seen a Russian customer rise from his table and stoop and kiss the hand of a Princess who was serving him.

Now, however, the place was empty, but for Nicolai himself, and a sailor from the merchant marine sleeping at a corner table over an unfinished vodka. The staff gathered round Nicolai at the bar staring at the empty tables with anxious eyes. Instead of the usual noisy chat they were all whispering. The cook, who had a small personal stake in the ownership, came out and the usual conversation about the future began again.

"What do you think is going to happen, Nicolai – can we survive here?"

"I don't know, Countess, I really don't know. However, I can tell you that I have just been given notice. Today was the last day that I will play at the Pera Palace, and unless I can find a new post, I won't be able to afford dropping in here anymore."

"Oh no Nicolai – I'm so sorry – so sorry," came a chorus of voices from all around followed by a short silence as they all contemplated the fact that, as customers like Nicolai dried up, their employer was unlikely to be able to carry on for much longer, and that they too would shortly to be out of a job.

"We'll simply have to go," said the cook. "There is not going to be any work round here for Russians, even if we are allowed to survive when the city falls."

"What do you mean, Dmitri, what are you saying?"

"Look, if we stay, the chances are that we are either going to have our throats cut, or we will be left on some seashore waiting to board ships to take us away, destitute and without anything to call our own. Look at what has just happened in Smyrna. The stories of massacres may or may not be exaggerated, but one thing is certain: the whole Christian population has been success-fully forced out, either by death or deportation from the town. Why shouldn't we expect the same thing to be repeated here? This is the ideal moment to get rid of the whole non-Turkish population in one fell swoop – Greek, Jew, Armenian, Russian – the lot."

Nicolai said nothing but he felt that Dimitri's words did make sense. Smyrna was a clear example of what could happen here.

"But what about the British, and the allied fleets," said one of the other waitresses.

"Well, what about them? They were all there in the bay of Smyrna weren't they? Did they do anything – did they raise a finger to…"

At this comment a lot of shouting and cross arguments erupted as Nicolai sipped his lemon and vodka, trying to decide what his own little family should do.

"Did you hear the story of the porter at the Russian Orthodox Church?" the cook called out over the noise. By now, he had already downed two more straight vodkas.

"It appears that the small hostel next door to the church was managed by a Russian nun known as Mother Feodora. This hostel employed a Turkish porter who had loyally worked for them for more than 15 years, from before the war. Anyway, it seems that Mother Feodora was chatting to him yesterday and said – 'Ahmed, what is going to happen when Mustapha Kemal enters the city with his troops from Smyrna.' Ahmed answered…"

Here Dimitri paused, filled up his glass with his next vodka and swallowed it down savouring the silence as his audience waited –

"The porter answered – 'Madame you know well I have

always loved and respected you. When the massacre begins I myself will kill you quickly so that you suffer no pain at all."

At this he began roaring with laughter, but was somewhat disconcerted to find that no one else found it amusing at all.

Nicolai sat for a few minutes more, looking at the worried and, in some cases, terrified eyes of the staff. He had already heard this story – it was going the rounds of the bars. Sometimes it referred to a Catholic church, sometimes to the loyal porter in an embassy. It did not really matter whether there was even the slightest element of truth in it or not. It was symptomatic of the feverish atmosphere in the city. Here lay a city of a million people over half of whom were waiting in dread for what was going to happen next.

Nicolai got home before dark and immediately started talking over the position with his mother.

"You must get away from Constantinople. We don't belong here mother. Why should we stay and suffer the consequences that may be visited on these people? It is only an accident that we are here in the first place."

"Yes, Nicolai I agree. We can go to Vienna, and from there possibly to the Veneto. My mother had two sisters. One was the Countess Berchtold – you know, I've told you about her, the wife of the former Austrian Foreign Minister at the time of the outbreak of the War. I don't think that she had any children, but I know she is alive and is still in Vienna. We have been in contact in the last two years. Then the other sister, also obviously my Aunt, was married to an Italian Conte who had an estate in the Veneto. They, I do know, have children who I presume would be your age or probably younger. I haven't contacted her for some time – what was her name? – oh, yes, the Contessa Maggi."

"Mother, we could send your Viennese relatives a telegram. It shouldn't be too expensive to take the train. We will only need to sell one of your pieces to give you plenty of leeway."

Nicolai was thinking ahead fast - considering all the possibilities – when Natalya quietly said –

"And what about Miss Sima, Nicolai?"

There was a long silence. In all his worries during the day about what was necessary for his mother and brother after he had lost his job, Nikolai realised that he had not considered the position of the woman he loved. Nicolai reflected how during the most tragic of circumstances, when Sima first heard of the death of her only brother, her first thought had been of him. What would Nicolai do? What would be Nicolai's reaction? How can he help me? Yet, faced with his own problem, he had put their future life together to one side, while he resolved the question of his mother's safety. Now his mother's gentle reminder brought him up sharply.

"Mother, mother, my mamushka, I thought you understood from the start that I was talking only about you and Alexei."

"But Nicolai...."

"No, mama, there are many reasons why I cannot at this stage accompany you. First I cannot impose myself on your relatives' charity – I, a grown man without any work or income – until you have yourself been welcomed. The position is quite different for you and Alexei."

"Come, family sentiment and obligations do not depend on the age of the...."

"No, mama, you don't understand, the problem lies in me, not my uncles. In any case, I can't abandon my Sima – she is to all intents and purposes my fiancée – and there really is no way that Karekin would allow her to accompany me to Vienna or anywhere else, even if we got married quickly. And frankly mama, I wouldn't blame him."

"So?"

"So, mother, I must remain here to face the future with Sima – and you and Alexei will...."

At this point, his cheerful, grinning brother rushed into the room; grabbing his mother round her still slender waist, he kissed her full on the lips; then turned and hugged his brother kissing him on both cheeks. He threw his fez at the hatstand, missing it completely. Karekin had insisted for some time, even before the collapse of the Greeks, that his staff should wear the Ottoman symbol and not the panama hats of one side or the flat caps of the other. He then collapsed onto the chair with a great beaming smile on his face.

"Well – why the long faces – what's going on?"

Both Nicolai and the Countess suddenly realised that in all their discussions about the future, they had failed to think of Alexei's position. He had been working for Karekin for over a year, ever since the departure of Haik and Paramaz to Smyrna. Karekin had been good to him and it had been a help for the Androv family all round. Quite apart from the fact that they had not thought for a moment of Alexei's possible feelings on the matter – he was, after all, 16 – they had ignored any obligations he might have towards Karekin.

Since coming into contact with the continually debating Avakians, the Androvs themselves had fallen into the habit of discussing matters together rather more fully than they had done before. This was increased by Alexei's own growing self-confidence, if not actual maturity, as he grew from a naïve 14 year-old into a lively 16. Now both Nicolai and his mother talked at once, explaining the impact of Nicolai's loss of his job, and their fears about the anticipated arrival of the Turkish nationalist army.

Alexei's own feelings about the Avakian office and his work there had become complicated over the last few days. He had been very fond of Haik and the news of his death had cast a gloom over the whole office. Once he had returned to work, Karekin displayed no outward sign of grief before his staff. Meanwhile, Paramaz had returned to the office to take over his former duties. Alexei had long since forgotten the dramatic confrontation between Haik and Paramaz, but the return of Paramaz brought it all back. He recalled the fear in Haik's eyes as the knife was picked up, and the burning hatred in Paramaz's eyes as his clumsy attempted sexual assault on Alexei was thwarted. Nevertheless, like everyone else he sensed a subtle change in the young man. He looked ill and was obviously not sleeping well. Within a day of Paramaz's return, Karekin had taken Alexei off his packing and checking duties, and brought him into the inner office where it became clear that he wanted him to replace Haik with all the letter writing, the filing and the general office work. Alexei's French was excellent, like all the old Russian aristocracy for whom it was often their first language, and his written English was improving the whole time. Two years in Bolis had already given him that Bolsetsi gift of switching immediately into whichever language was appropriate in any social circumstance.

Meanwhile, Alexei saw other young emigrés of his class and background wasting away without any work or hope of any future, drifting into driving taxis or carrying loads or, even worse, hovering on the edges of the sex trade. He was accordingly very grateful to the rather stern Karekin whom he no longer feared. Though a cheerful extrovert, Alexei was also sensitive to the feelings of others, and he was aware, without quite understanding it, of Karekin's increasing dependence on his own presence in the office as an antidote to the sorrow caused by the loss of his only son.

Alexei's grin faded as Nicolai began to explain exactly what he and the Countess had been discussing, and the plans they were considering. Alexei allowed Nicolai to drone on, saying nothing but disconcerting him by staring at him with increasing intensity. Nicolai stumbled to an end and Alexei immediately said –

"Very well, my brother, I hear you, but Nicolai what about Miss Sima. What are you proposing? Just to leave?"

Nicolai looked at his young brother and thought to himself – 'My God, my light-hearted, thoughtless, young brother has grown up without my realising it'.

It seemed he had two responsibilities – one to do his best for his mother and his dependent brother – and the other to look after the woman he loved. It was also clear to him that the Ottoman-born Greeks, Armenians and Jews of the city had become fearful, not only of a possible massacre when the Kemalist army broke into the city, but of the near certainty of a wholesale forced emigration, as had happened in Smyrna. If these actual Ottoman citizens considered themselves to be at risk in this way, how much more certain was it that the Russian refugees from Sevastopol, without any rights of residence at all, would suffer even worse. This was the moment for the Androvs to leave and seek out their relatives before there was any chance of a forced exodus, in murderous conditions.

But what about Sima? He was not married to her and there was no way she could leave with him if he left – Karekin would not allow it, and it would be dishonourable of him even to suggest it. So he had already decided that he would have to stay whatever his mother and Alexei did. But doing what? After the short silence which had greeted Alexei's comment, Nicolai finally said –

"You are right – I myself will not be able to join you for some time until things are more settled here, and mother is aware of that."

"And what, brother, are you proposing to do? Come crawling into the Avakian firm?"

"Oh, Alexei please – my love – my brother – we are not competing. I am trying to do my best for everyone."

Alexei looked away for a moment then turned and smiled at Nicolai – "I'm sorry, I am truly sorry – please continue."

"As it happens the thought had crossed my mind that Mr. Avakian might offer me a job when he hears of our dilemma, but I couldn't bear the thought of it. It was one thing for you, Alexei, to work for him – quite another for me, the fiancée of his daughter – completely dishonourable."

"Oh I understand you completely," said Alexei

"Well, I don't," snapped Natalya, "It's nothing but male pride. Here in Constantinople the culture is heavily family-oriented. It is absolutely normal – indeed to be expected – that sons follow in their father's footsteps and sons-in-law move naturally into their in-laws businesses. Look, Nicolai, think – suppose you had married the daughter of Count Voroshin – you remember him, our neighbour on the other side of the river. You wouldn't have thought twice, would you, of working for him on his estate."

"You know that that would have been quite different. It

would not have been a matter of a weekly salary. Quite different."

"Well, even if you are right, for better or worse, you are no longer in a position to have such scruples. You can't go on playing in second-rate orchestras all your life – not if you want to get married and have a family. I'm right, Alexei, am I not?"

"I'm afraid you are, mother. I'm sorry, Nicolai – as I said, I do understand your feelings, but mother is right."

There was a short silence after this last comment. Then Alexei stood up. Putting on a great beaming smile to soften what, he was about to say, he said firmly –

"Mama, Nicolai, I am sorry if this makes things more difficult for you, but I cannot just cut and run and abandon the Avakians because things might be getting difficult for them. I understand completely what you are saying but I just can't run away. Yes, yes, I can see what you are thinking – I know that my being with them is not going to help them in any way – but I simply can't walk out when they might be facing another massacre."

Nicolai and the Countess now joined forces and produced argument after argument, while Alexei stood obstinately by his decision repeating that, as he was now 16, he was entitled to his own position. It might have gone on all night, until Nicolai came out with an argument that finally swung the case against himself.

"But Alexei," he said "mother has to go, and one of us has to go with her."

At this point Alexei hesitated for the first time. But now the Countess turned on Nicolai.

"Come – that's nonsense. Complete nonsense. I can see that it would make things easier if I left for the moment and joined my sister in Vienna or my other sister in Italy – but needing to be 'looked after' that's rubbish."

The discussion continued for some time, but now that both Nicolai and Alexei's responsibilities were evident, it only remained for the details to be worked out. The Countess would leave for Vienna as soon as possible while Nicolai and Alexei would remain and take their chances for the moment with the arriving Turkish army. Once the situation was clearer, once Sima and Nicolai were able to travel together, and assuming nothing terrible happened, the family would hopefully be reunited. Meanwhile the Countess would be able to look out for, and report on, any prospects for Nicolai in the west.

Accordingly the very next day two telegrams went out – one to the Countess Berchtold in Vienna, and the other to the Contessa Maggi at an address in the Veneto. Once the decision had been made, there was no need for any further delay. The closer the moment came for the arrival of the victorious Turkish army, the more difficult it might be to get reservations on the Orient Express.

Within a further day a telegram arrived back from the Countess Berchtold, which read –

"Situation here in Vienna still not good – but you are of course welcome. Please send date and time of arrival. Will meet you at the station."

Yet another jewel was now sold and a First Class seat (the Countess insisting that she did not require a sleeping berth) was reserved for her on the train. She was due to leave on the mid-morning train on the 2nd October.

CHAPTER 17

Mikael and Elena

The whole town of Piraeus appeared to be in deep mourning as Mikael and Elena stepped off the launch that had carried them from the Italian Navy frigate lying at anchor outside the port, and which had brought them away from the horrors of the dying city of Smyrna. Almost all the ramshackle buildings surrounding the port had black drapes of all kinds hanging from the first floor windows. Where there were any flags flying they were all at half-mast. Many of the restaurants, smart or shabby, were closed, and those few that were open sported no musicians, no dancing, no joyous groups toasting all and sundry with glasses of ouzo.

There were scarcely any bureaucratic difficulties as Mikael and Elena and the two children – Andreas and Anya – clambered onto the quayside. Impoverished, bankrupt and desperately poor though it was, Greece had made it clear that she was prepared to accept every human being who was a refugee from the new Turkey being born on the other side of the Aegean, regardless of their race or their religion; the Greek nation state, redeeming itself by a new tolerance born of adversity.

Mikael of course, both as a streetwise Bolsetsi and having served in the Greek army for over a year, spoke Greek fluently. He imagined, as he stepped onto Greek soil for the first time, that he was about to witness the heart of classical Greece; a modern westernised capital, a people looking back to the glories of the Parthenon and the Periclean golden age. Instead, he was taken aback by the shabby provincial aspect of the life he saw around him. But Athens itself would surely be different. It was not. Used to the splendour and effortless grandeur of the 2,000 year-old Constantinople, he could only see the unsophisticated quality of this other centre of Greek culture.

During those first few days, as he and Elena tried to work out what they were going to do, Mikael saw that his ideas of the Kingdom of Greece as the heir to the glorious classical past, was romantic nonsense. It was Byzantium which was at the heart of modern Greek culture, not classical Athens. Mikael had always referred to the city in which he was born as 'Bolis'. He knew that this was the Armenian version of the Greek 'Polis' which simply meant 'the city'. What he had not realised was that the Greeks of old Greece also referred to Constantinople as 'Polis'. There were innumerable cities in Greece and the Greek world generally with the suffix 'polis' – Alexandropolis for instance. But only one of all these towns was referred to as 'Polis'. If you said in Piraeus – I am going to Polis – you meant and were invariably taken to mean that your were going to Constantinople – not to any other city.

Mikael still had some of his precious gold coins, and even Elena had managed to save a few valuables as she had hurriedly packed her case in Smyrna. This would give them some weeks grace to decide what they could do. They managed to find some modest lodgings in Athens, just ahead of the increasing exodus of desperate and mainly penniless refugees pouring in from

Smyrna and the Ionian coast on the Jennings' fleet and other vessels, fleeing just ahead of Kemal's ultimatum.

Mikael and Elena had found comfort in each others' arms – but if ever there was a marriage of convenience this was it. Mikael knew perfectly well that he did not have the same feelings for Elena as he had had for Olga Avakian. Yet he was unable to analyse in any depth the reasons for the difference. Mikael had always acted first and thought after, but his experiences with the Greek army in Anatolia had mellowed his character and made him more sensitive to the feelings of others. He was no longer the out-and-out extrovert and was more interested in analysing his inner feelings.

It was certainly not a matter of physical beauty or sexual attraction. Battle-hardened soldier as he was – he had been serving in some army or another, starting with the Reds in the Russian Civil War, since 1917 – he had never had a problem satisfying his sexual needs. Nor was it a matter of sharing background or common culture. In many ways, even though Elena was Greek and Olga Armenian like himself, he had more in common with Elena than with the *haut bourgeois* Avakians. Was it, he wondered, because Olga had rejected him while Elena had accepted him almost too willingly? Did he perversely hanker after Olga, because he could never have her?

Elena, on the other hand, had never known what it was to 'love' a man, as opposed to just living with him. She felt affection for the father of her two children, but it had never really amounted to more than that. The days of intimacy in the bedroom over those few days she had lived with Mikael in Smyrna, had been satisfactory enough, but really not much more than her former life in an arranged marriage.

Yet here they were, inextricably thrown together, forced by the turbulent political situation all around them to sink or swim together; Elena, because she needed someone to help her, burdened as she was looking after two small children, Mikael, for the more subtle reason that by helping her and taking responsibility for her children, he was making up for the lack of direction in his own life.

Mikael, of course, remained an Ottoman citizen. He still had his old passport and 'nufus' – papers carefully retained through all the vicissitudes of the last two years. On top of that, his mother and sister were still living in Makrikoy in Constantinople so far as he knew. But how was he to get back – and indeed would he be allowed back if he tried getting a boat? Rumours of what was happening in and around the city were raging in the Greek capital. Kemal's Anatolian army was already at the Straits staring at the British garrison in Chanak, and waiting patiently on the Asian side to enter – or to storm – the city itself. People talked fearfully of another massacre, of a burning and sacking next to which the drama of Smyrna would pale into insignificance.

Passage up the railway line to Salonika and even beyond was easy enough. But would it be possible to get through Eastern Thrace and on by land into the city. Adrianople was still held by the Greek army whose lines went up to 30 miles from the city itself.

Mikael wandered the streets. In the gloomy atmosphere in Athens, he found people friendlier than might have been the case normally and ready to speak freely to strangers in the cafés. Mikael had in the course of his years in the Greek army lost his 'Polis' accent and the Athenians did not recognise him as a 'yoghurt-baptised' one – the pejorative term they were already using to refer to the Ionians fleeing from the Ottoman Empire. He listened to all the views being freely expressed around him, but in the end simply got into an even more muddled state of mind. Mikael had always been forthright and able to make decisions, whether for better or worse. But now he dithered.

Already there were large numbers of people sleeping on the streets. As the refugees from the Jennings fleet began drifting in to the town, whole families, completely destitute, began sleeping in the ruins of the Acropolis. Any building which might be empty became a dormitory at night. The National Opera house was filled with family after family, taking over the boxes – the orchestra stalls – the grand stairs. Makeshift camps sprang up all round the town, and winter was yet to come.

Then, with Mikael still undecided, as September began to

draw to an end, a revolution broke out. Led by Mikael's old commander – Colonel Plastiras of the 42nd Evzones – the Venizelists swung into power on the back of a military revolt. At long last, Constantine formally abdicated on the 27th September and was hurried into exile. Venizelos himself was despatched at speed as Ambassador to Great Britain. Mikael thus found himself in the middle of his second revolution. But this was nothing like those events six years ago in Rostov at the start of the Russian Civil war. No one had a good word left for 'Tino' as he fled, and there was no fighting or opposition in the streets, although, in good Greek style, there was plenty of noisy argument, sometimes ending in fisticuffs.

But none of this affected Mikael's position directly. He could see that he had no real future in Athens as more and more refugees flowed in on a daily basis. There was no work – no prospects. What about the army? Only a few weeks ago, he had been a respected senior sergeant. Now, the Greek government could no longer even afford to pay its basic civil servants, never mind an army.

But the railways were still running.

The branch of the Simplon-Orient express that ran down to Athens was still operating. This line ran on from Salonika through Adrianople and Eastern Thrace and on to Constantinople. Eastern Thrace was still held by the Greek army, intact and in their neat encampments right up against the Chatalja lines manned by Harington's forces. Mikael was well aware of the odd military situation. Kemal and his nationalist army was now fully in control of the Asian side of the Straits. Harington's small but significant British forces held Constantinople itself, the European side of the Bosporus, and with the small garrison of Chanak on the Asian side of the Dardanelles. Then there was the large and powerful Allied fleet patrolling the straits and preventing – or so it would seem –the Turkish nationalists from crossing. Then finally, there was the unbeaten remnant of the Greek army in Thrace, on the other side of the British.

All this extraordinary turmoil had not prevented the administrators of the Compagnie Internationale des Wagons-lits et des Grands Express Européenes from doggedly continuing to run their trains from Athens northwards and from Sofia eastwards and into the Imperial Ottoman capital. Thousands of peasants who had lived in communities for centuries might be trudging hopelessly along trails from their homes to heaven knows where, but the elite bourgeoisie of Europe still wanted to travel. The trains ran, but they had to go through many more checkpoints.

After days of deliberation, Mikael at last made up his mind. He decided he had to get back to Constantinople, even if this meant risking another Smyrna solution. First he ascertained that he could buy the necessary through tickets to Constantinople – they would of course be travelling third class. He then hurried back and confronted Elena in their tiny apartment.

"Andreas, my boy, would you please take Anya down to Madam Sophia. I spoke to her on the way up and she is expecting you to stay with her for an hour."

Elena looked up in surprise as the children left.

"Elena, my love, will you marry me?"

It was not the most romantic of proposals. The abruptness of the sudden question and the rather brusque tone of Mikael's voice seemed to belie the words. But then Elena had long since realised that she could not expect 'tenderness' from Mikael – that was not his style.

"What – what are you saying?"

"It's clear enough isn't it. For heaven's sake Elena, you don't want me to go down on my knees, do you? I am asking you to marry me."

"But Mikael, why now? What's the hurry? I'm sorry, don't stare at me like that. I appreciate your offer but…."

"Elena – you have two children who are entirely dependent upon you. I am already a raddled 30 year-old. We are not mooning teenagers. We need to hold on to each other in a world which is falling apart around us. My suggestion is quite clear. I think we need to get officially married."

Elena shook her head. Her hesitation was not, as Mikael had thought, because she was hankering after any great romance or love affair. She had fled first in fear and terror from Odessa to Crimea. She had then fled from Sevastopol. Finally she had had to flee in dread and horror from Smyrna to Athens. She longed for security, for a feeling of safety, but there was something about Mikael's manner that disturbed her. She had come to understand his reserved, proud and prickly character, but couldn't he just once say that he loved her – or barring that, a confirmation of his affection.

"Mikael – please believe me, I am not insensitive to your offer, but look it's impossible. I am a married woman and I don't know whether my husband is still alive or not."

"Oh, that's impossible. You can't go through the rest of your life wondering whether Gianni is still alive or not. Look, my dear, the fact is that I am determined to get back to Bolis. My mother and sister are still there and it is my home town. Athens holds nothing for either of us. With all the refugees pouring in, there is no way I could ever find any work. How are we going to live here? Neither one of us are Greek citizens – you are completely stateless and I am an Ottoman subject. Once in Bolis we have a home, we have help with the children and I have good prospects for work. I have the legal right to return, but in case of any difficulty at the frontiers and checkpoints we pass, you must be my legal wife. Oh Elena, you do see that, don't you?"

The more Mikael talked the more he was sure of his position. There was a short silence – then Elena said –

"Mikael – I can't do it. You know that for both of us, there is no marriage without a church ceremony, and there is no way that I could take the oath before God that there is nothing preventing us from getting married."

"But – it is the state's marriage certificate we need – not the good Lord's sanction".

Even as he said these eminently sensible words, Mikael, who was himself a devout believer, knew that Elena was probably right. A church marriage was the only real option open to them and it was not possible.

Nevertheless, he was not going to give up. There was no certainty about what was going to happen or what lay between him in Athens and his goal on the landline to Constantinople. Surely, if the worst came to worst, they would probably be able to walk across whatever frontier might exist and then into the city. Once there, he knew he would be able to manage. Papers! Papers? Come, all he needed to say was that the marriage documents had been lost. He knew the Ottoman world backwards – he would manage. But was the world they were returning to still Ottoman?

"Very well, Elena, if necessary we will claim we are man and wife and that our papers have been lost. As my wife, you are also an Ottoman citizen. But whatever happens we must leave – you do see that."

"Yes Mikael, yes. I am in your hands as indeed I have been since you walked back into my life – my God, was it only three weeks ago? I will get the children ready and mentally prepared for yet another flight. But you must give us a few more days."

"I will need that in any case to get the tickets. Oh Elena, I know this is the right decision for us. You are brave. I love …."

And with this last remark unfinished, Mikael and Elena kissed – affectionately and lingeringly. That night they made love for the first time since arriving in Athens, a gentle love in stark contrast to the passionate and violent love of their days in Smyrna.

CHAPTER 18

Harry

Back in Constantinople events were moving fast. It was not that time had slowed down – it went on at its inexorable pace regardless of human affairs – but more seemed to be crammed into each day, and on each day anything could happen. In the great game being played out between London and Constantinople, between

Athens and Ankara, between Harington and his political masters, and between the last Ottoman Sultan and Mustapha Kemal Pasha, every day, every hour brought some new twist, some new possibility.

Yet in the midst of all the political and military turmoil, the wheels of Whitehall and the Admiralty bureaucracy continued to turn. The very next day after Harry had returned with Olga from Smyrna, he received notice that his court-martial was to be held on the *Iron Duke*. It had been decided that the case would be heard by a senior officer, who was being sent out to Constantinople by the admiralty for the sole purpose of presiding over the hearing. He was to be aided by two officers that he would himself be appointing from the junior officers available on the station.

When asked by telegram, Harry had already replied that he did not feel the necessity for legal representation. He received a further notification that with the senior officer appointed to hear the case, a prosecuting counsel would be arriving at the same time, who would be presenting the case against him. This had not changed Harry's mind.

With all the hard work and nervous energy expended in his recent days in Smyrna; in the midst of all the satisfaction he had experienced working alongside Jennings, on an effort that he felt was truly meaningful; through all the feelings of fulfilment he had felt throughout those days; Harry had not entirely forgotten the crisis looming in his own life. It was not his conscience that was bothering him. In his own mind his conscience was clear. The more he examined his decisions on that day as the city began to burn, the less he worried about the judgement he had made at the time.

Despite these thoughts, there was inevitably something daunting about legal proceedings of any kind, likely to cause butterflies in the stomach however convinced you are of your position. The cold calculating manner in which things you had done, or words that you may have uttered in the heat of the moment, are displayed in a public forum for all to consider and dispute, would cause anxiety in the staunchest and coolest of men. Decisions, which may have looked simple to Harry at the time, could easily be made to appear irrational, muddled, perhaps even treasonous under scrutiny. It was not that Harry feared any deliberate malice from anyone involved in the procedure. It was simply the whole clinical atmosphere of a 'court' – any court – which left him apprehensive.

The worry at the back of his mind was aggravated by the fact that he had kept the whole matter to himself. His colleagues in the East Mediterranean station knew of the impending trial of course, but Harry had not wanted to strain their loyalty in any way by discussing the matter with them. This was almost certainly an error of pride on Harry's part, as his fellow officers would have welcomed the chance to discuss with him and give moral support. However, the fact that he had been suspended from duty caused an inevitable separation from his professional peers, and this was exacerbated by his departure almost immediately for Smyrna.

Of course, as a responsible British officer, it never crossed his mind to mention any of this to the Avakians. What was it to do with them? He only allowed himself personal emotional release in a long letter written to his father after he had been suspended, and before setting off for Smyrna. He knew that his father would be disappointed in him. To Colonel Bridgeman, surely, disobeying a direct military order must be the greatest crime a man could commit. Harry had spent a lifetime trying to earn his father's approval. Now he felt he had finally forfeited any hope of obtaining it.

It was not in Harry's nature to try and excuse or mitigate the consequences of his actions – least of all to his father. He had simply written an exact and detailed account of what had occurred from the moment he had accompanied Admiral Brock to the interview with the newly-appointed Turkish governor – General Nur-ed-din – to the moment he had loudly called out 'boats away' and had authorised the picking up of 200 survivors from the waters of the bay. This long letter had taken him four hours to write, but in the end it had been a cathartic experience. After he had posted it, he had been able to depart for Smyrna in

a happier frame of mind – though the forthcoming legal procedure remained a source of underlying anxiety.

The notice served on Harry stated that the court-martial
would open on Wednesday, the 4th October, and would be heard
in the stateroom on board the *Iron Duke*. He was informed that a
launch would be waiting to pick him up from the Galata Bridge
at nine o'clock on that morning. This was in less than a week's
time.

Sitting in his hotel room near Taksim, staring at the telegrams
and the notices, Harry felt alone and vulnerable. In one sense it
was irrational. His actions were not a 'hanging offence', either
figuratively or literally. His many years of humdrum but good
service would surely count for much. The trouble was that with
no one to talk it over with, his mind wandered over remote and
unlikely possibilities, which any objective observer would have
rejected immediately.

And all the time he dwelt on his own personal dilemma, there
was the larger political crisis to consider, with a very real possibility of war. These thoughts occupied him for a full 24 hours,
and then suddenly, took their proper place as matters to be
coped with in life, like any others.

A final telegram arrived on the morning of the 29th
September, the same day that Harington received his instructions to deliver the fateful ultimatum to the Ankara nationalists.
In two or three short sentences it changed Harry's outlook
forever. It read –

*"Letter received. Am arriving Sirkedji station Simplon-Orient express
morning Monday 2nd. Don't worry son. Dad."*

Suddenly, from the unreasonable gloom of the last 24 hours,
Harry swung back to the euphoria he had experienced while
working with Jennings on the quaysides of Smyrna. Every single
word of the telegram meant something to him, even the signa-
ture. His father had never signed his letters, even those sent to
him at his boarding school, with the word – Dad. Everything
about the telegram gave him a feeling of happiness; something

he had been desperately seeking all his life without realising it. Not that Harry himself analysed it quite like that – he just felt better and immediately put his worries aside.

The next day was Saturday the 30th. Harington still had the ultimatum in his pocket. Turkish soldiers were probing the Chanak bridgehead, grinning at the 'tommies' behind their barbed wire, and exchanging ribald sexual innuendo with each other. Neither side could understand the other, though the body-language was clear enough. More British soldiers were arriving in Stamboul from Malta and Egypt. The British cabinet was murmuring wilder and wilder defiance, while the Turkish nationalist army had already passed Ismid and were camped in lines not too far from the city on the Asian side. The Turkish cavalry had not withdrawn and remained inside the neutral zone at Chanak, while the British cabinet continued to wait for Harington to deliver the ultimatum and for war to begin.

But Harington held his hand. He had already begun preparations to hold the conference which had been proposed at the Curzon-Poincaré meeting seven days earlier, but to which the Turks had not as yet replied

In a sense, Harington's refusal to deliver the ultimatum, carefully prepared by the cabinet, and sent to him with clear orders to pass on to the Turks, was as clear a breach of his duty as Harry's disobedience at Smyrna – though further up the chain. Harington, as the commanding officer of the British army of occupation, was under just as much compulsion to follow the orders of the constitutional civilian authority as Harry had been, when he defied the orders of his military superior.

On this Saturday, as it became clear in London that the ultimatum had still not been delivered, there were several in the cabinet – in particular Lloyd George – who now wanted to have the ultimatum sent at once directly to Ankara. They were not even prepared to wait for the conference at Mudania, proposed by Curzon and Poincaré at their dramatic meeting and due to commence on the 3rd October. They pointed out that the Turks had still not agreed to the proposed meeting.

It was at this time that Venizelos reappeared in London, having been appointed as the new Greek ambassador by the new government in Athens, after the forced abdication of the King. Lloyd George became excited all over again, now proposing that the remains of the Greek army still in Eastern Thrace, only hours away from Constantinople, could be called upon to help in repelling the Turkish nationalists. He simply could not accept that his cherished policy of creating a strong new Greece to act as a surrogate for the power of the British Empire in the Eastern Mediterranean, had totally failed. In his frustration, there was even a suggestion that General Harington should now be censured and possibly recalled for disobeying his orders to deliver the ultimatum. Lloyd George was acting entirely under the impetus of the traditional Gladstonian Liberal distaste for the Turks, coupled with a romantic philhellenism. Churchill and his group, on the other hand, believed with some justification, that to withdraw from a confrontation would be the thin edge of the wedge spelling the beginning of the end of Empire. Only Curzon stood firm against both points of view, convinced that the whole matter was exaggerated and that diplomacy could sort it all out. He managed to earn a delay from his cabinet colleagues. No further telegrams were sent to Harington for the moment, and the Foreign Office made further contact with Kemalist representatives in Europe. They immediately passed on his views and his hints as to the eventual outcome for the city and for Eastern Thrace, to Mustapha Kemal himself, newly returned to a hero's welcome in Ankara.

On the other side of the equation, the Turks were also in some disagreement with each other. Kemal was being pressed to ignore the Allies. It was now clear that the French and Italians would no longer oppose any moves into Europe. The Turkish army, now numbering over 200,000 battle-hardened veterans, could pour into Europe. Once across the straits, the small and demoralised remains of the Greek army would surely be completely unable to stop its advance. Not only Eastern Thrace would fall like a ripe plum, but also Western Thrace, and even Macedonia and Salonika could yet be recovered.

Mustapha Kemal was not impressed. His reply to these advisors was –

"What do you want? Do you want the cry to go up throughout the Balkans – 'the Turks are coming, the Turks are coming'? After which we will have everyone against us again. No, I am ready to send a delegate to meet with the Allied representatives at the place they have suggested. Let's see what they have to say. So long as we get no ultimatum which we could not in honour accept, we can at least see what they propose."

This acceptance was at last communicated to Harington. A conference at Mudania was to go ahead on Tuesday the 3rd October. It looked as if direct war between the British Empire and the Turks might be avoided. But the question of what was to happen to Constantinople remained open.

Meanwhile, Having sent a suitable message in reply to his father, Harry stepped out to visit the Avakians in Makrikoy, with a smile on his face and a light heart.

CHAPTER 19

Spiro's Future

"The baby is already over six months old and must be baptized as soon as possible. Paramaz, do you have any idea at all whether he has already been baptized, and if so what his name might have been? Didn't the mother say anything at all to you before she died?"

That morning Karekin had invited Paramaz to sit with the rest of the family after the breakfast things were cleared away, so they could make some final decisions on all the outstanding problems that had arisen as a result of Smyrna.

"I'm sorry, sir, I really have no idea at all. We were surrounded by panic-stricken crowds. Sometimes it looked as if they might tread on the lady. She was lying on the road bleeding and I was trying to make sure she was not trampled. I never heard her utter a word."

"Very well Paramaz – but are you sure she was Armenian? When I asked George yesterday he was hesitant. He rather thought she was Greek, but then he said that you would know better as she spoke to you as you were helping her."

Paramaz hesitated, but then began speaking quickly as he saw everyone staring at him.

"She said a few words in Armenian, sir – but then she would have known by then that I was Armenian, since she must have heard George and I talking to each other."

"But you just said that you hadn't heard her utter a word."

"No…er…what I meant was that I hadn't spoken with her at any length, and only heard a say a few words."

Karekin shook his head. He remained puzzled by everything he was being told about Smyrna – not only by Paramaz but, also, by Olga. Armineh, too, on whose commonsense advice he could usually rely, had been unable to help him. He was well aware that she too suspected that there was more that Paramaz was not saying – he was not however aware that she was hiding from him what she thought was the truth behind Olga's reticence and Paramaz's evasions.

"Very well, very well. We have to be on the safe side and proceed on the basis that the baby has not yet been baptized. I have arranged with Father Haroutune that we will baptize the baby tomorrow. Tomorrow is a Sunday and it can be done very conveniently after the morning service. Now let us see … Paramaz, as the saviour of this little lad you must clearly be the godfather. Who will be the godmother?"

There was a short silence as Karekin looked round the room at his three elder daughters.

"Nerissa, my soul, I think this is a duty you should take on."

Karekin did not pause, or wait to see if Nerissa agreed. He may have been liberal when it came to giving his daughters a superior education, but that did not extend to letting them thwart his will when it came to any important decision he made for them.

"Now Paramaz – do you have any preference for a name? He

may be ending up as my adopted son – but you will be the godfather and will be naming him at the font – and in a sense it is you who have given him life."

There was a silence. Paramaz had already stood up to leave. The silence stretched out as the family looked at him with curiosity. Paramaz had tears in his eyes and looked distraught and tired. He shuffled his feet and said –

"I don't know – I don't know. Can I leave it until tomorrow please? He must at least have the name of Karekin as he will be the only Avakian male. Oh God!"

No one said a word as Paramaz turned deathly pale and walked out of the room into the kitchen. The silence was broken only by Seta who started quietly weeping for no reason, but stopped at once when Nerissa took her hand and squeezed it tight.

Karekin cleared his throat, quite unnecessarily straightened his tie, and eventually ended the uncharacteristic silence, saying – "Well, well, girls; whatever the name, it is certain that you are going to have a new brother." He stared at Armineh, who looked back at him impassively, then crossed her arms and looked down as if bringing a chapter in their lives to a coded end.

"Now we must talk about Spiro. His situation is, of course, quite different. No, Seta, don't look at me like that. There is no way at all that we can adopt him into our ..."

"But baba, he has lost all his family where ..."

"Baba, you can't just send him away, he ..."

There was an immediate outcry from the four girls, who knew at once where Karekin was heading. Armineh, who had already talked it over with Karekin in the privacy of their own bedroom, said nothing.

"Look, my girls, this is not a question of race or nationality – it is a matter of practicality and consideration of what is best for the lad. He is not a baby – he is not even a small child – he is 11 or 12 and has already been brought up in the Greek culture. He speaks Greek first and then Turkish, and has only a few words of Armenian picked up in the streets. He needs to be with his own kind who can give him the love and attention he needs."

"Oh, father, are you suggesting that we would not be able to give that love and attention?" said Olga quietly.

"Baba," said Nerissa, "he could go to the local Greek school here. We wouldn't force him into any Armenian ways. Come, you yourself said he is not a child, he doesn't have to be adopted or anything like that – he can stay and live with us, like Paramaz and Talin."

"Nerissa, I don't believe that that would be right for him; if he had been eight or below, I might have considered it. But he is approaching young manhood. If he had been a year or two older he would have been shot or taken away, and would not have survived at all. No I have decided, and I have talked it over with him. Look, I won't try to say it will be easy. Of course he cried. After all his trauma, he has come to rest here and has found comfort and shelter for the few days he has been with us. But I feel that if he remains with us he will eventually have a crisis of identity, whether he goes to a Greek school or a Greek church or whatever."

"But, father, you can't just throw him out or send him to one of those awful orphanages," said Sima, as the four looked at Karekin anxiously.

"No – of course not – of course not. Really girls, that's not an option at all. What I've already done is to speak with a couple of my Greek colleagues at the Exchange. They both happened to know of a Greek couple who have a farm about forty miles from here on the other side of Chatalja – near Sinekli. The family have lived and farmed there for generations, and there is a good Greek school nearby. They have just lost their only son who was fifteen and they have no other children. I am told they have indicated they want to adopt a Greek orphan and have been looking out for months."

"But baba – who are they?"

"Baba – what are they going to..."

"How can you be..."

"Oh, come on girls! You could surely give your father more credit. Just listen and stop interrupting for heaven's sake," said Armineh sharply.

"Well – I don't intend to go on about it much longer. I have arranged to go with Spiro on Monday to meet these people. It's less than two hours away on the train and they will be meeting us at the station. First, I will meet them and see where they live. Spiro will also be able to tell me what he thinks. My intention is that unless he really hates it, or if I myself find it unsatisfactory in some way, I will leave him with them. I will help them to deal with any legal matters later."

"But..."

"No, no, listen. I intend to leave with him a return ticket and some money just in case. If anything goes wrong he will always be able to return. For heavens sake, it's only a couple of hours away. Don't shake your heads like that – the lad is 12, and has been through much more than the difficulty of adapting to a new family and a new way of life. I really have decided and..."

At this point the front door bell rang.

"Nicolai" called out Sima and jumped up and ran to the door.

Harry, smiling from ear to metaphoric ear, walked in on the surprised Sima and planted a firm kiss on her cheek, no longer surprising anyone by this open show of affection. Two years in the Avakian atmosphere had changed Harry forever.

"See, I too now know where the bell is – that makes me part of the family doesn't it?" said Harry, putting his hat down on the small table by the front door.

"Come in, come in my boy," said Karekin reverting immediately to his rather heavily accented English. "A coffee – yes – yes. But look we have all sat round the table long enough – let's go into the sitting room."

Harry duly kissed everyone as they passed into the sitting room – Armineh going to the kitchen to see to coffees, and Seta going up to her room. Olga, surprisingly overjoyed to see him, took his arm and sat him down next to her on one of the sofas.

"We were discussing Spiro's future" she said.

Karekin had taken up his favourite position, standing with his back to the fire with his arms held together behind him.

"Now, Harry – don't say anything Olga – I would really like to hear what you think we should do or advise Spiro to do about his future."

Harry, still in a state of euphoria as a result of his father's telegram, felt the warmth of Olga's arm still tucked through his as they sat together. He loved this family and suddenly – like the flash of an electric spark – it came to him that over the last few days, from the moment he had first met Olga again at the Ottoman Hospital in Smyrna and the hours that they had spent together since then, he...

"Well, sir," Harry hesitated as he saw the three women were staring at him with greater intensity than usual. His natural inclination would have been to try to ascertain what the old man wanted him to say – and then say it. He decided, however, to come out with what he really felt.

"I see the difficulty. However, I would like to say, at once, that this young man does not pose anything like the same problem as that of the baby brought back out of that inferno by Paramaz. Spiro seemed to me to be an intelligent lad who knows what and who he is and who has already weathered one of the worst experiences any boy can go through – namely the brutal killing of his own mother in front of his very eyes. It is tricky I can see that. He is not quite old enough to be left to make his own way – yet he is too old to be treated like a child.

"Hmm... My own instinct would be to go to the Greek Patriarchate in town and talk with some of the priests there or perhaps one of the administrators. They are bound to have arrangements already in place. There have been droves of Greek refugees coming in to Bolis from all round the Black Sea. Look, Spiro can have a word with them and they could help him decide."

There was a short silence. Both Sima and Nerissa had almost gasped when Harry had said 'Bolis' rather than 'Constantinople'. Olga had not even noticed – she felt comfortable with this man and had hardly heard a word of what he had actually been saying. She knew, with her usual instinctive feeling, that she would be likely to agree with whatever he said about the future of the boy.

She looked up with affection at her father. He continued to

stand ramrod straight as usual in front of the fire. It was still only the 30th September and the fire was not lit every morning until October 1st. She wondered idly why it had been lit today. She saw her father start smiling at Harry's words, and heard him say –

"That's it Harry, my thoughts in essence almost exactly. The only difference is that there is no way, no way at all, that I would think for a moment of leaving the decision to a bunch of clerics – especially that Greek lot. My God, you've seen the way they have treated the Ottoman government from the moment the British took over. Hubris – hubris – they are now about to suffer the consequences of their ridiculous attitude once the Kemalists arrive. Passports issued for their flock indeed…"

At this reminder of how the Greek patriarchate had acted in those early years of the British occupation, Karekin totally lost the thread of what he was saying. In any case the three women had now clearly capitulated.

"Nerissa, my soul, go and tell your mother that Harry is staying for lunch. No, no – I insist. Meanwhile I'll tell you what I have decided."

For the next hour or so, as family members moved in and out, contributing comments as they passed, the Spiro situation was hammered out and considered from all angles. Nerissa, not wanting to miss a word, had hurried back, and everyone was eager to give their views. Only Olga remained surprisingly quiet and thoughtful, still clinging on to Harry's arm.

Lunch was served and still the discussion went on, though now the talk began turning to the baby and the christening to take place the next day.

After lunch, Olga rose and, before anyone else could say anything, she turned to Harry and said,

"It's a beautiful day, crisp and cold but wonderfully bright. Let's take a walk together in the gardens."

CHAPTER 20

Instincts

Despite the fire in the sitting room it was still September – just - and the weather though crisp and fresh was sunny and bright. Harry tried to recall the last time he had strolled through the trees of the orchard at the bottom of the lawn in the Avakian garden in this way. When was it? Olga held his arm as they walked through the French windows of the sitting room and out onto the long veranda which ran along the back of the house.

Harry knew the way through the woods as they slowly strolled in the early afternoon sunshine, absorbed in their own reveries. As they walked past the little door set in the stone wall which led out into the street beyond, Harry suddenly remembered. Yes of course – it was at the end of that awful tea-party over a year ago, when that overly passionate young Armenian man...what was his name... ah yes Mikael, and the good-looking Turk Selim had almost come to blows. It came back to him in fine detail. He had walked this way with Nerissa demurely holding on to his arm, both of them keeping a discreet distance behind Sima and Nicolai, so they could have some time to themselves.

And what about Olga – where had she been on that occasion? He looked down at the beautiful girl at his side, clinging on to his arm more tightly than the young Nerissa had, and recalled she had been taken up in tears to her room by her brother as the party had broken up in disarray.

Harry had learnt a lot about Olga and her problems during their time together after he found her at the Ottoman Imperial Hospital. Olga had told him almost everything about her life in Smyrna before the fire. They had talked then and at even greater length during the voyage on the USS *Lawrence* as it brought them back to Constantinople. Harry had understood at once, that she and Selim must have been living together during the months before the Great Fire. She and Selim had considered themselves to be man and wife and were intending to marry when the circumstances allowed.

Still, they had not actually been married.

The Great War had undoubtedly changed attitudes, but not quite so far as to amount to social acceptance of impropriety. Harry was not even quite sure what he himself thought about it. He had not been 'shocked' at the revelation Olga had confessed with unthinking and honest naiveté. His upbringing, however, had been pre-War and it was difficult to get concepts like 'fallen women' quite out of his mind. Surely nice girls from good families did not go to bed with men before they were properly married in an official ceremony, did they?

They were walking together in companionable silence while Harry continued to muse. The circumstances of Olga's relationship with Selim had undoubtedly been difficult and both of them had clearly shown a long-lasting and true fidelity to each other. They walked on quietly until Olga saw the bench in a corner of the wall and suggested that they sit for a moment.

Olga had not as yet told anyone about the baby though it was now nearly a month since she realised she was pregnant. In a singular, but surprisingly pedestrian confrontation, she had finally got round to telling Armineh the full events of that 13th September, ending with the death of Selim. Sima was also present as she outlined all the circumstances; the arrival of Haik and Paramaz; the desperate attempt to get Selim out of the house as the flames approached; the three soldiers in the street outside; and finally the escape from the flames at the hands of the unknown Turk who had saved her from the advancing fire. She had not said a word about the rape – this she would keep to herself - though she hinted at some brutality before she made her escape. The revelation to her mother and her elder sister of the affair with Selim was both matter of fact and unsentimental. Sima and Armineh could see that, for Olga, the trauma and emotion of those days arose from the death of Selim, not from the brutality of the events she had witnessed.

But Armineh was no fool. She saw clearly what Sima could not see: that Olga had no longer been a virgin when all these terrible events happened. And that meant Olga's love for Selim had been consummated. Once that was understood, the rest of the story began to make sense; not only Paramaz's version, but also his evasiveness. Obviously the boy had some merit in him after all. He was surely seeking to save Karekin the embarrassment and shame of learning that his daughter and Selim had been openly living together.

It was all so extraordinary. Here was Karekin, a man of deeply liberal views, well-known throughout the city as a free-thinker, keen on education and with enlightened opinions on the role of women in society; yet the instincts of his wife and eldest daughter were to protect the fact that his second daughter had been living for some months with the man she had loved for many years; while for her part Olga, who was now carrying her lover's child, seriously contemplated passing off the coming child to her father as the result of a brutal act of rape rather than an act of love. In one way or another, it appeared that all three women instinctively believed that Karekin would be unable to accept that his daughter had been openly living with a man without being married.

Olga was genuinely tired as she and Harry approached the old wooden bench set back against the old stone wall. She needed the rest. Added to the physical tiredness, was the mental fatigue of knowing that she was at least a month pregnant, but unable, as yet, to share this knowledge with the people she loved.

Olga had never been a great thinker. Living with Selim, knowing that on their return to Constantinople, they would be married, she had existed in a state of euphoria, one day at a time. She loved her work, she looked after her patients, and had worked hard. Then she would return to the little first floor apartment in the house of Madame Derounian, bringing home with her kebabs, pitta and fruit bought on her way home. She would lay the little table and there would be a surge of joy in her heart as Selim came in. Whatever she was doing, she would drop it and run to him, and he would enfold her...his lips...his hands...What did Olga care about what people might think? She had told Mdme. Derounian they were married. She had not really been dishonest – she felt in her heart it was so.

But now she was home with her family, it was no longer so simple. Now Selim would never again be there to talk to; but there was his child, and suddenly convention and propriety were muscling in. She wasn't frightened, but she was confused. She had only been back a mere three or four days, yet it seemed like ages. She would have to speak up one way or another soon.

"Harry, that was lovely. Do you mind if we sit and talk a bit?"

"My dear, why not?" replied Harry.

Olga sat and curled her legs up underneath her as Harry sat alongside and stretched his out into the path. There was another comfortable silence as they looked around. Then Harry said,

"Look, the trees are just beginning to turn. It'll be a bit longer before the leaves actually begin to fall, but some of the colours are just starting to change. Down here it isn't all that dramatic, but you should see the autumn in England – in a good year it can be really amazing."

"Harry, you appear to be so joyful and full of life today – is there any particular reason?"

"Well, well, I didn't realise it was so obvious. There is, as it happens. My father is coming to Bolis and will be here on Monday, and I..."

"Oh that's marvellous. Your own father coming all that way just to see you. How wonderful. Why is he...no, no, why not...Where will he be staying? Oh Harry, I'll tell mama – he must come and visit us here."

"Olga wait – you're so ... well never mind. Aren't you curious why he should be coming all this way after all the years I've been stationed here?"

"Who cares about the reasons. The fact is that your own, your very own papa is travelling for three days just to visit his son. You must be ..."

"No, wait a moment – I must tell you – no more evasions, no more secrets. The fact is, I am facing a serious court-martial, which is due to be heard on Wednesday. You know what a court-martial is, don't you? Well, my father heard about it and is coming out to give me his support."

The step had been taken, and now Harry spent the next fifteen minutes pouring his heart out to Olga. He explained the conditions in the Bay during those fateful days; he spoke of his decision and the inevitable result; it all just came out. Unlike the first meeting between them in the little café up the hill beyond the hospital, when they were both talking together, at the same time, interrupting each other constantly, now Olga sat quietly and listened carefully to every word. As the explanations went on, Olga eventually said –

"And your father's reaction to all this?"

It was like a floodgate opening in a dam. Like water pouring out, at first in a straight stream and then spreading out on all sides, Harry began talking about his father and everything that he had felt about him over the years. This turned inexorably into what he believed that his father had thought about his only son: the coldness, the lack of any physical warmth between them, his continual fear that he would not come up to his father's expectations. He began to get confused, trying to stem the flood of words. He talked about the way he wanted to emulate his father, and almost in the same breath how he wanted to be very different.

"My God, Olga – even now I crave a hug from my father and to hug him back – imagine, I, a grown man, an officer in His Majesty's Royal Navy."

"Well, why don't you then, it's not difficult."

"He wouldn't understand. We don't do things that way in England – it wouldn't be manly. We would end up being embarrassed with each other."

"All right, all right – but even a handshake can either be warm and full of love, or it can be cold and formal. Harry, I'm looking forward to meeting this baba of yours."

Olga jumped up from the bench, her eyes lit up with enthusiasm, as Harry sat staring up at her, contemplating with wonder all the confidences that had come tumbling out of him. Olga had no idea why she was so animated, or why she was bubbling over with delight – she simply held out her hand and grasping Harry's, she pulled him up.

"Come, let's walk on, and now you can listen to me while I tell you about my baba."

They began walking together again, arm in arm, naturally, without affectation. They soon came out onto the lawn on the other side from where they had started. They were now facing back towards the house and saw that Armineh and Karekin had come out onto the veranda and were seated at the white wrought-iron table having their coffee. Nicolai was there as well sitting next to Sima. They were holding hands quite openly; Nicolai was grinning somewhat inanely, while Sima looked even more demure and self-contained than usual. Olga stared for a moment as Sima called out to her, but then steered Harry back into the orchard and out of sight.

Now it was Olga who was doing all the talking, matching Harry's personal revelations about his relationship with his father, with her relationship with her own. But in her case, the approach was radically different. Harry had been pouring out hidden feelings of which he had only been vaguely aware. It was a relief to bring it out in the open at last. The mere act of talking about it to this woman, whom he had come to know so well over the past two weeks, had been enough. But in Olga's case, she was seeking answers from someone she could trust; she had after all already placed herself fully into his hands in Smyrna.

She wanted to be told what she should tell her father – but her thoughts were irrational. She wanted Harry to give her the benefit of his advice, but somehow to give it without knowing the real nature of the problem. As she talked and they strolled on, kicking up the leaves that had already fallen, they eventually got back to the same wooden bench on which they had been sitting earlier. Olga sat and began fiddling with a bracelet, looking down at her hands. Harry sat down beside her and again stretched his long legs out, putting his clasped hands behind his head. He felt totally relaxed and contented. He was at peace with the world and with himself and ready to continue listening to Olga's thoughts about her father's character, although he was fully aware of most what she said.

Harry had had to make a substantial leap of trust in disclosing to Olga the details of the forthcoming court-martial – something he would not normally have disclosed to anyone outside the Service, least of all a foreign national, and even less to a woman. In the same way, Olga, fiddling indecisively with her bracelet, was now contemplating making an equal leap of trust in disclosing something deeply personal to someone outside the immediate family circle.

Just as Harry had overcome his professional pride in coming out with the details of his troubles, so Olga was having to overcome her family pride by coming out with the ultimate confidence. She had reached the stage that she had to confide in someone before telling her mother – and that someone was going to be Harry.

"Harry, I've been rambling on about my papa and our relationship as father and daughter. I have been going on about it because I need to talk with someone outside the family who knows us both. Frankly, I need some objective advice."

"Listen Olga, I've been all ears, but I do urge you not to come out with an intimacy without thinking deeply first. So often people come out with confidences they later regret. I will try to help and be as honest as possible, but I have not had all that much experience in what I presume is a family problem. I am not a..."

"I know the man you are. I have seen how you dealt with Spiro. I trust you; I want you to know about my problem which has been playing terribly on my mind. I know that I can confide in you."

Harry turned his head, pulled up his feet and brought his hands down in front of him. Now looking straight into Olga's eyes, he nodded and waited.

"You know that Selim and I were living together those last few weeks before the fall of Smyrna. I don't really know what he was doing there and I was never interested in finding out. For me it was enough that we were together, that he wanted to marry me and that we would be able to live together as man and wife once the political situation was settled and we could get back to Bolis. Harry – I was blissfully happy. After all I had been dreaming about this for six years."

There was a short silence. Harry, who had never experienced such a passionate revelation before, felt a shameful wish to look away. Instead, however, he held firm and continued to look directly into her eyes. Then she suddenly looked away herself, and looking down at her bracelet she said –

"I am pregnant. I am bearing Selim's child who will be born in eight months time."

CHAPTER 21

Nicolai and Sima

Nicolai had turned up at the Avakians somewhat unexpectedly after lunch immediately after Olga and Harry had strolled down into the garden. He had kissed Sima hurriedly in the hall and then asked to speak to Karekin. Sima, neither as clever as Nerissa nor as emotional as Olga, was nevertheless more perceptive than both at seeing the reality behind formal words. They had talked about this moment many times before and she realized at once what this hurried, unscheduled visit meant, coupled as it was with a rather cold and nervous formality. She blushed for a moment but said nothing, taking Nicolai by the hand and into the sitting room where everyone except Harry and Olga were now sitting waiting for coffee.

"Ah, Nicolai. You're a bit late for lunch my boy. It was 'mantu', my favourite – you missed a treat – but come, come. Coffee of course."

"Well, no thank you sir. I rather wanted to have a word with you in private at some time please, if that would be possible."

Karekin looked across at Armineh, who said nothing and would not even return his glance. Alexei had already told Karekin of the family's decision that the Countess should go to visit their relatives in Vienna. He had also informed Karekin of his own personal decision not to leave with his mother at this time. Karekin had of course passed this on to Armineh and they had already discussed the possible implications of the Androv family decision in the current political climate. They weren't aware Nicolai had lost his job with the Pera Palace orchestra. However, clearly, the political crisis looming over the future of the city was also affecting the relationships in their own family.

Nicolai was always a little more formal in his speech than the Avakians, or even his own younger brother, but it was clear to all of them that he was now being at his most – aristocratic! With an involuntary sigh, which he quickly muffled, Karekin stood up from the hardback armchair, which he regularly preferred to any of the sofas. Putting an arm round Nicolai's shoulders, and pretending not to feel the slight involuntary withdrawal, he ushered him from the room and into the study.

But it was Karekin ironically who was nervous, not Nicolai. Nicolai was worried how Karekin would react, but years of training by his English governess, coupled with the instincts of a born Russian aristocrat, came to his aid. He was both calm and clear as to what he wanted, whereas Karekin was quite unsure of what he would reply, assuming that he was right about what Nicolai was after.

"Sir, I know that you know of my feelings for Sima – feelings which I believe she shares for me. Your kindness to my family has given me some hope that you might look kindly on the continuation of our relationship."

Karekin stood by his desk, one arm as usual behind his back, the other with fingers splayed on the desktop; then, sitting down, he swivelled his chair round so he could look straight at Nicolai and nodded at him to continue.

"Sir, as I believe you know, my mother is leaving on Monday to go to Vienna where she will be staying with her eldest sister – the Countess Berchtold. The situation in Vienna is currently as desperate as here, so she might be going on to her other sister who is married to an Italian Count – Count Maggi – whose estate in the Veneto is still intact."

"Well – yes, yes, very well – go on my boy."

"I am not going with her, largely because I wish to resolve my situation here with your daughter. In short, sir, I wish to marry

Sima. Whilst I have not yet made any formal request to her, I believe that she knows of my wishes and approves, subject, of course, to what you and Madame Avakian might think."

By this stage of Nicolai's painfully formal speech, Karekin knew precisely where it was leading. The first, somewhat incongruous thought, that struck him, was that in a family of young girls, all of marriageable age, this was the first formal request for the hand of one of his daughters he had ever received from a young man.

A silence now fell between them, and continued for a short time – both men quite comfortable with it. Now that the question had finally been put to him, all the discussions between him and Armineh fled from his mind. Quietly, he brought out his beautiful amber beads and began clicking them, not nervously but deliberately – passing them slowly between thumb and first finger. He made a little gesture indicating that Nicolai should take a seat. Nicolai declined, preferring to continue standing. It was now his turn to get nervous as he waited for Karekin to speak.

Eventually, Karekin, looking up, said, as kindly as he could, and avoiding any suggestion of criticism,

"Nicolai, my boy, how will you manage – where are you proposing to live with Sima and what will you live on. You could hardly manage to provide for her and any future family on your wages from the Pera Palace."

At this point Nicolai finally took the chair Karekin had indicated, and sat down, realising that he hadn't even mentioned that he had lost this job.

"Well, sir, I anticipated your question. First, I have already given up my job at the Pera Palace. With the political situation as it is, they simply can't afford to keep up the orchestra in the same numbers as before."

He swallowed, his mouth dry, anticipating some sort of an outburst from Karekin at this revelation. Surprisingly, he saw that Karekin was not the slightest bit disturbed by this news, though he said nothing. Nicolai continued –

"The reason, sir, for my sense of urgency is that I wish to take

Sima with me to Europe. I don't suppose that I'll have much more chance in finding good work in Vienna than I've had here. But my uncle has a fairly extensive estate in North Italy, and I have high hopes that he will welcome having a member of the family with experience in this field as an Estate Manager. He is getting old and will be needing someone to help him soon."

Once again there was a silence as Karekin digested Nicolai's increasingly more hurried and passionate words. They had been speaking in English – their best common language, though Karekin had to reflect a bit more on the true meaning behind the words.

"I would add, sir, that I have several jewels still left to me by my mother. These are at a high premium at the moment in view of the political uncertainty and I am in the process of selling some of the bulkier items, which should give us some starting capital and a cushion in case of any problems."

"Have you considered, deghas," and here in the middle of the English they were talking, Karekin deliberately used the Armenian word, which could mean both 'my boy' and 'my son' – "that as my potential son-in-law, you would be most welcome to join the merchant house of 'Avakian & Co'."

Every word seemed to be loaded with significance in this conversation. Nicolai noted immediately that Karekin had not said 'Avakian, Levonian & Co' the current official designation of the firm. However, his reply was quick and decisive –

"I deeply appreciate your suggestion. You have already done a lot for my family – it has been the making of Alexei for a start. My mother told me that you might make this offer and urged me to accept it with gratitude – but, sir, I cannot. I have to try to establish my own future if I can."

"I can't agree with you. I could understand you might feel a gulf between our differing cultural backgrounds – between Russian landed gentry on the one hand and Ottoman merchant adventurer on the other. But why would you be prepared to accept an offer of work from an unknown uncle, as against an offer of work from your prospective father-in-law?"

The truth was that Nicolai was not at all certain why he felt there was a difference or why he could accept help from one and not the other – so said nothing. Karekin then continued –

"Bear in mind, Nicolai, that you will be requiring my daughter to share the same risk you choose to take by going off to Italy, or anywhere else without any immediate prospects."

At last Nicolai found his voice –

"I would like to add, sir, that in the current situation anything at all could happen. I doubt that we will actually end up in a Smyrna situation, but who knows, who knows? Everything about this city is in the melting pot and at least if we can arrange a marriage quickly, I would be in a position to take your daughter out of it. As you know I have acquired a Nansen passport and if a Smyrna solution was in store for us here, such a passport might well be worth more than an Ottoman document, easily repudiated by whatever government is finally established. I admit I don't think it will come to that – but it might, it might, who knows."

Karekin thought to himself that this was the first really good argument he had heard – there was more to this boy than noblesse and impeccably good manners. He stood up and again using the word 'deghas' smiled at Nicolai and said –

"Deghas, you are welcome to ask Sima for her hand in marriage – and if she accepts you, you have my blessing for an early marriage – but on one absolute condition."

"Oh my God – Oh what... er ... yes, sir, what would that condition be?"

"I want your solemn word, Nicolai, one on which I can absolutely rely, one in which your personal honour will be at stake, that if matters do not work out either in Vienna or the Veneto, you won't just try to make do in order to salve your pride, but will come back here to make your life in this city and in my merchant house."

"I accept your condition, sir. I accept it wholeheartedly and with thanks," said Nicolai, grinning from ear to ear. "I would never put Sima through any kind of penury just in order to salve my pride as you put it. I would add, though, that all this depends on whether, in a month or two, there is still a city here in which you or I would be welcome – or more to the point, whether the merchant house of Avakian & Co. will still be in business."

Karekin burst out laughing while the inane grin on Nicolai's face gave way to a chuckle. This relieved the tension between them. Karekin rose from his seat and put away his beads. He walked round the desk and put his arms round Nicolai's shoulders who had jumped up, this time receiving Karekin's embrace without any awkwardness. They walked together out into the sitting-room, which was now empty, and from there into the garden to join Sima and Armineh, who were sitting at one of the white wrought-iron tables, staring across at the orchard.

They looked up as the two men, Nicolai just ahead of Karekin, walked through the French windows and onto the veranda. Karekin still had his hand on Nicolai's shoulder as if he was pushing him forward – a rare gesture on his part. Both women immediately knew the question had been put and permission granted, but neither said a word.

Karekin took his hand off Nicolai's shoulder and, nodding at Armineh, he turned and went back into the sitting room without a word.   Armineh understood immediately and, muttering something about seeing to the coffees, hurried off after Karekin.

Nicolai was now more nervous than he had been with Karekin. He wasn't concerned about Sima's feelings for him, but he was aware of the weakness of his own current situation and prospects. Even before Karekin had pointed it out, he knew how little he was offering this very practical woman. He was well aware of the views she had always expressed on the realities involved in going into a marriage

Now, suddenly, he was unsure of her response. He was proposing to take her away with him to throw themselves on the goodwill of an extended family who even he hardly knew. On top of that, he was stateless and had an aging mother to look after as well. Would she be prepared to join him in building a satisfactory life for themselves, and for any children, far away from her family and the city she had always called home? He moved round the table towards her and then bent and took her hand in his.

"Sima, my sweetheart, my darling – will you marry me?"

There was hardly a second's hesitation. Sima knew what she was being asked to accept. A home of their own was nowhere in sight; the joy of children would have to be put aside until Nicolai could find his feet; there would be uncertainty even in where they would live. It was all so different from the arguments she had urged over and over again to her younger sisters. Nevertheless, this was the man she wanted to be the father of her children – this was the man she loved. She jumped up out of her chair, almost before he had finished his sentence. She put her arms round him and managed to gasp out –

"Oh yes, yes, Nicolai. Oh yes … yes … my love."

Standing there in the garden, with her chair fallen back behind her, the table rocking dangerously as Nicolai leaned back heavily against it as Sima threw herself into his embrace, they kissed. It was all so natural.

Eventually, after Karekin and Armineh returned, in answer to Sima's cries, they all sat round the table; the coffee arrived together with a bottle of Karekin's best champagne brought by Marie, who tearfully embraced Sima. As practical details began to be discussed, Olga and Harry first emerged, arm in arm, from the orchard. Olga waved at the seated group, and rather hurriedly turned away, pulled Harry back into the trees before anyone could call out. Well, there was plenty of time – there was plenty of time – perhaps.

CHAPTER 22

Confidences

Harry was over 30 and had the self-confidence that came from having been in a position of command over other men for at least the last four or five years. He was also a fairly standard product of the British education system, which produced men of assurance and imperial potential. He believed he had been a good officer and was proud of his record as such. The forthcoming court-martial, a professional hazard faced by many men before him, had not affected this belief, nor his own self-confidence. But Olga's quiet confession, put to him without dramatics, left him unable to say a word.

Harry had changed enormously since the end of the war and during the two years of his mission in Constantinople – but not quite enough to be able to cope with something like this. He was an 'only' child. Like so many of his class and times he had moved straight from an all-male boarding school into the military, in his case the navy. He had had little experience of women and none whatsoever of 'pregnancy'. "I am pregnant," she had told him. What was he supposed to say? Why were the words said to him?

At the same time, he had been with this woman almost the whole of every single day from the moment he had returned to Smyrna. They had worked together on Spiro's behalf; she had supported him in facing the nightmare of what had occurred on the quaysides; they had talked together for hour after hour on the USS *Lawrence* and ever since. Talk between them had become so effortless and meaningful that he felt he had to make a real effort to understand exactly what she was saying. Of course, he understood the biology of her statement – what he did not understand was what help or support she thought he could offer. He recalled that his first reaction to the revelation of her liaison with Selim had been judgmental. These thoughts passed through his mind like a flash – but, as it turned out, she was not expecting any immediate answer, only a sounding board –

"I am happy about it, Harry – I am truly happy and not afraid. I am only sorry that somehow I lost the moment to tell Selim before he died. I did suspect the possibility at the time, but I waited to be sure and then.... and then.... well, events took over and it was too late."

Harry leaned back against the stone wall for a moment.

Then in a gesture of alliance, almost of complicity, he stretched his hand behind Olga's back and round her far shoulder, holding her firmly. He didn't speak, but his mind was going through all sorts of mental gymnastics as he wrestled with the revelation of their liaison before proper marriage. It was as if the natural outcome of such a liaison – the arrival of another life, a baby, anxiously awaited and looked for – changed his whole attitude. Background, culture and upbringing are of course paramount in forming opinions, but circumstances and emotions can override them, particularly in the case of men with staunchly independent characters. And this was what was happening to Harry.

"Anyway, Harry, I haven't told mother yet, but I will be doing so, probably this very evening. I have no fears in my mind about it. But it is father, Harry, my father! How can I put it to him – what is he going to say – what is he going to think? Already I can see that everyone is scared about making it clear to him that I was living with Selim during those two months. If we can't even tell him about that, how will he take the knowledge that I am actually pregnant. Oh Harry, I am so scared of losing his love."

At last Harry had sailed into clearer waters. At last he knew what this girl wanted from him. She needed the sort of reassurance that he wished he'd been given ten years ago, by a loving father. As he turned towards her, a new and yet deeper warmth and elation came over him. The combination of his father's telegram that morning and this girl's confidence in him, was making this a day like no other he had ever experienced.

"Olga, you know that I'm not experienced in the sort of problem you are dealing with, but on the matter of your father, I believe I have come to know him well enough over the years, to give you my opinion. Firstly, my dear, you must tell him soon and not leave it hanging over you. Tell him immediately after the baptism ceremony for Paramaz's baby tomorrow, – and Olga, tell him yourself, don't be persuaded by your mother to leave it to her. And just tell him the truth – no excuses, no hiding anything."

Harry had been talking quickly with considerable emphasis. He was anxious to have his say before he could be interrupted – but for once Olga was listening patiently to every word.

"In my opinion, he may well find it a difficult to accept your decision to live together. His generation would undoubtedly have expected you to wait, however difficult the circumstances.

But once he has taken that on board – and after all the circumstances were pretty exceptional – the arrival of a baby next year will not faze him one jot. Formal marriage or no formal marriage it is his first grandchild. Oh dear, he may be irritated a bit at first, he may have wanted things to have turned out differently, he may finger his beads as he works out how to deal with it in practical terms, but the arrival of a baby won't hurt him. Good God, Olga, he'll probably be delighted."

Harry took a deep breath. Olga stood up, eyes gleaming. Then, she bent down and gave him a soft kiss, which lingered for more than just a moment, directly on his lips. Then she straightened up and said –

"Thank you Harry. I knew I could rely on you and your good sense. Come, enough revelations. It's as if Nerissa was here orchestrating our talk to make sure that we don't lapse into idle chit-chat. Let's go in. Thank you Harry – my mind is clear."

Even by Avakian standards the talk, the animated discussions, the kissing and hugging, the overwhelming warmth and delight over the news of Sima and Nicolai's forthcoming marriage was impressive. It lasted for the rest of the afternoon. In Ottoman Armenian circles, an engagement was usually the excuse for an enormous party, funded always by the girl's father. The marriage itself, usually organised by the bridegroom's family, was normally a quieter affair for the two families and their more intimate friends.

However in this case, the circumstances made this more difficult. The political situation was so tense that a traditional engagement party might have seemed gratuitous. As the conversation rumbled on, Nicolai soon realised the decision was largely out of his hands and was going to be decided in the usual Avakian manner of everyone talking at once. New bottles kept arriving at the table, and Harry and Nicolai were becoming dazed, as the discussions raged. The consensus, however, was much as Nicolai wanted. Everyone agreed that the actual wedding should take place as soon as possible. Inevitably this meant a month at least.

Everyone started calculating.

Armineh thought to herself that she would need this much time to send out invitations, prepare for the actual day and take time with Sima for such practical matters as dresses and the reception. Sima knew she needed the time to sort out her own things. She would have to look into the rooms at the Patakis house, for at her own insistence it had been agreed that after the marriage there would be no question of coming to Makrikoy. They would start their marriage together in those rented rooms, as by then, the Countess would have departed. Without anything being actually said, it was accepted that Alexei should be persuaded to come to live in Makrikoy, but he would have to be consulted.

Karekin was also pleased by the resulting calculation of the time available. He had come to the conclusion that, one way or another, the political situation would be resolved by that time. The question of what would happen to the city and to the dynasty remained unknown – but violence was now unlikely unless the Greek army still in Thrace on the other side of the Chatalja lines decided not to accept what had been decided, without their participation, at Mudanya. On the other hand, the dread phrase 'exchange of populations' was already being bandied about by the great and the good, and this continued to leave a terrible question mark hanging over everybody in the city.

Nicolai, in a state of bemusement as all these decisions were taken around him, would have wanted an even earlier date but understood that a month was the irreducible minimum. He, too, calculated that his mother would need at least that much time before she would know anything more about the feasibility of their own move to Vienna.

Olga? Well Olga was as happy for Sima as everyone, but in the end her thoughts remained on the coming evening and the news she was going to be giving to her mother.

The afternoon wore on and Harry and Nicolai, both already more than mellow from Karekin's excellent champagne, prepared to leave – Nicolai mumbling about the need to see his mother and Alexei and discuss the news with them. Karekin indicated that he would go with them in order to see Father Haroutune and start the necessary arrangements for a wedding. Armineh had noticed that Seta had become a little tearful from all the excitement, so suggested that she accompany her father on the trip.

After everyone left, the Avakian women were left alone in the house, which had suddenly become very quiet. Armineh, who had been bustling about all afternoon while the talk raged around her, finally sat down heavily in the sitting room and contemplated her three daughters.

"Well, my daughters, are you all ready for the baptism ceremony tomorrow. Nerissa, you have to hold the baby all the time. Make sure he is changed before the service. There is a place you can do it in the sacristy before the morning service ends. Remember, only hand him to Paramaz at the font."

"Yes, mama. You'll be next to me, won't you?"

"Of course – but your father will not be at the font. Traditionally as the father of the infant he will be hovering about at the back – which is where he prefers to be anyway at these occasions."

"Do you know who will be coming," said Sima.

"We will all be there, of course, but I have not invited anyone else outside the family. The Androvs – well they are family now anyway – will be there. And Sima, I'm sure you won't mind, but I have also sent a message round to George. After all he was there with Paramaz when the baby was saved, wasn't he."

There was a short comfortable silence.

Then Olga, who had said nothing for some time, sat up straight on the edge of the sofa and turned to address Armineh directly. She felt an unaccustomed rush of blood to her face and said rather more sharply than she had intended –

"Mama – the word she actually spoke in Armenian would literally translate as 'my own darling mother' – I have to tell you, all of you, something about Smyrna."

There was again a short silence, no longer quite so comfortable.

"You all know now that I met Selim quite by chance about six months after I first arrived in the city. What I have not said – at least not directly – is that we took a little apartment together in the Armenian quarter and lived together. You know exactly what I mean, my darlings, don't you. We lived happily together right up to the moment when the Turkish army entered the city. Our plan was to get married as soon as we got back home."

"But how…"

"What was…"

"Please wait. Selim had a couple of rooms in the Turkish quarter. I never saw them or went there. He would go there sometimes whenever I was on duty at the hospitals where I worked."

Sima and Nerissa were enthralled, even though they had both already guessed what she was telling them. Neither of them was taken aback. Nerissa considered herself both a very modern woman, and an enlightened liberal. It all seemed so right and romantic. Sima was more mature and more old-fashioned, but she was so happy with her own romantic fulfilment, that she too could only nod her head. Armineh said nothing but stared hard at Olga. She had long since realised that this was the case, but although she wasn't 'shocked', her upbringing had been totally different and she totally and utterly disapproved. She didn't judge, she didn't blame, but she disapproved. It was against everything she believed in. Such behaviour was subversive and conducive to the sort of anarchy she saw all around her.

Olga could sense her mother's disapproval; she felt the tears springing to her eyes, but she swallowed and went on as best she could –

"Oh dear, this is difficult. My loves – I must tell you what I've been bottling up for days. I'm pregnant. I will have Selim's child, in eight months."

The switch of feelings in the three women who were listening was immediate, enormous and extraordinary. Sima and Nerissa suddenly realised the consequences of two lovers living together. Sima immediately saw the cultural and social costs and the practical difficulties to be overcome. Nerissa was equally shocked by the product of this romantic attachment, which otherwise had all the elements of one of her favourite 19th century English novels. In the space of a sentence, the talk had turned from romance to physical passion. As always, she was struck dumb by this turn of events.

But Armineh stood up. She still disapproved, completely and without equivocation. She stared down at her daughter, who looked back up at her with silent tears running slowly down her cheeks. But here was a reality that had to be faced. It was nature. Bending down, she took Olga's head between her hands and kissed her on her forehead, saying –

"Oh dear – you silly goose – you silly, silly goose. Are you all right? Have you started feeling sick? Come, come, my darling – we have work to do and we must start planning."

With her tears now turning to tears of relief, Olga bent forward and clasped her mother round her knees burying her head in her mothers long, soft grey skirt. Mumbling into the skirt so that they could only just hear the words she said –

"Oh, mother – I do so want to have Selim's child. I really loved him – and mother he loved me. I…"

"Hush child – calm yourself. Of course you are going to have the child – and look, look at the wonderful aunts he is going to have."

Sima, sitting on her other side, leaned across and hugged Olga, in a rush of emotion. Nerissa sat for a moment, angry with herself at failing to extend the immediate empathetic support shown by the others. Then she too arose and gave her sister a warm embrace

CHAPTER 23

The Christening

Step by step, Paramaz walked, with his two little sisters beside him, each holding on to his hand, one on each side. The scene was strange and desolate – there were boulders everywhere of all shapes and sizes and he had to lead the two little girls round each one, in some cases having to lift them over. Even at this stage in the dream, he was already afraid, but he had no idea of what.

Suddenly, in front of them as they walked round yet another boulder, his father stood, gripping a sword in one hand and holding up Paramaz's mother who was leaning against him with the other. Even as he stared at them blood began pouring out from between his mother's legs and she began to sink to the floor, despite his father's efforts to keep her standing. Until this moment there had been an eerie silence as he had walked on with the girls – but now he heard the words 'Manchus – manchigus' (my son – my darling son) as his mother sank to the ground with her arms outstretched towards him.

His two little sisters let go of his hand and ran to the man who had been holding on to his mother – but it was no longer his father. His father had somehow become a large distended naked man with an erect penis, who with one sweep of his sword, struck off the heads of the two little girls. Then he advanced upon Paramaz, now with a spear held aloft – the sword had somehow disappeared.

Paramaz shrank away in horror but his feet were stuck to the ground. He could not escape – but now the father/apparition melted away and in his place stood some sort of androgynous figure, having no recognisable features. But Paramaz knew who it was – he knew exactly who it was. Still the figure advanced, sometimes looking like a boy of 17, sometimes like a young girl of 15, indistinct and blurred, but always with a sweet smile which drove terror into Paramaz's heart. It continued to advance, without appearing to get any closer. Why wasn't it already upon him? But then at last the hands of the figure came up and touched, with a caress, each side of his face – and the lips of the boy/girl stretched forward for a kiss.

In a frenzy of terror and repulsion, Paramaz found his father's sword was now in his hand. Fearful of the lips touching his, he raised the sword and struck and struck. Blood was everywhere. He dragged at the clothes of the dying figure, tearing them off one by one – striking again and again – but still the thing smiled up at him. Would the clothes never end – what was this creature? As he pulled layer upon layer away, the body seemed to shrink. Each time he struck again at what was left. At last, the sweet smile had gone – and there before him lay a baby. Dripping with blood Paramaz bent to pick it up, but it was no child – it was a snake spitting its venom into his eyes. It started to ... and Paramaz screamed, waking up covered in sweat and cowering in fear.

Night after night, ever since his return, with only slight variations, Paramaz had dreamed this dream. Once awakened by the terror, he could never get to sleep again but would lie in his own sweat waiting for the dawn to break. Had he killed his Kurdish abuser in that cave all those years ago, or was that also just a dream? Surely, surely he had not intended to kill Haik – surely it was accidental? And the brutal rape and murder of his mother on the death march, couldn't he have done something – anything – instead of thinking only of his own survival?

Often this last memory brought tears to his eyes, and sometimes he could turn his head and doze. But the repetition night after night of the same awful dream was leaving him weak and overly sensitive during the day, to the point where he was having difficulty dealing with even the simplest of tasks set him by Karekin.

It was early in the morning of Sunday the 1st October – the day the baby, rescued from the horrors of Smyrna, was to be christened into the Armenian Gregorian Church as the adopted child of Karekin Avakian. Paramaz had awoken with a start, sweating and in a state of complete mental panic from the nightmare which had enveloped him.

Armineh was up early on this morning. There was no longer the necessity to chivvy along her daughters. There was no longer an untidily dressed Haik who had to be told to straighten his tie and tuck in his shirt. But the organisation of any event was still hers to manage. The baby had to be washed and changed. She had no idea of the baby's real age, but she presumed he was coming up to one year's old. Certainly he was over six months.

Either way, this was not a month-old baby christened in swaddling clothes – the children's white christening dresses, saved since Sima was born, were of no use. Coolly and with only a slight shiver, she went to the old cupboards and brought out some of Haik's old clothes. There they lay, smelling of mothballs, lovingly stored away for the use of the first male grandchild. Not a tear dropped from her eyes as she picked out a suitable dress for the new baby.

Even at this late stage, the family weren't clear what the full name of the little boy would be. Karekin had already stated firmly that he would be prepared to 'adopt' the little boy, who would thus carry the Avakian surname – and that he would be the boy's father. The boy's godfather – an important role in Armenian families – would be Paramaz. Nerissa had agreed to be the godmother. In all Armenian christenings, it was the role of the godfather to name the child. Normally, there would have been family discussions first, and often, there were family traditions to be observed – but in the end, it was the godfather's decision. The family had indeed discussed it somewhat cursorily but assumed that Paramaz would name the child after Karekin. So it was that as the family gathered to go to the church near Taksim, where Karekin's favourite priest – Father Haruotune – presided, no one was quite sure what the full name of the little boy would be.

Despite all the political uncertainty and the worries swirling round the city, driven all the time by increasing knowledge of what had just occurred in Smyrna, the family party was full of joy and anticipation. Two carriages had been ordered from the station. This was the first full day since the tragic news of Haik's death had first burst upon them, that the family had been able to relax a little and turn their minds towards the future. Sima's happiness from the previous day was contagious, and there was a feeling that they were all ready to resume a more normal life. The sorrow over the death of the only son and brother in the family would remain always in their hearts. But for now, the four girls were wearing their best clothes and their most fashionable hats; the weather was getting colder but was still crisp and clear;

and everyone was in white, even Seta, who usually preferred blue. Olga was sporting a large hat with a wide brim, but the other three were wearing the currently fashionable, pert, 'cloche' hats.

Talin carried the baby. Paramaz was attired in his dark office suit and was the only one not smiling, looking tired and anxious. A few months before, Seta had been given one of the new black box cameras, just coming onto the market. She had been fascinated by it and was duly going around, snapping at everyone. She pointed the thing and clicked at each of her sisters as they clambered into the carriage; at her dignified mother and father as they too boarded; at the horses; at old Abdul grinning away at all of them; and, of course, at the baby. She had already become a good photographer, having learned not to make everyone pose as was the fashion, but snapping away to catch the moment. Unlike most, she could afford the waste of the occasional mistake or blurred image as people moved. Everyone was cheerful, smiling at the camera and at the baby, except Paramaz, who turned away whenever the camera was aimed towards him.

The Androvs were already in the Church when the family arrived and filed in. Morning service had ended, but there were still strangers and acquaintances in the Church. Harry, who had never before attended an Armenian church service was there, having already gone to the morning service earlier, out of curiosity. The Levonians, including George and Tamara were of course there. Of all the Church sacraments – baptism is probably the most relaxed and joyous, even more so than weddings, which tend to have a more serious, pompous, element. Everyone was still smiling after all the kissing, hugging and shaking hands had been completed.

Father Haroutune was robed in his full ecclesiastical robes and was helped by three deacons and a young 'vartabed'. Karekin might well believe that it was all anthropological nonsense, but he was not going to be outshone in the christening of this little boy, who was to be his adopted son. The service began with everyone gathered round the font at the far end of the nave; Karekin hovering at the back of the crowd – the traditional place for the father. As always, all the questions and answers, the prayers and the promises, the ritual phrases, were between the godparents and the clergy.

The baby was held by Paramaz, who rocked the child and kept him gurgling happily as the service dragged on. Armineh was there ready to help if necessary. Nerissa stood by him watching with wonder as Paramaz replied to the rituals, looking down with real affection at the infant staring back at him with big, brown, intelligent eyes. The older girls were close by and the only member of the family anywhere close to Karekin was Seta, who was still darting about taking pictures.

The climax finally came. Father Haroutune stretched his hands out and took the child from the arms of Paramaz, who almost looked reluctant to hand him over. Then firmly holding the infant who looked a little surprised, he turned to Paramaz and said, intoning the words in a full bass voice –

"What shall be the child's given names in Christ."

Paramaz looked straight at the priest and said quietly –

"Haik Karekin."

Father Haroutune held the child over the baptismal font – dipped his hand into the warm holy water and made a cross with the water on the child's forehead. Haroutune always took the precaution, particularly in the case of the older infants, of arranging for some boiling water to be added before the service. He called out in his warm and resonant voice –

"I name this child Haik Karekin and I … "

But Karekin no longer heard what the priest was saying. He held himself stiffly upright, his arms hard to his side. There was no way he was going to react in public, but he could not help the wetness in his eyes as he stood still. Seta was by his side like a shot and her hand crept into his, as full tears came into her own eyes.

Poor Father Haroutune – somehow no one now seemed to be paying much attention anymore as the service continued to its predestined conclusion. It was not a resumption of grief, it was just that this congregation all of a sudden went elsewhere, all in different directions. George became distressed; Nerissa looked on with amazement as little Haik was handed back to Paramaz;

every member of the family seemed to want some physical contact with a neighbour; Nicolai's arms went round Sima's shoulders; Olga took and held onto Harry's hand gripping it tightly. There were only two people who appeared unaffected – Paramaz was calm rocking the little boy back and forth, looking down into the smiling eyes – and Armineh, who touched no one, but looked at all her family one by one to make sure that none needed her help.

Then the tension broke.

"In the name of the Father, Son and Holy Ghost for ever and always," called out Father Haroutune raising his arms and making the sign of the cross over the whole congregation.

Then the hullabaloo commenced – people gathered round Paramaz and little Haik – there were smiles and tears as Seta ran round taking pictures of perhaps this last occasion when all the family would be present together. Only Karekin was not there. He had turned and walked out, slowly but deliberately, before the blessing.

CHAPTER 24

Sirkedji Station

It was the day after the baptism ceremony and autumn had at last arrived. The morning was overcast and there was a steady drizzle of rain throughout the whole of Thrace. The rain poured down on the Greek army, still in their neatly arranged tents on the other side of the Chatalja lines; on the British forces, holding those same lines on the European side of the straits; on the British force garrisoned in Chanak on the Asian side; on the Turks, grinning at the British troops only yards away on the other side of the wire outside Chanak; and on the Avakians.

The family were up early, getting ready for the departure of Karekin and Spiro for Sinekli to meet the Kafides family. Sinekli was less than two hours away on the fast trains out of Sirkedji station heading for Adrianople. These trains, even the slowest ones, did not stop at the suburban stations along the Marmara coastline. Accordingly, Karekin and Spiro had first to take the local train back into the city. The carriage had been ordered and had arrived, and a coffee taken out to Abdul by Talin. Karekin, impeccably dressed as usual, came down the stairs to join the others at breakfast.

Spiro had already gulped down some bread and honey with Talin in the kitchen, and was waiting there fidgeting. He was both nervous and excited at one and the same time. After all the drama and terrors of the those last few days in Smyrna, he had found great relief and security in this household, and he was fearful of leaving, though keyed up at the same time. He was at that stage in life when he was sometimes only a child, tearful at his memories, and desperate for physical comfort from any adult male or female. But at other times, he was a boy capable of jumping into the sea to save himself, ready to stand up for himself against the world and with the stirring of sexual feelings in his groin, that he could not quite control.

Spiro had arrived in the Avakian family with absolutely nothing except the clothes he stood up in. These had been stitched out for him by an American sailor on the Lawrence and consisted of odd cut-up remnants of sailor's uniforms. Armineh had already clad him with clothes originally belonging to the 12 year-old Haik. In her thrifty and careful way, these had been cleaned, ironed and stowed away over five years ago. What had been in her mind? Male grandchildren, perhaps. Either way, Spiro had worn these and had been walking around, trailing a faint smell of mothballs, for the last week. This morning, before daybreak, Armineh had arisen and prepared a small case into which she had packed more of these clothes, together with a new pair of shoes and at the last moment, throwing in an old child's short tennis racquet and a couple of ragged white tennis balls that had been a treasured possession of her now dead son.

"Good morning", said Nerissa, looking up at Olga as she came running down the stairs. "Why are you wearing those clothes?"

"Because I'm going with Baba and Spiro – and can't you see

it's raining."

"What – what's this. What's this," spluttered Karekin looking up from his tea.

"Baba – please don't fuss. I want to see what Spiro is getting into. Look, I promise I will be very discreet – no talking out of place, or contradicting anyone. But baba you know that I feel responsible for the boy – and anyway it will be company for you on the way back, if Spiro stays."

Olga, having now arrived at the table, kissed her father and ran into the kitchen so he was unable to raise any objections. She emerged holding Spiro's hand. He had been stoically waiting in dread and anticipation all this time. But Olga's warm embrace, her murmured words urging him to be brave, the firm and loving way in which she held his hand and led him out, was too much. To his intense irritation and embarrassment, his lips began to tremble and by the time they were out in the hall, the tears were trickling down his face. Swallowing hard, he managed to hold back any actual sobs. While the rest of the family stared at him, he put his arms around Olga, and buried his head in her waist.

As Olga glared at her father and the others as if they were to blame for causing the boy's distress, Armineh quietly rose and, making no overt attempt to comfort anyone, took up the case, which had been by her side and said –

"Well, well – come, it's time to be going. Seta, go and get your father's hat, gloves and coat. Olga, my love, please be sure to take your winter coat – it's a cold day already and it will be even colder in the countryside. Now Spiro – look, here is an old coat that used to belong to my son, you tried it on yesterday, remember? Good. Do you think that you could also manage to carry this case? Try it. It's quite heavy. I don't want Karekin to carry it if you can do it."

"Yes, hanum, I'm sure I can," said Spiro, swallowing his tears and coming round the table to take the coat. He put it on and then hefted the case, feeling it's weight. All of a sudden he was 12 again, and not eleven. He knelt in front of Armineh, took her hand and raised it to his forehead. Where Karekin might have pulled his hand away, Armineh said nothing thus giving a touch of dignity to what might have seemed an absurd gesture. Instead she let him keep hold of her hand and leant forward and kissed him on the top of his head.

Olga smiled gratefully at her mother. Then suddenly it was all action and within minutes the three of them had gone.

In Stamboul, the Androvs were also up and about at daybreak. Even though the Direct-Orient express was not due to leave till just before midday, Nicolai wanted to get to the station early without rushing. There were two large trunks to manage – a carriage to be obtained – and, at the other end, a porter to be hired.

For Alexei this would be the first time in his life that he would be separated from his mother. The Countess loved her younger son, but, for her, this separation was not such a great wrench. In her world, sons left their mothers and went off to serve the state in the army or some other capacity quite early. That was life as she had been brought up to expect. It had been normal for her to watch Nicolai go off to war, albeit a different kind of war than what she had expected. At the same time, Nicolai had automatically taken on his role without much thought or regret. But Andrei's position was subtly different. He had begun life on the family estate in the traditional manner of the Russian landed aristocracy. His father had arranged for him to start his studies by attending the local village school, at least until he was nine, after which a tutor would have been appointed.

But in 1914, when Alexei was not yet eight, the Great War had broken out and Count Androv had gone to war himself. Alexei had stayed on in the house attending the same village school, which no longer had the teacher the Count had employed. When he was still only ten, the Revolution had begun in St. Petersburg, and Alexei soon found that he was no longer welcome in the village, and lost all his boyhood friends. This was followed within months by the Civil War when his brother Nicolai went off to war, leaving him alone with only his mother. She had fled with him to the family property in Crimea, and

there he had remained with her until the evacuation from
Sevastopol.

So Alexei had had no father since he was eight, not even an
older brother to guide him, until he came to Constantinople and
was taken on as an apprentice by Karekin. Apart from the significant difference in their ages, his reaction to the forthcoming
separation from the Countess was in a way similar to Spiro's
feelings this morning – a mixture of nervous dread and excited
anticipation.

The Androvs arrived at Sirkedji station far too early – but it
was at the exact moment that Harry also arrived to meet his
father. He was dressed in civilian clothes. He waved at the
Androvs as he stepped out of his carriage, tipping the driver
handsomely to wait for them outside the station.

Sirkedji station had been completed only thirty years or so
earlier. The station had been built, in part, for the short-haul
local railway line going through the small suburban towns strung
along the north coast of the Marmara Sea. This was a busy line,
heavily used by the residents of these little towns. Its principal
purpose, however, was as the terminus of the various Orient
expresses – the Simplon-Orient – the Direct-Orient – the Balkan
- and so on. The Simplon-Orient had started its first run from
Paris the year before the station was completed, although the
breach cut into the great Theodosian walls at Yedikule to make
way for the lines had already been constructed.

The building had an ornate oriental façade and included an
excellent café, with tables outside, and a good restaurant inside
on the main platform. The entrance hall had a great, round,
stained glass window at the street entrance end, with a polished
marble floor and cut-glass chandeliers hanging from the ceiling.
The façade had no dome or minarets – which would have been
blasphemous – but nevertheless the architecture was reminiscent
of a mosque – or at least a small oriental palace.

When it had first opened for business, it was, for a short time,
a fashionable place to sit and have a coffee and watch the arrival
of one of the great trains that had travelled three days from the

west. But by now, these trains were running at the rate of more than one a day, and the station no longer held such allure. There was gas lighting and gas heating installed for the winter months – and on this day, the 2nd October – both were functioning.

After all the necessary arrangements and preliminaries had been settled by Nicolai:- tickets checked, porter engaged, timings carefully checked yet again, Harry, who had been hovering nearby, suggested that everyone revert to the station café. There he commandeered two tables, which were pushed together. He reminded the Androvs that an Avakian group were coming that morning as well, and that it would be worth having extra chairs available, so they would have somewhere to sit. He thought it would only be Karekin and Spiro travelling – but perhaps Sima might be coming as well, just to the station. The Avakians would be taking the fast local train to Adrianople, and would be without luggage, so it was unlikely they would arrive until an hour or so before the departure of their train.

Alexei may have been in a state of apprehension, but he was bubbling over with excitement. The atmosphere of an international railway station, with all its comings and goings, lifted everyone's spirits, as they gathered round the table to take their coffee and pastries.

The Simplon-Orient on which William Bridgeman was travelling from London was due to arrive dead on time at 8.30. The local train to Adrianople on which Karekin and Spiro were going to Sinekli for the day would leave at about 10.00. Finally, the Direct-Orient express for Vienna, already at a platform in the station would start boarding at 11.00, to leave within the following hour.

Shortly after the party had settled down, the local suburban train pulled in to the station, a little late but well ahead of the Simplon-Orient arriving behind it. Karekin and Spiro came out of the carriage, followed by Olga. Olga took Spiro's hand, and seeing Harry and the Androvs at the café, came over while Karekin strode off to arrange the tickets. As Olga moved round embracing everyone, Spiro smiled shyly all round, but eagerly shook Harry's hand, pleased to acknowledge the man who had referred to him as 'my friend Spiro Pantelis effendi'.

Just then the station loudspeaker announced that the Simplon-Orient had just passed Yedikule, entered the city and would be arriving within the next five minutes. Everyone checked the clocks and their own watches, and it was indeed exactly 8.25. Harry jumped up.

"I've got to go. I'm meeting my father off this train. I'll bring him back to have a coffee after we deal with the luggage, if he's not too tired."

He smiled at Olga and went over to the arrival platform. Karekin finally arrived at the table, kissed the countess on the cheek, shook hands with Nicolai and Alexei and sat down to order a coffee. Olga kept her eyes on the departing Harry. Only she knew how much this meeting meant to him and she was curious to see how they would greet each other.

The great train, hissing steam and moving slowly, and with immense majesty, lumbered into the station. Already the brown-coated attendants of each sleeping car were leaning out opening the door of their carriage from the outside. Turkish and Kurdish porters stood leaning on their trolleys, some already booked by those waiting to meet passengers, but most waiting to be hired as the passengers alighted. People travelled with heavy luggage, and Harry, remembering his own arrival at this station two years ago thought of hiring a porter himself – but then decided to wait and see what his father needed. William Bridgeman, a Colonel in the British army, had served in many colonial wars, mainly in Africa, before he retired. He was used to travelling light if his wife wasn't with him.

With a hiss of steam and a final shudder, the monstrous machine came to a halt, and there was an immediate babble of noise – whistles – shouts – the loudspeakers blaring out incomprehensible words to which no one paid the slightest attention. The single sleeping car marked 'Londres' which had started out from Victoria station attached to the Golden Arrow Express, was usually the first of the sleeping cars after the engine. This coach would have been shunted onto the rail ferry at Dover. After arriving at the Gare du Nord in Paris, it would then have moved cumbersomely round the 'ceinture' and attached to the Simplon-Orient waiting at the Gare de Lyons for its three-day journey to Constantinople.

Harry's heart gave a butterfly lurch as he caught sight of a young Naval Lieutenant helping his father down the steps of this first coach. Olga, going over to the newspaper kiosk to get a newspaper for Karekin, watched as Harry strode forward. She saw Harry stretch out his hand and grasp his father's hand. They stood like that staring at each other for a moment. She couldn't hear any words, and was not even sure that they were talking. And then... and then ... in the middle of a public place, with the 'natives' all around them, Colonel Bridgeman sloughed off the habits of a lifetime and clasped Harry round the shoulders and squeezed him in a semblance of a hug. It did not last more than three seconds, but Olga's heart leapt for joy as she saw that neither Harry nor his father showed the slightest sign of embarrassment as they parted.

Harry had been right to wait. Colonel Bridgeman only had a small Gladstone bag, which Harry immediately took charge of, and turned to lead the way. He found that the young Naval Lieutenant was still standing alongside, waiting to be introduced.

"Ah, Harry my boy, er... yes. This is Lieutenant Jones of the Royal Naval Legal department. Mr. Jones this is my son Captain Harry Bridgeman."

"Good morning sir", said a voice, which could have belonged to the 19 year-old Haik.

"Good morning," said Harry shaking hands, somewhat confused by the reference to the legal department. "But I thought the prosecution team had already arrived – or so I was told."

"Er... well yes sir, that is indeed so – but I am your defending counsel."

"What the..."

"Now, now Harry, my boy, don't let's go off at half-cock. I will explain everything as soon as... But hello who do we have here?"

Olga, consumed with curiosity and anxious not to leave before meeting this man, of whom she had already painted a somewhat negative mental picture, had come forward holding her newspaper. Harry turned and saw her and then unaccountably blushed and stammered out –

"Sir, this is a friend, Miss Olga Avakian – Miss Avakian, my father – William Bridgeman."

Olga, already modifying her mental picture, gave one of her devastating smiles – Nerissa would have cringed – and stretched out her hand for a firm handshake.

"Ah, Mr. Bridgeman, we have been expecting you. Please come and meet my father and share a coffee with us. I'm sure you must be tired, but we have to leave within the hour to catch another train and it would be a great pleasure if you would join us."

The Colonel was rather pleased that he had been interrupted and didn't have to go into any explanations with Harry right away. If he was surprised at the pure English accent of this beautiful, elegant woman who had just been introduced to him, he did not show it. Instead nodding at the hovering Harry to come along with the bag, he gave his arm to Olga and said –

"Well, well – let's go and have that coffee. What an amazing railway station…"

Harry could only gasp in surprise and trail along behind, with the mysterious Lieutenant Jones in tow, as they joined the party at the café table.

Two previously distinct outlooks were coming together in this meeting between father and son in an exotic foreign railway station concourse. The old Colonel had been unable to show his only son, born when he was already over 40 years-old, as much affection as the boy had craved. This had not been because William Bridgeman did not feel love – it was because, like so many at that time, he genuinely believed it was bad for a boy to receive overt signs of affection from a father. Only his wife knew that he would sometimes steal up to the young boy's bedroom at night, stare down at the sleeping child and give him a light kiss, fearful that he might awake and catch him out. Then, as he grew, Harry had left home at an early age – boarding school – university - an early entry into the navy, and then the War had separated him from his father. But for Harry, throughout these years he had struggled with an unacknowledged yearning for his father's love.

Meanwhile, as William Bridgeman had grown older and wiser, he had come to see the rather ridiculous Edwardian idea that it was 'bad form' to show a son too much affection as the misguided psychology it was. Now that his son was a grown man, his character already formed, he no longer felt it necessary to hide or suppress his feelings. Well, only up to a point. He was an English gentleman after all.

Olga's excitement, Harry's joy at the arrival of his father, and the obvious fact that the Colonel was not only determined to enjoy himself but was clearly doing so, infected everybody round the table. The general atmosphere of the station with the great trains gently steaming in and out in the background, with the hustle and bustle of the well-dressed crowds, allayed any slight anxiety about the coming partings and there was a sense of heightened delight. Karekin, also in great spirits, ordered champagne to toast the Countess. Harry made a few belated attempts to rise and leave, but the Colonel airily waved him aside.

Within minutes, the Colonel knew the relationship of everyone round the table. He fell over himself to be as charming to the Countess as Karekin was – and indeed managed much better, Karekin's spoken English not quite up to the challenge. They sparred away with an old-fashioned courtesy which delighted the Countess, as she sat back enjoying the attentions of the two grand gentlemen seated on either side of her. They, too, found that they were enjoying each other's company as well as that of the Countess – surprising perhaps in view of the enormous cultural difference between them.

The time passed quickly and and before long, the first departure – that of Spiro accompanied by Karekin and Olga – was upon them. Spiro, halfway between tears and excitement, solemnly shook hands with everyone. Then they left to walk to the platform at which the train to Adrianople was waiting, with Spiro, mindful of his promise to Armineh, lugging his case and refusing help from either adult. This finally broke up the party. Promising to visit as soon as he could, William Bridgeman said goodbye to the Avakians, and he, Harry, and Lieutenant Jones left to pick up the carriage retained by Harry earlier, still waiting patiently in the street outside.

The Androv family watched as the Adrianople train pulled out. Then at last it was the moment for the Countess to get on board the Direct-Orient express bound for Vienna, the second of the company to leave the Imperial city forever.

CHAPTER 25

The Mudania Conference

The refusal of General Harington to deliver the ultimatum, drafted by the British cabinet to the Turkish nationalists, had at last defused the situation a little. The possibility of a new war had diminished, though it had not disappeared. Lloyd George had appealed to the Dominion governments for support at Constantinople in emotional terms – referring for instance to all the graves in the Gallipoli peninsula which might have to be abandoned. The Australian government had reacted fairly positively though not enthusiastically, but the others – New Zealand, Canada and South Africa - had been distinctly cool. Above all, neither his Conservative partners in the coalition, nor the British public in general, were at all enthusiastic about the renewal of formal hostilities, while the French adamantly refused to support the British government in any way.

So it was that arrangements were made between Lord Curzon and the French President Poincaré for Harington to go to the little port of Mudania, on the Asian side of the Marmara Sea, to meet with representatives of the Turkish nationalists. The Turks had finally agreed to this. Both the French and Italian colleagues of Harington – Charpy and Mombelli – were to be present. The Turks would not allow any Greek to be present. The Allies agreed for a Greek general to be present nearby on a

Greek ship, just outside the three-mile limit.

Mudania was a typical, small eastern Mediterranean port. It had whitewashed houses straggling up a low hillside, nestled round a small sheltered bay. The little town had old timbered Ottoman houses and cobbled streets, but no stone buildings of any great size. The long pier, the only pretence to a harbour, was simple and free of any major buildings. There were shabby cafés and taverns on the other side of the cobbled street facing the pier. The population numbered about 5,000, half of whom had been Greeks until a few weeks before.

Harington decided to travel to the town, which was only a few hours away by sea from the city, in a fairly ostentatious manner by boarding the *Iron Duke* and sailing with Admiral Brock himself. They anchored in the little bay, half a mile out from the shore. All the local actors in the negotiations had agreed there should be no provocation on either side in Chanak, while the Conference was in session, and the Turkish cavalry retired a few hundred yards, though not to the extent of leaving the neutral zone.

The drizzle and overcast skies of the previous day, when the Androvs and the Avakians had met at Sirkedji station, had now turned to heavy rain. As Harington stepped onto the pier from the launch, which had brought him from the *Iron Duke*, a furious wind and sea-spray sprang up leaving him fairly wet, though not exactly drenched. Generals Charpy and Mombelli had already arrived on the pier and were sheltering behind a low wall.

The conference was to be held in the former Russian consulate – the only stone building of any size anywhere near the pier. It was bare and cold, though some Turkish carpets had been hurriedly draped about the low whitewashed rooms in an attempt to provide some semblance of furnishing. There were not enough chairs, so in the end Harington, Charpy and Mombelli were the only ones seated on one side of the table, facing General Ismet Pasha, the Turkish nationalist representative, seated on the other side.

Stubborn and wily, deaf when it suited him, Ismet – in touch with Kemal in Ankara by telephone throughout – was a good deal shrewder than appearances allowed. The telephone line had only just been laid down a few days before and went directly between the Conference room and Kemal's headquarters in Ankara. Whenever matters became difficult, Ismet either pretended not to hear or would immediately insist on checking with Ankara, while he considered a suitable response.

The conference went on all day, with Ismet jumping up and down and going to the telephone at least twice every hour. Harington not only had to consider the requirements pressed on him by London, but found that time and again, the French General was acting as a mouthpiece for Ismet. Constantinople was no longer the top of the agenda; the problem was Eastern Thrace – the small area of Europe, which had remained in the control of the Ottoman Empire in 1912 after the end of the Balkan Wars. This area had been given to Greece, by the Treaty of Sevres, signed, only two years before, by the Allies and the Ottoman government. Greek troops still patrolled Adrianople and a Greek administration still ran the province up to the Chatalja lines only 30 miles from the city walls of Constantinople.

By one of those quirks of historical and geographic development, Eastern Thrace, the area which the Turkish nationalists were demanding be returned to the Turkish state, was home to a majority of ethnic Greeks, whereas Western Thrace, now firmly within Greek borders, had a majority of Muslims. This hadn't mattered so long as both parts were part of the multi-national Ottoman Empire; but now with two exclusive nation-states vying for control, it had become a problem which these four gentlemen sitting round the table were forced to consider.

With the French and Italians ready to give in to Ankara on every point, it soon became clear that the British, too, were ready to give in on most matters affecting Constantinople. Without a shot being fired, sooner or later it was going to be handed back to the Turkish army. The Turks hinted that for their part they would not press their demand for Western Thrace, which had been given to Greece by the Treaty of Neuilly, so long as they could have Eastern Thrace back. They insisted on an immediate transfer from the Greeks and Harington was concerned problems would arise if there was insufficient time for a trouble-free handover. The Turkish demand to take over Constantinople, immediately, was also out of the question.

In the evening of this first day, Harington left for the *Iron Duke* to retire for the night. He stood waiting on the pier for the launch to arrive and as the rain drizzled down he looked at the Turkish soldiers on duty at the pier – the first Kemalist soldiers he had seen. He turned to his interpreter and said –

"My God, Blunt, they look a really grim lot."

"Yes, sir, not very smart or disciplined – but I bet they're tough fighters."

"Listen, Blunt, I would like to speak to them. Please interpret for me." Then turning to the dozen or so men, he asked if any of them had been prisoners of the British during the war.

"Certainly, effendi – Gaza camp," replied one staring at Harrington, while three of the others also nodded.

"And were you well enough fed?"

All four former prisoners broke into smiles for the first time – nodding vigorously and offering Harington a bedraggled cigarette, which he declined just as the launch pulled up to the pier.

The next day, the discussions went on and on, and in a fit of impatience, Harington produced a hastily scribbled draft agreement telling Ismet that these were his final terms beyond which he would not go. Furthermore, this very afternoon he was proposing to return to Constantinople, returning the next day for the reply. True to his word, Harington left that afternoon on the *Iron Duke*, sending a wireless message to General Marden, now in command of the Chanak garrison, warning him that it looked as if the conference was going to break up. He authorised him to be ready to open hostilities against the Turks, forcing them to leave the neutral zone. Then, once back in Constantinople, Harington made sure that all the military arrangements for holding on in Constantinople itself were in place in case no agreement was signed.

The fast local train to Adrianople steamed out of Sirkedji

station, made the great loop round the grounds of the Topkapi Palace, ran along the old Byzantine sea walls and eventually through the great Theodosian Walls at Yedikule and out of the city. Spiro sat in the first class carriage with his face pressed against the window, staring out as the little towns, all still separated from each other and from the city by fields and open country, passed by. He had seen trains in Smyrna, but this was the first time he had ever sat in one. The trains he had watched, rumbling over the river near the Caravan bridge, had almost all been freight trains of one kind or another. Spiro had never imagined such opulence and comfort as he now saw around him. Karekin and Olga chatted together in Armenian, and unable to follow, Spiro concentrated on staring out at the changing scene.

Once the last of the little towns along the Marmara coast was passed, the railway line turned inland into a totally agricultural area. There were few roads and those that did exist were merely dirt tracks. Where these tracks crossed the railway line there were no barriers of any kind. The landscape was treeless and would have been completely flat and depressing save for the evidence of careful human husbandry. Yellow fields of sunflowers, grown for vegetable oil, were dotted about, adding a touch of colour during the summer, now looking parched and crestfallen in the drizzling rain as they waited to be ploughed back into the land. Spiro, who had often gone for family picnics in the lush well-watered countryside around Smyrna, found this treeless scene sad and desolate.

The train passed through the Chatalja lines where Allied troops, mainly British, were still posted in small encampments. As the train moved on, these small camps opened out into the main Greek army camp. Spiro thrilled to see line after line of smart white military tents, with the flag of the Greek Kingdom proudly fluttering at the top of a tall white pole. It all looked neat and orderly and completely secure. Spiro knew nothing about the politics, which were fashioning his life, though he was beginning to pick up on some of the attitudes and anxieties of the adults. Although he was an Ottoman citizen, just like Karekin and Olga sitting chatting next to him, he had been living under a Greek administration since he was eight – his most formative years – so the presence of the Greek army seemed natural.

It remained difficult for him to reconile the three to four years of childhood security with the 13 days of nightmare of only a week ago. The dichotomy between the emotions of an 11 year-old child and the growing awareness of a young man, plagued Spiro. On one level, he knew he would never see his father or his brother Costas again, but on another he could still fantasise that they might suddenly re-appear, here, in what looked like a Greek community. Indeed at his most childish moments, he could even deny that he had seen the brutal death of his mother. Who knows, she could have survived! He could have misinterpreted what he saw, couldn't he? Spiro continued to stare out of the window as the train steamed on through the countryside.

Then the train pulled into its second stop on this route – Sinekli station. The station was a pleasant two-platform affair with only a few people waiting. Most of these clambered onto the second-class carriages at the back. However, there, standing on the platform, looking up and down the train, was an elderly couple dressed very formally in black, and easily recognisable as the Kafides family. Slightly behind them, was a fairly elderly man, dressed more colourfully in working clothes. They didn't move as they watched Karekin get down from the carriage and then turn to give his hand to Olga. However, as Spiro clambered down, dragging behind him the precious case entrusted to him by Armineh, they moved shyly forward.

"Mr. Karekin Avakian?" enquired the elderly man extending his hand somewhat diffidently, and speaking Turkish.

"Certainly – and do I have the pleasure of speaking to Christos Kafides effendi?", replied Karekin smiling broadly.

The man nodded his head, then turned and introduced his wife Saroula, and then his neighbour, Mukhtadir, the farmer who tilled the land next to his, and had driven them into Sinekli in his cart to meet the train. Spiro said nothing as more introductions were made. He shook hands with Mr. Kafides, looking down at the ground, and then with the Turkish neighbour – Mukhtadir - who winked at him as he looked up. Spiro smiled for the first time that day and then found himself enveloped in the voluminous skirts, smelling slightly medicinal, of Madam Kafides. Saroula kissed him on his head as she held him to her and then said – in the first Greek spoken that day to Spiro –

"Welcome – oh, welcome, young man. I, who have lost a son – and you who have lost a mother … We'll do – yes, we'll do well."

She took his hand and he relinquished for the first time his grip on Armineh's case, which was gently taken by the grizzled Mukhtadir. The little party moved off the platform and into the dirty, shabby street outside the station. There was still a slight drizzle. Here, rather like at the Cobancesme station in Makrikoy, stood a short line of carriages with their drivers huddled under the covered hoods. Further on, stood a large farm cart drawn by two strong horses. It became clear that Mr. Kafides was a little embarrassed by the open cart, and said to Karekin – nodding towards Olga –

"Avakian bey – I will hire one of these carriages for you and your daughter to travel in shelter"

For the first time speaking in Greek, Olga laughed out loud, took off her hat and swung her long hair in the rain saying –

"No, no, sir – I love the rain – I prefer the freedom of open carriages. You and papa go in the closed carriage by all means, but Spiro and I will go with Mukhtadir Bayram effendi."

Then, helped by Spiro, who kept falling in love with her over and over again, she clambered aboard the cart. Saroula had already ensconced herself in the front and was handing back big black umbrellas, which had been under the front seats.

Christos Kafides, a conservative farmer of the old school, had been a little shocked by the way this young lady had interrupted the talk between the two male elders – but he rallied and considered that this must be how it had become in Polis. He politely extended his hand for Karekin to clamber aboard as well. Dressed as he always was in an impeccably tailored grey suit, Karekin, would have preferred to go in the carriage offered, but he put on his most charming smile, opened up one of the umbrellas handed to him, and sat down with the others. The two horses started off, trundling over the cobbled streets and moving sedately through the shabby town which gave way, abruptly, to the flat treeless countryside.

All around them was the evidence of small well-tended farms. The neatness of the farmyards he passed, and the well-managed aspect of the agriculture, was unlike the usual disorder of most small Balkan farms that Karekin had ever seen. Looking on all round him and later going on a tour of the Kafides farm, Karekin saw that this was the result of generations of tender care by mainly Greek peasants, who had worked the land for centuries. The people had lived under an Ottoman government, and while it would be an exaggeration to suggest it was in any way benign, it had at least ignored them, did not discriminate against them because of their language, and allowed them to manage their own land and worship at their own churches.

There were fat cows and pigs in abundance and evidence of well-stocked and well-looked after farms stretching to the far horizon. There were Turkish peasants' farms as well – though without the pigs – but the majority were Greeks. As they trundled on, they passed only one small mosque, but Karekin had noted at least three tiny Orthodox churches.

The two men may have been irritated by Olga's intervention, but it had broken the ice. Greek became the language they spoke for the rest of the day. Both Christos and Karekin wore a fez; Mukhtadir was bareheaded. After leaving them at the farm gates, he indicated that he would return to take them back to the station in the late afternoon.

Karekin and Christos didn't really develop an easy relationship. Christos was shy and a little in awe of this Ottoman effendi from the big city. Karekin, never very good at general chit-chat, remained a bit stiff and aloof, unable to relax until he was taken for a tour of the farm after lunch. He then found himself interested in the pure 'business' aspect of farm management. As they walked round, Christos explained which were the cash crops, which the crops to be sold locally, and which were purely for the farm's own consumption. Christos lost his shyness and Karekin his reserve.

When they returned to the farmhouse and were seated in the formal sitting-room, Christos raised a matter which had been at the back of his mind for some time –

"Avakian oglu can you advise me as to what is happening in the city? What is going to happen? Who is going to govern there?"

"I'm afraid I really don't know. I hope that the Sultan will remain in some position or another, but one thing is certain, either way Polis will become Turkish again soon, of that there is no doubt."

"And here in Thrace?"

"Again I cannot say – but Thrace was annexed to Greece by solemn treaty and the British pride themselves on not treating treaties as mere scraps of paper."

"Well, perhaps, but look what happened in Smyrna."

"Yes – but that was not a treaty situation – the Greeks were there as occupiers and nothing had been agreed between the parties involved. No, no, the situation here in Thrace is different. The British signed an agreement with the legitimate Turkish government, and the Greek government. They'll act like they did over Belgium – that's the sign of a Great Power"

"Oh dear – I am not so sure Karekin effendi. Even Great Powers act only in their own narrow interest. I fear... I fear that it is going to be Smyrna all over again."

"I understand Kafides bey. I know how terrible it can be when Turks arrive, enraged and bloodthirsty ... Surely it is different here. I lost a son in Smyrna but ...."

Conversations something like this, were taking place all over Eastern Thrace as everyone, Christian and Moslem alike, waited to know what the great and good were going to decide for them.

By fairly early in the afternoon, it appearedclear that Spiro was going to stay with the Kafides. For their part, they needed some young blood on their farm. He, on the other hand, needed a new permanent home amongst a Greek community. He may have been a bit shy of the formal Christos, but he had clearly warmed to Saropula and she to him. Karekin could see that Olga was happy enough with what she saw. And so matters were settled and Spiro took up his case to the room that had formerly belonged to the Kafides son.

When Karekin and Olga left to catch the early evening train, Karekin pressed an envelope containing some gold coins into Spiro's hand, telling him to keep it safe, and not to open it except in an emergency. Spiro had spent the whole of the afternoon after lunch running about the farm, delighted with the fresh air and the sense of freedom. He loved the animals and was already making friends with the local farm labourer who worked at the farm. He was ready to settle here, desperate as he was to belong somewhere again after all the trauma of the last three weeks. What did he know or care for the wise and clever men sitting round a table in a bare room on the other side of the sea? Surely, surely he was home again at last?

On the very next day after Harington left Mudania on the *Iron Duke*, he returned on a Royal Navy frigate, leaving Admiral Brock in the city to continue preparations in the event of a military attack by the Turkish nationalist army. Further down at Chanak, General Marden received firm instructions to begin his attack on the Turkish cavalry at a certain hour, unless contacted otherwise. Harington was also armed with a telegram from London, authorising him to contest any military action within the neutral zone, if and when the current negotiations broke down, as was expected. Furthermore, he was authorised to issue yet another ultimatum threatening war if the Turks did not withdraw.

Charpy and Mombelli were waiting for him on the quayside. Once again the three generals, with their interpreters, went into the bare white-washed room in the old Russian consulate, and gathered round the table opposite Ismet Pasha. Once again, matters were discussed, the future of whole peoples, whole provinces, were bandied about from one side of the table to the other. But the atmosphere had changed – there were now only a few points of disagreement left. Ismet paced up and down the room on one side of the table as Harington did the same on the other, while the French and Italian generals looked on. At last, eliciting a quiet sigh of relief from Harington, Ismet stopped his pacing and said loudly –

"*J'accepte!*"

But what exactly was it that he had accepted – what had these four men, three representing the victorious and arrogant Western powers, and one representing a growing new nation-state, decided round this bare table.

The Convention of Mudania settled many minor matters and left open others to be dealt with later at a conference to be held in Lausanne. But its principal agreement – flashed round the world by telegraph – was that the Turks were to be free to cross the straits, to enter Constantinople, and also to take over Eastern Thrace. The Greek army was to start evacuation immediately and to retire across the River Maritza into Western Thrace, giving up the whole province and the city of Adrianople at once. Turkish gendarmes, numbering over 8,000, were to enter the province on the heels of the departing Greeks. There had not been a single Greek representative in Mudania at any point throughout the conference.

Already, men in frock coats were beginning to speak of new concepts, sanitised to sound benign, like 'exchange of populations'. What this anodyne expression meant in practice was cleansing the state of ethnic communities the Turks no longer wanted; who might be of a different religion or a different skin-colour, regardless of how many centuries they may have lived there, or whether they wanted to leave their ancestral homes.

These were civilised and reasonable men, who believed they were dealing with a problem in a humane and logical manner. But no Ottoman Sultan, however ruthless and fanatical, would have dreamt of imposing such a heartless solution on the diverse peoples living within the old Empire.

Spiro would have understood nothing of such things. Within a day or two of the departure of Karekin and Olga, he was settling into his new life and home. He began learning about animals and crops and new skills, which he hoped would help his new, adopted parents. What did those respectable men, many with impeccable liberal and humane credentials, care for the likes of Spiro and his new family? While the Kafides family carried on with their hard-working, everyday lives on land which had been theirs for generations, the statesmen were planning the final conference to settle, once and for all, the affairs of the dying Ottoman Empire; a settlement which would throw thousands more people off their lands and from their homes, the consequences of which would still be reverberating a hundred years later.

CHAPTER 26

Harry and his Father

Once the Avakians had left on the Adrianople train with Spiro, Harry and his father, together with Lieutenant Jones, clambered aboard the carriage, which had been patiently waiting outside the station. As it clattered across the Galata Bridge, there was a silence among the three passengers. The cover was closed as the rain continued, though it was open at the front. Sitting next to his father, Harry sat back and let his thoughts wander. The young lieutenant, sitting on the seat facing backwards, ignored the rain as he leant eagerly from one side to the other, taking in the views of this extraordinary city. The carriage was following the sea road to avoid the steps that climbed up to the Grande Rue. Here it was – the only city in the world to be partly in Europe and partly in Asia – the world's desire; the imperial city of Eastern Rome, the seat of the most successful Caliphate in history and the capital of the longest-lasting Empire the Moslem world had ever produced.

But while Colonel Bridgeman and Lieutenant Jones were looking round and marvelling, as the wonders of the city unfolded, Harry at last had time to consider who this Lieutenant was, and why he was here at all. He was determined to tackle the matter once all the formalities of registering at the Park Otel were completed, and he was alone with his father.

"Father, can you tell me why the Lieutenant is here with

you?"

"Listen, son, don't jump to any conclusions without some reflection. Court-martials are not all that different in the Royal Navy to those in the army – and I have had experience of these affairs in my 40 years in the Service. The formal atmosphere can be intimidating, and one can easily be dominated and overawed by the occasion. That is precisely how they are meant to be; you will usually be facing an officer whose whole, and indeed sometimes only, job is to prosecute and to portray the defendant as totally in the wrong. There is no malice in this – it is his job and all men will try to do their job as best as they can."

"Yes, very well father, but you forget that I was involved in one of the Navy's most notorious recent court-martials. You remember, when Admiral Troubridge was accused of dereliction of duty in allowing the Goeben and the Breslau to slip through his fingers, and to arrive here in this very city in such dramatic circumstances at the start of the war."

"Yes, well, that's a perfect case in point. Do you think for a moment that Troubridge would have been acquitted of all charges, as he was, if he had not had an experienced military lawyer to put his case so much better than the old duffer could have managed by himself."

"Well, what are you saying father – that I am 'the young duffer'?

"No Harry, but you need someone who can present your case for you, succinctly and unemotionally, and with the professional expertise which you inevitably lack."

"And this Jones fellow – he's very young – what experience..."

"Trust me Harry. I have just spent three days and nights with him closeted in a swaying railway carriage. He spent the whole time going through the documents given to him by the Admiralty. We talked together whenever he wasn't going through them, and though he may not be the greatest legal eagle, he knows what he is about."

"How did you find him?"

"Oh that – well I just went round to the Admiralty. They told me that they had offered you a defence lawyer and that you had refused. Well I countermanded that by offering to pay for the expenses of an officer to come with me to act on your behalf – subject of course, my boy, to your agreeing. They agreed and..."

"Father, are you saying that you have paid to..."

"Oh tosh Harry – don't be ridiculous. Now listen, the court-martial is the day after tomorrow – so you only have the one day to discuss it with Jones."

And so it was, that Harry spent the whole of the next day closeted with the young Lieutenant Jones, going through all the events of that fateful two or three days he had spent on the HMS *Lion* in the bay of Smyrna. Now that the actual court-martial was upon him, the thought of all the formalities of the courtroom, the pleadings, the speeches, and the reading of witness statements, began to cause all the familiar butterflies in his stomach. He was already imagining his arrival alongside the *Iron Duke* on a special launch dressed in full dress uniform. He pictured himself climbing up the gangplank and onto the deck; the curious stares of the sailors as he arrived; the boardroom where the trial would be held; the salutes, the handshakes, the false smiles hiding nervousness. But it was only his imagination working overtime, for things turned out rather differently.

The next morning – the day Harry was going to spend going through his case with the Lieutenant – as they were all break-fasting together in the hotel, two letters were handed to him by one of the hotel messenger boys. One was a formal note from the East Mediterranean Naval Command. This was short and terse, informing him that the *Iron Duke* had sailed that morning with the Admiral and General Harington on board and would be away on the other side of the Marmara for a day or two. Accordingly, the court-martial was now to be held at the Harbiye – the old Ottoman military academy, the headquarters of the British administration of the city, and the shore headquarters of the Navy. The message confirmed that the proceedings were not scheduled to take longer than a day, as agreed between the prosecuting officer and Lieutenant Jones for the defence. The opening statements would start at 10.00am the next morning and the note was a formal notice requiring Harry to attend at that time.

The second note was from Olga, written the night before.

"Dear Harry," it read, "we have just returned after leaving Spiro with the Kafides. It all went very well and you will be pleased to hear that both baba and I were happy with the situation. I don't think that it will take more than a day or two for Spiro to settle in, and I hope he will be able to make a new life for himself there.

It crossed my mind that you might be busy tomorrow, dealing with preparations for the trial. This may mean that your father will be on his own. I am free all day and, if it is of any interest, I would be happy to show off some of the interesting sights of the city to him. Nerissa will be finishing her classes in the early afternoon and my father will be at his office all day, but has invited everyone to Tokatlians for tea at four o'clock.

I will quite understand if your father is too tired or would rather stay with you during the day. In any event I will call at the Park on my own at about 11.00am and no doubt we can make any further arrangements, as I hope your father can at least accept my father's invitation. Respectfully yours, Olga."

"Er...father," said Harry after handing him the letter to read, "don't worry, I'm sure you won't want to traipse round the town in a carriage with this young lady. Really she won't mind a bit, we'll have a coffee together and then she ..."

"Good heavens, Harry, stop talking nonsense. I can't think of a better way to spend a morning. You'll be engrossed with Jones. No – no. But, listen, what is this Tokatlians she is talking about."

"It is the smartest restaurant, tea-room and dancing spot in Pera. It's where all the fashionable Armenian marriages take place – they have a church right next door. Many Greeks have their wedding receptions there as well."

Olga arrived about an hour later.

Tension in the city was running high, but neither the Colonel nor Lieutenant Jones was aware of it. Even Harry, who would normally have picked up on the changes in the air, had so many other thoughts on his mind, that he too was oblivious. Everybody was aware of the departure of the *Iron Duke* with Harington effendi on board. Whether Greek, Turk, Armenian, Russian or Jew, it was common knowledge that four or five generals were going to be sitting round a table at the little fleapot of a port across the Marmara – Mudania. It was expected that the basic terms for the future of the Empire and the city would be worked out there.

If no settlement was reached, and war broke out, anything at all could happen – even a bombardment of their jewel of a city. The revolution in Greece, and the flight of the King, had given some hope to the Greek community, who were aware that it was Tino's return, after the monkey's bite, that had so soured relations between the Greeks and the British. Maybe they might get Polis for themselves after all.

Speculation was rife in the febrile atmosphere of the city. Anything, anything at all, could happen. There was no going back on the new situation in Anatolia created by the resurgent Turkish nationalists – but as for Eastern Thrace and Constantinople itself, their fates were still undecided.

Like the perfect host he always was Karekin arrived early at Tokatlians. He was not entirely sure how many people were going to turn up for the tea party to which he had liberally thrown out invitations – but, in any event, he took a table for eight in the grand *thé dansant* room. Nerissa was the first to arrive. She often came here – it was a favourite spot for her and Vahan to meet after her classes at the university ended. They both loved dancing – Vahan, a natural musician who had studied music at the university before the war, was an excellent dancer. Nerissa did not have the same skill, nor did she have the natural grace of an instinctive dancer, but it was her one and only social talent and she worked at it, with her brain rather than her body.

She saw Karekin sitting alone, and came to join him at the table. After kissing her father, she sat and looked round at the salon she knew so well. She reflected that despite all the social changes wrought by the war and it's aftermath, this room had scarcely changed at all since that day in April 1915 when, as a shy young girl of sixteen, she had chaperoned Olga in this very spot. Here Olga had sat with her, holding Selim's hand under the table, neither of them saying much to each other, while she sat dreamily looking on, as officers of the army of the Ottoman Empire had danced away the whole afternoon with elegant and well-dressed ladies in their arms. Old Europe dying on its feet, with Gallipoli and about half a million deaths, only days and a few miles away.

The grand room was still much the same – a glass roof with a large and rather vulgar chandelier hanging from the centre of the cast-iron struts. Dark mahogany walls with potted palms, and other green foliage, dotted round the room. There were now more tables and less of the greenery, and that touch of privacy between one table and another, which had been carefully created in the past by the siting of the potted trees and shrubs, was no longer evident. The dance floor was larger than it had been in 1915. Quite apart from the fact that more people now danced, the American rhythms in fashion required a larger space. The dancing itself was no longer so formal and statuesque.

Nerissa smiled as she recalled the dancing on that occasion, seven years ago, when she had been so worried about the relationship Olga was rushing into. This brought her back, with a bump, to the thought that Selim was now dead – dead in the same fire that had burned up her beloved brother Haik. A tear came to her eye. She looked away from her father, who was examining the teatime menu, and wished that Vahan was here. She had sent a note to the Asadourian house inviting him to join them all – but she wasn't sure if he was back yet from his trip into Anatolia.

The next to arrive was Colonel Bridgeman, with Olga on his arm. They floated into the room – the Colonel clearly in a high good humour, both chatting away to each other. The Colonel was introduced to Nerissa and they all sat down, while Olga went over all they had done together during the day. It seemed to him, as he sat back and listened to Olga talk, that more had happened to him in the last two days since his arrival in this city, than since his retirement. But what was really important to him was the extraordinary sea change in his relationship with his son. He had never, for a moment, appreciated the effect that his telegram was going to have on Harry when he composed and sent it. There was never any conscious decision on his part to close the emotional gap between them. But from the moment of that first long handclasp, and the embrace that followed, their relationship had changed irrevocably for the better.

Each discussion brought a deeper understanding between them from their first meeting then followed by long exchanges in the afternoon at the Park Otel. The morning's leisurely tour of the city in the company of a beautiful and elegant young woman, who was so easy to talk to and who charmed him without flattery, left William Bridgeman in a contented state of well-being. The city had worked its magic.

Last to arrive was Harry, accompanied by Lieutenant Jones, and this made a perfect six. Tea was ordered. William Bridgeman and Karekin drew together and chatted about the options facing Harington in Mudania, the present military position, and where the parties to the conflict were heading. Meanwhile, the others danced. Jones turned out to be a good dancer and Nerissa enjoyed herself. Harry was a good deal more uncoordinated and didn't know any of the new American dances – but then neither did Olga. They could do the waltzes and the more old-fashioned dances, and Olga remained unusually quiet in Harry's arms.

When the party broke up, the English group to walk back up the Grande Rue du Pera, the Avakians to take a carriage back to Sirkedji station, Olga leant up and gave him a kiss on the cheek – in public! – whispering into his ear – "Good luck, Harry, good luck for tomorrow."

The next day, Harry arrived at the Harbiye military academy in good time. He was dressed in his full ceremonial uniform and was accompanied by the trim and dapper figure of the young lieutenant. As they stood at the hotel entrance waiting for the carriage to take them to the steps of the Harbiye, Colonel

Bridgeman, standing alongside, had grasped Harry's hand and
said –

"Good luck, son, good luck. Don't worry. I only hope that
faced with the same circumstances I would have had the moral
courage to act as you did. Orders are orders – but sometimes,
just sometimes, common humanity must come first. I'm totally
with you, Harry, my boy. Totally – whatever happens."

Then, fearing even now that he had gone too far, though no
longer embarrassed anymore by this evidence of emotion, he
smiled and turned away as the two young men clambered into
the carriage which trotted off round the square and headed for
the Harbiye.

CHAPTER 27

The Court Martial

Harry's vague ideas of what the proceedings would be like had
been largely correct except that the case was heard in a large
formal room in the Harbiye, rather than on the *Iron Duke*.
Lieutenant Jones and the principal prosecuting officer had put
their heads together, and quite a lot of the evidence had already
been agreed between them, without the necessity of calling
everyone. There were three officer-judges hearing the case –
one, the chairman, sent from London by the lords of the
Admiralty, sat in the middle with one officer on each side of him.
These two were senior officers from the East Mediterranean
station, sent from the Alexandria base, both of whom Harry
recognised, though he had never spoken to either of them.

There was, as he had imagined, a lot of procedural posturing
by the prosecutor and young Jones. There was the usual
obsequious address to 'my Lords', and 'my respected friend'.
There was plenty of 'with the greatest respect' when the speaker
was about to state that the witness being questioned, or the
opposing Counsel, was talking rubbish. If it came to 'with the
greatest possible respect', one knew that a fairly deadly insult was

about to be uttered. But in the last analysis, it was all fairly low-key, and there was very little fireworks from either quarter.

The radio operator on the *Iron Duke* was called and gave his evidence clearly, producing all the relevant forms and notes he had made on the day. Among one or two other witnesses, two of the officers on the Lion gave their evidence in a quiet and embarrassed manner, not daring to look at their former Captain. Apart from Harry, Jones called only one further witness, over and above those called by the prosecutor. This was the young midshipman who had been on duty throughout the whole incident. He was called to give evidence regarding the actions of the old sailor, who jumped overboard to rescue the young girl, who had been turned away from the *Iron Duke*, and who could be seen floundering in the water close to the Lion.

Eventually, Harry was called to the stand. Lieutenant Jones first took all his service details. Then he was asked to set out, in his own words, what had occurred on that day in the Bay of Smyrna. Harry spoke for several minutes, finishing in mid-sentence, unclear on how to continue. Then to everyone's surprise Jones simply said 'thank you' and sat down inviting the Prosecuting Officer to cross-examine.

The prosecuting counsel took Harry through more details, many purely formal matters for the record. He finished with two or three questions, which stood out in Harry's mind as being fairly significant. These, as shown on the court records, which Harry got a chance to see later were –

"Did you accompany Admiral Brock on his visit to General Nureddin?"

"I did."

"The Admiral required permission to put a party of marines ashore for the sole purpose of picking up, and escorting on board, British citizens who wanted to leave. Can you recall what was said at that interview? Please tell us in your own words what was said and what was the atmosphere?"

"General Nureddin was in a very excited state. Originally, he refused to shake hands with the Admiral and said very clearly that he considered the British to be the principal enemy of the new Turkey. The Admiral was tactful, but very persistent, on the question. He kept insisting that his only concern was the protection of British nationals, and pointed out that French, Italian and US boats were already doing the same. Immediately after this, he assured the new Governor – "that in every other respect we are entirely neutral in this situation."

"What did you think of that, Captain?"

At this point Harry had hesitated before replying, though this was not recorded in the dry official account, where the reply was simply –

"I find it a little difficult, sir, to set out my personal reaction as at the time it was mixed, and I have had the time since then to reflect on it. However, I believe it would be fair to say that I quite understood and admired the Admiral for the calm and tactful way he was dealing with a man who was clearly in a highly emotional state of mind. However, even then, it was not entirely clear what the Admiral meant when he assured the general with those words. I certainly took them to mean that they applied to the attitude to be adopted by any patrol which was given permission to go ashore."

"Is that all Captain?"

"No, I must admit that even then I thought the Admiral had gone a step too far, I made no comment and accepted that it was probably the least the Admiral could promise to be sure of getting the permission needed."

"Were you aware, Captain, of the pressures being applied by the government in London?"

"No, sir, I was not – nor would I have expected the Admiral to discuss such matters with me."

Then after some more points to clear up any ambiguities came the final questions –

"Captain Bridgeman, did you see the sailors on HMS *Iron Duke* pouring buckets of water down on swimmers attempting to grab hold of trailing ropes?"

"I did."

"Did you assume that they were acting under proper orders?"

"Yes."

"Were the sailors on the deck of your ship under your orders to remain at their posts?"

"They were."

"Did one of your sailors disobey your orders and jump overboard to rescue one of those swimmers who was swimming away from the *Iron Duke*?"

"Yes, Sir."

"Did you discipline that sailor?"

"No, I did not."

The trial ended shortly after with two short speeches by the Prosecutor and the Defending Counsel. The summations were followed by a short statement from the leading tribunal officer. He confirmed that judgement would be handed down formally within a month, and that meanwhile Captain Bridgeman was to remain suspended on full pay. The Court then rose and the court martial was over.

Outside in the corridor, Harry shook hands with the officers from the Lion and returned to the hotel.

He had remained calm and correct throughout the proceedings. However, the effort of concentrating on all the testimony, and answering the questions that had been put to him in as truthful a way as possible, had left him mentally exhausted. The moment he arrived back at the hotel he began to shiver and feel the cold. William had been waiting all afternoon in the lobby and jumped up and strode over to his son when Harry walked in.

Harry gave him a wry smile, and William Bridgeman, in public view and against decades of training, clasped his son in a tight embrace. Slowly but surely Harry's shivers, which only William Bridgeman had seen or felt, subsided and still his father held on. What was it about the atmosphere of this city that made it possible for the old Colonel to act so out of character – or was it perhaps his true character emerging after years of suppression.

Back in his room, Harry told his father all that had transpired, as well as the gist of the two summing up speeches. Then, with two extra pullovers, as he was still feeling cold, he dropped off to sleep, exhausted but still smiling at his father's last words as he left and closed the door behind him –

"Harry, my boy, I'm proud of you – truly proud, whatever the authorities might finally decide. You acted like the honourable man I always knew you were."

The Prosecution Speech

Members of the Tribunal, representative of the Lords of the Admiralty, this case is somewhat unusual in that there is no dispute of any kind as to the facts. In this respect we have a situation unlike most other Courts Martial. There is no question here of 'missed signals', or uncertainties as to what orders were given, or who said what to whom. The facts are clear, and both the defence and the prosecution are in total agreement as to what occurred within the British Fleet in the Bay of Smyrna on the 13th September 1922 – what signals and orders were issued by the Commander of the Fleet – Admiral Sir Osmond de Beauvoir Brock, and what were received by the Commanding officer of HMS Lion – Captain Harry Bridgeman, against whom these charges have been brought.

I will not, therefore, repeat before you the facts, all of which have already been carefully considered throughout the day. All you are asked to decide, My Lords, is whether the facts as agreed constitute an offence under the various Navy Acts, and what course of action is recommended.

I am sure that I do not need to emphasise that this is not a Court set up to determine whether the actions of Captain Bridgeman were morally correct or not. We are here simply to decide whether the defendant had any right to ignore the clear orders of his immediate superior.

No Navy or any military unit could operate properly if it was not clear that orders should be obeyed immediately and without question. When Captain Bridgeman himself ordered his men to 'lower the boats' in order to go to the rescue of some of the refugees, he did not need to argue his case with them. It did not cross his mind for a moment that his orders would not be obeyed at once. He could rely on their training to act quickly and without question. Without such a certainty, no army, indeed no disciplined body of men could ever function efficiently.

This principle applies with particular emphasis to the Royal Navy. In all ships throughout history, every sailor of whatever rank, depends on everyone else around him. The whole safety of an individual ship, and indeed that of the whole fleet, depends on the certainty of the chain of command. Suppose the Admiral wishes the fleet to move to starboard, he signals the first Captain to turn, and then signals the next alongside to make an equivalent manoeuvre, knowing that any fatal collision need not worry him, as the first Captain would have obeyed immediately.

Consider, My Lords, how impossible it would be if admirals could not be sure that their orders would be carried out to the letter by their captains, or if captains could not be sure that their orders to ordinary seamen were not equally obeyed immediately.

I would not seek to suggest that the conditions were not difficult – but the maintenance of discipline and order is even more important in such circumstances. How could Captain Bridgeman know under what pressures from his political masters the Admiral may have been labouring. Regardless of the circumstances, it was not his place to decide how the Royal Navy should react to the events that were unfolding in Smyrna on that day. It was, after all, only by virtue of the British taxpayer, and the British government, that he was there in the Bay of Smyrna at all.

My Lords, this is essentially a simple matter. Did Captain Bridgeman disobey a very clear order issued to him directly by his superior officer. You need look no further than that. If he did, he must be found guilty and should be dealt with as such.

The Defence speech given by Lieutenant Jones

My Lords, the Prosecuting Officer has in his final address pointed out that there is no dispute as to the facts in this case, and has accordingly not dwelt upon them in any way. However, I feel that I must refer specifically to one or two of these undisputed facts.

Firstly, it has been mentioned several times during these proceedings that Captain Bridgeman was present when Admiral Brock gave General Nureddin his word that the British would remain strictly neutral, and that this personal knowledge of the defendant makes him somehow more culpable. However, I do believe that it is a vital aspect of this case to analyse what was meant by that neutrality offer. I would suggest that the neutrality promised could only refer specifically to the events unfolding in the city. The Admiral had to make sure that the General understood that any patrol the British sent ashore would remain strictly neutral while

232 CONSTANTINOPLE END OF EMPIRE

ashore. It was the necessary precondition that General Nureddin demanded from the Admiral in order to allow British marines to operate on the shore to bring off their own nationals, as the French, Italians and Americans had already been doing for days. Neutrality meant not interfering with whatever was going on, on shore. No marines were to be landed – no bombardment would be made - to influence whatever was going on in the city.

The Admiral's signal to the fleet, which is the basis of the order which Captain Bridgemen is accused of disobeying, was to the effect that no 'refugees', whatever their race, should be allowed onto any British ship. 'Refugee' has a clear meaning, my Lords; it could only refer to all those unfortunate people milling about on the quayside looking for some way to get away from the approaching fire. A drowning man is not first and foremost a refugee – he is simply 'a drowning man'. Captain Bridgeman's actual orders and actions avoided the picking-up of any people, obviously potential refugees, on the waterfront and was directed only to picking up people already in the water in danger of drowning. He specifically ordered his boats not to approach the shoreline, but only to pick up people in distress already in the sea.

I would repeat that a drowning man or woman is not a refugee. When witnessing a man about to die in the sea you neither consider his race nor his political status

The signal that Captain Bridgeman sent back to the Admiral may have been a little too firm and perhaps a bit unwise for a Captain to his commanding officer, but it states the position clearly, and I will repeat it here in full. It read –

"There is no breach of neutrality in saving any human beings regardless of race, in distress in the sea. Three hundred years of Royal Navy reputation requires us to save even outright enemies from drowning, when we can."

The only intention of this signal was to make it clear that he accepted the fact that he had been present when the unfortunate promise had been given to General Nureddin, but that he wanted the Admiral to understand that he considered that his actions did not in any way jeopardise that promise of neutrality.

Of course I accept totally the Prosecutor's argument that it was not for Captain Bridgeman to decide whether the Admiral's policy of strict *neutrality was correct politically or not. But, as I have tried to show, the actions of Captain Bridgeman had nothing to do with the policy of strict neutrality, which applied to the situation on shore. I would simply say that the signal sent showed that while he was happy to accept the Admiral's decision in every respect, he believed that picking up drowning people from the sea did not breach that promise or policy in any way.*

In lowering the boats to pick up survivors drowning in the water, Captain Bridgeman believed he was acting well within the scope of his orders, and that it was a matter of using his own initiative in difficult circumstances. In this respect, I would add, my Lords, that he had already been warned by his second-in-command that his men, experienced sailors, were getting highly restive as they were forced to watch people, including women and young girls, drowning all around them; and this agitation, as evidenced by the old sailor who jumped overboard, was likely to lead to a loss of morale and was a factor that he was entitled to take into account when making his decision.

Finally, this brings me to that veteran sailor and the failure of Captain Bridgeman to discipline him. Is it really suggested that on bringing up the drowning young girl, Captain Bridgeman should then have clapped the man in irons – and then what – thrown the girl back into the sea to establish that the honourable British Navy was being strictly neutral?

I must, therefore, put it to you that Captain Bridgeman's actions were not only morally correct but were also not contrary to the spirit of the orders he had received. I repeat that he was most careful to make sure that none of the boats launched from HMS Lion that day were to go anywhere near the shore. In the end he was entitled to use his initiative in these difficult circumstances, circumstances of which his superior commander might not have been fully aware.

Accordingly I would invite you to treat the matter as one not requiring any further action.

CHAPTER 28

Departures and Arrivals

Two days later, William Bridgeman and Harry arrived at midday at Sirkedji station. His father was to catch the two o'clock afternoon Simplon-Orient Express, with its one coach at the far end marked 'Londres'. The day after Harry's return from the proceedings at the Harbiye had been spent sightseeing. He and his father spent the morning taking carriage after carriage and going round the city visiting, one after the other, all the famous sites and monuments, which visitors had stood before for over a thousand years; in particular, going into the mosques, which Olga had not felt able to take William.

In the afternoon, the Colonel, anxious to stretch his legs further, and to put some colour into Harry's cheeks, persuaded him to accompany him on a full-scale tour of the great Theodosian triple walls. These began in the north at the ruined old Byzantine Palace – the Blachernae – right on the Golden Horn, then went across the peninsula and down to the Ottoman fortress of Yedikule on the Marmara coast.

The Colonel had read up all the military manuals and dissertations about these formidable walls, which had made Constantinople virtually impregnable throughout the Middle Ages. The great land walls had never been breached in one thousand years, until the arrival of gunpowder had, in the end, changed the balance between missiles and walls forever.

On that particular afternoon, it was cold but bright. William, relaxed and in fine fettle, strode out at a pace which belied his increasing years. He took notes at all the important places along the wall, where the manuals indicated particular weaknesses or strengths. The countryside still came right up to the walls, with no buildings on the other side for some distance.

There was hardly a single point along the whole stretch which had not witnessed some dramatic event in the city's history. Almost every one of its one hundred towers had some myth or story attached to it. The Colonel noted the famous weak spot where the river Lycus ran into the city and where the ground, and perforce the walls themselves, sloped down on either side of the valley. Finally, they duly lingered at the one place where the walls had at last succumbed to the pounding of the great cannon and had been breached for the first and only time in 1453 by the Ottoman conqueror of the city – Mehmet II. This event above all others had symbolized the end of the Middle Ages. The triumph of the 'gun' over the hitherto dominant 'wall'.

In that dramatic and decisive year the last Byzantine Emperor – Constantine XI – had died as the Ottoman army surged over the walls. His power and his empire had by then been reduced to the city alone; all the rest of his empire had been lost to him. Ironically, now nearly 500 years later, as the Colonel and Harry strode along the same walls that the last Byzantine emperor had defended with his life, the power of his ultimate successor, the current Ottoman Sultan, was also reduced to this one city – all his power having fallen away, exactly as it had to the Byzantine.

Perhaps Mustapha Kemal Pasha was right in referring always to the decadent, effeminate and corrupting influence of this half-European and half-Asian city – the only city in the world that could be described as such. Perhaps she deserved the rape that was threatened by the avenging Anatolian army, drawn up on the other side of the straits.

The following afternoon after this military stroll, the Colonel and Harry arrived at midday in good time to have a lunch together in the portico of the restaurant at Sirkedji station. They were comfortable and relaxed in each other's company, perhaps for the first time in their lives. The city might be effeminate and even decadent – but it had worked its charm as always.

"Harry, my boy, what is going to become of Constantinople? What a city! What a city!"

"I really have no idea, father. It's clear that the agreements at Mudanya is going to return Eastern Thrace, and even Adrianople, to the Turks, and that inevitably will include this city. But what the regime here will be is all still in the melting pot."

"What do you mean – isn't it clear that the Kemalists have won and will simply take over"

"Well that is the most likely. However, pathetic old man though the current Sultan may be, don't be misled by all the noisy nationalist demonstrations we have been seeing in the streets. Of course all the young men are excited and appear to be wholly 'republican' in their feelings in view of the total defeat of the Greeks – but there is a deep-rooted emotional attachment to the Ottoman dynasty in the majority of the people here; a pride embodied in their sense of identity for over 500 years."

A quiet voice behind them said –

"I agree with you entirely young man."

Both the Bridgemans looked up startled. There, behind Harry's chair, stood the tall, impeccably dressed, figure of Karekin, already removing his hat and gloves.

"May I join you?"

"Certainly, sir, certainly, with pleasure. I was seeing my father off," said Harry jumping up and bringing over another chair after shaking hands. "What brings you, sir, to Sirkedji."

"Why, the departure of your father of course," said Karekin calling out to the waiter for a coffee. "How could I let such a distinguished visitor depart from my city, my world, without a proper farewell."

Only a few days ago, William Bridgeman might have felt uncomfortable at this sort of openly stated sentiment, but now he beamed with delight, and the three of them drifted into a wide-ranging discussion of the future facing the city. The Mudanya conference was still continuing. Whilst they did not put it quite like that, they agreed that there was absolutely no 'historical imperative' as to what might yet happen, and they bandied about solutions with joyful recklessness.

Eventually, the moment came when the Colonel had to board the train, waiting opposite them on Platform 1. Karekin rose, too, and shook hands –

"Last week I was here to be present at the departure of the Countess Androvna – the mother as you know of my first prospective son-in-law. Now here I am again, Colonel, to see you off. I wonder how many more departures I have yet to face from my town, my birthplace and that of my forefathers."

Karekin smiled warmly as he continued shaking hands, in an attempt to lessen the solemnity of this last comment. The Colonel and Harry strode away as Karekin turned and left the station.

Welcomed by the brown-uniformed Wagons-Lits attendant, waiting at the door of his coach, William Bridgeman turned, looked at his son and embraced him tightly, in public, yet again. Whether it was the city itself or the diverse people who lived in it, the atmosphere had worked its magic on these two English gentlemen. The Colonel boarded for the three-day journey to London and Harry turned and walked briskly away without another word.

What indeed was to become of Constantinople? Harington was still occupying the city as Allied Commander of about 5,000 troops. This might have appeared puny, compared to the 80,000 tough Anatolian peasants facing them across the straits, but this 5,000 represented a still mighty empire. An empire, furthermore, that counted among its boundaries, more Moslem subjects than any other state in the world. Sheltering behind the British occupiers, the Ottoman government still existed with a nominal authority only over the city itself. The old Sultan, Mehmet VI, indecisive and fearful, still sat on the throne – not only Sultan and ruler of what was left of the Ottoman Empire, but also Caliph, representative of God on earth, protector and ruler of all the faithful – the Moslem Umma throughout the world.

In the other camp, was Kemal, already quite clear in his own mind. There would be no 'Mussolini' solution for him. The idea of moving the capital back to Constantinople, and wielding power as Prime Minister under a dynastic throne, was not what he had been fighting for. As for the concept of 'Caliph', he looked on it as an obsolete relic of a religion he no longer believed. But he kept these opinions carefully to himself. He saw the reality behind all the noisy clamour of the professional and middle class nationalist minority. As matters stood, the conservative and pious

Turkish lower classes, together with the elite in the cities, remained deeply loyal to the dynasty. So he stepped softly. He began by introducing the questionable concept that the Sultanate as the temporal power in the Empire could be separated from the Caliphate as the spiritual power.

It was more than questionable, it was a complete misrepresentation. From its inception, the office of Caliph belonged, by tradition and acclamation, solely to the strongest ruler in the Moslem world. As the Ottomans had held the title for so long, the continuance of the caliphate had become hereditary in all but name. Mustapha Kemal was going to confound them all.

By now the Conference at Mudanya had come to an end. The documents had been signed by all parties to the accord. It soon became common knowledge that Adrianople and Eastern Thrace were to be returned to the authority of the Turkish state. Furthermore, 8,000 Turkish troops and policemen would be allowed to cross the straits in order to take control over the area and the Greek army would have to begin immediate preparations to abandon the province and leave without raising a finger in opposition. This was despite the equally solemnly signed Treaty of Sevres. This treaty had allotted Adrianople and eastern Thrace to the Kingdom of Greece, clearly defining the area to be annexed to Greece.

That treaty was now consigned to the dustbin, unlike the guarantees given by solemn treaty to plucky little Belgium ("more than a mere piece of paper"), the repudiation of which had aroused such moral indignation in the British public only eight years previously. The British Empire had begun its slippery slide, both from its high moral position and in its political reach. It was undeniable that the peace, which Harington had sifted out from the morass into which British policy had fallen, was most welcome. It was equally true that any armed conflict would have been needless, and probably futile. Nevertheless, in the longer scale of history, Churchill and Lloyd George were right. The retreat over the crisis of Chanak marked the high-water mark of the British Empire, and its turning point. From the Mudanya conference onwards it was downhill all the way and within a mere thirty years ...

But still the question remained – what was to become of Constantinople? Mustapha Kemal was now in Bursa, halfway between the two wings of his army, one facing the peninsula leading to the Bosporus, the other facing Chanak ready to pounce on the Dardanelles. With the decision taken to hand over Eastern Thrace to the nationalists, Kemal now appointed his friend Refet Pasha to be the new military governor of that province, replacing the Greek administration. Then he declared that Refet's headquarters were to be in Constantinople itself. This was a particularly brilliant decision. It was well within the spirit of what had been decided at Mudanya, but it had the effect of introducing into the city, right under the noses of the British and the Sultan, a high-ranking representative of the Ankara government.

The Galata Bridge again!

Four years after the arrival at this same point of General Franchet d'Espery - desperate Frankie – and his dramatic entrance into the city on that symbolic white horse, another steamer, with Refet Pasha on board, approached the same spot. It was the 19th of October, scarcely a week had passed since the signing at Mudanya. The whole harbour was awash with hundreds of small boats sailing out from both the Asian and European shores – all festooned with the red and white flags of the new Turkey. There was a cacophony as all the ferries and steamers on the waters hooted and shrieked their sirens. Thousands of people milled about in the streets – the bridge itself was impassable, filled with excited men. At the Stamboul side of the bridge a great cluster of women stood ululating; more significant was that most were unveiled, with their hair uncovered in full public view, and not a single look of disapproval went in their direction. It was a portent of things to come: Arab culture – Arab mores – Arab language – even the Arabic alphabet, all about to go into the dustbin, and these unveiled women, standing at the far end of the Galata Bridge, symbolised what was to become one of the most deep-rooted and radical revolutions in history.

As the steamer carrying Refet Pasha finally drew alongside the bridge the noise was deafening. A huge roar arose from the crowds as Refet stepped ashore. Of course the vast majority of the crowd were Turks – but this was Constantinople not Smyrna. Thousands of Greeks, Jews and Armenians, less enthusiastic perhaps, but nevertheless in the midst of the enthusiastic crowds watching a moment of history, together with foreigners from all over the world. Harington had made sure that there would be no British soldiers present in uniform. Karekin could not have kept away. He invited Johannes Levonian to walk down to the bridge with him, but Johannes, fearful and apprehensive declined. George, however, was equally curious, and agreed to accompany Karekin. After all, instead of the arrival of an army, here was the historic arrival of one man.

Smiling broadly, Refet stepped ashore onto the quayside under the bridge. Youthful looking, with the Ankara style fur kalpack on his head, he looked immaculate and 'modern' in every sense. His moustache was turned up in a sharp point, similar to that of the former German Kaiser and the wretched Enver Pasha, but somehow without the arrogance. As the crowd shouted enthusiastically, he was met by the aide-de-camp of the old Sultan himself. No one, outside the officials waiting on the quayside, could hear a word of what was being said – but Refet shook hands with each one, expressing his religious devotion to the Caliph, and the persons representing that office. However, he carefully refrained from making any mention of the Sultanate and never once referred to the doddering elderly Mehmet VI. Karekin, who had managed to get into the room of a friend's house in Karakoy overlooking the bridge, saw the Sultan's ADC turn visibly pale at one point, though he had no idea why.

There was no white horse for Refet as he struggled up through the crowds onto the bridge. Here an open topped car was waiting for him. He stepped in and stood smiling but standing stiffly to attention, a small and elegant figure as the car drove slowly off. His first stop was at the tomb of Sultan Mehmet

II – the Ottoman conqueror of the city. As Harington had ruefully been reminded, the people of this city – Greek, Turk, Jew or Armenian - never forgot a single moment of their history. Everything they did, every event, held some significance from the past. All along his route, sheep had their throats cut ritually and prayers were recited.

Refet had come with a personal bodyguard of no more than 20 gendarmes. Officially, he was only the military governor of Thrace on the other side of the Chatalja lines, and had no authority in the city. But such was the emotional atmosphere of the majority in the city, it was immediately apparent that all power had finally and irrevocably passed from the Sultan's government. Furthermore, it soon became obvious that the days of Harington's command at the head of the British occupiers, were also numbered.

With Refet's landing, and his triumphant procession to the tomb of Fatih, Karekin saw, with his own eyes, the fall of the dynasty to which he had given political loyalty all his life. He turned to George, standing next to him at the window watching the events unfold on the streets below, and said

"Well, well, George – this is the end of the Ottomans. Sad in a way, I suppose, but on the other hand it looks fairly promising doesn't it – the crowds are in a good humour."

"So it would seem, sir, but nevertheless I have persuaded my father to book a passage for the whole family on a boat leaving in a few days, bound for Famagusta. We haven't had a summer holiday this year and have booked a hotel on the slopes of the Troodos mountains for a two-week holiday. Don't forget, I was there and saw what happened in Smyrna – three days of discipline and good humour soon turned to riots and eventually bloodshed and rape."

"Yes, but George this is Bolis!"

"So what, sir. You see all the emotion and passion – it could so easily turn violent. Look at these crowds, do you think that the small British force here could stand up, for one minute, to a mob intent on breaking into giavour homes or churches."

"You're understandably prejudiced by your experience in

Smyrna. There are no specific, defined 'quarters' here. No, no, a bit of unpleasantness here and there, perhaps, but on the whole, all will be well."

"I hope you're right sir, I hope so. However there's no harm in our taking a short holiday now. Our house and our street in Bebek is known to be largely Armenian."

Two days later, George and Tamara left with their parents for their holiday in Cyprus. Before leaving, Johannes and Karekin quietly confirmed several business engagements bringing their partnership to an end, but also making prudent arrangements for dealing with affairs in the event the Levonians were unable to return, or the Avakians were forced to leave in a hurry.

George's fears were not unfounded, but for the moment the centre held. However, the pent-up passions of the last three years during which those who supported the Ankara nationalists had had to keep a low profile, now burst out into the open. The authority of Harington's police force dissipated and began to flow away, while the doddering, garrulous old Sultan, at the Yildiz Palace, became totally irrelevant.

A vacuum of power arose in the city. While Ankara had finally and completely prevailed, it was even now uncertain how it would all end. The nationalists were nearly in full control, but not completely. Constantinople drifted into a semi-anarchy, as the various parties involved jockeyed for position, and preparations began to send representatives to Lausanne to hammer out a final and hopefully lasting peace between the Ottoman Empire and the Allied governments with whom they had technically been at war for over eight years. It was against this backdrop that the Avakians and their friends, were still having to make decisions about their future.

CHAPTER 29

What's in a Name?

Small children, whether they have big brown eyes, flashing blue ones, or small black ones, adapt quickly to new conditions. Vahan watched six year-old Rehia playing with a doll Ara had bought for her in the Kapali Carsi, when on his way back home from work in Garabed's retail shop.

Nouritza Arabian, the only other survivor from the massacre that had destroyed all the Asadourian women, had been unable to trace any of her rather remote relatives, after the little party returned from the village of Chehan to Constantinople. Accordingly she was staying on at the Asadourian house to look after Rehia during the day. This enabled the four men to continue to go to work as before. Ara had always left the shop and warehouse earlier than the others, in order to prepare the evening meal, and this arrangement continued.

But the little house was cramped, so Nouritza arranged to get lodgings nearby, with another widowed lady. She would arrive at the Asadourian house in the morning and would leave as soon as Ara returned.

The Asadourian house was just to the south of Taksim Square near the Park Otel, in an old Ottoman building on Osmanli Sokag, one of the steep roads running down to the Bosporus. From the first moment that the little girl had stepped into the all-male household, she had totally disrupted their routines. It was not just a question of having a female in the house. It was more than that – her liveliness and continual chatter completely disoriented the four men.

Garabed, stern and with a short fuse, was totally enthralled by his new daughter. She was not spoilt by him – he remained the conservative paterfamilias of old – but he had noticeably mellowed. The fact that his daughter, like him, could only speak Turkish, had created an immediate bond. An old-fashioned Ottoman, Anatolian, Armenian, Garabed had never concerned himself with his previous three daughters. There was no question of educating them beyond the age of twelve, and he had left the details of obtaining husbands entirely to his wife.

But then, unprotected by Vahan's status as a Turkish officer in April 1915, those that were married and in other families were slaughtered in the first wave of deportations that hit Caesaria that month. That had been followed, as he had always known in his heart, by the murder – for surely that is what it amounted to – of his beloved and gentle wife, when she too was forced to trek out of the town, with the last of the remaining Armenian women and children. Garabed believed that he had lost every female in his family.

He was a healthy and active male and he had missed his wife. His last loving sexual encounter had been with Ara's mother, under the night skies during that desperate escape across the Anatolian hills. But that too had eventually ended in abduction, and ultimately rape and death, for the woman he had loved. In neither case had he been able to protect the women in his life. He suffered survivor guilt to a degree quite unsuspected by Vahan. Sensitive to others' feelings, Vahan understood the concept of survivor guilt, but having escaped the horrors himself, lacked the firsthand experience of the torments his father was going through. Raffi, on the other hand, having still been at home when these terrible events occurred, had gone through the experience but lacked the insight to understand the concept of survivor guilt. Poor Garabed could not get the gentle Mariam out of his mind, but found himself drifting to the little back streets parallel to the Grande Rue de Pera, which Raffi had coarsely recommended to Vahan.

Garabed would never have thought there was much complexity to his character. But here he was, a survivor of the terrible events of 1915, making a living in an environment in which he was not really comfortable. Inevitably, he blamed the Ottoman dynasty for all the ills which had been visited on him and his family since that April in 1915. But he remained an Ottoman gentleman at heart. He only spoke Turkish and he had lived his life in the manner and style of an Ottoman citizen of good standing, with the sole exception of religion. Even in that, he was closer to his pious Moslem neighbours than they were to the new nationalist rulers. He prayed, not in the western style with his hands and palms together, but with his arms raised up to either side, and he was used to seeing his women servants, and even one of his over-pious daughters, touch or kiss the floor at the name of Christ – in a decidedly Moslem fashion.

Of course he had not remained completely untouched by the nationalism of the late 19th century which had affected everyone – Turk, Greek and Armenian alike. Nevertheless, he distrusted all these bright young men in the ARF and other revolutionary organisations. He disliked all their glib talk of 'blood', 'martyr-dom', and 'national destiny' – the blood to be shed always being that of others, particularly that of the peasants and farmers of the interior. Garabed worked with these simple country folk. He could see that they only wanted to get on with their lives; he liked them, whereas the revolutionary nationalists rather despised them. He was wary of all those city-educated revolutionary academics, urging the farmers on to martyrdom.

Yet he had made sure that his sons received a good education from those very same academics, some of whom, in fairness, had sacrificed themselves to come and teach in the provinces. He was proud that they spoke good Armenian – that they read Armenian literature and poetry – that his eldest son spoke excellent English and a little French. But for all that, there was a residue of something he couldn't analyse. Not envy; it was a sort of distance, which separated him from his two sons, a distance which didn't extend to Ara, the farmer's son and now his own adopted son.

And, above all, it didn't apply to Rehia.

Raffi didn't have the slightest trace of survivor guilt. He wouldn't have understood the term. He was not the least bit sorry that he had survived, where so many others had perished. Why should he feel guilty about it? He had won through entirely by his own unaided efforts. He hadn't been selfish; he'd tried to help others survive, notably his young friend Dikran – but he couldn't help the fact or feel guilty that Dikran had died in his arms.

Vahan, on the other hand, had been living in Constantinople

throughout those terrible months. He had no personal experience of what it meant to be hunted and cut down, merely
because he belonged to a particular ethnic community. He had
no idea of the inchoate jumble of emotions, which swirled about
in Garabed's head. When he saw the distress in his father's face,
he thought it was continuing sorrow for the loss of his wife – and
he knew nothing of the guilty monthly visits to the shabby rooms
in the seedy streets nearby.

Both Vahan and Raffi adored the little girl and, as so often
happened, it was the cheerful, unthinking, insensitive, extrovert
Raffi, who treated her roughly like a boy, who became her
favourite. Vahan had come home early on this particular day. He
watched as Rehia talked non-stop to the doll, playing some game
of imagination he could not comprehend. This was his sister – his
full-blood only sister, the only surviving daughter of his father. It
was a wonder she wasn't already spoilt, yet it was only a few
weeks since she had first arrived – they would have to be careful.
Despite all the turmoil in the city, the news of the Mudanya
agreement, the arrival of the dapper Refet, dinner parties and
social activities continued. This was, after all, sophisticated
Constantinople, not grim Ankara. Even among the supporters of
the Kemalist nationalist movement, 'kef' still ruled – it could not
be changed overnight. So it was that on this afternoon, Nerissa,
with Seta in tow, was due to come for an early dinner with the
whole family.

"My father believes that the Ottomans are at last finished and
that Mustapha Kemal Pasha intends to get rid of them once and
for all. What do you think sir?" asked Nerissa.

The conversation round the dinner table was in Turkish.
Nerissa and Seta were the only ones not entirely fluent, being
more at home in Armenian, English and French. Poor Garabed,
even after all these years in the city, could not get used to the idea
that a 20-year-old girl could openly address him like this. But he
was learning.

"My girl, I cannot believe that he will be able to dismiss them
just like that. The Sultan's government is crumbling, that's for

sure. Refet Pasha is slowly going to take over the city. But to get rid of the dynasty that has ruled us for 500 years. No, no. It won't be that easy. I think he will depose Mehmet, it's well within our tradition, and make his son, or some other member of the family, Sultan in his place – but only as the nominal head of state – like constitutional monarchs in the west."

"It's not only the government from the Yildiz Palace which is disappearing, father. The British, too, are being eased out and I don't think they like it," said Vahan. "Day by day Harington effendi has less and less authority and Refet has more and more. There may not be anarchy, but there is a power vacuum. Though the police are still around, they no longer know from whom they should be getting their orders. The old Ottoman officials are slowly resigning, but as yet Refet can't take full control."

"No anarchy, yes," called out Raffi finishing his soup, "but the streets are no longer quite as safe as they were even a few days ago. Nothing racial, or anything like that – at the moment, at the moment – but there are a lot of plain criminals about and there is a hesitancy in dealing with them, as they hide their purely criminal intentions behind nationalist patriotic slogans."

"Are we going to face a Smyrna here then, Raffi?" piped up Seta, shocking the unfortunate Garabed even more – surely the girl was only 15 wasn't she.

"No, no, Seta, no. I think that at last we can forget that awful episode. Since Mudanya, there will be no more fighting. There will be some sort of triumphal parade on the part of the better-disciplined sections of the army, but most of them will be shipped straight across the straits and directly into Thrace. The fear of another Smyrna has passed for good."

There was a murmur of agreement all round.

The light was fading as the dinner came to an end. Madame Arabian took Rehia up to bed and left for home shortly after. Rehia rather clumsily shook hands with Nerissa and Seta and, after kissing her brothers and father, skipped out, not deigning to hold Nouritza's hand. They all moved into the sitting room while Ara went out to make the coffee. The conversation turned to the decisions that soon needed to be made about Rehia.

"Look, baba, surely Rehia is going to go to an Armenian school." Raffi and Garabed had been talking together, but the others now started listening, and the discussion broadened out. "If that is so, she should use her Armenian name. She was baptized Satenig – and Satenig is what she should be called."

"Baptized?" said Vahan. "I'm not so sure brother. There were scarcely more than a few hundred or so Armenians left in the town when she was born – and none of the churches were functioning after the priests were all murdered."

"Well, yes, I think you may well be right," said Raffi, remembering that he had been forced to watch the public hanging of all his own schoolteachers, "but it's not relevant. Mother named her Satenig and Digin Arabian, for instance, always knew her as Satenig. Above all, how can we put her into an Armenian girls school with such an obviously Turkish name."

Garabed sat forward on the hard chair he preferred, leaning on his stick with both hands. This was his daughter they were talking about – but what was for the best, he simply didn't know. He looked at Nerissa who hadn't ventured an opinion yet. Now, encouraged by his questioning look she said –

"The real problem is Rehia herself, not whether she will have any difficulty in an Armenian kindergarten or school having a Turkish name. Since first learning to speak, she has known and thought of herself as Rehia. Her mother – oh I'm sorry, sir, but Gulmaz hanum was the first person Rehia knew as her mother – called her Rehia. In her own mind she is Rehia. Requiring her to change her name may cause resentment; a feeling that we are trying to force her to forget her 'ana'. I would be very careful how you set about it."

"Oh come on Miss Nerissa," called out Raffi. "She's only six – she's a little girl. Possibly a day or two of tears, but then she will be Satenig again, if everyone calls her that. She'll have forgotten Rehia within a few weeks."

"Actually, Nerissa," said Vahan interrupting, "you can't dismiss the school and culture problem. I accept that what the teachers or the other children might think for a day or two is irrelevant – but her name is symbolic of other things as well. Is she going to be a little Turkish girl, brought up in the Armenian culture, or is she to become an Armenian girl, raised as part of the Armenian community, without any doubts or uncertainties?"

"Another thing," said Raffi, "she must be baptized sometime. She's our sister, her name is Asadourian, by right and by law. How can we give her a Turkish Christian name – it's a contradiction in terms. She has to go back to the name she was given by her biological mother. Frankly the sooner we all start referring to her as Satenig, the better."

Garabed sat straight up on his chair, his hands folded over his stick, with his chin now resting on his hands. He saw Nerissa's point very clearly – Rehia came easily to his lips. But his dear wife, who had borne all the suffering alone in giving life to this little girl, who had died with her in her arms and, shielding her with her own body as she fell; her last words were probably a whispered – 'Satenig'. He was always so good at decisions – what was wrong with him? He looked across at Seta and, despite himself, he gave her too a smile, inviting her comment. It was clear she had wanted to say something. However, despite the ease with which she participated in family discussions, she recognised that in this household, she should not express an opinion until invited to do so by the father. She almost felt like raising her hand, like at school. But then she saw the old man raise his head from his stick and smile at her. Thus encouraged she said –

"Oh, sir, I'm sorry to interrupt but I would like to say something – don't look at me like that Nerissa, Barón Garabed has indicated that...."

"Yes, yes – go on, my girl, tell us what you think."

Seta blushed, for suddenly everyone was looking at her. Then she looked up and saw Ara giving her a great big secret wink and that gave her even more encouragement.

"Sir I do think that my sister has a point. Forcing Rehia suddenly to change her name, as if we want her to forget her 'ana' and her first six years of life, will seem to her unjustified and she will resent it – and perhaps all her life. It's not, Raffi, just a matter of a few tears and then everything will be fine. It's the sort of thing where you end up lying in bed, hugging your doll and thinking my secret name is Rehia. On the other hand – oh dear, Daddy always tells me to try and avoid that phrase – she is Armenian, she is your daughter and your real sister and the problems of culture and community will.... Ah well. Could I ask why shouldn't she have both names? Her baptized name will be 'Satenig Rehia Asadourian'. It can be explained to her that she is a very special girl and has two names. Some will still call her Rehia – some can start by saying Satenig, though it would be best if there was some consistency. I remember that Haik used to be called Moug as a sort of nickname, up until he was eleven. This didn't prevent him being called Haik at the same time. I mean if..."

Seta at last ground to a halt. Blushing by now a deep crimson, she suddenly realised that she had stood up in the middle of her contribution – and she sat down with a bump.

There was a long silence as Seta looked down at her hands, now primly folded on her lap as Sima had taught her. Then at last Garabed raised his head from his folded hands and said – not using words like 'my girl' or 'my dear' –

"Oriort Seta you have settled the problem sensibly. I compliment you. You, Raffi and you, Ara can start calling her Satenig as soon as it has been explained to her that she has two names. I will for the moment stick to Rehia. Everyone else can decide for themselves. She will be baptized next week – Satenig Rehia – and I won't stand for any black-robed priest complaining that the second name is not a Christian one. Eventually, she will make up her own mind over which name she prefers."

He stopped for a moment and looked at everyone in turn. They all remained silent. It was as if by arriving at a decision, he had reasserted his position as head of the family. It only needed a look for him to quell the objection that Raffi was about to raise. Vahan too swallowed what he was about to say.

Then he turned to Nerissa and said –

"Miss Nerissa could I request a really great favour, one which might not be easy for you but which I would really appreciate..." Garabed would have blundered on with Turkish-style compliments forever, without getting to the point, but Nerissa cut him gently short, saying –

"Barón Garabed – please ask me, I will happily do what I can."

"Hmph...Could I ask if you would take on the task of explaining to Rehia, in the way I believe only you can do – the coming baptism service and her two names, one named for her by her 'ana' and the other given to her by ... given to her by ... by ..."

"Her real mother," supplied Nerissa quickly. "Certainly, Barón. In fact, I am free for the next two days and could come tomorrow after breakfast – but please explain the position to Digin Arabian. I think I would like to start by taking....", she swallowed, but then smiled, almost as stunningly as Olga, at everyone "Satenig Rehia out to look at some of the boats."

Seta beamed with pride at her wonderful sister, as they got ready to take the carriage to Sirkedji for the return home.

CHAPTER 30

Panic in Thrace

Rumour and fear! How is it they spread so quickly? One person tells another, he passes it on to the next with a dramatic flourish to make it more interesting. It spreads and envelops and crosses whole countries in a flash. The news of the final decisions arrived at in Mudanya began to spread in this way among the Greek farmers of Eastern Thrace. What everyone heard was that the Turkish army was crossing the straits to return after four years – that same avenging army that had wreaked such a terrible vengeance in Smyrna only a few weeks ago.

The Greek army, in fairly good shape here, despite scare-mongering reports to the contrary, was massed on the other side of the Chatalja lines. But it was not gouing to be allowed to make a last stand. Greece itself was in utter turmoil. A revolution had broken out and King Constantine had fled. The country was bankrupt and had been abandoned by the British, who had egged them on so disastrously in the first place. Britain, too, had had its own form of revolution with Lloyd George the first casualty, his government fell and he left office never to return.

But what all the thousands – the hundreds of thousands – of these ancient tillers of the soil saw, was the sight of the Greek army hauling down its flags and marching away; away from Adrianople, away from Constantinople, across the River Maritza and out of Eastern Thrace. Thereupon, the rumours redoubled in force, as these people who had lived in the province for generations, whose ancestors and way of life could be traced back centuries, began to hear the dread words – 'exchange of populations'. Words which well-meaning men in Western European sitting-rooms thought up as a 'tidy solution' to a tedious problem, but to the people involved, meant new horrors and the abandonment of the only lives they had ever known.

So it was that one by one, and then in the hundreds, and finally in the thousands, these people, mere statistics to the men in London, Paris and Washington, began to up sticks and move.

"But Kafides bey, my friend, why are you leaving? Why? Has not our Ghazi, Mustapha Kemal himself, confirmed that no one is to be harmed. This is your own land. I remember well your father discussing crops with mine, and his clever brother, your uncle, who left and went to the city. How can you just leave like this?"

"Mukhtadir effendi, I know, I know, but see what happened at Smyrna. There too, the Ghazi said that no one was to be harmed – but what happened is not just rumour or speculation. You heard what this boy has told us. Do you think he is lying, my friend? My old friend – I do not fear my neighbours, I never have. But it was not 'neighbours' who carried out all the rape and killing in Smyrna. I fear the outsiders who come among us and stir up hatreds that never existed before."

"But Costas effendi, everything you own, everything you have worked for, all your memories, your friends, are here, here. You were born here, you were circumcised ... er... I mean baptized here. All you have or have ever had is here. How can you just up and leave?"

"Haven't you heard, my friend, that they are all going to meet in some town in Switzerland? There, they will decide the fate of all the populations living in eastern and western Thrace. Those of Moslem faith will be forced to move either here or to Anatolia, while those, like us, who live here as Orthodox Christians will have to move out. They don't care what language we speak or what beliefs we hold. Should I wait to be thrown out and find myself at the end of a long queue – or should I try to keep ahead of the mass exodus to come?"

Spiro stood by the side of his new foster-father. He had been on the farm now for about two weeks and, already, the days spent with the Avakians were an age away. The memory of those few days of warmth and kindness were fading, whereas the horror of those last two weeks on the quays of Smyrna were returning to plague his dreams. His new parents were kind but firm and Costas urged him to learn as quickly as possible all about the farm and animal husbandry.

The young Turkish – well, he spoke Turkish – hired help arrived early every morning and had been told by Costas to arouse Spiro if he was still sleeping. Spiro struggled out of his bed on hearing Ali shouting at him outside his window. He would immediately join him – milking the cows – leading them out to graze – dealing with the hens – the goats, and everything else that needed seeing to in the morning. Only after three hours of work did they both come in to eat the breakfast prepared by Saroula and ready for all of them round the kitchen table. Costas also grew tobacco, but this was more specialised work and he told Spiro that this would become his particular expertise next year, when he would be taught all there was to know about the growing and marketing of this cash crop. For now, he should apply himself to learning the general principles of running a small farm.

Spiro was essentially a city boy, and struggled initially to adapt to the rigorous work and the early rise before dawn. But the routine and the physical labour soon came to soothe him and daily, he suffered less and less from bad dreams. Within days he took on strength and looked more and more like a young man, and less like a child. For the first time since that dreadful day of the 13th September in Smyrna Spiro had begun to feel settled.

But for Spiro, these satisfying days was going to be a mere interlude in a the continuing tragedy of the disintegration of the Ottoman empire. On the very next day, after Spiro had listened to the conversation with Mukhtadir, Costas told his wife and Spiro that they were going to leave and join the hordes of farmers and peasants already trailing across the plains towards the old Greek frontier, now destined to become the new one.

As if in sympathy with the tears shed by all the people forced into exile, the heavens opened and the rain poured down. What roads existed – mostly just paths – turned to seas of mud. Neither the hired hand nor Mukhtadir turned up that morning as Spiro and Costas got out the cart and began filling it with the things Saroula put out at the door – mattresses on the bottom – then the better carpets, the sewing machine, a roccoco mirror, pots and pans, knives and spoons, the useless old grandfather clock that had stood in the hall and which could not, simply could not, be abandoned. Then the clothes and Spiro's own bag, originally packed by Armineh with all the clothes that had belonged to Haik, some barely unpacked, joined the growing pile. Finally the same three umbrellas which had sheltered Karekin and Olga all those days ago were placed on top.

The river Maritza was over a hundred miles away and the question which exercised Costas was 'fodder' for the animals. He could only move all these belongings on the overladen cart, if his horses could drag it along, and they needed to eat. Then, there was the herd of cows? He only had five, but while they would provide milk on the way and would constitute the nucleus for a new herd, they too needed fodder.

In the end Saroula provided the answer – neither she nor Spiro would ride on the cart. The top of the cart would be covered with such straw and hay as they could gather together. The hens would be settled onto the hay, the tools would be packed in under the straw, as would what food, cheese, olives and bread they could manage. For the two adults, it was heart-breaking as they contemplated their denuded home. For Spiro, mixed in with the fear of the future, there was nevertheless also an excitement and a sense of being closer to his foster-parents in shared adversity.

At the last moment, just before setting out, Mukhtadir turned up. This moment would be repeated over and over in both the Ottoman world and, within weeks, in the Kingdom of Greece as well. The knowledge that they would probably never meet again; the strange feeling of shame and sorrow on the part of those remaining as they said their farewells to their neighbours whom the bright young academics and nationalists on both sides assured them they had hated; the anticipation and fear of the ones being forced to leave, abandoning everything they had known and loved; all was the same, both for the Greek-speaking Moslems having to leave the Greek Macedonian countryside and the Turkish-speaking Orthodox having to leave the old Ottoman world.

They said little to each other – there really was nothing left to say. The rain fell unceasingly as slowly, churning up the mud, the little procession moved off. Costas, walking ahead with his scythe over his shoulder; Saroula, following, leading the two horses pulling the creaking cart; Spiro, bringing up the rear, driving the five cows who plodded on following the cart. Mukhtadir stood and watched as the little party went on over the flat plains into the distance. He didn't wave, but watched until they disappeared from view. Then, with a sigh, he turned into the empty farmhouse whose door swung open to see if there was anything left worth taking back to his wife.

Costas, of course, had not simply stumbled away from his house without having some idea of where to aim for. He knew that he could not just strike due west to take the shortest way to the Maritza. There were swamps and impassable roads that way, if any roads at all. He decided to make for the railway line and then follow it all the way to Adrianople, and from there they would cross into Greece. Unfortunately, thousands of others throughout the province had the same idea. So it was that travellers, still riding comfortably on the carriages of the 'Compagnie Internationale des Wagons-Lits et des Grands Express Europeen' – the Orient Express –stared out of their windows at line after line of Greek peasants trudging, mostly on foot, with their chickens round their necks, their wheelbarrows and carts heavily laden and soaked through, their animals and all other worldly goods, passing on each side of the railway lines. The French directors complained both to the Greeks and to the British authorities in Constantinople that all these people were interfering with the efficient running of their services.

Within a few days, Spiro and his new family found themselves part of this long line of refugees, soaked to the skin from the incessant rain. Small children, younger than Spiro, staggered along carrying any number of items, draped round their little bodies, some obviously useful, but many not. Their glazed and tired eyes looked up with wonder as the trains of the Orient Express passed by in each direction, with the 'haut bourgeoisie' of Europe staring back at them with little comprehension or compassion. Even pregnant women walked rather than add their weight to the overloaded carts and the oxen pulling them.

The Kafides party had almost reached Adrianople, not far from the railway and road bridge crossing over the River Maritsa into the old borders of Western Thrace. They were about 30 miles away when the whole line of carts, animals, wheelbarrows and exhausted people came to a complete standstill. Far away across the plains, whenever the rain lifted, they could see the minarets of the old town in the distance. But now everyone and everything was completely stuck – jammed along the so-called road on both sides of the railway line.

"Spiro, it looks as if we'll have to stop here for a while. I'll take one of the horses and ride up and see what's happening up ahead. In any case – look, the horses are exhausted and I don't think we can keep driving them anymore. The cattle have been managing to graze fairly well, and they can digest this poor hay better than the horses. What we'll do is let the horses come with us if they can – but in future we'll get the cattle to pull the cart."

"But can they do it, sir – they're not oxen but milk cows."

"Well, it won't be good for them and they'll be very slow, but we can't go any faster than the lot ahead of us anyway. The horses won't survive if we keep them pulling the cart."

Spiro and Costas untethered the horses and took the two strongest cows and managed to hitch them. Costas kissed Saroula and patted Spiro on the head and rode off, up past the long line of refugees. Spiro settled down and Saroula produced some stale bread and cheese for him. They had already been travelling for over a week. Spiro sat back against the cart, chewing at the bread and looked around him. They had stopped right next to the railway line. The trains that passed were moving very slowly in view of the closeness of all the people and animals on either side of the track. All along the railway lines and paths, going back for miles and miles, there were now thousands and thousands of exhausted men and women walking along blindly in the rain with everything they possessed either in carts or wheelbarrows or on their backs. None of them, not one, had the slightest idea where they were going, or what they would do when they got there.

It was statistically inevitable that among all the thousands trudging along, there would be some women who would go into labour somewhere along the line, and this now happened only yards away from where Spiro was sitting in the rain. There was only an old man with the woman, perhaps her father, vainly holding a tattered umbrella over her head. A little girl, clearly the woman's daughter was sitting crying beside her mother as she moaned and rolled about. Eventually two women, covered in wet blankets shuffled over through the mud and persuaded the little girl to move away. One of them held up a blanket over the woman, both as an added shelter from the rain, and to give some semblance of privacy as birth took place in the middle of death. Spiro wandered across and stood by the little girl, who had stopped crying. He smiled at her and handed her the remains of his bread, now softened with the rain. In other circumstances, she would never have taken it – but today it was different and she stuffed it into her mouth in one gulp, not saying thank you, or even looking at him. Spiro turned back and sat down again

There were no relief organisations – no soup kitchens – no medical facilities anywhere – it was a picture of medieval proportions, unfolding before Spiro's questioning eyes. None of the statesmen whose decisions had provoked this exodus would ever have believed such scenes were taking place in the second decade of the twentieth century. Meanwhile in the midst of all this misery, modern trains full of affluent passengers, passed every few hours with brutal efficiency, while thousands of human tragedies were taking place on either side of the line. Trains emanating from Paris, Milan, Vienna, Bucharest ...and Salonika!

Costas soon returned, trotting back through the fields away from the lines of hopeless refugees. It appeared that all the carts, the cattle, the people and their animals were jammed solid on the bridge over the Maritza leading into Western Thrace and the Kingdom of Greece. No ethnic Greeks were being allowed into Bulgaria further ahead, though Armenians - merchants and small shopkeepers from the little towns in the province - were allowed to enter. Costas told Spiro to be ready to move, as once the great line shuffled forward again, as it surely would, there would be no time to gather things together.

The rain never stopped. Costas settled down next to Saroula, holding her tight and comforting her as best he could. All three huddled close together, Spiro held an umbrella over his new parents. A train slowly moved up the tracks alongside them. Somewhere between here and Constantinople, something must have blocked the line, as the train shuddered to a halt, steam rising from under the carriages – the whole monstrous machine clanking and hissing. Spiro stared up at the big clean window of a first class carriage. There, a lady dressed in furs with a large brimmed hat looked back down at him. Opposite her sat a gentleman reading a newspaper. Spiro felt embarrassed about his shabbiness– after all, he had stared at plenty of ladies like this one in the smart cafés on the quaysides in Smyrna – but now, bedraggled, dirty, unwashed for days, soaked through as he now was, he found he could not meet her eye. He looked away as the train hooted and moved away. Then, suddenly, it came to another shuddering halt.

That very morning Mikael, Elena and the two children had finally arrived in Adrianople. Getting the tickets in Athens, and making all the necessary arrangements, had proved more difficult and more costly than Mikael had first envisaged. Everyone was looking for tickets to Salonika and northwards, but as it happened, few people wanted to go on from Salonika to Constantinople. So, in the end, by booking and paying for his ticket right through to the city, Mikael had finally got his four third-class seats.

One of the extraordinary features of these chaotic few weeks, as the Ottoman empire came crashing to its final end, was the way in which some aspects of life continued as if nothing had changed, for one group of people; whereas another group of people, would be suffering the drama and horrors of the collapse of organised civilisation. Mikael had seen this contradiction during the civil war in Russia and here it was again in Athens. There was terrible hunger and disease in the streets of the little capital as Greeks from all over the old Ottoman world, came pouring in. Yet at the same time, Mikael had been able to send a telegram addressed to Nairi and his mother, informing them of his survival and warning them that he was trying to get back to their home in Makrikoy.

At last the day arrived when the train left Athens with Mikael and his family aboard. It stopped for a few hours in Salonika, coaches were uncoupled and reattached and then it trundled on, along the mainly one-way track along the Aegean, finally turning north to go along the Maritza and into Adrianople. Already, before the train even entered the province of Eastern Thrace, Mikael could see the enormous difference between his seat in this modern twentieth century train, albeit only a wooden third class one, and the devastating sight of the lines of refugees they were passing by outside.

The fearless, brave and even arrogant Mikael, no longer existed. He had matured immeasurably. He was now responsible for a companion and her two children. Anya slept with her head in Elena's lap, and Andreas dozed next to Mikael with his head nestling against his shoulder. And Mikael found that he was nervous – anxious to the point of butterflies in his stomach – worried in a way that he had never been throughout all the vicissitudes of the Anatolian campaign, even at moments of extreme danger. He accepted that he had no idea at all – none – as to how he was going to get Elena and the two children through to Bolis. He didn't even know, at this point, under whose authority Eastern Thrace now was. He thought vaguely of leaving the train before it entered the Allied Zone and walking into the city.

But the first hurdle passed without incident. The train steamed slowly into the station with signs stating unequivocally "Adrianopolis". There had been no frontier post, no guards demanding passports. Mikael did not know it, but he was just ahead of the game. It would not be more than another few days before the signs in the station were removed and replaced by "Edirne". And even before that happened, Turkish gendarmes would already have arrived and set up the old frontier posts, abandoned for the last four years.

The little family party had to change trains here in Adrianople to catch the next train coming through Bulgaria and going on across the plains to the city. Adrianople was in turmoil. Thousands of people with all their possessions and their carts were in the streets moving, or attempting to move, in all directions. The Greek administration was packing up, and the only authority present in the streets were small bands of Greek cavalry riding past, ignoring the population on their way out of town.

Mikael and his little group did not, indeed could not, move far from the station. They gulped down a coffee and some bread at a small café and hurried back into the warm comforting embrace of the Compagnie Internationale des.... Within another hour they had taken their seats in the only third class carriage on this particular train, added on here to the Direct-Orient express coming through Bulgaria from Vienna. Mikael was now almost sick with anxiety. With a lurch and a hissing of steam, the train moved out of the station, out of the town and onto the great flat Thracian plains. Mikael stared with increasing fear and trepidation at the two lines of bedraggled people on either side, as the train lumbered slowly forward, hooting at the donkeys and cattle wandering across the tracks. The train stopped and started, coming to a complete halt and sat for about ten minutes.

Mikael looked blankly out, registering only the fear that he too might have to join this mass of wretched humanity and trek back into Greece, if he could not get his charges into the city with him. Then with a sudden lurch, which churned his stomach all over again, the train started moving again between the two lines of refugees, only to come to another shuddering halt with all the carriages clanging into each other. Mikael stared down out of the window at a boy, soaked to the skin, sitting leaning against a ramshackle cart by the side of his mother and father, holding an umbrella over them. The boy looked up at him as the train stopped. For just a moment Mikael thought that the boy looked familiar. He smiled and gave a little wave as the train lurched forward again. This woke Andreas who had been dozing again.

"Who were you waving to Uncle?" he said as the train began at last picking up speed.

"On, no one in particular," replied Mikael. "A little boy who looked a bit like your cousin. Come, it's no use your looking out; we've passed him and it couldn't have been him anyway – these are all farmers from Thrace trying to leave before the Turks arrive. Come, sleep some more, we will arrive at the city soon, and we may have to get out and walk a bit."

And with a sigh of escaping steam, Spiro's last remaining relatives, the last survivors of that big, happy, extended family, passed away down the railway line heading for the great city of Constantinople. He hadn't recognised Mikael, who he had only seen for a few days and in the most traumatic of circumstances. Looking up as the train disappeared down the line he saw the line of refugees ahead begin to move forward at last. He hurriedly shook Costas and Saroula who had dozed off in each other's arms. Then for the first time ever, he called out to them – "Father, mother, get up – get up, we're going at last."

CHAPTER 31

The City Waits

Two weeks had already passed since the Countess Androvna had left the city on the Direct-Orient express bound for Vienna. The Greek army had departed from the province of Eastern Thrace. Refet Pasha lorded it over the city, and British authority was wilting away with every hour that passed. Turkish gendarmes, considerably more than the 8,000 agreed at Mudanya, had poured into the province on the heels of the departing Greek peasants. Attempts were being made by these arriving policemen, all hard nationalists of the new breed, to prevent those who had not already left earlier, from taking their cattle and their farming tools. Admiral Bristol, who had not even been at Mudanya, was nevertheless indignant, claiming that the terms of the conference were such that these 'pesky Greek farmers' were not entitled to remove either their animals or their tools – and he sent telegrams to all and sundry to make his feelings known. Happily, by now, no one of any consequence was interested in what Admiral Bristol had to say.

Fortunately for Mikael and Elena, they had passed through the province, on their international express train, a day or two before the Turkish police arrived. These gendarmes had reopened the frontier posts and taken over control, right up and down the railway line as far as Chatalja. The little family could not have timed it better. They passed through the Chatalja lines and entered the neutral zone of the city, just after the Greek authorities departed. They were, therefore, sitting comfortably in their express train while the control posts were still manned by the old Ottoman officials, backed up by British personnel who were clearly less and less interested in the arrivals and departures. Within days, these polite officials would be replaced by Refet's men, and the British would be withdrawing, almost entirely from the frontier control.

As it turned out, apart from a cursory glance at Mikael's Ottoman papers, followed by a hasty murmur about the loss in a fire of 'his wife's' papers – he, Elena and the children passed through to Sirkedji without a hitch.

The Mudanya conference had not touched directly on the matter of the city itself. All the old questions, which had been going round for over four years, remained unanswered. What was to become of Constantinople and the variety of diverse communities living there? That it was going to be returned to the Turks, had become a foregone conclusion, and it was on that basis that the basic agreements had been made. But the fate of the non-Turkish peoples, was unresolved, as was its status as the capital city. For a fearful Bolsetsi, everything was pointing towards deportations of one kind or another. The example of Smyrna remained at the forefront of everybody's mind. Everybody claimed to know some story or some piece of gossip relating to the population of the city. The British were going to leave, but, in their absence, could the army of discontented Anatolian peasants on the other side of the straits be controlled?

Meanwhile, as the city waited, looming in the background of all the rumours and the gossip were the dread words – 'exchange of population'. The 100,000 or so Armenians in the city of course had no one to be exchanged with, however they knew what deportation, if it came to that, was likely to mean in reality. It was the Greeks, at least 40 per cent of the population, who listened to the rumours with increasing fear as they digested the news coming out of the countryside of Thrace. Nevertheless, in the midst of all this uncertainty, people continued to work, to have babies, to eat out at the wonderful restaurants along the Bosporus, to love each other and to marry.

Sima and Armineh worked together in planning for the wedding. It was decided they would be married in the small local Armenian church in Makrikoy, which the family rarely attended. Father Haroutune would preside. It was not going to be a grand affair, though Sima did want a traditional wedding with all the Christian trimmings. She had listened to her father's confirmed, secular cynicism about the clergy, and about organised religion, all her life, and as a result, she didn't have any strong religious convictions. But on this one instance, she wanted to be conventional, she wanted it all done in a proper manner – and in this, she was reverting to her natural instincts. The church was booked for the 1st November, and this was to be followed by a small reception at the home, for which purpose caterers were organised by Armineh.

During the next days Sima went often to the Patakis house, not just to be with Nicolai, but to set about arranging the rented rooms for their coming life together. A letter had already arrived from Vienna. The Countess was living with her sister, the Countess Berchtold, in fairly comfortable surroundings, but she had written to warn that conditions in Vienna were worse than they were in Constantinople. Electricity was often cut during the day and the heating in the apartments was erratic. Vienna, it would appear from her comments, had become a bulging capital city without a country to govern. Bureaucrats, landed gentry and officials from all over the old Hapsburg Empire were returning to Vienna, without anything left to do. There was no work and little joy.

However, she wrote that she had already spoken to her other sister – the Contessa Maggi – and that in Italy, the situation was different. The old Count still retained all his land. There had been no social revolution and it did not look as if there would be. She wrote to add that he had already indicated to her – his sister-in-law – that he would welcome her coming to Padua where they lived. Furthermore, he was encouraging about the suggestion that Nicolai might also come, and be employed in the management of his estates in the Veneto.

Meanwhile, Nicolai had found some work with a Greek shipping firm, who required a clerk to write letters in English and French. Nicolai's Greek was non-existent but his Turkish had become more than adequate. As it happened, there were plenty of Greeks in the city who could speak English, as also many who could speak French. But those who could manage both were few, so Nicolai got the job.

Despite Harry's advice, Olga had not spoken to Karekin after the baptism service. Karekin had walked out at the end of the service before all the kissing, hugging and shaking of hands could start. He had walked for a short time, aimlessly, up the Grande Rue du Pera, not exactly grieving all over again, but simply remembering his son yet again, his good spirits, his moments of shyness, and his triumphant ones. Tears prickled – it was all still too soon. He would do his best for the little boy baptized this morning, but he knew in his heart that he could never come to love him as he had his own son. At one level, he was irritated that Paramaz had sprung the name Haik, like that, at the last moment. However, he had seen immediately that all his womenfolk, taken aback at first, had been delighted. Eventually he wandered back to join the rest of the family. The Levonians had invited everyone to a grand restaurant on the Bosporus in Bebek. The carriages were all ready and they were only waiting for him.

Lunch had gone on at that waterside tavern, plate after plate arriving as they ate, until six in the evening and everyone was exhausted by the time they all arrived home. Either way there had been no time for Olga to broach any subject, never mind one quite so sensitive.

The next day had been the trip to Sinekli with Spiro and once again Olga had been unable on the return journey to raise the matter, as she had never been alone with her father. But with the passing of each day it became more and more difficult. Meanwhile she was seeing Harry almost every day – either he would come to Makrikoy and would have lunch, or she would meet him in Pera and they would go somewhere together. After the days and days of rain that had poured down earlier in October, the weather had brightened again. They passed days wandering round the older parts of the city, the covered bazaar, the various Byzantine ruins, Prinkipo, Rumeli Hissar, and even one, crisp afternoon, following the same route Harry had walked with his father down the old walls; although on this occasion Harry had taken the precaution of hiring a carriage to lumber along the road which ran alongside, to which they reverted when they got tired and which saved them from having to go the whole distance on foot.

Like so many people who lived in wonderful and historic old cities, Olga had taken it all for granted. She had seen more of the famous sights of Jerusalem, which she had visited with the rest of the family as a tourist before the War, than she knew of her own city. But Harry had become an enthusiast over the two years of his life spent here. He took her to back streets in old Stamboul, the cemeteries of Eyup, villages in the woods of Sultan Su, all of which she had never seen. And every day, without fail, he would urge her to speak to her father to explain what had happened and what was her current condition. And every day his heart, still filled with the joy of the five days spent with his father, became ever more enamoured. He found himself begrudging the time he could not be in her company. His heart raced with pleasure every time she ran up to him at their rendezvous in Pera, or when she opened the door to him, on arrival at the house, walking up past the fields alongside the Vali Effendi racecourse.

Harry was 30 years-old. He knew that he was falling in love. But he also knew, too well, that Olga had been deeply in love, for over six years with another man, who had died only a few months before. Furthermore, he also knew she was carrying this man's child. How could he impinge on her grief? Wouldn't it be totally insensitive of him to make his growing feelings known to her? He felt that with a woman like Olga, it was almost impossible to gauge what she might be feeling towards him. Her natural vivacity, her Avakian enthusiasms, and the outpouring of warmth that was such a part of her character, aimed directly at him when they were alone together, appeared to be aimed at others, equally as much, when in company. It was very confusing, and it was so very un-English. Harry dithered. However, on the matter of telling Karekin about the pregnancy, he was firm and could see that she was making herself ill with the thought of speaking to him. So one afternoon, as they sat in a café in Karakoy watching the ferries coming by, before they strolled back across the bridge for Olga to return home, he said –

"Olga, my dearest, this must stop. You simply cannot go on keeping from your father what has happened."

"Oh Harry, I will, I will. It just seems so difficult to get him alone and..."

"Nonsense, you are simply finding excuses. Think, think how much of a strain it must be on your mother, being unable to talk to Karekin about what must be a worry for her. I know that she promised to leave it to you, but that was now days and days ago."

"All right, all right, I'll speak to him soon."

"No, no. That's rubbish and you know it, my dear. You'll speak to him tonight – tonight Olga. I really will be upset if you put it off anymore. I'm coming to Makrikoy tomorrow after lunch. I want to hear about how it all went from you, or I..."

"Or what, Harry?" said Olga somewhat mischievously.

"Or.... Oh I don't know." Harry laughed as did Olga. "But honestly Olga, I really will be hurt, I mean it."

Olga looked back into his eyes and their eyes clashed. It was Olga who turned away, but she could see that it would, indeed, wound him, and that realisation brought her thoughts sharply into focus.

That night after supper, she asked Karekin as they arose from the table, if she could talk to him in his study. Karekin was surprised. Haik had occasionally asked to speak to him privately in his study in this way, particularly if he had been naughty as a young boy and wanted to confess some misdemeanour. But this had never happened with any of his daughters. He looked across at Armineh, at the other end of the table, but she deliberately looked away, refusing to let him catch her eye, and started ostentatiously helping Talin to clear away. He suddenly felt anxious, and took out his amber beads as he walked ahead to the study where he sat at his desk and motioned to Olga to sit on the other side.

"It's about Smyrna isn't it? It's something that I don't know about isn't it, my soul?"

"Oh, father, yes. I haven't told you everything about my life there yet."

Karekin fingered his beads, clicking them as quietly as possible and looked straight into his daughter's eyes. She flushed ever so slightly but then looked straight back. The blood slowly rose to her cheeks as she continued –

"Father, after I had been in Smyrna for some months I suddenly met Selim quite by chance in the street. Father, you knew that throughout those days during the War I loved Selim and that he loved me. Oh, baba, you knew, you knew in your heart that I had not forgotten him... his visits ..."

She trailed off. Karekin said nothing but continued fingering his beads. Olga swallowed and looked down, but continued –

"We decided after that chance meeting that despite opposition from both our parents, we were going to marry. I was living at the time in small rooms at the back of each of the hospitals. Selim had a room in the Turkish quarter. We got a small apartment, just two rooms, in the house of a Madame Derounian in the Armenian quarter near the cathedral. We lived together there for about three months right up to the moment that the Turkish army poured into the city. Baba, he was in the city clandestinely. We couldn't have got married there – but we lived together as man and wife."

Karekin still said nothing. Completely incongruously, as she was talking and as he listened, he thought of those times ten years ago when the eight or nine year old Haik would sit there stammering out some peccadillo, some bad thoughts he had had, or stealing something from the kitchen, lying to his mother or losing his temper with Marie. His young son would be craving some form of punishment or absolution to rid himself of guilt. He would usually oblige in some way, but with a light heart. He had always been firm with Haik, but, oh God, the boy had never caused him any real anxiety. Were boys perhaps easier to bring up than girls – ah, my son ...my son... Karekin sat up with a start dropping his beads onto the floor – Olga had stopped and was looking at him anxiously.

Coming to the end of what she was saying, Olga was aware that Karekin's attention had wandered for a moment. Then, with a lurch of her heart she heard the beads falling to the floor. She had never seen this happen before and assumed that her father had thrown them down on hearing what she had just said. And so they both sat, staring at each other, both silent and both totally misunderstanding each other. Despite all the fears that all his women – the three girls and Armineh – had feared about his likely reaction to this information, Harry had been right and they had been wrong. Karekin despised mere convention. He didn't care a jot about what so-called society might think. He accepted that in the current circumstances, he was taking a risk bringing up his daughters in the way he had. But he was no hypocrite. He would not open them up to liberal influences and then condemn them for acting on the basis of that upbringing.

But his thoughts were in turmoil, edging away all the time to his dead son. He, too, misunderstood the position, thinking that Olga was merely trying to expiate her own feelings of guilt and that she was only seeking some words of penance or atonement from him – something he felt he could not supply with any conviction. The silence dragged on until at last – at last – Olga without looking at Karekin, said quietly –

"Oh father, baba – I am pregnant. I am going to have Selim's child in about seven months time. I am happy about it. I want to hold a bit of Selim again. Oh father, I ..."

Karekin's mind cleared as if a bolt of lightening had pierced a great fog. He rose, kicking aside the forgotten beads, and came round to Olga who till then had not shed a single tear. Lifting her from the chair he enveloped her in his arms. Holding her tight as she began crying, murmuring –

"Oh, my daughter...my daughter....," over and over again.

Nothing further was needed. They both knew that everything between them was going to be fine. Karekin realised that this must be the reason why Armineh had been acting so strangely over the last few days. Olga realised that Harry had been right all along. It came to her that even if her father deep down, disapproved of her actions, the arrival of his first grandchild delighted him, unequivocally ...

Some days later, as October passed and as the day of the wedding approached, Alexei moved out of the Patakis house and came to live in Makrikoy. There was not the slightest hesitation or even a frisson of grief when Armineh arranged for him to move into Haik's old room.

CHAPTER 32

Love and Marriage

Mikael, Elena and the two children arrived at the shabby, and run-down, house of Vartuhi Sarafian in the centre of Makrikoy in a state of high euphoria. Almost up to the very last moment, as they stepped out of the train, Mikael had worried that an overzealous official would suddenly appear and demand to see their papers. Elena had no papers of any kind. She had been born a citizen of Imperial Russia, before fleeing with Wrangel's defeated army from Sevastopol two years ago. Settled in Smyrna with the Pantelis family, sheltered by a benevolent Greek administration, and nurtured in a welcoming extended family, she had never bothered to sort out any nationality for herself and her children, although, in point of fact, there was no nationality she could have adopted in the circumstances.

They had been lucky, and now Mikael was determined that he, and his little adopted family, would never again go through such days of uncertainty as they had suffered over the past week. From the moment that he got on to the train in Salonica, to the moment that he finally walked out of the station at Sirkedji and into the hustle and bustle of the Stamboul crowds, he had been in a state of nervous anxiety, far worse than anything he had ever felt in battle.

He was going to marry. Once married, the marriage certificate, coupled to his own papers – the valuable Ottoman 'nufus' – would be enough. It never crossed his mind that the poor peasants he had seen trekking wearily along the railway line to an unknown future in a bankrupt and poverty-stricken Greece, had perfectly acceptable and legally valid documents. What was the use of all these documents if the nation-state enthusiasts, those respectable men with their cold logic, wanted everybody to be tidily picked up and put down where they 'fitted', rather than where they were born or where they wanted to live.

As they talked it over, Elena did not see it that way.

"Mikael, we both want a church wedding, in accordance with

our beliefs. We already talked this over in Athens, remember? Can we take vows before God, when I am a married woman and don't know for certain whether my husband is still alive or not?"

"Elena, I remember our conversation perfectly; we've been through all this before. But listen. You parted in the panic in Odessa over five years ago. All sorts of things have happened since then – but it is inconceivable that he wouldn't have got some news back to his family in Smyrna, if he was still alive. There was a sizeable Greek community in Odessa, and many have been trickling out since the civil war ended. Letters have been coming out over the years, as well. No, no. Listen. We go to a special confession, we see a priest, either here in Makrikoy or at the Patriarchate in Bolis, and we see what they have to say."

There was a silence between them, created largely by Elena. It was only the second day after their fortuitous arrival back home in Makrikoy. Mikael's mother Vartouhi was not very happy about a marriage which was going to include two stepchildren – and Greek ones at that – but she was so overjoyed at having Mikael back home again, that she would have accepted any nationality as a daughter-in-law. Nairi was over the moon right from the start – she, more than her mother, was aware of how her brother had matured. Andreas and Anya weren't consulted, but they were fond of Mikael, so there really was no problem.

So why did Elena hesitate and look for excuses?

She had never experienced love in her relationship with her husband. She had not expected it. In that first, long conversation with Mikael, on the boat which brought them both out of Sevastopol two years ago, she had surprised him with the cool way she described what a loveless marriage had meant for her so far as the bedroom was concerned. Mechanical. It was her duty and she would perform. However, she had expected affection to grow and fill the void and perhaps even turn to love. But this never came – perhaps they had not been given the time. The silence lengthened – but before Mikael could come out with any more comments, she said quietly –

"Do you love me, Mikael, or do you just want a ready-made family?"

Now the silence was on the other side. Mikael had never spent time analysing his feelings. This had nothing to do with immaturity – but a character trait. He knew that the driving, all-consuming passion he had felt for Olga Avakian, all those years ago, was quite different to his feelings for this Greek woman. Which of the two was 'love'? Mikael didn't like being confused in any way. As always, he knew exactly what he wanted. Philosophic discussions about what might constitute love were of no interest to him. Anger and impatience came to his aid.

"Elena, my sweetheart, I've told you before that I am not the type to go down on my knees, or bring you expensive bouquets of flowers or chocolates or whatever. If all that I have done for you and with you over the last six weeks has not been enough to prove my love – then you are not the woman I have taken you for. I am prepared to lay down my life for you and your children. If you had been forced off that train and had to trek back to an unknown future all the way to Greece, you know very well that I would have got off too and shared your fate with you."

Tears came to Elena's eyes. He was surely a good, if brutally honest, man. He was right; no one could have done more; he had saved her and her children. She didn't want chocolates or expensive flowers – that wasn't what she was after. She was going to marry this man and entrust him with her future. But somewhere deep down in her consciousness, she was aware that he had never said – 'Elena, I love you'.

Brushing away her tears, and with a smile of genuinely unalloyed joy she said –

"Oh Mikael – yes. Let's get married as soon as possible – here in your home town – in the Armenian church. Please, Mikael, as soon as possible."

For the past week, Nerissa had been visiting the Asadourian home regularly, almost every afternoon, after the University closed at about 3.00 pm. As Madame Arabian was always there looking after Rehia until Ara returned from work, there was no longer any worry about her being alone in an all-male house-hold. She found the task given to her by old Barón Garabed was intellectually more stimulating than she had imagined. Explaining to the intelligent little girl, step by step, all the circumstances that had brought her to this house, in this city, was fascinating. She was determined from the start that this was not to be a tale of terrible massacres, of the premeditated cruelty by one section of a population against another. Satenig was not to become an enemy of Rehia. The tragedy of her true mother's death was not to be laid against her affection for her ana.

In this, she found she clashed with Raffi. He wanted Satenig to be told the facts – that his mother had been brutally murdered, egged on by the ideologues and the authorities; she shouldn't be spared the knowledge that this was only one small incident in a planned genocide, which had largely succeeded.

"Look, Nerissa, I'm not suggesting that you have to frighten the little girl. These are matters, which must be clothed in the language a six year-old can understand. But it would be wrong to make them seem anything less that what they really are. Sooner or later, she will find out the truth, and you will be doing her a disservice not to prepare her for it."

"But Raffi, it is not necessary to burden her with all that at six years old. How can she reconcile the 'truth' with the kindness and love she received in the village, and the care and security she got from her ana. There are always two sides to every issue and I..."

"My God – a true Avakian position. Listen, face up to it. Just because there are two sides to an issue, that doesn't mean they both carry equal weight. On one side, we have the planned extermination of over a million helpless people, and on the other, we have many, perhaps even thousands, of small acts of kindness shown by individuals, often against their own leaders' decrees. There is no bloody equivalence – none, none at all."

Raffi was now getting red, but Nerissa was no longer going to be abashed by strong expressions of feeling by others. She no longer blushed and looked away, but said quite sharply –

"Raffi, please don't swear – it doesn't strengthen your argument one little bit."

Raffi bit his lip and said –

"I'm sorry Oriort Nerissa, I'm really sorry – but I do feel deeply about this. She is my sister, you know. I would not want her to grow up without an appreciation of what happened to her family and why."

The conversation continued, Nerissa admitting that, while she accepted Satenig would, sooner or later, come to understand the truth of why she had two names, but that six years-old was too early. At this stage, she need only know that her true mother had died and that her ana had looked after her out of the goodness of her heart.

However, when she talked it over with Vahan some days later, she found that she was changing her mind again. When she reported her conversation with Raffi to him, he said –

"Nerissa, my soul, it's inevitable that Raffi takes a one-sided view of these things. After all, he was personally touched by the events of 1915. He was there when I was not. However, you know he has a point. Surely, you can't take a middle course in describing what happened in April 1915. It has to be simply and roundly condemned, with no 'ifs' or 'buts'. There are some things in life that cannot be dealt with in the tolerant, liberal Avakian way. There can be no moral equivalence in this matter and, on that, Raffi is right."

"But Vahan I am not for a moment making that point, nor have I ever done so. I am simply saying that it is not good for a child of this age to be forced to face up to a conflict between the truth of what happened to her biological mother and the love she feels for the only actual mother she can recall. It is too much to take in all at once."

Vahan looked at this girl, with whom he had been 'going out' for the last two years, and he knew that he loved her. He also knew she didn't love him – at least not yet. But for all his quiet and sensitive spirit, he was in his own way as stubborn as his brother Raffi – and he was going to marry her. She did not know it yet – but he did. They were looking straight into each other's eyes and he almost blurted out – 'I am going to marry you, you know'. What he actually said was –

"Nerissa, my soul, you must do exactly as your conscience

tells you. My father may be a bit brusque and not highly educated, but he was always an excellent judge of people. He asked you to take on the task of explaining the two names to Satenig, and he means you to do it as you think fit."

That afternoon, when she left to go home, Nerissa not only bent down and gave Satenig a great big hug – but also, for the first time, leant forward and gave Vahan a quick, tentative, kiss on the lips as she passed out into the street. But Nerissa was not thinking – not then – in any way of love or marriage.

Sima, the practical sister; the one who always claimed that she only ever thought of men as potential fathers of her children; the one who had always scorned her sisters' romantic notions of the chemistry of love; the one who was only going to marry when she found the man who could provide for her; was hopelessly and happily in love with a man who was unlikely to be able to do any of those things, at least for some time. The day of her wedding drew closer.

Olga would undoubtedly have married Selim, if they had both survived the holocaust of Smyrna. She had always taken the line, instinctively and not overly analysed, like Nerissa, that the only really important matter in considering marriage was love, by which she appeared to mean sexual chemistry – the overwhelming desire for another person. But ironically, the more she remembered the relationship she had had for over three months with Selim, the more confused she became. For the first time she began to question whether it had been just a physical attraction between them. If desire was all that really mattered, then weren't her parents and society right to have expected her to wait until the union could be sanctioned by…. by who? God? Society? Olga began to get a headache whenever she started thinking back on the events that had all seemed so right, so inevitable in those last three months in Smyrna.

She was incapable of the sort of self-analysis that was second nature to Nerissa. She only knew that it was Selim's character which had, at some early stage, become the important factor in their happiness together. It was the beauty and wonder of his spirit, of his kindness, of his roughness, that had made her ache for him to come home and which she thought about during the day when she was not at work – not the beauty and wonder of his body. So what did that mean? What did that say about chemistry?

Olga knew that her friendship with Harry was deepening. She couldn't tell how far his feelings for her had developed, but she could see that he went out of his way to seek her company. She was grateful to him for having pushed her into speaking to her father. She was never shy in his company – she loved their trips together all over the city, and they were always cheerful and fond of each other – her shyness was in her own mind. She was glad he knew her secret. But knowing as he did that she was expecting another man's child, how could she encourage him in the attentions he was giving to her. Somehow, she felt that it would be morally wrong on her part to openly welcome any advances. It was almost like ensnaring a man – she shuddered at the thought. But Harry had not, as yet, said anything to her directly. Perhaps she was creating a problem that didn't exist.

It never crossed her mind that Harry might have been having similar thoughts about her.

Olga was not the sort to keep things to herself and as the day of Sima's wedding approached, she and Nerissa drew closer. Sima and Armineh had their heads together, continually, in lengthy discussions about the wedding. Whenever Sima was not sitting arguing over some trivial matter with her mother, she was away organising things at the Patakis house. She may have been in a romantic daze where Nicolai was concerned, but, as always, she was also highly practical. So it was that Olga, who would normally have been more likely to confide in her elder sister, talked instead to Nerissa. In addition, they both felt alienated from all the marriage preparations; Olga, with just an element of regret for the wedding she could not have; Nerissa, thinking it was all a lot of unnecessary fuss. They both accepted, on a purely practical level, that marriage involved more than just the couple, but was a social act in which society as a whole had an interest. A sacrament in which the church had an interest? Very well that too perhaps - but all the surrounding fuss had nothing to do with the Church's interest in the matter, even if you believed in it.

Olga needed to talk to someone and she turned to her younger sister who, in the past, had always been critical of her and, what she described, as her frivolous attitude to life. But things had changed – life had progressed – both of them were more mature, and so one night in Nerissa's bedroom –

"Oh dear, Nerissa, I am really tired of all this talk about the wedding. Why can't people just give their vows to each other and get on with it?"

"Because, in the end, it is simply a contract, which has to be witnessed and, in which, all civilised societies have a stake."

"But that stake is just about property rights, and inheritances and...."

"No, not only that – it binds the man to the woman and to all the children of that woman so that...."

"Nerissa is that all it is? Didn't we used to believe that it was primarily a matter of two people living together, and that all that was necessary was that they should love each other."

"You may have believed that – but I only agreed that was how you arrived at your choice of the man. Love, I agree, is the vital factor in that choice – not your future, or the future welfare of any children. But Olga, once your choice is made, the right of society to intervene, to witness, to register and in the last resort to make the rules, must be accepted.

"And the church?"

"Oh poof Olga, neither you nor I believe in the right of some priest, some guru, some mullah, some rabbi or some shaman to prognosticate, bless or condemn. We tend to go through the motions dictated by them, largely because that is how society likes to organise these things. I doubt it will last another hundred years."

"And what about me? I'm going to have the child of a man who is dead and can no longer marry me."

"Oh Olga, my darling, my soul, just be thankful that your child is going to be born into a family where he, or she, will receive as much love and security as any child born into a family with their father present."

"Well I suppose so… but have I the right to want another man? Would that not be the height of selfishness? Is it even possible in view of the depth of feelings I had for another?"

"My dear sister, you can't repress any genuine feelings you have for some other person, just because you once completely loved another. But Olga, your moral position must, absolutely must, be dependent on the man knowing of your condition and accepting it completely."

"Oh Nerissa, even if he knows all the circumstances, should you allow yourself to indulge in fantasies about him, or encourage him?"

This question was followed by a long and quite comfortable silence, as Nerissa took time to grasp the full meaning of her sister's question. Then she said –

"It's Harry isn't it?"

"Yes. I think he likes me; in fact I think it might be going much further than that. He knows about Selim, and about Selim's child. I've been careful not to encourage him in case …Oh Nerissa it's so complicated – in my own mind I mean. I like him – we have fun together when he takes me to places in my own town, which I've never seen. But I worry that my attachment is …oh. I don't know …artificial – as if I am looking for someone to help me out of my current predicament. He saved me from myself in Smyrna, and I know he likes my company but he doesn't say anything. It is all so English."

"Are you sure that it is the English in him, and not that he is worried that he shouldn't pressurise you? After all, it is only three months since you were living with a man to whom you were truly devoted. He might be feeling that it would be selfish to press you at this stage. Remember, if Cyrano de Bergerac is the great literary hero for the French, Hamlet is the equivalent for the English, and you know what he thought of his mother's 'o'er hasty remarriage'."

"My God Nerissa, you are so intellectual it's positively indecent. But I don't know, my love, I don't know. It's all in the air. We are all just waiting …"

CHAPTER 33

Olga and the City at the Crossroads

A conference had to be convened sooner or later to sort out the incredible muddle into which the whole situation in the Eastern Mediterranean had fallen, since the defeat of the Greeks and the burning of Smyrna. The Mudania discussions and agreement had finalised the basis for an eventual territorial settlement; but the status of the Imperial city itself, still occupied by the British propping up the tottering Ottoman dynasty, had yet to be decided. Looming in the background was the policy of population exchange, another name for ethnic cleansing. What this could mean for the cosmopolitan population of the city was too dreadful to contemplate – yet the tidy-minded bureaucrats of all the nation-states involved in the situation, were working behind the scenes on actual blueprints.

Surprising though this appears in hindsight, British diplomatic circles had first thought of holding a limited conference, between themselves and the Turks in Smyrna, just before the Anatolian army began moving towards Chanak. On hearing of this proposal, Lord Curzon observed to a senior foreign office official – "As to a conference at Smyrna, my dear Crowe, not even Nero held a symposium amid the smoking ruins of Rome."

That proposal was dropped within a day or two, as the Chanak crisis developed and the Nationalists drew ever closer to the Imperial city. Then came the Mudania conference, where the men on the spot sorted out, as best they could, the purely military arrangements for the territorial settlement. But a full conference of all interested parties was still needed and, after much discussion, Lausanne was the venue selected. Lausanne was on the direct line of the Simplon-Orient express between Paris and Constantinople, and it possessed good hotel accommodation. The conference was going to have to consider the whole future of the collapsing Ottoman Empire – above all the legal status of the straits and the city which controlled them, a matter of vital concern to the whole world.

Accordingly, everyone had to be present, not just the participants in the war. That included the Americans, who had never
actually ever declared war on the Ottoman Empire, and the new
Soviet Russia, still pariahs on the international stage. The participation of America meant the necessity of including the impossible person who occupied the position of the American High
Commissioner in Constantinople – Admiral Mark Bristol.
Crowe's comment back to Lord Curzon, when, at the height of
the Chanak crisis, it was proposed that America might be given
the task of looking after British affairs in the event of a new war
between Britain and the new Turkey, was on the lines of –

*"I really cannot agree to the suggestion that British interests should be
confided to the preposterous Admiral Bristol. If he were a person less
hostile to the Christian populations of the city and less petty and vindic-
tive in his personal attitudes it might have been a good idea to entrust the
care of our interests to the USA."*

As the panic-stricken Greek farmers of Eastern Thrace
continued to pour out of that province; as the authority of the
British occupation forces continued to melt away in the face of
Refet's charm offensive; as the already negligible power of the
Ottoman administration in Constantinople frittered away, and as
Mustapha Kemal imposed his will on the city from the backwa-
ters of Ankara, the delegates began arriving by train at the
wholesome, but immeasurably boring, city of Lausanne on the
shores of Lake Geneva.

The wedding of Nicolai and Sima – the first of the Avakian
girls to leave home – had come and gone. Alexei was still recov-
ering. In Armenian weddings, there is no tying of ribbons round
the couples' foreheads, or gold crowns, but the best man is
required during most of the service to stand between and behind
the happy couple, holding a cross aloft over their heads.
Needless to say it was considered to be unlucky if the cross
drooped or failed to remain permanently over the heads of the
bride and groom. This was fine if the best man was tall and

strong. But both Sima and Nicolai were tall, while Alexei, desperately anxious not to let his brother down, was fairly short. No one
had told him of the little techniques available for holding up a
heavy gold cross. Fortunately, Father Haroutune did not believe
in lengthy ceremonies, and, by occasionally shifting from the
right hand to the left and back, Alexei kept the gold cross bravely
aloft.

Sima and Nicolai had gone straight from the small reception
in the family home in Makrikoy, to the Patakis house. The
Countess Androvna, now moved from Vienna and settled in her
sister's apartment in Padua, had already written with confirmation that the old Count Maggi had warmly welcomed the idea
that Nicolai should come to Padua with his new wife, with a view
to taking over the management of his estate in the Veneto.
Nicolai had already started a crash course in Italian. He went
every evening, after returning from work, to the little apartment
of a somewhat impoverished, but excessively genteel, Italian
lady, a flotsam left high and dry in the city after the death of her
Greek husband during the war. She had no children and
immediately fell for the reserved and well-mannered Nicolai.
Nicolai learnt quickly. But, whether the polite and refined
conversations which Nicolai had with her for two hours every
evening, in her dark and cluttered rooms, was going to be much
help to him in dealing with stubborn peasants in the Veneto
countryside, was another matter.

The impending departure of her eldest daughter had
galvanised Armineh. She was continuously closeted with Sima,
preparing cases, packing and repacking, insisting on the absolute
necessity of one item one day, and rejecting it as completely
superfluous on the next. There was then the question of dividing
those items, which simply had to accompany them, from those
that could be safely shipped separately. Karekin took little part in
all this preparation – but already bills of exchange were lodged
with his agent in Lancashire and his bankers in Milan. Letters of
credit in Sima's name were already with her papers. Alexei had
spent three whole days at the Italian consulate having Sima's
Ottoman passport checked and counter-signed, and Nicolai's

Nansen passport issued with a visa. Alexei claimed that holding up the great gold cross at the wedding was nothing, compared to the sheer tedium of waiting in the dingy corridors of the Italian consulate, added to the frustration of dealing with bored bureaucrats, in both Italian and Ottoman offices.

The movement of some of Karekin's commercial balances out to his European agents and bankers was not just in case Sima and Nicolai were in need of ready capital. There was also an element of prudent insurance against the possibility of a Smyrna solution for the Greeks, Jews and Armenians of the city. Karekin looked on in despair as the Ottoman world appeared to be disintegrating in front of his eyes, or rather crashing about his ears. It was becoming clear that no one, Turk or Christian, had much respect for the person of the current Sultan, the garrulous and timid old Mehmet VI, surrounded, as he was, by fearful and indecisive old Stambouli courtiers and ministers. Refet Pasha was now the only credible authority in the city, and day by day the counterbalance and power of the British was being whittled away.

However, despite the slippage of authority and the powerful nationalist propaganda; despite the shouts of the students gathering to watch and cheer the Turkish troops marching through the city to join the gendarmes already in Eastern Thrace; there remained a residual respect and love for the dynasty that had commanded the city and the Turkish people for centuries. The students, the section of any population most susceptible to strident propaganda, might shout enthusiastically –

"Down with the old rascal at the Yildiz" – but the majority of the quiet and patient working people of the city felt differently. Many of them, both Turk and non-Turk, were aware that the heir to the current Sultan, his cousin Abdul Medjid, was waiting in the wings to take over. A robust, honourable man, he had enlightened views, an artistic spirit and was modern in outlook. He was a devout Muslim, but also had sympathy with the nationalist movement.

Nothing is inevitable in history. The future was all in the

balance and Karekin felt he must to be ready to move in any direction, at a moment's notice, for the security of his family. Of course, he had absolutely no wish to leave the city. He had no desire whatsoever to move away from the life, the culture, the memories and the friends he had made over 50 years in this beautiful city. Despite all the fear and trauma of the events that had taken place to his people in April 1915, despite all the pain that each community had inflicted on the other – Greek on Turk – Turk on Armenian – everyone on the Jews – a residue of the underlying respect for the religion and culture of other faiths and peoples, which had maintained the Ottoman dynasty for centuries, still lingered. Karekin had plenty of Turkish friends and business associates who felt the same way, despite all the propaganda directed at them.

The academics in the schools and universities, fabricating lies and myths, and all the small-minded bureaucrats gathering in Lausanne, went about their business of stating pedantically, roundly, baldly, above all without basis in historical fact, that the peoples of the Empire had always hated each other, and been unable to live peaceably together. Accordingly, the only solution was to separate them with lines on a map.

Nationalism! As soon as geography is looked at in detail, the naturalness of a so-called national border melts away, and the horror – the absolute and peculiarly 20th-century horror – of ethnic cleansing emerges. This 'exchange of populations' was designed, by officials and sectarian academics, to ensure that a 'people' and their 'land' coincided exactly. But it was precisely these abstract divisions, which were so unnatural and, in practice, so cruel. And it was worth noting, that no former Ottoman Sultan, however ruthless or despotic, would have contemplated, for one moment, such a solution.

Harry, waiting in a sort of professional limbo for the decision of the court-martial, had spent almost every day since, either at Makrikoy or visiting favourite sites in and around the city – always in the company of Olga. The continual rain and cold, of the first weeks of October, had given way to balmy skies and warm sunny days in November, They strolled over ruins, looked at old castles, picnicked at the Sweet Waters, swam off the islands. There was no constraint between them; they enjoyed each other's company unreservedly, and the easy nature of their relationship, established in such dramatic circumstances in Smyrna, continued. But Harry was quite unable to get rid of the looming presence of the dead Selim. It was not just the thought that he had been Olga's first love, a love she had faithfully maintained for over six years, and which had been consummated. It was also that Selim continued to exist in the baby Olga was carrying.

Olga was enjoying a contentment that she had believed impossible, following the events of 13th September. The welcome and support she had received from the whole of her family had so delighted her, that in true Olga-fashion, her mood had swung right round to a complete disregard for the social difficulties her present condition would cause, once it became obvious. She knew that her baby would be surrounded by love, despite being without a father, and this gave her a happiness that, at last, overcame her grief at the death of her lover.

Yet, perversely, her joy, radiating from her open, expressive features, became a barrier for Harry. In the midst of his own volatile feelings, he could only watch her and observe her happiness. He came to know every nuance of her expressions, and he concluded that she was happy – happy in her memories of Selim – happy for the baby growing inside her – and above all happy at not having, or needing, any further emotional entanglements. He now knew that he loved this woman and wanted to spend his life with her. But it was no use – it was too late, the chance had gone. He had already been approached by the Admiralty with news that, subject to the results of the court martial, he would be posted to the headquarters of the Eastern Mediterranean fleet in Alexandria, and should begin making preparations for leaving. He began thinking of his own departure from the city, and out of the lives of all these people, who, in different ways, he had come to love.

Events now began crowding in on each other. An anti-nationalist ex-minister in the old Ottoman administration, who had continually campaigned against the nationalists of Ankara, was arrested by Refet's secret policemen right in the middle of the main street in Pera. He was dragged away, gagged and put aboard a boat. He was taken by night, with the lights dimmed in order to avoid any British patrol boats, to the Asian side and put into the hands of the nationalist army. Once there, he was brought before the local commander, who interrogated him and then had him led in chains, with only a few guards to accompany him, to the local prison. Word was carefully spread around of the route he would be taking. On the way he was surrounded by a mob inflamed by propaganda – now shouting 'traitor' traitor' instead of 'giavour', 'giavour'. The guards, forewarned, melted away, and he was brutally murdered by the mob, in scenes reminiscent of the death of Archbishop Chrysostom in Smyrna, two months before.

The Sultan now became seriously alarmed. Memories of the fate of the odious Abdul Hamid, mixed with reflections on what had happened in Smyrna only two months before, left the garrulous old man in fear for his life. On the 4th November, following one of Mustapha Kemal's lethal speeches before the assembly in Ankara, the deputies had voted in favour of a declaration stripping Mehmet of the title of Sultan, but, for the moment, retaining his title of Caliph. Stating that this would separate the temporal power (the Sultanate) from the spiritual (the Caliphate), Mustapha Kemal hinted that the Caliphate would pass to Abdul Medjid.

It was not that Kemal had the slightest reverence for the title of Caliph. For him it was outmoded, medieval, like Selim had often said to Vahan –

"It's an Arab thing – let it go."

But there it was, for better or worse, for the first time in the history of Islam, there was to be a separation of the temporal from the spiritual power. That day – that very day – the National Assembly ended their session with prayers; prayers, which the principal nationalist ministers did not attend, but which, for the first time in history, were recited not in Arabic, but in Turkish.

Since returning from Smyrna, Olga's moods had swung between grief and despair on the one hand, to a rather brittle joy and euphoria on the other. But once she had settled Spiro permanently with the Kafides family in Thrace and after, at Harry's urging, she had brought Karekin fully into the picture, she began for the first time to think of Selim's family – his sister Yasmin and his implacable mother Halideh hanum. After sending Yasmin a note, she heard back from her that the Ankara authorities had written a cursory official letter to her mother. This had stated that Selim had been in Smyrna with the army as it entered the city, but that he had disappeared and was believed to have died in the fire that had 'accidentally' broken out and destroyed the town. This note, sent direct from Ankara, had been signed by a certain Ali Ahmet, who no one had heard of, but it was written on paper with the Ghazi's personal heading. Yasmin told Olga that it stated, categorically, that Selim had died a heroic death as a full Major in the Turkish army.

The balmy days of early November continued and at last Olga, acting purely on instinct and without giving it enough thought, decided that she had to go to see Halideh hanum and tell of her approaching grandchild. She did not confide in Harry or anyone else. She simply made an arrangement to meet him for lunch after her visit. Harry suggested that they meet at the Pierre Loti café and then visit the mosque at Eyub which Olga had never seen inside. Neither of them knew that this was the spot, five years ago, where Karekin had witnessed the death of his great friend – Doctor Manuelian – and had been forced to abandon him in his last moments.

Olga did not send her note to Yasmin, but directly addressed it to Halideh. She didn't think the situation through – happy as she was at the thought of the coming child – secure as she was in the love and support of her own family – she simply charged ahead with her plan. After all, she felt, the child was as much Halideh's grandchild as it was Karekin's.

So, there she was in the elegant sitting room in the apartment block, half way up from the Galata Bridge to the start of the Grande Rue du Pera. It was only after she arrived, and was let in by the maid, that she realised that Yasmin was not going to be present, and was probably at work. This also meant that Halideh had not told her that Olga was coming.

Halideh came in almost at once, and forced greetings were exchanged between them, until the maid reappeared with a tray of coffee and some pastries. Halideh, who looked pale and was chain smoking, silently handed Olga the letter received from Ali Ahmet effendi from Ankara. For the first time, Olga began to question her decision to come to this house of grief and stir up matters which might be better left alone. However, while she might have been thoughtless, she was no moral coward. She could have said some comforting words, remarked on the fact that Selim appeared to have been promoted and then quickly got up and left. That would have been that. Wouldn't it be better that way? The two women sat silently as Olga's mind raced. Halideh thought that she was still reading, still taking in the news – but it wasn't that at all. Olga was facing up to her own impulsive action, everything suddenly seemed to be warning her to remain silent and not to add to this woman's grief in any way. Just go!

But she didn't. Surely Halideh was as much entitled to the truth as Karekin was. Ironically, her thoughts turned to Harry and his arguments that had persuaded her to open up all the truth to her father, and how she had been wrong in trying to avoid it for so long. She would make every effort to present the truth as kindly as possible, but at last she decided to tell it all as it was. So, leaving out that she had also been working at the Armenian hospital, she told Selim's mother of her appointment to work as a senior nurse at the Imperial Ottoman hospital in Smyrna. She then went on to speak of her chance meeting with Selim in the street, of their love, of their life together at the house of Madame Derounian. She described as gently as possible Selim's shatterd knee and broken leg, her inability to get help for him, and his death in the fire which swallowed up the whole street.

Halideh never uttered a single word but just stared at Olga, smoking cigarette after cigarette, stubbing each one impatiently before lighting another. Olga became more and more uncomfortable but at last came to her final words –

"I helped him to put on his uniform at the end, and he died a full officer in the army, which he had joined voluntarily the year before. I have to tell you Halideh hanum that we intended to marry as soon as we returned to Stamboul. I also wanted to tell you that I am pregnant and expecting Selim's child – your grandchild."

There was a long silence as Halideh continued to stare at Olga, who now blushed as the blood raced to her head. Then speaking slowly and deliberately Halideh rose from her seat and looking down at Olga said –

"So, Miss Olga, what you are saying is that my son was in Smyrna on some clandestine mission for the Ankara government. There you met him and seduced him into your bed. No – don't interrupt me. This clearly must have taken place in the giavour quarter of the city as I know that the Moslem quarter was not touched by the fire. So, if you had not persuaded him to live with you, my son would almost certainly be alive today."

"Halideh hanum …please …I …"

"No. Let me finish. Quite apart from your sluttish behaviour in sleeping with a man to whom you were not married, you then totally failed to help him when he arrived at your door wounded and in great pain. I don't know, as you have not explained, how you yourself managed to get away from the fire – but it is clear that you abandoned my son to die in the flames that your people had probably started in the first place. You left my son to die and saved yourself. You have only ever brought me grief and pain from the moment I first set eyes on you. Now please leave this house. I never want to see you or hear from you ever again."

Olga, stunned and in a state of complete shock, struggled up from the sofa. There were such barbed elements of truth in what the implacable lady was saying, she could not think straight. In a trance she moved to the door where the maid was now standing, and out into the hall. Then as she reached the front door of the flat a shrill voice called out –

"I curse you, you loose woman; who knows whether my son really is the father of your bastard child. May you both perish together when your time comes!"

And Olga left the apartment.

Olga had no idea how she managed to get from Pera down to the Galata Bridge and onto a ferry going up the Horn to Eyub. She remembered nothing of the trip there, or stumbling through the cemetery, up the hill to the Pierre Loti café. Harry was sitting at a small round table for two, reading a book, as usual – he never went anywhere without a book in his hand – as she walked up from where the carriage had left her at the bottom of the path, halfway up through the trees of the old Moslem cemetery. Olga had blushed redder and redder as the words of Halideh had burned into her, but there weren't, as yet, any tears. Nor had she cried either on the ferry or in the carriage from the ferry station. But, as she arrived and saw Harry sitting there with his head buried deep in a book, the tears began coursing down her cheeks and she stopped in her tracks.

Oh God, it was true, it was all true. She had abandoned her lover hadn't she? She was a slut wasn't she? Would Selim have got into her bed if she hadn't willed it, wanted it? And above all, it was true that if he had stayed safely in the Turkish quarter he would be alive today.

As Harry at last looked up from his book, Olga sank down onto the little wrought-iron seat on the other side of the table.

"My God, Olga, what is it, what is it my darling – what has happened." Harry jumped up and came round and held Olga tight round her shoulders. At this, Olga finally burst into sobs.

Sobbing, and unaware that Harry was now kneeling beside her holding her hand, she came out word for word with what had happened and what Halideh had said. Then in a frenzy of self-loathing, she stood up making Harry who was still holding her hand stand up as well and blurted out in a mixture of sobs and hysterical laughter –

"But, Harry she was right, she was right. I did abandon Selim didn't I. Surely I …"

"Oh nonsense, Olga, absolute nonsense. You were desperately seeking the only way you could to get him out of the house."

"But would Selim have died if I hadn't persuaded him to come and live with me in Hasmig Derounian's house. Oh God, Harry I am a slut – I did persuade him. Oh God, how will I face my child when he asks after his father?"

"You were both deeply and honourably in love. You were both adults, you both knew what you were doing. How can you be responsible for what occurred in Smyrna later – for the fire and destruction in one section of the city."

"I abandoned him – I abandoned him – she was right, I am a loose woman, yes, she called me that, oh heavens when she cursed me and ..."

"Olga, stop it, you know none of this is true. Here is a woman who desperately needs to blame someone for the death of the second man in her life. What does she know of the circumstances in which you were struck unconscious as you sought help? Come, my love, come, bear up, I ..."

And then it happened. Harry might never have been able to refer in words to his love for Olga. However, standing there outside the shabby little café, with his back to the crazy patchwork of gravestones standing at all angles which comprised this section of the cemetery, still holding onto Olga's hand as she tried to wipe her tears with the other, he leant forward and kissed her full on the lips. He was totally oblivious to the one other couple sipping tea at another table nearby; indeed entirely oblivious to the whole world around him. Standing tall and strong, his lips on hers, he held her tight and his strength and support flowed from him directly to her in the embrace.

Olga, crying and in a complete maelstrom of emotions, felt herself held tightly by this man, in whose company she had been almost every day for the last month. In one section of her mind, she knew that the inferences made by the relentless old lady, regarding her actions during that dreadful day in Smyrna two months ago were completely unjustified – but it had all been so close to a part of the truth. Almost every event in the past can be seen in more than one way – however unjustly. But she thought of none of this consciously. She was after all Olga, not Nerissa. All she felt was the strength, which seemed to be passing from him into her. As oblivious to all around her as Harry was, she returned his kiss as they stood there under the trees, for a whole minute – for an eternity.

CHAPTER 34

The End of the Sultanate

It was the 17th November, the day before the projected departure of Sima and Nicolai on the Simplon-Orient Express, for their journey to Venice and, from there, on to Padua and the Maggi estate. The weather, which had been so gentle and warm for the past fortnight, had at last broken for good. The usual winter blight of the city, the cold winds blowing down the Bosporus from the Black Sea, had begun. The rain was bucketing down, as Karekin hurried, on that well-travelled road past the Vali Effendi racecourse to the station at Cobancesme, to catch the morning train into the city. The sky was overcast and the umbrella, only good enough to protect his coat, could not prevent the water splashing onto his shoes and the bottom of his trousers.

Karekin was becoming worn out by all the events that were pressing in on him – political and personal. It was, of course, as always, Armineh who had been dealing with all the practical details – the things that Sima should take with her – the trunks to be packed – the sheets and the towels and the blankets to be included; the separation between those absolutely necessary items, that would go in the trunks accompanying them on the train, and those which could be sent on as freight by sea, once they had settled in. But ultimately, it fell to Karekin and his office, with the enthusiastic participation of Alexei, to deal with the documentary formalities.

Tired, almost punch-drunk though he was, he revelled in his

capacity to deal with it all. He had it all worked out; every detail of the departure of his eldest daughter to her new life in Italy; every detail of how and where he would take the family, in the event that Lausanne decreed an 'exchange of population' for the city; a school for Seta in Switzerland. Karekin strode on, even smiling at the rain.

Only the day before, he had faced up to yet another change in family circumstances. In the morning, as he was dressing before going down to breakfast, Armineh had warned him of a possibility that was likely to arise that day.

"My soul, I think that today you are going to be approached by Harry."

"Harry? Oh you mean Bridgeman effendi. All right, all right, don't glare at me. Yes – yes, the Englishman who has been here almost every day for weeks, who has that wonderful, but elderly, father. What does he want?"

"Karekin, you are deliberately irritating me. Look, I'm in a hurry. It's Sima's next to last full day and we still haven't decided on everything. Anyway, what do you mean 'elderly father', he wasn't much older than you."

"Oh yes he was – anyway, elderly in his conservative views."

"Karekin – stop. Surely you have noticed that this young man has been paying a lot of attention to Olga. You didn't think he was round here all the time for us, did you? They have become very close since that first meeting in Smyrna. Olga confided to me last week that Harry asked her if she would marry him – in that café above the Eyub mosque of all places."

Karekin, who had indeed been teasing his wife, pulled up short. He'd been aware, who could not have been, that ever since coming back from Smyrna, Olga had grown close to the Englishman. For six years, he'd watched Olga's love for Selim develop, and eventually had even supported her. He understood her feelings and emotions better than any of his other children. He had seen the enormous affection she had bestowed on this Englishman, and she seemed happier in his company. However, he had not seen the same passion as she had shown towards Selim. He'd assumed she wouldn't encourage the Englishman in his attentions. Olga must have changed in some way that he had not appreciated – was it the coming baby?

"And what, my love, did she say back to him?"

"She has, informally, accepted him."

"But Armineh – Armineh – does he know about the baby. I can't....we can't....it would be quite wrong....I...."

"Come, come – you've always said that however silly our girls may be, they do know right from wrong. I understand that she told Harry all about her pregnancy even before she told any one of us."

"Good heavens – and despite all that, he still wants to marry her. Does he realise that...."

"I'm going down Karekin. He's a good man. He will make a good father to the child which, to all the world, except just a few, will be his. But of course ... of course, another of our children will be leaving us. Olga said they will be leaving Bolis very soon, as soon as they are married. Listen, they will be here for lunch – could you come early from the office. I will arrange a late lunch for everyone."

And so it was that Karekin had found himself sitting behind his desk in his study that afternoon, only yesterday, listening yet again to a young man asking for the hand of his daughter. As he strode on under his umbrella down to the station, he reflected on how different the two experiences had been. Nicolai, young, penniless but passionate, and ready to fight for what he wanted, if necessary. Harry, older, much more mature, reserved and secure – equally ready to fight, but coolly presuming that he wouldn't have to.

"Harry, my boy, I do want to be clear on one thing. I understand that you are aware that Olga is now nearly three months pregnant and is expecting Selim's child. You only met Selim once, I think, at that awful tea-party here in the summer, over a year ago. He was an honourable man. I could have accepted him as a son-in-law, despite the strong opposition of both mothers. But look, are you prepared to take on my first grandchild as your own. Please think about it – are you sure?"

"Sir, I accept the responsibility and I don't need to think

further. I believe that my love for your daughter will sustain me in this. It is not only blood that counts in these matters. I will be the natural father of this child when it arrives, for everyone, except a very select few here in Bolis. In any case, I will be with the child as its father from the moment of birth. Do you believe that I won't be capable of loving the child as much as those that I trust will be graced to me and Olga in the future? Come, sir, you will have many more grandchildren, and in my eyes they will all be equally cherished."

"Well, well, Harry, you couldn't have put it more fairly. Tell me what exactly are your immediate plans."

"I'm not entirely sure, sir. I'm still awaiting the verdict of the court-martial. It is highly unlikely that I would be cashiered, even if the verdict goes against me. It would appear I'll be posted to the headquarters of the Eastern Mediterranean fleet in Alexandria. But sir, above all, with your permission I hope to arrange our marriage at the soonest possible moment."

"But if the decision does go against you."

"I cannot say – but these are decisions which I will make with Olga's help. Either way, we cannot stay in Constantinople much longer. Anticipating a favourable decision from you, sir, and knowing as I did that I have Olga's ...er ...love ...er ... consent, I have begun making arrangements for a secular marriage at the British Embassy. We need to move quickly and I'm sorry but neither of us wanted a church..."

Karekin strode on and down onto the station platform beaming with delight as he recalled Harry's embarrassment in revealing that he and Olga wanted a civil marriage. This had not worried him one little bit. What a joy that at least one of his daughters was going to avoid those meddling priests and their silly, long-winded rituals.

He was still smiling as the train pulled in. It was all under control. Everything was at his fingertips. My God he could cope with anything.

As it was still raining, he took a carriage from Sirkedji station and eventually arrived at his office. Alexei was already at his desk, having taken an earlier train, as were the rest of his staff.

He decided that he would work for the morning, but would then walk down to the Galata Bridge and over to the Patakis house with a view to offering his help with the forthcoming departure. He nodded at Alexei and motioned him to come into his office.

"Alexei, finish those letters you are working on and then leave and go back home. Armineh went out without her coat this morning. Please get her coat and then go straight back to the Patakis house and lend a hand there, if necessary. I will see you there."

"Yes – thank you sir. Er… by the way, a letter was delivered this morning by a boy from the Armenian Bureau for Missing Persons. It is addressed to 'N. Avakian' and was forwarded from the Imperial Ottoman Hospital in Smyrna. Knowing that your middle name is Norair they have assumed it is for you. There is no other N. Avakian in the city. Here it is."

"Very well – thank you", said Karekin lightly, putting the envelope to one side, "I'll look at it later."

Alexei nodded, turned and, taking his umbrella, left the office to walk back down to Sirkedji. There he took the next train back to Makrikoy.

It was still early in the morning of the 17th November. Tim Harington had arrived early at his desk in the Harbiye. He too, like Karekin, was reflecting on what had happened the day before. In the morning he had been sitting at his desk when he was told that the old Sultan's aide-de-camp was in the building, asking to see him. Harington went down and found that the man in question was the Court bandmaster, and not the officer referred to. Knowing that this man was the father of one of the Sultan's wives, he realised at once that it was likely to be important and confidential. Accordingly, he invited him up to his office, making sure his own A.D.C was present.

"Greetings, effendi. How can I help you?"

"Your Excellency I have come from the Palace at the express request of the Sultan."

"Yes. I have already been warned that if the Sultan required to get in touch with me urgently and secretly, he might use your services."

"Your Excellency, everyone at the Palace has become disloyal. The ministers have all resigned, and yesterday, even his personal doctor, who has been with him for years, fled without a word. Sir, my master believes that he going to be murdered tomorrow at the Selamlik service. He is asking you to save his life by arranging for him to leave the city immediately."

"But what evidence is there? Surely there is no way that Refet Pasha would be party to such an outrage. No, no, your master is surely mistaken."

"Your Excellency I can only repeat that my master is desperate and begs your intervention."

Harington knew, as he sat at his desk this morning reflecting on these events, that he had acted both decisively and correctly in requiring the old bandmaster to go back to the palace and return with a letter, signed by the Sultan himself, setting out exactly what he wanted Harington to do. This had duly arrived and as he sat at his desk, watching the same rain that was drenching Karekin's shoes, bucketing down outside his window, he studied again the letter, which had been delivered by the bandmaster. The document had been written by the old Sultan in his own handwriting, and under his own personal seal. It read –

"Sir. Considering my life here to be in imminent danger, I voluntarily take refuge with the British government, and request that I be taken away from Konstantiye as soon as possible."

This pathetic note, written by the last descendent of a great dynasty, which had terrorised the monarchs of Europe for centuries, was signed – Mehmed VI, Sultan and Caliph of the Muslim Umma.

Harington had already been warned by the British High Commissioner, Rumbold, before he left for Lausanne, that he was to be responsible for the life of the old man. It was, however, one thing to be ready to act decisively, quite another to know exactly what to do. The Palace was well guarded with spies, reporting daily to Refet Pasha, everywhere. The problem was how to get the last Sultan of the Ottoman Empire out of his own palace alive, and without the intervention of the nationalists, who, in almost all respects, now controlled the city. Harington had spent the whole of the rest of the day, yesterday, discussing this with his two senior commanders.

The plan that they had finally adopted was that the Sultan and his son should spend the night in one of the kiosks at the far end of the palace gardens. This was not particularly unusual and wouldn't arouse suspicion. However, this elegant building conveniently adjoined a gate in the high surrounding wall of the palace, which led out into a square, itself bordered, on the other side, by the barracks of the Grenadier Guards. The plan was that the Sultan and his party should leave from this gate early in the morning. At the agreed time, the Grenadier Guards would be drilling in the square. Two ambulances were to be stationed in the square – Yildiz Square – and parked on either side of the gate. The gate was to be opened at the agreed time – 8.00am had been accepted as the best moment – by one of the palace eunuchs, or, if necessary, forced open. The intention was for the Sultan and his sons to go into one ambulance, and the rest of his party with the luggage and including the father-in-law, the loyal old bandmaster, should go into the second vehicle. Both ambulances would then drive straight down to the quayside outside the Dolmabahce Palace, where Harington himself, and a naval detachment of at least one hundred men, would to be ready to receive the fleeing party. The gate was to be covered by machine-gunners. Officers with loaded revolvers were to be out for a morning walk at as many points along the route as possible.

Harington could sit patiently at his desk, waiting and worrying, no longer, although it was still early. He took out his own revolver, buckled on his belt and went out to take his car down to the quayside. HMS *Malaya*, the ship chosen to transport the last Ottoman Sultan away from his capital, the only British battleship to have been largely paid for by a Muslim community, already lay out in the straits opposite the Dolmabahce.

Harington arrived well before 8.00 – the two ambulances were not due to arrive before 8.20 at the earliest, even if all went well. He strode up and down with his two aides. But 8.40 came and there was still no sign of either of the ambulances. His own thoughts, and the conversation between his officers, went to the Flight to Varennes and the failed attempt of Louis XVI to flee from Paris and the French revolutionaries. That had ended in complete disaster. Was this to be a repeat fiasco?

At five minutes to nine, already half an hour late, the second ambulance with the luggage and the servants arrived at the dock. But where was the first, containing the last Sultan, which had left earlier? In the pouring rain, almost a storm by now, as if nature was playing an impressive accompaniment to the end of an imperial dynasty, this second ambulance had taken a wrong turning and had wandered round on a longer route, hence its delay in arriving. But the first ambulance containing the Sultan should have arrived long ago. It had not, although it had left the Yildiz Square almost an hour ago.

The rain poured down. It was the 17th November and getting later in the morning. Back in Makrikoy in the Avakian house, Paramaz was looking after baby Haik. He had been given the day off – it was a Friday – and he was lying on his back in the hall letting the infant crawl all over him. He would throw him up and then catch the squealing infant, who was yelling lustily in a mixture of joy and delighted apprehension. Talin was finishing some chores and Marie was bustling around keeping an eye on the idyllic domestic scene. Eventually Talin finished and came to watch Paramaz and Haik rolling about on the floor. It was at this point that Marie made her fatal suggestion.

"Talin – it's been raining for days. This poor child has been indoors all this time. It looks as if it might be slackening. The little lad has had no chance to get out into the fresh air for days. Why don't you take him out for a walk in the pram."

"But Marie, it's pouring with rain."

Yes, fine – but I can see it getting lighter all the time. Take one of the really large umbrellas. Don't just go out into the garden and the wet grass, but put the pram hood up and walk on the road down the hill. Paramaz, you go and nail up that coal shed

door as Karekin bey instructed – and then go down and meet
Talin and help her to push the pram back up the hill – it's a
pretty heavy carriage. Now Talin don't go down as far as the
railway, go about halfway and Paramaz will come and join you for
the way back."

As it happened, Talin took much longer to get the child ready,
whereas Paramaz went straight round to the back of the house to
finish the task Karekin had set him. It was therefore about
10.00am before Talin set out carrying an enormous umbrella,
with little Haik staring out from his sitting-up position in the
cumbersome old carriage which had served the family for ages.
This pram had been used for all the children, starting with Sima,
and somehow had always been overlooked when it came to
buying new things. The rain here in Makrikoy was beginning to
slacken off, and the air smelt fresh and invigorating. Talin, glad,
after all, to be out of the house, trundled the old pram down the
road between the fields.

Constantinople had, before the war, always been one of the
safest cities in the world. Western arrogance and myth had
nurtured the legend that the city was one of darkened doorways,
daggers in the night, the decadent orient steeped in poison and
vice. It was a lie which went right back to the great days of
Byzantium, when those 'muddied oafs', the uncouth and
unwashed Anglo-Norman and Frankish Barons, passed through
the city on one of their interminable crusades. Finding
themselves in a sophisticated imperial city, where people wore
clean clothes and washed and bathed regularly, they suffered
from a deep inferiority complex. They retaliated by inventing
the myth of a decadent and depraved city. This story survived
and, years later, would be applied to the Ottoman successors.

While the rulers themselves, both Byzantine and Ottoman,
cheerfully murdered each other in a welter of blood, whenever
the question of a disputed succession arose, the ordinary people
lived in a city which, until the middle of the nineteenth century
was well-regulated and, above all, safer than any other city in
Europe. There were whole areas of London, Paris or Rome
through which no woman would consider walking. In

Constantinople, up until the end of the Great War, no woman, veiled or not, would ever be molested anywhere in any street.

But the arrival of the Allied forces – the so-called civilised Westerners – and the occupation of the city, changed all that. Drunken sailors weaving through the streets of Pera at night became a normal sight. Women no longer walked alone in the streets after dark. The city became home to criminals and riff-raff of all types and nationalities. However, Harington's police had been fairly effective, once the British took firm control of the gendarmerie. The arrival at the end of 1920 of the whole of General Wrangel's defeated army – a quarter of a million hard-bitten soldiers – had after all been successfully assimilated and accommodated. But now, as everyone waited for Lausanne, the city was drifting into near anarchy. The old Ottoman city police force had become confused, like so many others. The British presence was wavering; the Ottoman government was in total disarray with ministers resigning and disappearing on a daily basis; while the nationalists, although having the full support of every Turk in the city, did not yet have the political capacity to take over the police and the responsibility of dealing with criminal behaviour.

There was a power vacuum. The allies were still strong, but there was a great difference between having power, and having the will to exercise that power. What the Sultan had failed to take into account – this collapse of allied will – the criminal classes of the town had quickly come to appreciate.

It was not a matter of complete lawlessness – nor was there any element of ethnic conflict, as occurred in 1915. There was simply an atmosphere of suppressed excitement and anticipation, together with a mood of violence in the air, that vibrated in the city and spilt over, even into the quiet suburb of Makrikoy. It could have happened in any city.

The rain continued to slacken, but there was a fine wet mist in the air as Talin continued to walk down the road. She was about halfway down and approaching the edge of the Valli effendi racecourse, when she stopped to wait for Paramaz. She made funny faces at Haik, which had him giggling, when she saw, coming up the road towards her, out of the fine mist, three scruffy young men. If she had been a born Bolsetsi she might have said to herself 'Turk', using it Ottoman style, not meaning an ethnic Turk but referring to them pejoratively as uncouth Anatolian peasants. But these were not Anatolian peasants at all, they were the increasingly confident and uncontrolled riff-raff of the poorer quarters of the city, and they were looking for trouble and something to steal.

Talin was a brave girl, but she had been through a lot. She had seen her mother and father, and all her family, die of exposure and hunger in the horrific death marches of 1915. She was 14 and she stood helpless. The young men had stopped and stood in the rain staring at her without emotion, just cold and calculating. One of them began rocking the pram violently. Talin gave a scream – a screech really – and leant in to the pram, grabbing the baby Haik and pulling him out. She held him tight, pressed against her wet clothes. The child did not appreciate being yanked out of his dry and cosy shelter and into the rain and began yelling at the top of his lungs. Until that moment the young men had been grimly silent, but now one of them shouted viciously at Talin -

"Shut the fucking thing up."

Talin, now thoroughly scared, began rocking Haik in a frantic effort to quiet him down, but inevitably in these circumstances, he yelled even more. One young man was eyeing the pram somewhat dubiously, while the other was pulling out the expensive linen and blankets. It was at this point that Talin felt the hands of the third man stroking her buttocks, and probing front and back. Holding on desperately to the screaming Haik, she could do nothing but let out a scream herself – not a screech this time but a full-blooded scream.

Then, coming out of the mist further down the road, just beginning to roll up his umbrella as the rain had almost stopped, she saw Alexei hurrying up the road from the station. She shouted out – "Alexei!".

The early morning of the 17th November had been spent by

the last Sultan of the Ottoman Empire in the Merasi Kiosk at the far end of the garden of the Yildiz Palace, as arranged with General Harington. All night he had fussed about with the servants who were going to accompany him into exile, packing jewels and other valuables into the trunks that had been left in the kiosk the day before. Everyone carried revolvers and the atmosphere was tense. So this was what the great House of Osman had been reduced to – a frightened and timid old man, talking incessantly to everyone around him, a shadow of a monarch. Portraits of the great Padishahs of the past glared down at him from the walls. What could he possibly be afraid of? What could the nationalists have done to him? Even if the Turks repudiated the dynasty, there was no way that they could have physically harmed the last Caliph of the Moslem world. Mustapha Kemal may well have thought that it was all a bit of religious nonsense, ripe to be thrown out of the window into the dustbin of history, but he was a supremely pragmatic realist, and he would not have risked the inevitable odium of harming the old man.

But the paranoia of the atmosphere of the Yildiz Palace – the baleful spirit of the almost demented Abdul Hamid – Abdul the Damned – cast its fearful shadow over the last Sultan. He was sure that something tragic and dramatic was going to happen to him.

It was 7.00am. A large detachment of the Grenadier Guards was ordered out to parade for drill on the Yildiz square. The rain was pouring down, and the comments of these 200 men, no longer conscripts, but regular soldiers of the permanent army, could not be repeated in polite society. To be ordered out to 'drill' in such indescribably bad weather, and at such an unearthly hour, must mean that their officers had finally gone mad. But the drill began – left-right... left-right... about turn... and so it went on as two ambulances drove unobtrusively into the square and parked alongside a small doorway set into the high wall of the palace. The young soldiers had never seen this door opened. Now, as they drilled, from the corner of their eyes, they saw the door open and a party of men – all men – came out. The rain continued to pour down, and there was a lot of fussing about with umbrellas by all those who had just emerged from the palace. Trunks were carried out and loaded into one of the ambulances while the men continued to drill, marching back and forth and making a lot of noise.

Eventually, the first ambulance, into which two men had been bundled, drove off and out of the square. The second ambulance, which was crowded with as many as six others together with all the trunks, finally shuddered into life and turned round the square and followed in the direction of the first and out of sight. The drill continued for another five minutes and then unaccountably stopped, as pointlessly as it had started in the first place.

In the first ambulance Mehmed VI, the last Sultan of the 500 year-old Ottoman Empire, sat talking incessantly and smoking cigarette after cigarette. His talk was rambling and sometimes incoherent – but the gist was that he was not afraid of dying, but was afraid of being put on trial and being humiliated if he stayed. There was always the possibility of assassination – some fanatic, inflamed by the passions of the nationalists, might end the dynasty with a single shot. He rambled on unconvincingly, as the ambulance, carefully negotiating the badly pot-holed, cobbled road leading down to the Bosporus, drove on. There was only ten minutes more to go before they arrived at the dockside rendezvous, when there was a sharp sound like a muffled shot. The ambulance swerved violently and came to an abrupt halt with its front wheels over the pavement in what appeared to be a deserted and narrow street.

No one in the city, except the few directly involved participants, were aware of the drama being played out, as the last of the Ottomans made his attempt to flee the city. Certainly Karekin, as he sat at his desk, had no idea what might be happening on the wider political stage; he had enough problems of his own to deal with, and was far too busy to reflect much on what was happening outside the family circle.

It was a Friday. After Alexei had left to collect Armineh's coat,

Karekin found he could not settle down. There was really no point in trying to work. He decided he would close up the office and go over to help – or anyway watch – the preparations for the departure tomorrow. He called out to the remaining staff that they could all leave for the rest of the day and that he would lock up. He looked round – yes he had dealt with everything, he was on top of it all. He took up the letter handed to him by Alexei, which appeared to have been forwarded by the Armenian Bureau for Missing Persons – the Bureau he had helped set up four years ago.

It was the letter written by Burhan Celal two months previously, addressed by him to N. Avakian, instead of Nurse Avakian.

Karekin read it through quickly. It was vivid and well-written prose, and it was only as he approached the end of it that Karekin realised that it had been meant for his daughter Olga. But by then, he couldn't stop. He read it through again slowly, sentence by sentence, forcing himself to take in every word, every nuance of meaning of what he was reading. Burhan had been a journalist of repute. His articles had been read by a large readership, who had revelled in his elegant prose, his command of Ottoman Turkish and his great descriptive talent. This letter had been drafted with all the benefit of his notes, and had been composed to take the place of the world-famous article on the Great Fire of Smyrna, which, racked by guilt, he had never got round to writing. It burned itself, line by line, page by page, into Karekin's mind.

Suddenly every event of that terrible day in September became clear to him. Like a stroke of lightening, the whole mystery of those last few hours of the life of his only son was illuminated. So, he had dealt with everything had he? He had the situation at his fingertips had he? His mind reeled, and he shouted out into the empty office a blasphemous profanity, words which no one had ever heard him utter. He read the letter again and again. He saw himself in the streets as the flames drew nearer. He knew exactly what his daughter had meant when she was gabbling out 'Turkish officer', 'Turkish officer', when she appeared in the street, and which the writer of the letter had himself not understood. And then – and then – the rape!

At this thought Karekin groaned out loud and found he could hardly breathe. What man can hear of the rape of his own daughter and remain entirely sane. Yet she had said nothing – not a word of it to anyone – not to him, nor, more to the point, to her mother. His mind broke down, if only for a moment. He got up and paced round the office, picking things up and putting them down randomly. It was still pouring outside as he stared, unseeing, out of the window.

Then, sentence by sentence, he forced himself to contemplate the violent death of his only son. The son he himself had sent to Smyrna, deliberately sending him there in the company of his murderer. As he read, he groaned out again. Had every decision he had ever made rebounded against his own family? He stopped for a moment – had he perhaps misunderstood? He forced himself to read slowly, word for word, the writer's vivid description in the third page of his letter, of what he had witnessed when he first arrived outside the house from which Olga had appeared later.

"*This third day I went out again and found myself, early in the evening, in a narrow street in the Armenian quarter, not far from their cathedral. The cathedral was filled inside and out in the courtyard with wailing Armenians, mainly women and children with a spattering of old men. They were clearly taking refuge, but from what I could not then tell. Later, as I walked through the Armenian quarter I saw that many houses had indeed been entered and pillaged by the soldiers. Looting and even rape was proceeding in front of my eyes as our soldiers took revenge for some of the sights they had been forced to witness as the wretched Greek army fled through the Turkish villages of the interior a week earlier. Nevertheless it was a gruesome demonic atmosphere.*

I was standing outside a house, by chance the same house which figures later in this narrative, when I saw two young men emerge. They seemed to be Armenians, the only Armenian young men that I saw during the whole of that night. I saw the younger one run forward up the street. It looked to me as if he wanted to get hold of an empty cart lying propped up against the wall several doors down. The other young man hung back. The doors of many of the houses on both sides of the street were swinging open, or had been broken down. No one was at any window as far as I could see, though I had the impression that there were fearful and watchful eyes somewhere.

As the young man ran forward, three soldiers came out of the house outside which, the empty cart was standing. They were carrying bundles of what looked like carpets or clothes. At their first sight of the young man, they dropped these bundles and began taking down their rifles which had been slung across their shoulders. The running boy stopped and stared for a moment at the soldiers, and then turned to run back. I knew at once that it would be too late – his hesitation had condemned him as two of the soldiers already had their guns up and aiming. But then I saw the second young man pull out a revolver, aim up the road and fire three shots. Each shot went into the chest of the boy ahead who died instantly.

This was one of several incidents, which I will describe on the next page, but I have dwelled on it as it happened outside the same house, which was later the scene of my own shame. It is one of the surprises of the human condition how quickly civilised behaviour can disappear in conditions of extreme duress and danger. I myself had instinctively stepped back into the doorway of a house, and saw the young man who had fired the shots run forward and begin rifling through the clothes of the dead boy. Pulling down the boy's trousers, he found a money belt and took it. He then handed some coins to the three soldiers who were standing somewhat confused. He offered some to me, which I declined. I gave little more thought to the incident – there were corpses everywhere. I moved on and next found myself...."

Sentence by sentence, word by word, syllable by syllable Karekin read and reread this passage. Once again he could not breathe properly – the normally impeccably controlled and immaculately dressed Karekin, pulled down his tie and opened the buttons of his shirt. The bile rose in his throat and he ran to the washroom and thrust his head under the cold tap. It was no use, the heat and fever in him was inside his head and could not be assuaged by cold water. It was he who had helped to set up the Bureau for Orphans, it was he who had introduced this viper into his home, it was he with his liberal values, his worship of tolerance; Oh God! What had he done? – It was all his fault. Oh – my son – my son.

And at last – at last – as the image of his cheerful smiling son came to his mind, the relief of tears finally arrived as he fell to his knees onto the floor. He stayed there on his hands and knees for many minutes – banging his fist up and down on the floor until his hand began to bleed. This could not last and he rose. He felt dishevelled and went to tidy himself up. A cold and devastating anger now took hold of him – an anger he had not felt for years. Where was all the talk of tolerance, the urge to reconciliation? Forgiveness and reconciliation – the very thought made him groan out loud again. His son – his only son – who he had loved with a fierce pride – how could he ever forgive? Then, somehow, as he paced up and down, the passion of his emotions began to overwhelm his whole philosophy of life. Had he been wrong all the time? Perhaps the fanatic hard nationalists had been right after all – why should there be forgiveness or reconciliation towards people, or a person, who had caused such harm to him and his own.

There was now only one way he could relieve the terrible tension in his head. He would find out exactly what Paramaz would say when confronted. After hearing him out, he would avenge his son's death with his own hands. Then he would find out exactly who had raped his daughter – with money to throw at it, it would not be that difficult – and he would kill him too. He could not keep still – he kept pacing up and down. But at last, exhausted, he locked the office and went out into the city – his beloved city – and walked, seeing nothing.

In the city, in a desolate cobbled street somewhere near the Dolmabahce Palace, earlier in the morning than Karekin's purgatory, the rain was still pouring down. The ambulance, containing the old Sultan and his son Ertogrul, had mounted the dilapidated pavement and was standing stationary halfway down a deserted street. The houses loomed up on either side, but not a window was open – not a soul was looking down on the end of a dynasty. What was the hitch? Had the old man been justified – was there an assassin lurking somewhere?

'The world ends not with a bang but a whimper!' The

ambulance had simply had a puncture – but changing the wheel was taking a long time. The driver and his officer assistant got out, but in all that downpour, the two other occupants remained in the van, adding to the weight. It seemed to take forever, and still no one, not a single person, appeared on the street. It only actually took about 35 minutes, but it seemed like all day. Mehmed, the sixth of that name by the grace of Allah, had at last stopped talking.

Once the ambulance finally arrived at the dock, Harington, with a sigh of relief, hurried forward and escorted the Sultan and his party onto the waiting launch, and from there onto the deck of HMS *Malaya*. In the cabin that had been allotted to the fleeing monarch, Harington said –

"Your Highness, you are now on British territory. You are completely safe, I guarantee it. Where do you wish to go?"

"Harington bey," replied the last Osmanli, "I have no idea, no preference – I cannot think of my own future just at the moment."

"Well, sir, yes I understand. We were planning for the ship to go to Malta where you will be safe as the guest of His Majesty's government. This would give you the time to make plans for the future."

"For the future – for the future – what future? I am abandoning the city of my forefathers – forever. I have no future now, only a past."

Harington said nothing. It was not his problem any longer. The old man was safe and would go, while he had to face music, when news of the escape came out. He saluted and left the disconsolate old man, promising at the end to help send his wives and daughters on after him. HMS *Malaya*, already with full steam up, slowly moved away, passed round the point of the old Byzantine palace and the Ottoman Seraglio, and into the Marmara Sea, taking with it the last Osmanli Sultan forever.

Back in the Yildiz Palace, one of Refet's spies, realising what had happened, and in a fever of anxiety at not having antici- pated the escape, rushed to see Refet, who had had a sleepless night, sensing that something was afoot in the Yildiz. It took the man, running out into the pouring rain in his slippers, an hour before he could find a carriage. Bursting into Refet's room, he reported what he feared had now taken place, anxious, above all, at his own dereliction of duty. Refet smiled and told him to go back to bed and get some sleep. He then informed Ankara that they no longer needed to worry about having to arrest and deal with the ex-Sultan, as he had left of his own accord. Furthermore, and to cap the good news, he had done so with the aid of the infidel occupiers, inevitably nullifying once and for all any lingering support he might still have enjoyed. He sank back onto his bed as the rain began to slacken, and fell peacefully to sleep for the first time that morning.

Alexei could scarcely credit what he was seeing as he emerged from the light mist and saw Talin ahead of him, standing in the road, holding a distressed Haik in her arms, and surrounded by three menacing young men. He heard Talin scream and then shout out his name. He immediately ran up the road towards the group. The scene froze as the three thugs turned at Talin's shout to see Alexei, a mere boy, running forward waving his umbrella and shouting – "stop … stop … leave her alone," in an obviously foreign accent.

Three knives appeared in a flash, glinting in three dirt-grimed hands. Talin was still holding the now silent baby, who had been startled and shocked out of his own yelling, by Talin's terrified scream, right by his ear. Alexei was brave, but he had had no experience in street fighting, and he pulled up to a stop as he arrived to face the three. Now that they had a clear view of who they were facing, they began grinning, which chilled the frightened Talin, even more. She could not say a word, but she had the sense to slowly back away, step by step, backwards up the hill.

The tableau below her had frozen. There was no one about, and events could have gone in any direction. Alexei stood with his rolled up umbrella raised in front of him in a rather futile gesture of defiance, facing three young toughs, any one of whom could have knifed him, long before he knew what was happening. But for a moment, nobody moved. Then suddenly it all unfroze. Charging down the hill came Paramaz.

Paramaz, far more canny and streetwise than Alexei could ever hope to be, saw at once, the moment he came into view, what was happening. He saw Talin, turning to look back at him with tears in her eyes, holding tightly on to the unhappy Haik – his baby – his godson. He saw the 16 year-old Alexei further down, attempting to hold off the ruffians with a pathetic shabby old umbrella. He saw the three hooligans, the stolen bedclothes and the three wicked looking knives. He did not hesitate for a moment but started running down the hill.

It was the 17th November. The weather in Western Europe was not much better than in Constantinople. Lloyd George had already resigned, his government having fallen largely due to the handling of the situation in Constantinople. At the General Election, which followed his resignation, Gladstonian Liberalism had been rejected and a Conservative government came into power. Lord Curzon was confirmed in his office as Foreign Secretary, and so it was he who left London for Lausanne, on the same Friday, that saw off the last Sultan of the Ottoman Empire from the Imperial city.

The delegates were gathering. The reinstated Venizelos, unquestionably the ablest man at the conference, was already there, but in a very weak position. Lord Curzon met President Poincaré in Paris and, despite their mutual antipathy towards each other, they travelled down by special train together to the Swiss city on the lake. A certain Signor Mussolini, who had only two weeks previously taken power in Rome, also arrived by special train for the opening. In a style reminiscent of an Italian comic opera, he insisted on meeting his supposed allies – Curzon and Poincaré – outside Lausanne, before proceeding solemnly to the town.

Kemal had insisted that his friend, Ismet Pasha, who had conducted the negotiations with Harington at Mudania so ably, should lead the Turkish delegation at Lausanne. The Turks were convinced that the new nation-state they were creating – modern

Turkey – was not only immeasurably superior to the multi-cultural empire they were succeeding, but that as the conquerors, they could impose a conqueror's peace. In every direction they looked they appeared to be the equal of the Great Powers. Soviet Russia was their ally; France and Italy had become friendly; and finally in decisively repudiating Lloyd George and his government, the British had shown they would no longer oppose any of the new Turkey's demands.

In the event, despite all the odds stacked against him, Lord Curzon, 'that most superior person', did well, and Great Britain emerged with its prestige, so important and necessary for a World Empire, less dented than the last two months might have suggested. It was all very urbane and civilised. But in the end all those frock-coated, impeccably dressed, gentlemen making their way in special trains to this small town on Lake Geneva, would stand condemned for the one decisive and important decision that they were about to take – referred to then as an exchange of populations but better described as the forced 'ethnic cleansing' of the old Ottoman Empire.

Here in the Chateau d'Ouchy, described by an American writer as a 'pile of stone so ugly as to make the town hall of Hicksville, USA look like the Parthenon,' a decision was to be taken that raised rampant nationalism to the dominant creed of the rest of the century. It was to be a decision as ugly in its effect, as the building from which it emanated.

Article I of the convention which was put before the delegates at Lausanne stated clearly and explicitly –

"There shall take place a compulsory exchange of Turkish nationals of the Greek Orthodox religion established in the territory of the Ottoman Empire and of Greek nationals of the Moslem religion established in the territory of the Kingdom of Greece. These persons shall never return to live in Greece or Turkey, respectively."

This convention, enthusiastically accepted by the politicians and the foreign office dignitaries of all nations, and by political academics everywhere, as a matter of 'political necessity', was immediately, and remained ever after, the greatest example of the crude exercise of the power of the state over the individual.

If, in the end, the people of France had to suffer four years of harsh foreign occupation, and the people of Great Britain had to see their Empire collapse, and their liberal and tolerant way of life threatened, it was because this Article set the whole philosophical basis for the rest of the 20th century.

The criteria for the exchange, was religion – offensive enough some might say – but the rationale was the mystical notion of the nation. Over a million Greeks, a large proportion of whom could only speak Turkish, would flood into the already impoverished Kingdom of Greece, together with a further 100,000 or so Armenians. Although Armenians were not supposed to be included in the proposed exchange, Greece, even though desperate and bankrupt, accepted them without discrimination, requiring the commissioners dealing with the return of the Greek prisoners "to treat them with the same consideration as Greeks."

The question of whether Karekin and his family, or the Asadourians, or the Patakis family, would have to leave the only homes they had ever known was also discussed in tones of calm objectivity. However, as it turned out, for reasons largely of commercial advantage to the parties, Article II proposed that Greek Orthodox inhabitants of the city of Constantinople should not be included in the forced exchange. The convention stated, categorically, that no exchanged person would ever have the right to return to his or her native home. Spiro's new parents could never return to their farm in Sinekli. They had no idea what the future would hold for them, as they finally crossed the bridge over the Maritza. Yet even they were more fortunate than most of their compatriots. They, at least, had two exhausted horses, five milk cows and all their tools. They also had a bright 12 year-old son, who respected them, and had been a great help during their flight, and whom they had come to love.

But for Karekin, the beginning of the Conference of Lausanne on this Friday, an event for which he, and all the other politically conscious inhabitants of the city had been waiting for so long, no longer mattered at all. He walked and walked, seeing and hearing nothing, and, eventually, as if on auto-pilot, he found himself on the Galata Bridge. Leaning against the parapet, he stood and stared down at the ferries jostling each other, to tie up at the several spots where they were to discharge their passengers. He ignored the fine and now gentle rain falling on him. He never even saw the HMS *Malaya*, as it passed across the mouth of the Golden Horn and into the Sea of Marmara, on its way to Malta.

He was quite unaware of how much time had passed since he first read the letter. Wearily, he turned and began walking toward Sirkedji station. But then the thought of going straight home to confront Paramaz with his newly gained knowledge, was too much for him. Instead, he began walking up the hill towards his daughter's lodgings. There he would at least see Armineh, no doubt still helping Sima to pack for the Simplon-Orient tomorrow. His thoughts now turned to his wife. Thinking about someone else's feelings, instead of wallowing in his own distress in a welter of guilt and self-hatred, immediately eased him. He quickened his pace and turned into the cul-de-sac leading to the Patakis house.

He was let in by the domestic and walked up the wooden stairs into the sitting room on the first floor. The room was filled with trunks, all open, almost all filled to the brim. Standing in the middle of it all, looking hot and flustered was Armineh, who took a quick glance at him as he entered and said –

"Ah, Karekin, my soul, Sima is out with Nicolai for some last minute shopping and..."

"Armineh, my love I..."

And at that rather constricted cry, Armineh turned and looked at her husband for the first time. There was not a moment's hesitation. They were not a couple given much to overt displays of emotion, particularly outside the home, but there was no one else in the room. Armineh dropped the blouse she was holding and ran to Karekin's side, clasping him hard.

"Oh my God, husband, what is it – what has happened?"

"Armineh – wife – I don't know how to tell you. I have found out ... oh, merciful heavens ... I have..."

"Karekin just tell me. Whatever it is that you know or are afraid of, we will both cope with it better, if it is shared."

Karekin suddenly felt very tired. He could no longer shoulder it all on his own. Without another word, he handed Armineh the letter and sank down on one of the sofas.

It was a long letter – the article that Burhan had felt too guilty to publish. There was a long silence as Armineh read slowly. Her mastery of the Arabic script, of the Turkish language, had not been as thorough as she might have wished. But she read on calmly as, on a first reading, the description of the events on that narrow street in the Armenian quarter did not have any impact. It was only as she neared the end of the letter, with the appearance of Olga into the street from the same house from which the two young men had emerged, that the significance came home. Armineh paled as the realisation hit her. She put the letter down for a moment and rubbed her eyes, then quickly picked it up and continued reading. This brought her to the revelation of the rape, which she read almost with equanimity. When she finished the letter she looked down at her husband – dishevelled, with his head in his hands and in a state bordering on despair.

"My God, so that is what has been eating at Paramaz's soul all this time. That's why he is obsessed with the baby, that's why he named it after my son."

At the words 'my son' she choked and struggled to restrain her tears. Karekin at last looked up and said –

"I know I can undo nothing. I know that I can't bring my son back – but I will have a life for a life. One way or another, I will have my vengeance."

"Karekin, my soul, my love, don't, please don't. How do we know that it wasn't an accident? He may have been...."

"Nonsense. Look how the writer describes what happened immediately after the shooting. Turk though the writer may be, he saw that the rifling of the body and the stealing of the money belt was immoral, and he would have no part in it. But he too will die at my hands. Hypocrite! Rapist! They're all the same – I hate them all."

"No you don't hate them all, Karekin. Stop please. Consider

just for a moment that, but for the writer of this letter, our daughter would not be alive today. Has the manner of Haik's death changed everything for you. My darling, if the Turkish soldiers had completed shooting, and Haik had been shot by them rather than by Paramaz, would it make all that much difference to your peace of mind? You have already grieved and are becoming reconciled to the death of your son, as one of the tragic consequences of the death of a whole empire and a way of life – that still applies, whoever pulled the trigger.

"It's my son, Armineh. It is one thing to face up to the consequences of a national catastrophe and to learn to live with it – people have had to do that throughout history – but my own son, my only son, that I ..."

"But all the people who died in 1915, they were the sons or daughters of others. Is there no hope of forgiveness? Karekin, you have already accepted and lived through your grief – you can't begin all over again – it will tear at your soul and destroy you. You have to let go."

"Oh God, I can't. Help me, I can't. I have been at fault all along. I was wrong with all my liberal ideals – they have only led to my own son's death. My daughters – I forced them to have a liberal western education. What has been the result – one has married a penniless Russian count and is leaving us – and the other has been raped. My ..."

"Rubbish. Utter rubbish. That's enough Karekin. You are lacerating yourself for no purpose. Not everything is due to you or controlled by you. Now snap out of it!"

At this point, Armineh stamped her foot. And at that traditional sight, Karekin gave a wry smile. He stood up, and they embraced long and lovingly in the middle of that untidy messy room.

"Look, Karekin, we must go home right away. We will interview Paramaz together and at least find out his side of the story. Whatever he says, I accept that it would be quite impossible for either of us for him to remain in the house. But Karekin, while forgiveness might be too difficult, some sort of reconciliation is vital. We have adopted a new son – the baby Haik – it would be condemning him for the sins of others if he were now rejected or made to suffer in some way. Paramaz will have to go but...."

"And Olga?"

"Karekin, forget your male pride. Olga has chosen to ignore what happened to her on that terrible night. She has chosen not to tell anyone. Whether she eventually tells Harry after they are married, is entirely up to her. I hope that she does get round to it – perhaps when they have their own first child together. But, Karekin, she must not be burdened with this letter. It seems to me that Olga has coped with it like women have had to do over the centuries. She doesn't need the burden of your anger or your guilt, as well."

Holding hands as they rarely did, Karekin and Armineh left the room with a message to Sima and Nicolai that they would meet them at Sirkedji for the departure to Venice the next day. Unlocking their hands once in the street they took the usual train back to Makrikoy.

Paramaz, who had immediately taken in the situation on the road below him, charged on with passionate anger, and by the sheer force of his charge ran straight down onto the first youth, knocking him over with a single blow. Alexei, with a whoop of excitement, joined in, swinging his umbrella with a will, but was immediately stabbed in the shoulder. Blood began pouring out. Paramaz turned to deal with Alexei's assailant, striking at him hard over the head with the butt of his revolver which he had taken out as he ran – the same weapon which he had fired at Selim and at Haik all those weeks ago, and which he had kept with him ever since, although there was only one bullet left. Then, before that second youth staggered away, Paramaz too was stabbed just near the neck – and he too began spurting blood from the front of his throat.

Meanwhile, Talin had walked back, step by step, up the hill, clutching tight the baby, who had started crying again. The third man saw his two accomplices on the floor crawling away, and assumed that this newcomer must also have a knife. He sized up the situation in a flash, took the necessary few steps up the hill and grabbed Talin, raising his knife and threatening to plunge it into her body – or horrors, into that of the baby – the knife was raised against both.

Paramaz went cold – he did not realize the extent of the blood he was losing. He sank to the ground onto his knees, looking up at the knife poised so close to Talin and his baby – his godson Haik. Then slowly and deliberately holding himself up with one hand he raised the revolver – his hand did not shake – he aimed at the tableau in front of him and shot. The bullet went straight through the heart of the bully still holding Talin. He fell to the ground, instantly dead, without a sound, but with a look of pure amazement on his face. The last thought that passed through Paramaz's mind as he too sank to the ground unconscious, was the horrific realisation, which he had never accepted before, that he was, and always had been, a natural good shot. Alexei, holding his own shoulder in an attempt to stem the blood, came and knelt by the side of Paramaz as the other two youths, hearing the gunshot, staggered up and took to their heels down the hill.

The rain began again, falling gently as Talin stepped down to join the bleeding Alexei kneeling beside Paramaz, who appeared to be sleeping. Haik had stopped crying and sensing, somehow, that the crisis had passed, was wriggling to be put down. Paramaz opened his eyes and tried to sit up, but with every movement, blood spurted from his throat. He could hardly speak. Young though they were, Alexei and Talin had both seen enough death in their lives, to know that Paramaz was unlikely to survive. They bent to listen as Paramaz gurgled out some words.

"Oh God, Alexei, Oh God – it turns out that I was always a good shot. Oh Haik forgive me, forgive me."

"Paramaz – hear me, hear me – there is nothing to forgive," said Talin. "Look here is Haik – see, he is well, he is well – you saved him."

Talin bent down and placed the infant on Paramaz's chest. He was now lying on his back staring up at the sky, covered in blood. The infant Haik, remembering his play with Paramaz earlier in the morning and expecting more, bounced up and down on the dying Paramaz. The rain began to fall more heavily again, washing away some of the blood. Paramaz tried to sit up a little and finally blurted out –

"Asvadz, Asvadzim – Father – Mother – my sweet sisters – Oh God I never knew it, but I was, after all, always a good shot. Oh forgive me..."

But neither Talin nor Alexei understood a word – it all came out as a gurgle, as more blood spurted out of his throat. Only the baby, the infant Haik, reacted, as he crept forward still on the bloody chest and put his little hands out and touched Paramaz's eyes as they closed for ever.

The rain had stopped when Karekin and Armineh arrived at the Cobancesme station. They were both exhausted and didn't hesitate to wave at Abdul and take the carriage back home. Karekin had already calmed his fever, as they arrived, and followed Armineh as they walked into the hall and into the sad situation that confronted them.

None of the four girls were there, but the rest of the household were gathered in the hall. The family doctor had already come up from the town and was still tending Alexei's wounds. Haik, already washed and changed by Marie, was in her arms. The two men who had helped to carry up the body of Paramaz had already departed, and his body lay on the floor at the foot of the stairs covered by a dark sheet.

The explanations poured out, jumbled and frantic. Armineh went forward and took the baby from Marie and cuddled him, much to his gurgling satisfaction. Karekin listened and then, when everyone had stopped talking and everything had been explained he said –

"Poor Paramaz. He had a difficult life, in which nothing ever went right for him, after he was left alone with all his family massacred in that awful death march. He coped with it all as best he could, and saved the life of this infant – twice it would seem. We will have a service for him within the next few days."

He then turned and, leaving them all in the hall, went into the sitting room and for a moment, leaning on the mantelpiece, he stood silently staring down into the flames of the fire in the

319 THE END OF THE IMPERIAL CITY

fireplace. Then he took out the letter and without a further look, he tore it to shreds and fed them to the flames.

CHAPTER 35

The End of the Imperial City

The next day, a Saturday, the whole family gathered at midday at Sirkedji station. Alexei, already recovered from the wound, which had been fairly superficial, had gone ahead to get a table arranged for twelve at the restaurant on Platform 1. Two porters had been engaged for the whole morning until the train was due to depart. They stood patiently at the grand entrance to the station, leaning on their trolleys and waiting for Sima and Nicolai to arrive. The death of Paramaz had added a sombre touch to an occasion that was, for Karekin and Armineh, fairly ambivalent already. Their eldest daughter was leaving them, not only leaving their home, but leaving the city in which they all lived. The news of the departure of the Sultan the day before was now all over the city, and the usual gossip and uninformed speculation was rife. But Karekin no longer cared. Let them sort it all out, he had more than enough to worry about in sorting out his family's affairs.

The carriage containing Sima and Nicolai finally arrived, clattering up from the seafront onto the roadway in front of the station. Alexei, who had made himself the master of ceremonies for the whole occasion, came forward out of the entrance hall, extended his arm and handed down Sima from the carriage, as if she was a Grand Duchess of the Imperial Court, arriving at the annual ball. Sima was beaming, flushed with pleasure and heady with excitement and anticipation. Everyone had by then arrived and were all gathered outside the chandeliered entrance hall – Nerissa in a white dress and large floppy hat despite the cold weather – Olga, standing beside Harry, their hands touching but not openly holding each other – Seta, jumping up and down in excitement. Talin had not come – she was still upset and had elected to stay at home and look after the infant Haik. However, Marie was there – in tears almost the whole time – dressed in her best Sunday clothes.

As Sima, smiling broadly, stepped down from the carriage, the whole party burst into spontaneous applause, clapping as she ran forward to Armineh and hugged her tight. Karekin felt a mixture of enormous pride and sadness. He reflected on the fact that he had been married for almost thirty years, and now his first-born child was leaving home, as would his second girl soon afterwards. Was it all downhill now, all the way, as he became older and his other children left him one by one?

He shook his head, as if to rid himself of cobwebs. The words of Armineh, thrust at him yesterday, as he was about to give way to self-pitying despair, came back to him. She had pointed out that it was a form of arrogance on his part to assume that everything emanated from him, that everything depended on his will and affected only him and that he had to be in control. He smiled. He would be reconciled.

As Armineh and Sima embraced, Nicolai, still in the carriage directing the porters to the cases piled up behind, turned and gave a great shout of joy and welcome. Striding up from the seafront came a grinning Vahan with what appeared to be a huge bunch of flowers.

"You don't want all these, Sima," he said coming up. "They wouldn't all fit in the compartment."

It wasn't actually one enormous bunch, but four more modest smaller ones. Vahan was no Alexei, but nevertheless he managed to put some panache, for once, into the gesture. He handed one to each of the Avakian girls – including a blushing and extremely pleased Seta. The two porters laboriously loaded their trolleys with the six trunks, two hat-cases and several bits of hand luggage, which were accompanying the couple. Then they all trooped into the station and wandered over to the restaurant with its overhead canopy and a line of shrubs in large rectangular wooden boxes, separating the outside tables from the platform. There was no way anyone wanted to go inside, despite the chilly weather, and the restaurant was, in any case, fairly well sheltered.

A table was already laid for twelve, though they were in fact only eleven. Alexei had jotted down the numbers two days before and of course...

Considering the surrounding circumstances, it was a surprisingly cheerful party. As often happened in Bolis, and despite the fact that there were some more solemn Westerners in the restaurant, the neighbouring tables were sent round drinks by Karekin and even dishes to try. They were invited to join in the toasts, and reciprocated by raising their own glasses to the future of the two newlyweds. Karekin swelled with pride and emotion, and Armineh smiled.

Then the empty train, with the carriages all cleaned and prepared, pulled slowly into the station and alongside the platform and immediately, there was animated activity, although there was still half an hour before the train was due to depart. The brown-uniformed Wagons-Lits attendants were already at their doors with their lists of boarding occupants. The two porters, who had been given the carriage number and the compartment number, were already on their way up the train. Everyone began to stand at the table. The tears began. Olga and Sima embraced for more than a minute. Everyone hugged everyone – there were no more words. Bolsetsi Armenian 'goodbyes' were always notoriously long and over-emotional – but after two years of exposure, even Harry joined in.

Then, they all streamed out of the restaurant and up to the coach marked for Venice, and on to Milan. With a hissing of steam from under all the coaches – with a great cacophony of shouts and whistles, without which no train ever appeared to be able to start from Sirkedji station – with a great clanging lurch –the train hooted once, and slowly left for the West.

A week later – exactly the same group, but without Sima and Nicolai, gathered in a side room of the imposing British embassy just off the Grande Rue du Pera. Olga, stunning in a sort of compromise between a white dress and a gorgeous Turkish shawl, held Harry's hand throughout as they stood in front of a table completely covered with an enormous Union Jack. Two of

Harry's friends, fellow officers from the Lion, were present in full uniform. Tim Harington sent a warm note of congratulations. Harry himself was in civilian clothes, looking cool and dashing, but in the last resort, without that final flourish of impeccable elegance, exhibited by his new father-in-law.

The arrangements were carefully organised, and once again it was Alexei who sorted it all out. The lunch after the ceremony was in a private room at Tokatlians just round the corner; carriages for everyone for the ride down to the sea-front at Eminonu were ready after lunch; and finally, yet another bottle of champagne as Harry and Olga boarded the launch to the liner which would take them to the start of their new life together in Alexandria. It had all been much to Karekin's taste, though fashionable Bolis did not understand it at all. Yet another Avakian eccentricity.

One month later the decision of the court martial held in the Harbiye buildings was published. Harry was found guilty of exceeding his authority and disregarding orders from his superior commander. Extenuating circumstances were accepted, and Harry was given an official reprimand and put back in seniority, though not reduced in rank. On reflection, there was no way that the Court, faced with the standing and reputation of one of the Navy's senior Admirals, could have decided otherwise. The decision was sent immediately to Alexandria, where Harry and Olga were already settled.

Six months later the great and the good, gathered in the city of Lausanne beside the clear waters of the lake of Geneva, passed a final resolution requiring a compulsory exchange of populations between Greece and the new Turkey. The compulsory exchange was to be based on people's religious beliefs; the date of the finality of the decree to be the 1st May 1923. In Article 2, Greek Orthodox citizens registered as living in the city of Constantinople were to be exempted. However, the treaty made it clear that any Greeks who had already fled, would not to be allowed to return.

Who cared about Spiro and his new family, wandering homeless along the Aegean coast? Who cared about the many Turks of Macedonia, who had lived there under Ottoman rule for centuries, and only spoke Greek? Some of them even applied to change religion in order to remain. The nationalists were adamant. No exceptions! The nation-state, and its fanatical supporters, required 'land' and 'people' to coincide exactly. This conference, praised for tidying up a difficult situation, by generations of academic historians, ushered in a century of other experiments in 'ethnic cleansing', all in the name of the sanctity of the nation.

Nationalism and the nation-state cannot exist in a conflict-free condition. It cannot exist without claims, counter-claims, grudges and resentments. Whenever the nationalism of one group of people raises its ugly head, immediately as if springing up out of the very earth, the nationalism of another group will emerge in opposition.

There are, and there were, plenty of other possible solutions. Humanity is capable of many forms of civilised rule. 'But surely' said the gentlemen in their miserable and ugly Chateau, 'they all hated each other, didn't they? – We had better separate them.' People may hate other people for all sorts of personal and petty reasons. But hatred of a whole group is always a matter of deliberate manipulation by a ruling elite, usually supported by propagandists, ready to orchestrate myths shoring up one form of nationalism against another. Hate? The Spiros of this world wouldn't even hate the well-dressed urbane gentlemen of Lausanne who had so unreasonably ordered their lives – where they should go – where and with whom they should live – even which God they should worship.

On the very same day that the convention was signed Conrad Bridgeman was born to Olga Bridgeman in a nursing home opposite Regents Park, in the imperial city of London.

A year later the last acknowledged Caliph of the Moslem community – Abdul Medjid – the successor to the last Sultan, was sitting in the Dolmabahce Palace reading the Koran, when the palace was surrounded by troops sent from Ankara. He was summarily informed that he had to leave the city at dawn the next day. Mustapha Kemal had already decreed that Ankara was to be the capital of the new republic. After over 1,500 years as an imperial capital, longer than any other city in the world, it had now, at a stroke of a pen, become the second city of the republic. Kemal refused to visit the city. He removed the wily, cheerful Refet, and now in October, a year after the departure of the last Sultan, he abolished the Caliphate without a murmur of dissent.

Early the following morning, at half past five, the Caliph was bundled into a car. Orders had already been sent that there was to be no great send-off at Sirkedji station. So, unlike the departure of Sima and Nicolai, the exodus was to be hugger-mugger. Two cars, followed by a lorry carrying such luggage as could be packed in the eight hours notice, given for the move, drove out of the Yedikule gate and on to Chatalja, 30 miles away. Once again it was raining and the road being no better than the year before, the cars frequently got stuck in the mud.

Six hours after setting off the party finally arrived at the Chatalja railway station, which had been cordoned off from inquisitive eyes. The station-master here was Jewish. He had been station-master here since 1912. He had witnessed the whole of the political and military events which had lapped round the station. The arrival of the Bulgarians, the counterattack by the Young Turks, the German supply trains, the Greeks, the British and now the nationalists. He had remained loyal, as had almost all the Jews in the city, to the Ottomans throughout. He offered the exhausted Caliph his own quarters while they waited all day for the train nominated by the government to arrive. It was not due until the evening.

As the Caliph got ready to leave the station-master's little house to wait on the platform, he gave his thanks for the hospitality he had received from him and his wife. The good man, disregarding the nationalist officials looking on disapprovingly, bowed and said -

"Your honour, when our ancestors were driven out of Spain,

it was your ancestors, the Ottomans, who alone agreed to give us shelter and who saved us from extinction. Only through their generosity and help did we retain our religion, our language and our lives. As their representative at this moment I will serve you always as best as I can."

The Orient Express – it was the Simplon-Orient this time – steamed into the little station to make a special stop. Most of the occupants were already asleep and few of the green blinds were pushed aside to look out as the Caliph, the last reigning Ottoman and his little party, boarded the train into the coach, hurriedly arranged by the new governor of Constantinople the day before.

The Caliph tried to smile, as the officials and the local gendarmes gave him his last salute. The Governor who had at last turned up, handed his secretary passports, visas for Switzerland and a wad of money. The doors shut, the whistles blew, the train hissed out and the last Ottoman left the land they had ruled for 500 years.

Finally, three years later by a decree emanating from Ankara the name of the city founded by the Roman Emperor Constantine, with its myriad of alternative local names, perched half in Europe and half in Asia, was officially changed. It was in future to be known only as Istanbul. Notice was given that no letter addressed to Constantinople would be delivered by the Republican Postal services. Constantinople no longer existed.

The Problem of the Nation State

It might appear that Wilsonian democracy triumphed at Versailles in 1919 – but it did not. Within 10 years or so, democracy was virtually wiped out throughout Europe, despite the sudden arrival of a plethora of nation-states in place of the old empires. What triumphed at Versailles, and the years immediately following, was rampant nationalism and the worship of the notion of the exclusive, sovereign nation-state.

The complete failure of democracy between the wars, and for some time after, was not just a 'blip' in an otherwise onward march of the left. It was a popular movement of the Right, which manifested itself in all sorts of political movements – Fascism; National Socialism; Catholic absolutism; the Corporate state; Royal dictatorships; all appearing in the new nation-states. The idea that nation-states and democracy are synonymous is simply not true.

The triumph of the nation-state, in the period 1918-23, brought bloodshed, war, civil war and all sorts of problems with it. The spread of the idea of the nation-state to Eastern Europe inevitably created the problem of "minorities" as a political issue, a problem which still exists today. When a state claims to derive its legitimacy or its sovereignty from "the people", and then defines "the people" as a particular nation, the presence of other nations or ethnic groups within its borders, immediately poses a problem.

In the old 18th and 19th-century empires, where legitimacy was based on a geographic entity, or a dynastic loyalty, or an overriding culture, the problem of minorities did not arise in the same way. It was possible, for instance, for an ethnic German to rise to the highest position in a Tsarist administration, or for all sorts of diverse nationalities to help in running the Hapsburg state, or for Greeks to be the diplomats representing the Ottomans in international congresses.

But after 1918 and Versailles, that ceased to be possible. So what then became of all the minorities – and there were many. The Great War and Versailles gave a new 55–60 million people a state of their own – but in the process it turned another 25 million into 'minorities'.

How to cope?

Exterminating the minority, as the Turks tried with the Armenians, and as others copied later, is of course one solution – though perhaps not really generally acceptable.

Exchanging populations was another possibility; but how barren, how much a failure of political thought. In 1912, Salonika under the Ottomans was a vibrant cultural mix of peoples and religions. Even the dock workers routinely spoke 5 or 6 languages, with all the access to literature and poetry that implies. The population exchange between Greece and Turkey in 1923, followed by the Nazi extermination camps in 1940, left Salonika so much the poorer – only a uniform Greek culture remains in the city, now unutterably boring.

The suffering involved in forced exchanges was only a little less than extermination. All those homes of centuries deserted, all the friends left behind, all the fields tended lovingly for generations abandoned. Only through the blinkers of the nation-state worshippers, could this be acceptable.

What about stability? Suffer a few years, perhaps, of uprooting people who have lived in an area for centuries, but after that, awful though it may be for a few years, there will be no more problems – total uniformity will be achieved. However, uniformity impoverishes life. On top of that, as Hapsburg political thinkers emphasised, in the modern increasingly globalised world, the market is organised into much larger units. Are Bosnia, Kosovo, Montenegro, Croatia, Slovenia, Macedonia, etc. really viable as sovereign units – and what about further sub-divisions – why not Krajina, Herzegovina, the Hungarian districts of Slavonia – one could go on for ever.

Neither Selim, the nationalist, nor Vahan, the multi-cultural imperialist, could see what the future held, as they discussed the matter together. Nothing is inevitable in history and even though it seems as if only Selim's views prevailed and only the nation-state had a future, anything could have happened.

Could the Ottoman Empire have survived in some form or another. It might have, if it had evolved more accountable, democratic structures. An all-powerful compassionate planner, just looking at a map of the Empire in 1912, could have arrived at a whole host of possible divisions of the whole area, which would not have resulted in the sequence of events which eventually took place; in which millions were killed or driven from the homes they had known for centuries, and which still troubles the world today.

What happened in the end was that the powerful simply divided the spoils without regard to the consequences. The Ottomans, who were unable to reform quickly enough, do share a measure of responsibility for the debacle. However, the main fault lies with the nationalists – and western imperialists - who did not consider the costs when they destroyed the basically tolerant multi-national Ottoman Empire in favour of a myriad of intolerant, exclusive nation-states, Arab and Jewish, Serb and Albanian, whose petty, mutually exclusive, squabbles are still troubling the world a hundred years after the Empire which had encompassed them all disappeared.

Constantinople 1920

HAIG TAHTA

ISBN 9781 900355 58 2

Constantinople 1920, the second book in Haig Tahta's projected trilogy, chronicles the impending fall of the Ottomans and explores the circumstances and atmosphere of Constantinople during the British occupation of the city from 1920 to 1922. It carries forward the same characters from Mr. Tahta's first novel, *April 1915*, set in the Ottoman Empire at a critical moment following its fateful decision to join the Great War in November 1914. Olga, an Armenian girl and Selim, a Turk, are impossibly in love. Their relationship, much more difficult and problematic than Romeo and Juliet, develops and unfolds during the Greco-Turkish War, reaching its shocking climax in the burning of Smyrna. An historical novel of deep insight and high passions, *Constantinople 1920* brings to focus a time which echoed throughout the world and set in train events that would engulf Europe in flames a few decades later. Written with a rare sense of humanity and peopled with a plethora of characters, bold, sensitive, articulate and always fascinating, *Constantinople 1920* is that rare novel of ideas and drama that appeals to both the heart and the intellect.

To purchase this book or to find details about other Black Apollo publications, visit our website at
www.blackapollo.com